THE DARK IS DESCENDING

BOOKS BY CHLOE C. PEÑARANDA

THE NYTEFALL TRILOGY
The Stars Are Dying
The Night Is Defying
The Dark Is Descending

AN HEIR COMES TO RISE SERIES
An Heir Comes to Rise
A Queen Comes to Power
A Throne from the Ashes
A Clash of Three Courts
A Sword from the Embers
A Flame of the Phoenix

THE DARK IS DESCENDING

CHLOE C. PEÑARANDA

BRAMBLE

TOR PUBLISHING GROUP

NEW YORK

THE DARK IS DESCENDING

Copyright © 2025 by Chloe C. Peñaranda

Cover design by Lila Raymond
Map design and page design by Lila Raymond
Full page illlustration on page 400 by Pangolin2b
Sun images by Shutterstock.com

A Bramble Book
Published by Tom Doherty Associates / Tor Publishing Group
120 Broadway
New York, NY 10271

www.torpublishinggroup.com

Bramble™ is a trademark of Macmillan Publishing Group, LLC.

EU Representative: Macmillan Publishers Ireland Ltd, 1st Floor,
The Liffey Trust Centre, 117–126 Sheriff Street Upper, Dublin 1, DO1 YC43

The Library of Congress Cataloging-in-Publication Data is available upon request.

ISBN 978-1-250-35560-7 (hardcover)
ISBN 978-1-250-35562-1 (ebook)

Our books may be purchased in bulk for specialty retail/wholesale, literacy, corporate/premium, educational, and subscription box use. Please contact MacmillanSpecialMarkets@macmillan.com.

First Edition: 2025

Printed in China

10 9 8 7 6 5 4 3 2 1

*For the dreamers who gaze
at the stars—may you always find light
in the darkness and courage in the infinite.*

AUTHOR NOTE

Dear reader, I am a fantasy nerd to my core, and the idea of multiverses has always tickled my brain. We're seen mentions in prior books of Nyte not being in the realm he's supposed to be, and the concept of the Nytefall trilogy transpired from my fantasy series set in a different world, An Heir Comes to Rise. There are vague mentions of people in *The Dark Is Descending* which could potentially spoil the An Heir Comes to Rise series. If you desire to read both for the full crossover experience, my recommended reading order is the order in which my books have been published, which is as follows:

An Heir Comes to Rise, A Queen Comes to Power, A Throne from the Ashes, A Clash of Three Courts, A Sword from the Embers, The Stars Are Dying, The Night Is Defying, A Flame of the Phoenix, The Dark Is Descending.

However, if you discovered me through Nytefall, reading as follows will have the same effect:

The Stars Are Dying, The Night Is Defying, the An Heir Comes to Rise series in full, then *The Dark Is Descending.*

Though I also stress, you do not need to read An Heir Comes to Rise to follow and enjoy the Nytefall trilogy. It can be read completely on its own with no missing information.

Happy reading!

THE REALM

ARANIA

FESARIS

MISTVEIL

LAKE OF
NELTIS

VESITIR

PYXTIA

THE
UN

ALISUS

CONSTANTS   BA

VOLANTIS

PART ONE

The Darkest Days of Nyte

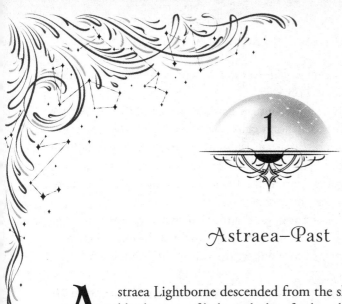

1

Astraea–Past

Astraea Lightborne descended from the skies like a shooting star, a blinding arc of light and silver feathered wings slicing through the darkened clouds above the city of Vesitire. The key in her hand pulsed with a fierce, radiant energy, mirroring the markings that snaked across her skin—ancient symbols glowing like embers over her flesh, their intensity heightening with each second. She could feel the weight of her purpose thrumming within her, grounding her even as she landed with a soft, lethal grace on a humble dwelling's rooftop.

The city loomed around her, an intricate web of bridges and towering spires. Tonight the vampires had attacked. Astraea took in the savagery of red eyes and leathery wings, but the nightcrawlers cursed to roam after dark weren't the only vampire race among those fighting against the celestials—her kind. Some didn't cast a shadow as they sank their fangs into the scrambling humans, consuming their blood. Others didn't have a reflection in the nearby shop windows as they held innocent prey in their arms, draining their victims with a kiss of death.

It hadn't always been like this. The vampires were once as peaceful as the fae, coexisting with the humans. Until someone entered her world who was never supposed to be here and sought to overthrow her reign as the star-maiden, ruler of Solanis, by poisoning the minds of her people and the celestials who governed against her. Nyte's father was the leader and instigator of that brutal uprising, but everyone knew he was nothing without Nyte—*Nightsdeath*—known as the realm's nightmare.

Astraea swooped down off the roof, and with a flick of her wrist she held the key aloft, watching it blaze brighter in response to her awakening magick, a beacon in the gloom. The vampires surged forward to the target she made of herself. Swift and deadly they came at her, their fangs bared and claws outstretched. She took a breath, the air sharp and cold, and then sprang into action.

"We can handle this," Auster called over to her, sending bolts of blue lightning to take out several foes at a time.

He always tried to send her away, but she could never stand by idle. Auster and the other three High Celestials wanted to encase her in glass for protection while they led the frontlines of this war. Though each time he suggested she stay out of the fighting irked her, she understood his concern. Astraea's chest pounded with fear for his safety too in the thick of their enemies. They were lifelong friends and he was her Bonded.

Astraea was reminded of the immense guilt that had festered inside her when she hadn't yet told him that they would never be able to forge their true bond now. For she'd tied herself to another: the realm's nightmare, and Auster's greatest enemy.

Nyte should be her enemy too, but at some point along the dangerous alliance she'd made with him to discover why their lands were shaking and the stars were dying out, the line between desire and hate had blurred, burned, then ceased to exist.

Now, as she sent a flare of light to cut through a swarm of nightcrawlers, she knew Nyte was watching. His presence lived within her, both a pleasant assurance and a nagging hindrance to her focus. He couldn't interfere with this fight, though his tangible wrath at sitting on the sidelines rattled through her.

"You're far more capable than he is," Nyte grumbled through her mind in response to Auster's concern for her. *"Behind you."*

She spun, shifting the key to a blade that sank through the chest of a shadowless. Even though they were her foes right now, she hated to spill the blood of those she didn't know the stories of. How desperate did this man have to be to side with Nyte's father and believe this was the only way his kind could achieve equality?

Astraea was determined to bring back the peace she'd dedicated her life to. Her Golden Age was shaking, and she was running out of time to keep it from collapse.

"I'd focus better without your input," she sent back to Nyte.

"I'd focus better by your side."

"You're not needed here."

"You wound me."

She didn't reply, though contrary to what she told him, talking to Nyte while she fought oddly kept her hyper-focused on slaying enemies.

"Did you know about this attack?" she asked, wanting to find exactly where Nyte was, but these vampires were unrelenting.

"No, actually," he replied with a note of disturbance.

"Then if you want to be helpful, you could find out."

"I can't leave while you're in danger."

"Like you said, I'm the most capable here. And I've survived much worse without you."

"You're having all the fun without me."

"I'll make it up to you later."

She shivered as Nyte stroked her senses. It was highly inappropriate given the circumstances. She dislodged her blade from a vampire's back.

"How so?" he coaxed.

"It might involve a bath, given we were interrupted."

Two vampires came running for her at parallel sides. Astraea took a second to flick a look over her shoulder and cast a smirk toward the shadows next to a high chimney. Nyte was very well hidden, but not to her.

"Arrogant," Nyte mused in delight.

He was referring to the fact she'd taken that moment to pin him, letting the vampires get dangerously close. She threw her stormstone dagger at the last second, precisely into the heart of one before ducking under the other's arms as they lashed out to grab her, simultaneously cutting clean through his knees with her key blade. Twisting as she stood, her next swipe cut through his neck and his body fell as a heap of limbs.

"You are an absolutely exquisite vampire slayer."

"Show is about to be over," she said. *"If you could please find out your father's motives before I'm forced to."*

"Since you begged."

"You can make that *up to me later."*

"I'll beg for you, Starlight. Only to make you scream for me in return."

Those were his parting words, and as Astraea retrieved her stormstone blade from the chest of the vampire, she cast her sight up anyway, disappointed he was no longer a spectator. Her mood dampened now that he was gone even though she'd pushed for it.

That she had fallen for the enemy was a secret that would shake the continent, but she wanted it to be free. Wanted the world to know, and in her fairytale mind they would accept it; one day they might even rejoice about it. One thing she treasured most about Nyte, though many would never understand, was how he didn't pretend to be anything he wasn't. Every dark and bloody confession he owned, and she believed he wasn't beyond redemption.

Astraea was the world's goddess of justice, thrust into this role to govern people in peace, amity, and equality. She only hoped they wouldn't question her judgment when it came to him.

Their bonding might have been forced as there was no other way to save her from a fatal wound, but part of her was glad for it. Knowing her attachment to him, her desire for him, had been a root growing deeper over the many years they'd spent together. Nyte had nestled into her mind, body, and soul. So slowly she didn't think either of them realized, or wanted to admit, what had been entangling them together from the start.

Astraea was snapped from her thoughts when a vampire dropped down from the sky, and she cursed Nyte now for distracting her from detecting it. She was thrown onto her back while vicious teeth snapped at her face. Holding him off by his shoulders, she was about to burn him inside out with her magick. She was saved from the bother when blue lightning seized the vampire and Astraea pushed him off. Seconds later, Auster's mighty stormstone sword plunged through the nightcrawler's chest.

As she caught her breath, Auster towered above her with a frown of disapproval and concern.

"I was daydreaming," she said sheepishly.

"Unlike you while in battle," he said skeptically, holding a hand down to her.

Astraea smiled sweetly, accepting the aid up and brushing herself off.

Surveying their surroundings, the other High Celestials—Notus, Aquilo, and Zephyr—finished off the last of the attack.

"I wonder what they hoped to achieve," Zephyr pondered, wiping the blood off his blade on a fallen nightcrawler.

Nyte would find out, then Astraea would know.

"Abominations," Notus spat.

She didn't like that term. How he could so easily condemn an entire species for the heinous acts of some of them. Three of Astraea's six guardians—each chosen from all races by her creators, Dusk and Dawn—were vampires. They had all raised her to be a fair and unbiased ruler. Her guardians passed on to their blissful Aetherworld decades ago with their sacred duty fulfilled. Astraea had to lead and discover herself now.

When more celestial soldiers approached, Astraea ordered them, "Start checking for wounded and clear the streets."

She stepped over bodies, heading for some nearby homes to account for innocents.

"You should go back to the castle," Auster said, following her.

"Why should I do that?"

"It's safer. Leave it to us to discover what might have brought on this attack and scout outside the city for others."

He always tried to shield her behind high walls. She'd never outright admitted this to him, but a lot of the reason why she'd stayed to govern in Vesitire rather than Althenia was to be free of Auster's and his brothers' suffocating measures for her safety.

Auster's sigh was audible as she disregarded his suggestion and knocked at the first home. When there was no answer, she entered gently, only to see immediately that the residents were all slaughtered. Four humans.

"We can't keep letting him pick off our people like this," Auster snarled.

Astraea's spine stiffened. Though Nyte's father was the leader of the vampire uprising, Auster and his brothers knew it was another that kept the enemy armies in line.

"Nightsdeath has to be killed."

She'd heard it a hundred times. Shit, she'd harbored that prime goal herself for a long time. But now they were bonded . . . and everything had changed.

She cried in her soul at imagining him dead, but she remembered one crucial thing.

"He can't be killed," Astraea mumbled.

The intense impression of Auster's eyes broke a shiver over her skin while her attention bored into the pools of blood soaking into the wood around the quaint cottage home.

"Of course he can," Auster said.

"He's . . . a god, technically. He can only be killed by something he's made of."

Acid burned in her throat to expose Nyte's weakness to Auster. Her heart was soothed over the fact that Nyte wasn't from this realm, and so nothing could kill him, even if Auster had this information.

"How do you know this?" he inquired.

"I've been hunting him, I told you. I figured it out."

Astraea's skin flushed with her white lies. Auster assessed her, and she couldn't get rid of the itching guilt over her body that if he stared long enough he would see the bond she'd forged with the realm's villain. Would he brand her a traitor? She liked to believe Auster would let her explain. After all they'd been through together, he would consider her heart, regardless of its dark choices.

Auster sighed. "Let's go; there's nothing to save here."

They spent the day cleaning up the savagery, rescuing the survivors, and implementing stricter measures of protection around Vesitire. The longer Astraea was left to ponder her own conclusions about the attack and watch them wash the blood of innocents off her streets, the uglier her resentment grew.

It didn't help that she hadn't a moment away from the High Celestials and their ramblings of disgust for the vampires and Nyte. Always him in particular. Her fists flexed each time they assumed every barbaric act had been perpetrated by him.

"You seem tense," Zephyr observed, creeping closer to her side. The others were talking among themselves in the castle's throne room.

"It's been a long day," she said.

Zephyr turned, blocking her view of his brothers like a shield for privacy.

"What do you know?" he edged carefully.

"What about?"

"The attack."

"No more than any of you."

That was the truth, but Zephyr was aware of her more *illicit* activities when she slipped out of these walls. She trusted him. When Astraea had found out Auster and the others were casting out their own people for having their wings poached, she'd made quite a protest. But though she might be the star-maiden, she was overruled where the celestials were concerned as the four brothers were god-blessed to preside over them. Brothers not by blood, but duty.

"You've been absent recently. Auster is beginning to grow suspicious," he warned.

"I don't need to be watched," she groused.

Zephyr winced, his face creased in apology.

"You have to reject the bond with him," he said, barely a whisper.

She knew this. When she'd first faced Auster after bonding with Nyte, she'd never felt foreboding fear like that, but to her relief Auster didn't sense her mating tie to Nyte.

"I know. I just don't want to hurt him."

"You're hurting him more the longer he thinks there's a chance."

Astraea's eyes pleaded silently with Zephyr. She wanted to tell him about Nyte so badly the confession strained in her chest. He would keep her secret, but she feared he might judge her harshly despite their close friendship.

Zephyr read her deliberation, taking hold of her upper arms.

"You can tell me anything," he said.

She nodded, but her lips remained sealed. She would find the courage to tell him soon. Right now, she only had one person on her mind as she discreetly left the castle.

Astraea waited for Nyte in the bell tower—a place that had become their secret home above the world. She sensed him near, but he was being stealthy, trying to catch her from behind unawares as she watched the city spilled with moonlight. Astraea spun, thrusting a hand to his chest with a surge of magick. Nyte tensed but held firm against buckling, grabbing hold of her wrist and yanking her against him.

"Always so violent," he said with a low lilt.

They shared breath through their heated stare.

"Why did the vampires attack?" she demanded.

"I've missed you," he said, reaching to tuck a lock of her hair behind her ear.

She pulled her arm free and tried an attack with her magick again. Her flare was swallowed by starry darkness. Nyte's wicked smile curved through the dissipating shadows.

"Tell me you had nothing to do with it," she said, pinning him with a glare.

The amusement dropped from his face.

"Do you think I would lie to you?"

"I don't know."

But her heart did. It pushed against her ribs, at war with her mind's uncertainty.

Nyte erased the small distance between them when he pressed her to the wall next to one of the open archways.

"Then I haven't made myself transparent enough for you to *know,* without hesitation, that there isn't a thing I wouldn't kill, a realm I wouldn't break, or a god I wouldn't forsake for you."

His hand wrapped around her neck as he stared her down with the intensity of the sun blazing in those amber irises.

"Blood will always run thicker than water," she said.

"As my mate, you are my blood. Though I can't bleed out my heritage, or for you I would. Tell me where this is coming from?"

His hand on her neck curved around her nape, angling her mouth perfectly to his.

"You are my damnation," she whispered across his lips.

"Oh my Starlight, our collision may be a masterpiece crafted for the walls of Hell, but should that be next where we meet, you would rule the underworld triumphant."

His lips slanted over hers and she was lost to him. Found in him. She was his eternally, and that's what frightened her the most.

Planting hands on his chest, Nyte yielded to her push, and she slipped around him. All her life she'd only known duty. To the people. To Auster. Before Nyte she'd come to terms with being as good as betrothed to Auster.

Nyte said, "My father claimed the attack was merely a test of your resources and strategy. He had spies watching the slaughter."

Astraea gauged the hesitation in his explanation. "You don't believe him?"

"I'm not certain. I don't know why he would lie to me, but he's never called for an attack without my knowledge. He claimed it was because I've been absent in my diligent pursuit of your capture."

"You can't lose his trust."

"Let me worry about my father."

Astraea knew that wasn't truly why her thoughts stormed and her heart raced.

"Tell me what's wrong," Nyte coaxed, voice soft as a plea, which she rarely heard from him.

"I love you," she blurted, with her back still to him.

The confession tumbled out of her. He'd given her those same beautiful words after their bonding, but she'd not been able to say them back. They were there . . . in her chest, sometimes they clawed up her throat and had been suffocating her for months, but she was too afraid to let them out. Now . . . she realized how much stronger she felt with him by her side, even when he couldn't be physically there. Now, more than anything, she wanted to prove to the world Nyte wasn't terror, he was hope to bring an end to this war with his father.

Nyte's advance from behind tightened her skin. When he pressed his front to her back, her body became pliable to him, and he wrapped around her like a shield from burden.

"Say that again," he murmured over her neck. His lips trailed from the hollow spot behind her ear, and her eyes fluttered closed.

"I love you," she repeated. Each word swelled more in her heart, convincing her mind it would all be okay. They could survive anything together.

Nyte groaned against her; the vibrations scattered across her chest like gentle sand and pebbled her breasts.

"As much as I've been longing to hear that, why does it trouble you?"

"Because I shouldn't. Because I'm afraid it's a choice I can't make. That loving you means I can't love my duty. The people will rebel before we can start convincing them to understand. It's going to break Auster and perhaps start a different war."

His hand on her waist turned her around, and he guided her until the back of her knees met the edge of the bed. He coaxed her down, and lust started to heat her skin with his slow, alluring movements hovering over her body, pressing her into the mattress.

"What do you need me to do?" he asked, so calm and ready to bend the world or break it for her. "Because you're mine now no matter what I have to do to keep it so. I'm determined to see to it that you have anything you desire."

Nyte was known as a nightmare in the minds of every species. He was wicked and cold and cruel . . . but Astraea discovered that his darkness could be warm if one ventured far enough to feel it. Nyte offered himself to her when he could have killed her. His wants had never been his own until this—their bond. He was willing to do or be whatever he had to for it, and that cleaved something inside her.

He deserved to be loved. To receive the devotion he offered.

"Be patient with me," she said quietly. Her legs tightened around his hips when they lowered against her.

Nyte pulled back from trailing kisses along her collar. He claimed her mouth, and her fingers threaded through his dark hair. Only for one long, promising kiss.

"For you, I'm as patient as the night that awaits the full moon. As calm as the stars that await the night. For you, Astraea Lightborne, I would wait in every lifetime of infinity." He smiled, and it was a treasure worth more than any diamond.

"Now," he said in husky murmur. "I believe there's begging to be done and making up to be had."

2

Astraea–Present

The moon was bleeding; casting our world in a red hue like the anger of the gods weighed down on us. It turned the blood-splattered snow around me even more sinister.

I'd lost my sense of morality as my purple blade drowned in crimson from the neck of another celestial.

If you're not with me, you're against me.

The chant followed everybody that fell by my hand, but words weren't enough to stop the darkness creeping over my soul with their deaths.

They weren't all celestials. Vampires, fae, and even humans were eager for the bounty Auster had placed on my head and those of my friends. Some were far more vicious and unrelenting, and if they attacked my friends, mercy was left behind in my retaliation.

My return from the stars began as they hunted, but now I had become more than the hunter: I was a harbinger of death. His maiden.

The dawn never rose again and the dusk would never fall. Worst of all . . . my soul remained severed from its other half. Nyte had left me in this world thrown into disorder and anarchy, but I was determined to bring him back.

Two weeks, and we were no closer to finding a cure for his curse of death-like sleep.

"You wouldn't be close to passing out if you left some for the rest of us," Nadia remarked. She approached tentatively, as did Davina. They were always cautious around me, as if one wrong word would trigger my explosion.

"You can't keep up," I said, leaning down to wipe the blood off my blade on the cloak of a fallen celestial. Catching a glimpse of Auster's constellation sigil on his navy cloak, I felt my guilt for the life I'd taken twist to resentment.

If you're not with me . . . you're against me.

I resented Auster most of all for what he'd made me become.

He had killed me over three hundred years ago, but I could still feel the twist of the phantom key as it lodged in my chest by his cold hand like it was mere weeks ago.

Well, it was—when he'd repeated history to force Nyte to forge our bond. Now Nyte's blood could heal me if I drank it. Or kill me if a weapon coated in it was plunged into my heart. It was a sick, twisted irony.

I fucking despised Auster.

And I mourned for him.

I despise that I mourn for him.

My mental tug-of-war became exhausting and deeply unfair. I could almost feel Auster watching, smirking as if aware of the control he still held, a shadow looming over my every thought. I was furious with him, yes, but I loathed myself even more for letting him linger. For replaying conversations that trickled back from lost memories, as if trying to discover the moment he decided I was his enemy. The moment he knew that he would kill me; all the while I had been oblivious.

When I turned, I was met with the concerned face of Davina.

We were at the edge of Vesitire's central city. We came here often to track and take note of their defenses. I couldn't be idle for a moment. If I wasn't arguing with Drystan over every slight theory that could bring Nyte back, I was focused on a rescue plan.

Auster had Eltanin. *My* dragon.

The audacity of Auster to capture Eltanin filled my body with fury, but above that, I feared what he might do to the young dragon getting closer to his second moon cycle that would see him grow again.

All that kept me from recklessly charging through the city and challenging him now was that Auster had the city completely under his fist. Celestial patrols were everywhere. Most commoners who caught a glimpse of me would want to capture me for the large bounty he promised. The city would become blood, rubble, and ash if I were to unleash Lightsdeath to get what I wanted with no consideration for others.

I couldn't let myself become that even if I was powerful enough to do it. Though I couldn't deny that all my recent failures made the thought of getting a taste of triumph tempting.

Lightsdeath lay dormant within me—a deadly gift of primordial power that could devastate the world if unleashed without my complete control. In an exchange to bring Drystan back, Death itself had done exactly what we hoped and given me this advantage—a power that could kill gods.

He wanted the end of Dusk and Dawn, my creators. After all they'd done, and for taking Nyte from me, it became my dark desire to end them myself.

I feared Lightsdeath could make me forget myself and lose the ability to tell friend from foe. I remembered Nyte's struggles with Nightsdeath long ago, and now more than ever I *needed* his help to learn to harness this new gift.

"Have you noticed there's a gap in the west wall? The guards are spaced enough apart that it could be a blind spot for us to slip inside," Davina said thoughtfully.

I tracked where she'd indicated. The gap was small, but we could make it through. Auster had a veil set by a mage around the wall to prevent me from stepping through the void and easily evading his soldiers' efforts to keep me out.

"Then what?" Nadia countered. She folded her arms, always wearing a calculating scowl as if she hated herself for *wanting* to be a part of this. "We'd be fresh bait on the other side of that wall."

"All we have to do is make it to Eltanin; then we'll have a fast escape with him." Davina replied. "Is he big enough to carry three yet?"

"Barely," I said.

What I learned from Drystan, who remained a prickly ally for finding a cure for his brother, was that Eltanin hadn't forged a dragon bond to me as a rider. Not like Drystan had with his great red dragon, Athebyne, freed from the Guardian Temple we visited months ago. Past their second moon cycle was when dragons were mature enough to consider a bonded rider, and so the urgency to get Eltanin back was amplified since Auster might manage to break him into submission and bond with him. It was rare and barbaric, but possible. Outlawed, of course, during the time of the dragons, but I didn't think Auster was bound by any moral or lawful code in his determination to triumph over me.

"Let's go," I said. "There's been enough blood spilled today."

I'd gained what I needed as my objective wasn't to find where to infiltrate, but *when*. Those who scrambled out to find me worked to my advantage as I squeezed information out of their last breaths before I killed them. Which led me to know Auster called for the citizens of Vesitire to gather at the castle in a few days.

I glanced at the tips of my black feathers brushing the snow as I unglamoured my wings. The stark color of them was a brand from Death—a dark omen to my kind, the celestials, whose wings were tones of silver. Despite this, I'd never felt more confident with my new touch of darkness.

Taking to the skies, I returned to Nadir's home where we'd been taking refuge the last few weeks. The mage lived in a precariously tall wooden structure hidden and protected by a veil of magick. They'd graciously offered to hide our band of the continent's most wanted.

Passing through the shield tingled my skin and flared my silver tattoos. Nadia and Davina would take longer to make it back on foot.

Inside the home, I barely acknowledged Nadir, who was sitting in the main room smoking something in their pipe as usual. A plant, which I'd come to realize had to be some kind of relaxant. I think they tried to pretend we weren't intruding on their peace.

Two levels up, I slowed by the room Zathrian was in. The door was slightly ajar, and no matter how many times I saw him lying in that bed, with Rose by his side, my heart sank with despair. The revelation of Zath being Nephilim—half celestial, half mortal—had come as a shock, but I was glad for it because the sword through his gut would have been fatal otherwise. Instead, he'd been unconscious since Auster's ambush. While Zath's heartbeat was a strong promise of recovery, Nyte's was as distant and shallow as a fleeting drum.

I passed Zath's room and headed up another two levels.

Every time I pushed open the door Nyte lay beyond, hope that he might have somehow awoken flickered like a candle in my chest. That he would be sitting up, and when those amber eyes found me, they would light up brighter than all the lost dawns our world had suffered.

Countless times now, that candle snuffed out the second I saw him lying in the same bed, as still as death. I didn't think there would be a time I wouldn't look at him and feel like a hand had punched into my chest and taken a tight grip of my heart.

Taking off my weapons, cloak, and boots, I climbed in beside him, hooking my leg over his and tucking myself into his side. He wasn't warm, but my magick glowed under my palm on his chest, heating both of us, and I reached for the shallow song of his heart. Relief flooded me when I found it, and I closed my eyes.

My moment of peace barely lasted a minute before I heard the steps march down the hall and burst into the room without a hint of a knock. My eyes flew open and I pinned Drystan with a glare. His eyes beaming of excitement was a grating contrast to my irritation.

"Dragon bonds," he said, grinning.

It was the brightest expression anyone in this house had mustered for weeks.

"Explain before I cast you out without moving an inch," I warned.

Things between us had been tense. Though we'd colluded in a ploy to get the power of Lightsdeath, that's where our alliance was supposed to end. He blamed me for leaving—*dying*—long ago and taking his brother away from him when Nyte closed himself off from everyone. Now it was again my fault Nyte was gone. I didn't know if my friendship with Drystan could be mended, if he would ever forgive me, but I wasn't giving up hope, even if I couldn't show it right now.

"Your bond with Nyte was already forged when the curse took him," he continued, "but what if it hadn't been before he fell under? What if you tried to claim your bond with him now, so he would have to claim *back*? What if it would have been enough to awaken his consciousness?"

"As you said, our bond is forged, so that's not an option anymore."

"What if another bond could do the same?"

I pushed myself up, frowning and turning it over in my mind.

"A dragon?" I concluded. Drystan gave me a nod of confirmation before crossing the room to where stacks of books lay.

He spent most of his time studying in his own room, but occasionally he brought his books and journals here. We never spoke, but I had to admit the company was welcome sometimes. Even in silence, sharing the weight of the burden between us for a while was a reprieve from bearing it all alone.

"Eltanin doesn't have a bonded rider. If we get him back by his second cycle, maybe with your persuasion he'll choose Nyte. Forging that bond could reach a part of Nyte's subconscious that might snap him out of his sleep," Drystan went on, flipping through pages.

I leaned on my thighs at the edge of the bed, contemplating.

My hope began to spark as I dwelled on the possibility. There had always been something *familiar* between Nyte and Eltanin that made me believe the black celestial dragon might choose Nyte as his rider.

Drystan thumped his book shut when he found the enchanted map that seemed to have been haphazardly used as a reading placeholder at some point. What I recalled about him, and what hadn't changed, was how chaotic and disorganized he kept his things. Yet he always remembered exactly where everything was when he needed it.

"You still haven't learned the concept of a bookmark," I mused.

It was an attempt at normality, kindness, but even that felt awkward between us. I despised the rift I didn't know how to disperse.

Drystan slipped me a look, debating whether he wanted to reflect on the past with me. His jaw worked, then he busied himself with papers.

"Do you remember everything from the past?"

"Not really. Most of the time I recall things in the moment, like just now with your inability to organize a thing."

"It's organized my way."

That twitched a smile onto my mouth.

"I'm sorry," I whispered. Drystan's shoulders locked. "I don't know where to begin."

"So don't." His sharp eyes cut to me. "Let the past die."

"I can't," I said desperately, pushing up from the bed. "You were my friend. The first I had beyond my suffocated life around the High Celestials and my duty."

"Then you *left* me. Both of you did, and I had *no one*. You can't blame me for healing that wound over centuries and denying you the blade to do it again."

That hurt so deeply, a physical wound would be easier to bear right now.

"I'm going to win this war. Nyte is going to wake up. Then we're staying right here with you until the end of our age."

Drystan held me with a cold stare, but his eyes flexed a fraction. He didn't respond, turning his attention back to his journals.

He placed the enchanted map he'd loaned me in the Libertatem on the table and slipped a new overlay on top of it. I strolled closer to catch a glimpse.

"There's sixteen more temples with dragon paintings across Solanis, which means sixteen dragons to free just like we did with Athebyne—I hope. You told Nyte to tell me your key is with the dragons. When you broke it, you sent the pieces to these temples, didn't you?"

"Yes. Your father was granted the ability to wield it without harm by my creators—I think they want me dead as much as Auster does. I couldn't risk the weapon in their hands, and they had us in that temple. So I broke it, and I knew that if I didn't escape Auster, you would understand what I meant and get it back without me."

"It was smart thinking. But do we really need the key back?"

"Being Lightsdeath is only half of what it will take to kill Dusk and Dawn. The key is the other."

Sometimes as I slept I thought I felt the key's pain. Heard the cries of broken power like a violin off-key. Grating, demanding someone to tend to the instrument to fix it back in tune. I wondered if ignoring the key's calls to be found and reforged would have any greater effect on me than a few headaches and restless nights.

"That could take months," he said, itching with our mutual despair. "But at least if Eltanin doesn't choose Nyte to bond with, we might have sixteen other dragons to try."

My hope grew into a larger flame against my will.

"You really think it could work?" I whispered.

Drystan flicked a look up, and it was the most caring emotion he'd shared with me. I'd come to accept his cold shoulder over the weeks. With no solutions and hitting endless walls with suggestions, I couldn't blame him for hardly being able to tolerate me.

"I really *hope* it can," he amended before pivoting. "Since you mentioned my father, have you seen him at all during your scouting of the city?"

"No," I said. In truth, I hadn't thought of him at all while my vengeance was acutely set on Auster.

Drystan paused at the door, making to leave. "Perhaps Auster has already disposed of him. A shame; I've been looking forward to doing it myself."

He said it so coldly and detached from any emotion. His indifference was a mask over his pain. Though he deserved to face his monstrous father and be the one to end him, as did Nyte, I thought it would also be the most difficult thing they'd ever have to do.

I was about to crawl back into bed when a familiar head of pink hair appeared in the doorway. My mouth opened but no words formed on my tongue. I'd never seen Rose look so tired and frightened than in these last weeks. She hardly ate and had barely said a word. In all the chaos of my own life, I hadn't seen just how much she'd come to care for Zath. Something was different about her now; there was a light in her eyes I hadn't seen in too long, which straightened my spine and skipped a beat in my chest before she even spoke.

"He's awake."

3

Astraea

I didn't know why I was nervous to see Zathrian. He was still the exact same person I knew, no matter *what* he was. Yet my hands clammed, my heart raced, and I faltered just past the door at the sight of him, propped up and *smiling*.

As if he hadn't narrowly avoided death. As if his wound wasn't still bandaged and healing. He was just . . . Zath. All bright blue eyes and dashing grin. When his gaze slipped to me, a whimper escaped my lips.

"I don't look that bad, do I?" he said, voice still thick from his long rest. "It's good to see you, Stray."

My brow crumpled to hear him call me by that name. To recall how much of a dear friend he'd been while I was finding my way.

I let out a breathy laugh, and the image of him blurred more as I edged closer.

"How is he?" I asked Lilith, who had been his savior. Her knowledge of nature made the medicines that kept him alive, and I was sure her magick had healing properties as well.

"He is healing well," Lilith informed me, straightening from checking the bandages over his bare torso.

"Doesn't feel that well," Zath said, giving himself a mocking inspection. His skin had lost its glow and tan and was now clammy and pale. His eyes carried dark circles despite the cheerfulness that added a sparkle to his irises.

"I'll get you some water," Lilith said.

He said to me, "I know I'm very good looking, but I'm spoken for, so you can stop staring."

My eyes flashed briefly to Rose, and her cheeks flushed, but her familiar scowl pinned on Zath, who winked at her. My body relaxed to see her spirit somewhat returning.

"You don't want me to speak for you; it won't be kind," she said.

"Come on, Thorns. Let me have a little fantasy in my comeback from death."

"You cheated," Rose countered.

"You're not glad I turned out to be a supernatural being and survived it?"

"Of course I am," she grumbled, crossing her arms.

"Nephilim," I said. His attention slipped back to me with a guilty smile. "Surprise?"

I shook my head, incredulous. "Why didn't you tell me?"

"How could I? You were already dealing with being told *you* weren't human."

"I wouldn't have felt so alone in that." I didn't mean for it to sound like an accusation, but I was hurt that he'd kept such a life-changing secret from me and carried it alone.

Being Nephilim would have been a lonely, hard burden to carry. The celestials had been away for a long time behind the veil, but now that they were out, Zath and his kind would be in hiding like the fae had from the king's forces not so long ago. Auster had regarded what Zath was with such disdain it boiled my blood now. The Nephilim were hunted and either killed nor outcasted.

"I'm sorry," he said. "Truthfully I've been in denial about what I am for a long time. I didn't want to believe I was different."

"What does it mean to be Nephilim?" Rose asked.

"That I'm even more charming than you knew before."

"You call yourself charming; I find you irritating."

Zath chuckled, but it turned to winces of pain as he clutched his abdomen.

Rose huffed, adjusting his pillows to make him sit back. The tender care she displayed even with a sour frown warmed my heart.

"So what is our plan now, star-maiden?" Zath mused.

"Your plan is to rest. You're not in the clear yet."

"As I hear; I've rested far too much. Of course, that dark bastard still has to best me, doesn't he?"

The light comment regarding Nyte's situation didn't land with the humor intended. Zath's expression fell.

"Is he—?"

"He's going to be okay," I said quickly, more to quell the fast rush of panic in myself than to assure Zath. "But as I would tell him if he awoke right now, you're not going anywhere until you can muster full combat without a wince."

Zath groaned as he tried to sit up more; obviously he wouldn't be lifting a sword anytime soon, never mind swinging it.

"Sounds like a challenge," he said, voice strained with the pain he was trying to distract us from.

"Stop being difficult," Rose fussed.

"Why does it feel like our roles have switched?"

Rose's jaw worked, and I thought in any other circumstance she would abandon him from annoyance, but she didn't leave. Instead she sat back in her chair, and it was only then I noticed the knitting equipment and a surprisingly neat half scarf.

I didn't get to question the unlikely hobby when she said, "What is the plan? I heard you've been scouting."

"We've been monitoring Auster's defenses, trying to find any cracks we can exploit to get Eltanin back."

"Eli?" Zath said, his brow pulled together with a wash of upset. Then it twisted to anger. "That asshole has Eli?"

My sad expression conveyed the confirmation.

That roused Zath again into believing he was exempt from healer's orders. Throwing back the covers, he managed to swing his legs off the bed, but his brace on the side and pause for breath gave away his lack of strength.

"I just need to stretch and wake up a bit more, but I'm coming with you when you go to get him back."

His skin was slick with a sheen of sweat, and his breath wasn't steady. I didn't argue against his determination, believing it would only make the stubborn ass push himself more and delay his healing.

"Death isn't easy to come back from," I said quietly.

He looked up with a wave of understanding.

"It seems we're forming a band of death-touched." With that, his eyes flicked up to Rose and a hint of fear creased around his eyes. "Though I very much plan to make sure you never acquire a membership."

"Worry about yourself," she said, but I thought her face softened at his care. Something she wasn't used to receiving.

"She's right," I said. "I'm not the scared and vulnerable girl of the manor anymore. I . . . remember a lot of who I was, what I'm capable of."

I thought about trying to explain the change in me, but Lightsdeath was still an inconceivable notion that I hadn't the chance to figure out for myself yet.

"I'm getting that sense," he said bittersweetly. "Being in your company is strangely intimidating."

I huffed. "No need to flatter me."

He smiled, and it dispersed some of the dark clouds that swirled around me.

"It's in the way you carry yourself now: as the leader you were born to be. Even the way you talk with confidence. It's . . . I'm so proud of you." My eyes stung, and I crouched in front of him, taking his hands. Zath added, "But it doesn't matter what you are or the power you have; you're still my friend, and I want to be by your side to help."

"Soon," I promised.

My gratitude for having Zath in my life was immeasurable. He wasn't a shield to guard me; he was a pillar of strength on and off a battlefield.

But I couldn't wait for him to heal to make my move toward retrieving Eltanin.

"How is he?" Rose asked quietly. I detected a note of guilt as she inquired about Nyte now when she hadn't over the weeks. She could hardly tolerate his company when he was conscious.

"As well as can be for now," I said.

"Zath might not be able to help, but I can. I want to come with you next time you go scouting."

"I'll let you know next time we head out," I said, though it burned in my throat as a lie.

I had been yearning to have both of them fighting alongside me for weeks, but now I would be acting without them. I was done with merely observing Auster taking his fill of my kingdom and basking in the manipulated minds of my people.

Bidding them goodnight, though I didn't know if that was accurate when the blood moon always dominated the sky, I left and was heading down the stairs when I heard Davina and Nadia. I found them in the main room in conversation with Nadir, their cheeks flushed from the cold trek back.

"The wings are so unfair," Nadia grumbled upon seeing me, brushing snow off her shoulders.

She glanced to an invention above the blazing fire pit that kept time for us. Nadir had a flare for unique things, and this used sand like an hourglass, except it spiraled slowly toward hour markers, tracking the whole day. The winter arrived thick and without mercy even in the daytime, but it was closing in on midnight and the late hours plummeted to lethal temperatures.

"You should get warmed up," I said to them.

Davina seemed to notice my somberness. She approached, reaching out and squeezing my arms.

"Tomorrow will be a better day," she said, always so optimistic that her presence along with Lilith's was often the only breath above water any of us felt.

I plastered on a smile, though it was hardly convincing. Tomorrow . . . well, not even Davina's warmth could chase away the foreboding chill creeping through me.

They headed to their rooms for much needed rest and heat, which left me alone with Nadir. I found their company strangely relaxing yet unnerving. They reclined in an armchair by the fire, bare feet propped on a wooden kitchen stool. Their emerald filigree pattered shirt was tucked into black pants, but most of the buttons were undone to expose the dark skin of their chest.

They smoked absentmindedly while their fingers idly swirled around a teacup. Their silent glances to me often made me feel that secrets could never stay buried. Even those I didn't know I was harboring.

"Self-sacrifice is in your nature," they said with a knowing lilt. Their eyes wandered lazily, likely the effects of whatever was in their pipe.

"I think it's in everyone's nature for those they love."

"Not everyone. Selfishness is often a victorious beast."

I'd had various suspicions about Nadir. Could they foresee things? Was their magick far more than a typical human mage? Did what they smoked in their pipe merely give them a convincing air of wisdom beyond their means?

Regardless, I sat with them. There was something about them that made me desperate for relief even if they could only provide mindless ramblings, which I had to find my own meanings within.

They blew out their next drag of the pipe and gave a lopsided smile. Their eyes had been yellow with a vertical pupil when I'd first met them; now they must have switched the enhancement in their starlight matter—a substance crafted from fallen star matter and spelled by mages for various cosmetic and practical uses—which changed them to an unnatural vibrant green with a circular pupil.

My sight flicked briefly outside, catching on the tall thorned stem with fluorescent blue flowerings. A beautiful, deceptively harmless plant, which was poisonous to my kind. Depending on the use and strength, it could incapacitate a celestial's magick and weaken their bodies.

"Does the nebulora make you wary?" they asked in reply to my wandering observation.

"I guess I'm wondering why you grow it."

They shrugged, nonchalant. "It's nothing personal to your kind. I have obsidian, which can harm the celestials too, and stormstone that is lethal to vampires. I have them all in forms you couldn't decipher."

That furrowed my brow. "Forms?"

"It's not always about possessing the weapon but having the cunning to use it in ways one least sees coming."

Nadir liked to speak in riddles. Usually I would indulge in the game, but I was too on edge.

"The nebulora is rather obvious."

"It is nearly bloomed to perfection; then you might never see it again."

I shivered involuntarily, eyes fixing on the glowing cosmic plant that grew from soil untouched by the white snow. When I thought of a weapon, sharp things and magick flares came to mind, but I stared at something so quiet and beautiful, knowing it could kill me in far more cunning ways.

"I left a gift for you in your room," Nadir said.

That took me by surprise. I didn't want to question their kindness, but it was unexpected to receive something now when we'd been here for weeks.

"What is it?" I asked warily.

"We can't have you unequipped as well as unaccompanied." Their eyes tilted down at me with a reprimand they didn't voice.

This was another instance that roused my suspicion over whether Nadir had some kind of clairvoyance. I didn't confirm I harbored any plans to leave, but I didn't need to.

"Thank you," I said.

"Unaccompanied where?" Drystan said, strolling into the main room. He came around the hearth, taking Nadir's pipe and inhaling long and deep. With the immediate relaxation he exhibited blowing out the smoke, I was starting to reconsider my desire to sample, or at least inquire about, whatever root it was.

"I was going to train tomorrow, but it seems my combatant will have to be the most sturdy tree," I lied easily.

Drystan hooked a brow at me, settling down on the rug by the fire, his knee bent and posture the most at ease I'd seen. Perhaps it was from the hope gained with our new prospective attempt to wake Nyte, and I only prayed the loss of that hope, if it didn't work, wouldn't crush more of his spirit.

"You have an immense power inside you, and you want to dally in swordplay?"

Nadir's lazy gaze slipped to me, a lingering meaning hidden in his answer. "She can't rely on one skill that could be taken away."

With that, my attention caught on the fluorescent blue flowering nebulora outside again with a jittering unease. A warning that no power was unstoppable.

"Are the falling stars affecting your magick?" Drystan asked me curiously, like I was a thing to study in his journals.

The stars were causing more destruction than ever before. I'd seen the gaps between them stretch apart, but this was the first time they'd started plummeting to the land as catastrophic rocks ablaze.

"No. I don't think the cosmic imbalance is affecting me like it has the other celestials."

"Maybe when we get Eltanin back we should wait this out—let celestial magick weaken so we have an advantage," Drystan pondered.

I shook my head. "My war is with Auster and your father, no one else. I want to spare as many of my people as I can, and waiting only gives them more time to turn innocents against me."

"Besides," Nadir interjected. "It would take decades for them to be substantially weakened, and it doesn't affect their ability to fight with mortal weapons."

Drystan hummed, taking another inhale of the pipe before passing it back to Nadir. Then he shifted to retrieve a small journal from his back pocket. I didn't impose on his moment of thought as he flicked through his own writing.

"I'm going to get rest," I announced.

Drystan didn't look up from his pages. Nadir gave me a small smile with a dip of their head, an unspoken tender farewell in their bright green eyes.

Back in my room with Nyte, I found Nadir's gift immediately. Combat leathers with a beauty like nothing I'd seen before hung beautifully on a wooden dress form in the corner. I floated toward it lost in awe, taking in the exquisite craft. It wasn't just black; the shoulders gave the illusion of dark purple tipped feathers made of leather. When I moved around the garment, the candlelight caught on different surfaces, and I found the sleek bodice shifted from black to an iridescent purple hue depending on the light.

I bathed in a tub filled with steaming water I assumed Nadir had also used his magick to place in this room. With a sulking heart and a lost soul, I watched Nyte with my chin resting on my folded arms over the bath's edge.

"If this plan doesn't work . . ." I started, but my words cut off, as I needed to swallow the lump in my throat. "I haven't posed the only other option we might have to try to save you. I think Drystan knows of it too, but he's hoping it will be the last resort. I don't think I could cross realms with you anymore. I have a debt to Death to pay here. But Drystan could take you back through the mirror to where you belong, and then the curse from this realm won't hold you. Maybe there you won't have to be the villain anymore. Maybe home is where you get to be . . . free."

A tear slipped down my cheek at the thought. Was it selfish to even try to bring him back with Eltanin and the dragon bond? Nyte deserved so much better than the cruel hand life and death had dealt him. He'd become what he had to in order to survive and protect his brother. Now he had a chance for a new life and I couldn't let him go.

He was so beautiful lying there that the pain in my soul swelled. I harbored so much love for him, and I didn't want it to ever stop, but it was also killing me inside no matter what was to come.

I sighed, washing my hair with a honey shampoo before getting out and drying off. Wearing only a cotton robe, I crawled over the bed, hovering over Nyte and cupping his cheek. I pressed my lips to his, but they were cold and I held back my whimper.

"You waited centuries for me. There's no measure of time I won't wait for you. Forever, if need be. In every lifetime eternal until we are triumphant."

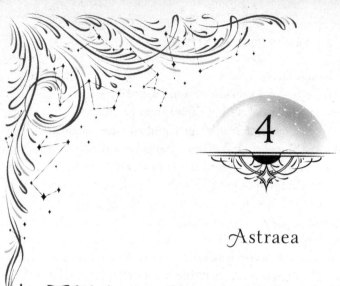

4

Astraea

If I had to guess, I'd say at least two hours had passed since I left Nadir's home. It wasn't without tethers of guilt making every step away difficult. Or it could just be the thick snow that made walking feel like climbing a mountain.

I would have flown but the sky was clear tonight, and with no cloud cover, I couldn't risk being seen.

My plan was . . . well, I wouldn't even call it such.

I knew I could be stealthy enough to infiltrate the city alone. Once within the walls, however, events could unfold a number of ways—my capture, having to wear more blood of my kin—but I hoped to free Eltanin without ensuing chaos while Auster was distracted by his address to the city.

Wishful thinking, most likely.

The only part I wasn't confident of was my restraint not to let my emotions act out recklessly when I saw Auster within reach. When I would have to watch him claim *my* throne, twisting the minds of *my* people, and remember how he had harmed *my* friends with no consequence.

Yet.

Wrath was coming for him. Wrath was me.

I wondered if the patrolled borders between kingdoms no longer existed, as the measure had been implemented for control during his Libertatem game by Nyte's father. Auster would have no reason for it. Perhaps he used the abolishment of the borders to appear even more heroic. He was the High Celestial who saved the continent first from a tyrannical king, then from its dark-hearted maiden and her villainous bond.

A breathy laugh escaped me at the thought. I found it both a humorous and delightful concept. It's exactly what Nyte and I were, except we would aim all our villainy toward Auster Nova and Nyte's father.

I kept aware and silent, watching the path ahead but focusing mostly on my hearing. After a stretch of time, I started to get a sense I was being followed. I hadn't heard any sure footfall or crack of branches, but weariness unsettled in my gut and my skin pricked with awareness.

If I was being followed through this woodland, my stalker was being *very* careful.

I flexed my gloved fingers and slipped one off. My magick was far stronger without the leather barrier. With a snap of my fingers a light sparked between them, a small violet pulse. The warmth was glorious, but I wanted whoever the pursuant was to think twice at the sight of my unpredictable magick.

They gave themselves up with a step too fast through the crisp snow, or perhaps they wanted me aware now.

I cast my hand out, fingers pointed, in their direction, but they were agile, and my magick splintered the side of the tree they ducked behind.

"You've lost your touch," he called.

My battle stance slackened and my magick cooled.

"Drystan?" I called out, mildly irritated.

"Don't stop," he said, appearing from his cover with a sword in hand. He twisted his wrist, advancing with it braced.

"What are you doing?" I bit out.

He shrugged, then attacked with no warning.

I gasped at the vertical swipe of his sword I twisted to avoid, then clumsily pulled my own weapon free. Our blades clashed, not giving me pause to calculate as he seized the advantage of my outrage.

"If you wanted to kill me you could have taken a dagger with Nyte's blood to my chest already," I said through gritted teeth.

My returning memories weren't so clear. On the contrary, they often confused and frustrated me wildly when they were like dreams: flashes of people and things and events that didn't fully feel real. I recalled Drystan was no fighter in the past, however, and that had severely changed over the centuries I was gone.

"Consider this a reprimand for your stupidity," he snapped back, continuing his unrelenting advance.

"You picked up some skills over the years."

"You've certainly lost some."

I was panting already. I really needed to train harder, and that's where my frustration came from: knowing how adept at combat I'd been in the past, and yet in this life I was barely pushing past novice against someone with real fighting skill. I'd used magick for efficiency against most people I'd fought so far, or I'd faced common folk and rogue vampires, whose skills in weaponry were hardly a challenge.

My coordination faltered when my ankle caught on a branch hidden by the snow. Falling onto my back, I hissed at the tip of Drystan's blade over my chest.

He smirked down at me. The amusement grated on my rising temper.

"Wanted to prove you could best me?" I grunted.

"I wanted to gauge how long you might last in your reckless endeavor," he said, removing the threat and popping the sword between his hands against the ground. "I'd give you less than a day beyond the city wall before you got yourself captured."

"Your faith in me is charming." I pushed up before the cold could seep through my leathers.

"Did you really think you could take on the task of retrieving Eltanin alone?" His ire creased deeply on his brow.

"It'll be easier for one person to get inside the wall and remain hidden. I planned to be back in a few days."

Drystan mocked me with a scoff.

"I can't decide if your arrogance is delusional or faintly admirable." His expression turned harsh. "There's no second chance for you this time. If you die, this world dies with you, either by Auster's corruption or Nyte's vengeance."

"I am Lightsdeath now; it was *your* plan to make me that, and I've stopped underestimating myself, so I don't need you to start."

We matched disagreeing stares while our breaths frosted the air between us.

"I know you, Astraea. You would have gone into that city and lost focus of everything the moment you had Auster in your sights."

"I know what I need to do, and you're only slowing me down."

I tried to brush past him, but I detected the shift of his arm in time to raise my sword to meet his. The heat of our glares through crossed blades was enough to dull the sharp chill of the night.

We were moving again and I led the attack this time. I honed in on him like I would with an enemy, seeing him as nothing but a barrier stopping me from getting to Eltanin and having Nyte back. If he wouldn't back down, neither would I.

My steps became a dance awakening from a distant place in my mind. It was then I realized that despite my vicious efforts, forcing his faltering offense through the trees, I would never harm him. There was a tear in my soul for what was broken between us, and as Drystan stepped around a tree, my next horizontal swipe lodged my blade into the timber.

I let go of the hilt, leaving it suspended there while I gathered my breath.

"So a world upended by war showed you can't fight with your books?" I said, reflecting on the man I knew from long ago, who always had a fascination for knowledge and arts but never with fighting.

Drystan huffed, a bitter sound. "A hundred books can sharpen a mind to be far deadlier than any steel. But what I learned was that books were often an escape from the rage and pain; fighting was the only way to keep those emotions from killing me by giving the pain back to the world."

That unexpected, deep truth was a slice far worse than what he could have inflicted on my flesh. I snapped my eyes to him, but he'd already dismissed the vulnerable words by sheathing his sword.

"We should go before the others notice and come after you too," he said with an icy distance now.

Then it dawned on me. "You didn't follow me to haul me back?"

His smirk lacked humor. "Of course not. We might have a way to wake Nyte up, and I'm not leaving it solely in your reckless hands."

I opened my mouth to argue, but Drystan suddenly straightened, casting a look through the depthless forest and holding a hand up to silence me. I turned rigid, then scrambled into a defensive position when I heard steps racing toward us.

"Shit," Drystan swore, raising his sword. "Nightcrawlers. Maybe a soulless or shadowless too."

"You all but called them to us with your unnecessary violence," I hissed.

He didn't get to retort when one of the vampires reached him. Watching Drystan in combat while it wasn't aimed at me just showed how much had changed. He was good. Great, in fact. He moved with as much elegance and form as I could hope to regain.

My sights fell to my sword, still suspended in the tree, and when I heard the snarls of more vampires approaching I cast my hand out toward it. A flare of violet light engulfed the blade, and I shifted my leg back for balance, crying out with the force it took to cut clean through the trunk with my magick-infused sword.

The tree toppled and several vampires faltered in their approach, trying to scramble from the path of the thick trunk instead. My hand wrapped around the hilt of the sword that flew toward me, my arm drawing back with the force. I barely got the chance to tighten my grip before my blade slashed across the first nightcrawler that narrowly missed being crushed by the tree. A loud *boom* resounded through the forest from it.

"Was that really necessary?" Drystan called, not faltering in his combat.

"It took out five of them at once!" I shouted back. "You're welcome."

"And likely summoned a hundred more."

Well, he maybe had a point there. Though I hoped we'd finish off the last of those here and be long out of range before any more heard the commotion and came.

All I thought about was killing. There was a certain dark exhilaration to it. I felt the slick tear of flesh and heard their wails as victory. I didn't see my satisfaction as wrong when it was either kill or be killed. I'd spent most of my short life back, almost six years now, being manipulated by Goldfell—the man who'd found me staggering lost through the woods when I first returned to this land and taken me in. He made me believe I was no better than flesh to keep him warm and a pretty prize to collect.

Now I was a reckoning to all who stood against me.

My magick sliced through the wings of a nightcrawler, and my blade plunged through his throat, cutting off his piercing cry. He was the last body to fall before all became silent save for the harsh breaths of me and Drystan.

"Let's go," I said, not waiting for him as I made haste away from the blood-painted snow.

We ran through the woodland, letting the icy air spear down my throat and set fire to my lungs. Soon the pain subsided, though I knew that blessing in the moment would be punishment to my body later.

I didn't stop until I broke out of the tree line and came to the familiar hill overlooking the glowing central city of Vesitire. It was so beautiful I forgot about the corruption that had spread within.

"What's your great plan to breach the heavily guarded wall?" Drystan muttered dryly, surveying while we kept to tree shadow cover.

"There's a blind spot between guards. Small, but if we're careful . . ."

His scoff dismissed that idea. "You're lucky I came."

He began heading down the hill, and his smug attitude was feeding my ire irrationally. Muttering curses under my breath, I hastily caught up to him, but he was heading away from the opening I'd indicated.

"Are you disregarding my way in because it wasn't your meticulously crafted plan?" I grumbled.

"Petty arrogance isn't really my thing."

"You've known of a route in all this time?"

My steps marched after him, but Drystan was so calm and composed.

"You might have ruled from this city for a century, but you were never locked inside. Being a prisoner breeds a particular obsession to discover every inconspicuous way out."

"You weren't locked inside," I argued. Though as I said it, I realized I'd never learned about Drystan's life with those walls after I was gone.

He said, "Nyte was the one with the freedom. He was useful to our father, especially with how destructive he became in your absence. I think my father knew that Nyte would turn on him and the city if he tried to keep Nyte by his side. Instead that was my role. The perfect prince, always poised and pretty in the castle, the one who would take over his throne someday and for whom he'd arrange a marriage for political advantage."

My heart sank for him. "I'm glad it never came to that." It was a pitiful statement, but I didn't have much else to offer.

"It nearly did. He desperately wanted me to wed one of the elder vampires to gain their allegiance." He chuckled in reflection, though it was bitter-coated humor. "She never would have agreed, so my father made me try to *court* her, make her fall for me. It wasn't the first time he suggested I win people over that way. Nyte was his weapon as good as steel, while I was his weapon as good as a courtesan. I guess you could say we're both very good at what we do."

I'd stopped walking with the terrible upset that hollowed my stomach. I stared after him with pity, though I knew he would despise seeing it. Drystan was so beautiful, and the way he could speak and lure someone in with carefully mastered stares alone made the realization slam into me.

"We don't have time for rest," Drystan said, turning back to me with hard eyes.

We both knew it wasn't why I stopped, but he didn't want to talk further on the matter.

"When you found a way out of the city . . . where did you go?" I asked; the question hung between us as fragile as glass.

"Anywhere. I couldn't get far, of course, but you'd be surprised by the many wonders that can be found somewhere you think is too familiar to be worth deep exploration."

It was the first time I'd felt a spark of inspiration for anything other than my rage and retribution. I wanted him to show me, to go with him and explore what he'd found, and then when the war was won . . . we could go anywhere.

I followed when Drystan turned and walked again. The tension between us felt thick, but there was a light I wanted to reach for.

"You wouldn't go on these ventures and not take note of them," I said, offering a token of conversation that might add a stitch or two on the cracks of our friendship. "Is that what you write in your journals?"

"Among other things."

I envied his ability to slow down enough to take in his surroundings and findings, then make sure he could revisit the memory anytime he liked.

"Would you ever show me?"

His brow hooked as he peered back at me. Then he drew a long breath.

"If we make it out of all of this, I might consider showing you. Or better yet, taking you."

I broke a small smile even though he didn't see it. I held onto those words as a promise, which added more determination to triumph in this war.

Drystan led us, ducking cautiously down the hill and around the city wall. A distant noise caught my attention, like the wind was on fire heading straight to us. Instinctively, my sight tracked up and my eyes widened.

"Shit," Drystan swore, taking off in a run, and I didn't hesitate to follow.

"The stars . . ." I trailed off in a panting breath as the snow made our retreat so much more laborious.

"The wrath of your parents, perhaps," Drystan deduced.

We'd only seen the fireballs from afar and sometimes felt the ground quake with their impact. This was the first time we ran from being the direct target of one.

With gritted teeth of frustration, sweat began to trickle down my spine as I thought we wouldn't clear the blast radius in time. I cast my magick out with heat, melting the snow beneath our feet, which allowed us to push our legs faster.

"You shouldn't have done that; your light is like a beacon," Drystan hissed.

"Would you rather we become buried a hundred feet under?" I snapped back.

I hoped anyone who might have seen the flare I tried to keep small would believe it to be related to the flaming ball hurtling toward our land. The red hue cast over us from the crimson moon along with the falling stars turned our world into a land of blood and fire. I didn't know how long we had before the destruction started to lay waste, leaving nothing for us to salvage if we managed to defeat Auster then the gods.

At least this star seemed small and would land outside the city where thousands of citizens lived.

The crackling from the meteor grew louder, and the heat grew against my back. Panic bubbled inside me, but we reached a cave near the river shore surrounding Vesitire's main city.

Drystan grabbed my hand, hauling me inside. I gripped him just as desperately as we huddled into ourselves right as the blast into the river shook the ground, trembling from my feet through my whole body. I threw out a shield of magick over the cave entrance, hoping it would provide *some* protection.

The star pummeled into the water, which would have drowned us in an instant if it flooded into this cave. My body tightened at the force battering against my magick, and for a moment I thought it would shatter through. The crashing against it felt endless, pushing and pushing against me.

"You can hold it," Drystan said, his voice a soft encouragement barely audible through the chaos.

He held me tightly, and the firm assurance of not being alone gave me strength enough to keep holding on with everything I had.

"I can't . . . hold it . . ." I said between strained breaths.

"You can let go now, but brace yourself," he said.

I didn't need to be told twice when magick was burning through my veins. I only managed one breath of relief before my next held as water swallowed us.

Neither of us anticipated the low wave would still be enough to knock us off balance and send us drifting deeper into the cave.

The water wasn't high enough to swim, and I could only let the shallow current take me until it ran out. Or, as our unlucky streak would have it, until we slammed into a wall and the remaining wave continued around the bend.

The water only lapped up to my elbows and thighs as I was on all fours, drawing breath with sharp adrenaline as I feared more water could come crashing through the cave at any moment.

"I've never enjoyed swimming," Drystan said; the pain in his voice drew my attention to him.

His boots sloshed through the mercifully shallowing water toward me before he leaned down and I accepted his aid to stand. Drystan studied me head to toe.

"Your head is bleeding," he said, not in concern but like that was a hindrance to our plan.

"Don't get any ideas," I muttered, pulling away.

Drystan chuckled dryly. "Believe it or not, I don't turn into a bloodthirsty beast at the scent of a little blood. Even yours."

"Good to know."

"Though it does make me irritable to crave it."

"I'm not offering," I grumbled, touching the wound past my hairline at my temple.

"Fine. I'll just have to find a snack when we get out of here."

I tried to focus my hearing, but my pulse was still erratic and loud. Every sound of water kept my adrenaline on a razor's edge. "Please tell me we planned to go this way and that there's another exit."

"This takes us under the second level of the city."

That would be a few hours in this dark, wet cave. I shuddered, trying not to let my spirit sink.

"Why didn't you tell me about this entrance before?"

"Because if you had a sure way in you wouldn't have waited a week."

He . . . might have been right about that. Though I wouldn't admit it.

"I don't think I like swimming either," I said, shivering at the cold water seeping into my skin.

"It's being trapped you don't like," he said. "You can't swim, but you did enjoy shallow lakes, especially in summer before that gloriously warm season became more and more fleeting, year by year. Don't you remember?"

My heart skipped because Drystan remembered such insignificant things about me.

He shut the door of amity that he'd let creep open before I could reply. "Come on. The faster we are, the less time we'll spend in here."

I had no choice despite my fear of confinement. We *had* to get inside the city and rescue Eltanin. My teeth bashed together and my steps were slower than those of Drystan, who marched confidently through the shallow water.

After a few more paces, he groaned, turning back to me as I hugged myself and followed pitifully.

"Take my hand," he said, like it pained him to offer.

"I'm fine."

He didn't speak, and our harsh stares battled each other. I could hardly see him in the fleeting light, but the water added some reflection, at least.

With a disgruntled huff I dropped my palm into his, and immediately he tightened his hold, all but pulling me along. It only took a few seconds for me to feel more at ease, secure. Holding onto each other would be a tether of security should another wave come, and I tightened my grip too with that thought.

"You could warm us both," Drystan said after a moment.

Now that I wasn't prickling with the anticipation of being drowned or being cautious to keep the light from being seen, my body started to relax and I reached for my magick. My silver markings glowed faintly, giving us more light to navigate the dark. Warmth started to trickle over me, and I sighed in relief from the cold, but it wouldn't dry us, nor would our feet have any chance with the shallow pool we had to walk through.

There was something about the dark that left no option but to be trusting; regardless, I knew my heart trusted Drystan even when my mind couldn't.

5

Astraea

Climbing up into the second level of the city from our cave entrance had proven to be the most difficult part. Many of the steps had worn and crumbled over the centuries this escape route had been abandoned. We made it to the top after nearly plummeting to our deaths a few times—at least that had been what Drystan rambled about constantly while apparently I had nothing to worry about with wings to catch me.

Our clothes were still uncomfortably damp, and while my magick had provided us some warmth, we were miserable in our current state. Not off to the best nor most competent start in this mission. We pressed ourselves against a narrow, dark alley wall. Our hoods were up, and coverings were over the lower halves of our faces. It wasn't uncommon to see suspicious looking persons like this around the city; they were usually assassins or unsavory mercenaries that people avoided the paths of. Yet we had to be cautious. One tip off would turn this place into a maze of a hunting ground, which we were all but locked in. Even if I had an opportunity to escape by flying, I wouldn't leave Drystan.

"We need to dry ourselves and get rest before we risk our lives again," Drystan said, still scouting the street to decide where to go.

Of course, if we were going to die in our quest to get Eltanin, better to be comfortable and energized. We were on the upper level of the city, which was thickest with Auster's forces. Every nerve in me was on high alert.

"I am highly insulted to be worth a lesser reward for my capture than you or Nyte," Drystan muttered, spotting a line of our wanted posters across the street.

I didn't deign to respond to that, slipping out of our cover to head down the street. Plain sight might be the only way to navigate the city. There were guards around, but they roamed as nonchalantly and unaware as the civilians. There was something highly satisfying about walking right by, undetected as their greatest enemies.

"Are you trying to get us captured before I can remember the feeling of dry socks?" Drystan hissed beneath his mask, falling into step with me.

"They'd have less reason to stop two ordinary looking citizens traveling out in the open than those skulking through the shadows."

After a short while our misery chose the next inn we came across; we'd been trying to hold out for the most bustling and tucked away establishment to lose ourselves in occupied crowds.

We ordered stew and bread, and our leftover coin afforded one room for the night. Sitting in a tucked away corner of the main room, I couldn't stop my sighs of appreciation when we were brought the hot food.

"If this is to be our last meal, I'm content," Drystan said, equally lost in the stew.

"Do you think the others have awoken to find us gone yet?" I wondered with a pang of guilt.

"It should be nearing morning, but we don't have a time teller."

"What if they come after us?"

"We can't really prevent that."

"You say that like you don't care about what happens to them."

Drystan looked off to consider. "Should I?"

My face fell flat. "Have you completely lost the ability to invite friendship into your life?"

"I have merely grown armor in the places that were once soft, Maiden. You should do the same."

The coldness in his tone stung. He used my title like a blade that cut back any vine of friendship growing close to him.

"You can keep trying to push me away, but I'm not going anywhere," I said, plunging my spoon back into the stew with a scowling look at him.

His lips curved into a small smile, but it wasn't endearing. "Didn't seem that way as you left to come here without even a farewell when this brash plan of yours could result in your death. Permanently."

"That was to make sure none of you meet the same fate."

I didn't expect Drystan to slam his spoon to the table, rocking our cups.

"That's why I don't have *friends*," he hissed. "They will always make you weak and force you to take stupid measures to protect them. Even then, they're likely to leave or die sooner rather than later."

Before I could respond, two parchments were slipped over the table between us by a hand. We'd been too lost in the growing heat of our conversation to notice someone had approached. Both of our hands reached for weapons, and I glanced up . . . then shock replaced my fear.

Drystan braced his hands on the table to rise.

"Sit, Prince. We don't want to draw attention. Others might notice two of the most wanted in all of Solanis," Tarran said, low and faintly amused.

His brown eyes danced from me to Drystan, but I was still, lost in my mind, which dragged forth flashes of memory after memory until I suddenly felt dizzy.

"Here to claim the prize?" Drystan snarled low, snatching up the posters with our faces on them. He scrutinized the parchment with a deep frown, and grumbled, "They got my nose all wrong." When he looked over at me, it smoothed out a fraction. "You look like you've seen a ghost rather than just a red-headed ancient bastard," he said.

Ancient. Tarran was an elder vampire . . . but he was also so much more than that.

Tarran spoke. "I hear you're regaining your memories."

There was a confusing note of gentleness but also tension in his voice. I could hardly bear to look up at him when I didn't know how to react. How to unscramble the past from the present to make sense of him.

"Why are you here?" I asked, choosing to stay guarded as I cast him a hard look.

"I'm watching all sides of the brewing tide so as not to be caught on the ship that's going down. May I?" Tarran didn't wait for a response before sliding onto the bench beside Drystan.

"Turning us in would surely strengthen Auster's *ship,*" Drystan said carefully. I noticed how his hand hovered over a small blade at his side.

"Perhaps, but I like to believe the structure comes second to the skill of the captain." His mischievous eyes slipped to me with that.

"Just explain how you found us here," I snapped, on edge about his presence and slippery allegiance.

"It wasn't hard. Even cloaked and hooded you stand out to anyone who knows what to look for." His head canted like I was prey in his trap as he leaned on his forearms. "There's a certain confidence in your swagger that's finally come back. It had me intrigued."

Drystan looked at us, puzzled.

"Did you know each other in your past lives?" he asked me.

My "no" was run over by Tarran's "yes."

Drystan shook his head like it would piece together how that was possible.

I closed my eyes on a long exhale. I didn't know why I wanted to delay the inevitable spilling of the truth.

"He's not just an elder soul vampire," I said. "He's the son of two of my guardians. A soulless and a fae."

The shock on Drystan's face was what I'd expected.

"No. That can't be true. How could you have kept that from Nyte and me?" Drystan leaned his elbow on the table, pinching the bridge of his nose, mulling over the past like he might have missed something.

Tarran said, "You could say back then Astraea and me were somewhat estranged."

I winced; the sharpness of his words was a dagger directed toward me.

"You made the vampires and me believe you wanted to capture the star-maiden as a gain for the vampire side of the war," Drystan said sourly. "Now I discover she's practically your family? Are you going to try to say your pursuit of her was out of endearment?"

I narrowed suspicious eyes on Tarran. "When did you want to find me?"

"Before you arrived in the central kingdom and practically announced to the world the star-maiden was back. I killed the Libertatem participant and took his place to be close to you and make sure you stayed alive, won, and found your key. I wasn't sure what I would do with you afterward. Of course, Rainyte intervened and got to you before anyone else could—me, Auster, Drystan's father. That was no surprise really."

"So what do you want now? To gain a strong alliance with Auster by handing me in?"

Tarran's eyes darkened on me, but he had no right to be insulted by the question given his convenient appearance here.

"Don't you think you'd already be in chains heading to the castle by now if I was?"

"Not if there's something else you hoped to gain before ratting us out," Drystan said.

Tarran cast him a bored look. "What if I came to give you something instead?"

Drystan crushed the wanted poster of himself. "We don't need souvenirs."

The look they shared was daring, but the intensity accompanied by the slight delighted curve of Tarran's mouth almost urged me to look away from their exchange.

"Auster has called the citizens of Vesitire to the castle tomorrow to hear his speech," Tarran informed us.

"I already knew that," I said.

Drystan swung me an accusatory look. "Anything else you know and haven't shared?"

I shook my head with a sheepish wince.

Tarran said, "I assume you want your dragon back. What if I said I can help?"

"We don't trust you," Drystan said.

"I don't have the time nor care to convince you to trust me," Tarran said, bored as he reached for Drystan's cup and took a drink. Setting it down with a casual sigh, he stood lazily. "Auster Nova is no fool. He won't let his guard down for this. My advice? The only way to distract him enough is to give him what he wants more than anything." His brown eyes landing on me sent a chill down my spine.

"I need to be the bait," I said.

"Not happening," Drystan rejected.

"My token of insight is that, while Astraea occupies everyone's attention, I have those loyal to me posing in Auster's vampire ranks. I can make sure they anticipate letting a lone shadow slip by into the side entrance of the library where a black celestial dragon is being cruelly shackled."

My gut twisted at the image of Eltanin chained where Nyte once was. Alone and afraid.

"What do you have to gain from helping us?" Drystan asked bitterly.

He shrugged, looking off through the crowded inn. "What do I have to gain from helping Auster?"

With that, Tarran turned and made to leave.

"Tarran," I dipped his name in darkness before he got one step. "You do anything that puts my friends in danger, I will kill you."

His cold eyes sliced back to me.

"You're good at killing, aren't you? Auster's words aren't all lies about you, Maiden."

"They're twisted lies. Ruling isn't without hard choices and living with blood on our hands."

This had turned into a far more personal conversation. One brewed from a memory of the past that severed the bond we grew up with while being raised by the same people.

"You should have made sure the blood on yours didn't leave vengeance in its wake."

A tense silence left in Tarran's shadow as he wove through the busy inn until I lost track of him. In truth, I didn't know if we could trust him or if this was his wicked way of having his revenge on me.

"What happened between you two?" Drystan asked.

"I took away someone he loved."

Drystan slumped with exasperation. I didn't elaborate.

"Then how the hell can we trust a word he says?"

"Because there's one person Tarran will always hate more than me, and that's Auster, all the High Celestials, really, for how they've treated vampires for centuries. He might despise me but he's the son of two of my guardians and I . . . I have to trust his heart is still a piece of theirs and wouldn't truly want to harm me."

Drystan sat in silence to mull over all I'd told him.

"If we use what he offered, if you expose yourself as bait, you need to tell me you're confident you can escape and fly to join me as soon as I have Eltanin."

My heart was pounding at the mere thought of what we both had to do. As I stared at the sodden wood of the table, my mind processed dozens of situations that could unfold tomorrow with this new plan.

"I have my role; you have yours. The most important outcome of this is that you get Eltanin back to Nyte. No matter what, agreed?"

Drystan knew my meaning. That should something happen to prevent me from making it to join him, he had to leave me behind.

"Shit." Drystan ran a hand down his face, then downed the rest of his drink. "If he wakes by bonding with Eltanin, and you're not there, I am not looking forward to dealing with his rage."

The stiffness in my shoulders relaxed when he didn't argue. Drystan's gaze turned to one of concern, but he slipped it away from me like he didn't want to admit it.

"I am rather looking forward to hearing what the High Celestial of House Nova has to say. A coronation announcement, perhaps?" I said with resentment.

Drystan glowered at the wall with that suggestion. "I doubt he'll wait much longer to claim that crown as the realm's savior from the corrupted star-maiden."

My heart darkened at the thought of Auster claiming my throne and spewing more false and evil words about me and my friends for his own merit.

"He can claim the crown, but he'll never hold the throne so long as I live."

6

Astraea

The streets were alive with a hum of excitement, a restless energy weaving through the crowd as they pressed shoulder-to-shoulder, moving toward the castle in a thick, unbroken wave. Murmurs of anticipation rippled through the people, punctuated by the occasional shout as children were hoisted onto shoulders for a better view or friends jostled to keep from losing one another in the crush.

It was only my dark resentment toward Auster that wished the atmosphere for his summons at the castle grounds was gloomy and unwelcoming rather than this spirited display.

Above the crowd, the castle loomed, its black towers catching the red glow of the blood moon, turning the sight eerily sinister. Banners unfurled from its stone walls, vivid and regal, swaying gently in the breeze as if welcoming everyone closer.

But they were navy, not deep purple. They had *his* constellation sigil, not that which represented the star-maiden. Auster's speech had already begun with the waving of the crest of the Nova House from the castle of Vesitire.

"Last chance to reconsider this plan," Drystan muttered at my side.

It was easy for us to stand by the wall of the inn we lodged in without attracting any attention from the people buzzing with excitement.

"See you on the other side?" was my response while I scanned for the right gap to slip into the throng.

With his silence, I cast him a glance. Drystan was fixing his face covering in place with a stare of apprehension at me.

"Just don't get yourself killed," he groused.

I couldn't help smiling under my mask. "Likewise."

He slipped away from me first; then it was my turn to force my body into the tight wave against everything in me that wanted to be anywhere else.

I'd always battled low tolerance for the compact suffocation of a crowd.

Maybe the panic came from my short life in Goldfell's clutches, which had sheltered me and made me afraid of the world. I didn't think it mattered how many memories I gained back; I would always be two people fighting in one body. The legendary star-maiden of the past, and the girl from Goldfell manor—still fighting to be brave and resilient.

My throat kept tightening even though the flow of traffic remained consistent and following it was easy. I pushed through a little faster but tried not to attract attention. I was one body in a sea of many, and this almost felt like being swept away by that brutal wave underground with Drystan.

My feet are on the ground. My magick is in my veins.

I breathed to make my irrational fear subside. Despite the thick, dark winter, my skin was beginning to become slick with sweat under my leathers. Looking high helped to spot the tallest part of the castle, which was growing closer now as I climbed to the top level.

Finally, the masses started to slow, deciding they were close enough.

Not me. I kept going, slipping through every gap I could.

My pulse built toward a crescendo like a war drum at the thought of how near Auster had to be. Was he atop the portico watching the people arrive and gloating in his new authority?

My panic of suffocation became irrelevant with the drive of my rage-fueled adrenaline as I weaved through the loud cluster of bodies. It was becoming more difficult the closer I got. I would have to start pushing to get any nearer, earning more attention than I could risk right now. A lot of people were taller than me, limiting my view of the portico. Through the movement . . .

There he was: Auster Nova, High Celestial of the House of Nova, with the power to brew storms and conjure lightning. He stood on the portico, radiating a calm authority that only made the crowd below more reverent. His brown hair, neatly half-tied, fell over his shoulders with an effortless grace. His jaw, strong and shadow-lined, was set with a serene confidence, his hands clasped behind him in that familiar stance that gave him an air of unwavering strength.

The crowd watched him with awe, as if he were a perfect, untouchable figure carved from marble. They couldn't see past the polished veneer—the dark cunning lurking just behind those steady eyes.

The people had once looked at me that way, as if my presence were a comfort and my gaze over them a shield against the world.

Now, Auster had painted me as their villain when *he* wore a gilded disguise over the cold ruthlessness he wielded like a blade.

Beside him stood another two of the four High Celestials—bound in brotherhood by duty if not blood. Notus hung back a step on his left and Zephyr on his right. The sight of my friend next to my preeminent enemy twisted me with nerves.

In our past, Zephyr had helped me devise a plan behind Auster, Notus, and Aquilo's authority that ruled all wingless celestials and Nephilim were to be exiled—we'd built a secret sanctuary for them. And if Auster discovered Zephyr had aided my escape from his ambush after the recent attack on Althenia, I didn't want to know what he would do.

Glancing over the High Celestials again, I noticed Aquilo was missing. I'd taken his wings when the rebel Nephilim and celestials had captured him after rescuing me.

Had Auster and Notus really held true to their law of exile and stripped their brother of his land and title?

I couldn't say I would feel bad for him if that theory was true. Aquilo had always been cruel and cold. Taking his wings had felt like the most just punishment considering his distain when he ordered the barbaric act upon his own people.

The whispering taunts of Lightsdeath started to swirl around me in the wisps of air, hushing the crowd to be heard. My skin hummed and I flexed my fingers, prickling with the power that wanted to come out. This kind far deadlier and more uncertain than the magick I could conjure without Lightsdeath.

I can't lose control now.

It seemed the more stress and anger that surfaced in me, the louder Lightsdeath became—nearly impossible to ignore.

Staring at Notus wasn't helping, but I couldn't tear my gaze from him while the whispers grew louder. The flashbacks of him standing by so coldly, watching Aquilo chain and whip me in the place Auster ambushed me . . . I could hardly stand still.

Scrunching my eyes, I clamped my hands over my ears. *I can't lose control.* This was a dreadful place, packed with civilians, for me to unleash a dangerous power that might not care how many lives were lost from my retribution.

If what lived in me now was anything like Nightsdeath, I couldn't take that chance here.

Auster raised a hand, and the restless crowd began to silence. It drew my attention up, and Lightsdeath diminished again. There was a sinister touch to the air, a darkness I didn't think the people of Vesitire were oblivious to.

"We all grow weary in the darkness and destruction our once beloved star-maiden has caused. In angering the gods who created her, she has cast a blood moon curse upon us. She let Nightsdeath lead an attack that slaughtered many of my people and destroyed my castle on the Nova province of Althenia. Together they have become the greatest threat our lands have faced. But I want to assure you we will not rest until the star-maiden is stopped and Nightsdeath is destroyed," he announced, his voice amplified by an enhancement of magick to reach through the crowd.

My fist flexed and I slipped through the bodies slowly, tracking him like a predator, with the desire to pounce twitching my muscles.

"She will not win in her reign of terror. Once she is found and put before the gods to answer for her crimes, I promise our daylight and balance will be restored."

Lies. Auster preached in the name of gods but it was his own ego that wanted me dead and his own terror that destroyed the Nova province to pin the blame on me and Nyte.

"I gathered you all here today, as we cannot waste time. Upon counsel with my brothers and the reigning lords of Solanis, we have decided that henceforth I should be crowned your king as only I can bring the star-maiden to justice. As she is my Bonded, it is a deeply painful but necessary duty I will fulfill. I promise to lead us back into the daylight no matter the cost."

He used our soul tie to his advantage, for now the people murmured their sympathy for him. How devastating it was that his Bonded was a cold, heartless maiden. Many people were bending to his false and hollow words. With the terror of the blood moon and a shaken monarchy, the people needed to cling to someone as a beacon of hope, and Auster was *so* convincing.

I couldn't breathe easily enough and pulled my face covering down, still slipping through the gaps between people, who started to mutter their disgruntled complaints, squeezing my way closer to the front.

I couldn't stop. Every fraction closer I got, taking in more details of Auster standing there proudly with everything he stole by spilling blood, my compulsion overpowered my rational thinking more and more.

Before I knew what I was doing, I'd slipped my hood down. My silver hair pooled out, icy air breezed across my nape. I didn't tear my sights from my greatest enemy. Far greater than Nyte had ever been to me, far deadlier than his father had been to the realm.

I didn't hear most of the commotion as people started to recognize me, but I didn't have to weave my way through tight spaces anymore. People moved out of my way and my magick raked across my skin in case any thought to lunge for me.

Auster finally found my cold stare promising death. Dark fury flashed across his hazel eyes before his hand hovered over his sword. I stood right in front of him now, the crowd parted completely, separated only by a stretch of path toward the portico.

"Any crown placed atop your head would slip with madness beneath it," I said, loud enough for him to hear in the tense silence that had fallen. "It's only a matter of time before everyone sees it."

My fists kept tightening with my loathing, weaved with heartache, to be face to face with him now. Vengeance for what he'd done clashed with fond memories that flooded over from the past. Our long history of growing up together, bonding as great friends before anything else. There would always be a part of me that ached deeply for what we'd become.

"Seize her!" Auster bellowed.

Even his own soldiers hesitated. When they did act to his demand, my magick flared to life in warning, creating sliver threads weaving over my palms and a warm swirling wind. More space grew around me as people tried to gain distance.

"This is between you and me, Auster Nova. Or are you too afraid to face me yourself?"

"You're bold to come here," he said.

"I'm not afraid of you," I challenged. "I won't hide while you foster fear and lies about me in the minds of my people. And I won't let you hide behind the villain you're trying to make of me either."

"It is your actions that have caused devastation to this realm, Maiden," Notus said.

Murmurs of agreement around me rattled my composure.

"Where is your Bonded, Astraea?" Auster goaded. "Where is the monster you chose over your own people and duty to protect the realm?"

I realized he was trying to make me stand trial in front of the gathered city.

I said calmly, "You don't fear him for what he's capable of. You fear him for the mirror he shows you."

Gasps echoed and my marked skin glowed a little brighter.

"Why did you come?" Notus asked.

I didn't dare glance at Zephyr, but I knew he stood tense beside them, likely wondering if I'd lost all sense of self-preservation in being here.

"You've been looking for me. Well, here I am."

"You're alone," Auster said daringly. He unclasped his cloak at his shoulder; someone took it from him as he stalked forward. Then he removed his circlet. "Did you come to fight me?"

"If I win, you let Eltanin go and leave Vesitire," I said.

His smile sliced cruelly and viciously.

"And if I win . . ." he said, hanging a pause for his delighted suspense. "You'll stay with me. I'm not beyond believing our Maiden can be reformed. That I can bring you back to righteousness."

His vile delusion broke awe through the onlookers. How merciful it was for him to find forgiveness after all I'd done.

He was good at this, I had to admit.

Maybe there was some truth in the new perception of me as the villain he was painting in the minds of my people, because while he was masterfully composed, I was ready to burn this city to the ground to reclaim it.

"Fine."

I was sure Drystan would be cursing me if he was watching. I hoped he was rescuing Eltanin beneath the library right now.

"I admire your will," Auster said, his voice growing closer as he came down the castle steps. More space was created around us, but all that existed to me was him.

Auster and my simmering fury.

"I can't say the same when yours has always been spineless."

"It's all a matter of perception, really. You've made me your villain only because I had the will to do what needed to be done to stop what you have become."

I kept careful attention on him as he stopped, facing off with me. He didn't retrieve a blade and neither did I.

"Like you said, a matter of perception."

I moved first, not in attack toward him, but around us. As I aimed my hand down, my magick cracked through the ground, digging deep; it took reaching for a touch of Lightsdeath to conjure the strength to shift back my legs and push down with everything I had. A flare of light broke in a jagged line, creating a large serrated circle around us. With a battle cry, I gripped the stone with my magick and lifted my palms as if I held it in my physical grasp. I floated us high on the platform now suspended above the gathered people.

"Impressive," Auster remarked.

"I won't let you hurt my people."

It took constant focus to keep the platform floating, but this was only between Auster and me, and if he reacted with his own magick against me, it would be catastrophic on the ground with so many innocents nearby.

"If you hadn't run from me when you came back five years ago, things would have been so much different," he said.

The bastard had the audacity to seem *pained*.

"I'm glad I did. Had you captured me after my memories were taken, being forced to live a life by your side would have been worse than what I'd suffered with Goldfell."

When I fell back to land, I'd awoken with my memories for a brief time. Auster had been waiting for me in the temple of Alisus; he knew it was where I'd be. I remembered he was the one who killed me, and I'd run from him, barefoot and freezing through the woods by Goldfell manor. The next person to find me was Drystan, who made sure I got away, letting me run into the arms of Goldfell, who kept me hidden in his manor for five years.

Despite Goldfell's cruel hand and spending years alone and hidden, the alternative that could have been had Auster found me without my memories—unwittingly in the arms of my killer—made me terribly nauseous to imagine.

"I mourned you long before I killed you, Astraea," he said, a slipped confession.

I gritted my teeth, turning the pain within me into something I could wield, and my hand cast out with a gale of violet light toward him. Auster's blue lightning collided with my magick just in time. Unlike when I battled with Nyte's power, there was no desire that ran through the currents of energy between us, only pure, dark loathing.

I couldn't die this way, but he could.

Though if I managed to kill Auster now it would solidify every evil he'd painted about me to those below. Reversing what he'd done was not going to be as easy as getting rid of him.

"Was I really that terrible of an option for you?" he yelled when our blast ceased.

We mirrored each other in our pacing around the perimeter.

"I never wanted this. It was you who couldn't stand that I chose Nyte."

"You never told me why."

"I did. It just wasn't to your ego's liking."

I struck again, and he ducked out of the way before sending a bolt my way. Pivoting, I threw out a light dart, and we parried like that for some time, exerting our heartache and vengeance on each other.

"You were my friend and I *trusted* you!" I shouted.

The tears that gathered in my eyes burned my skin as they fell, and I was glad for it. I didn't want to hurt inside because of him. He didn't deserve my heart.

For just a second, we locked stares and his brow furrowed in a way that haunted me. That flicker of regret turned to detached resentment so fast, but I'd let it weaken my guard enough that his sudden strike of lightning hit my chest. Cast off my feet, I had no choice but to release my wings, which caught me in the air.

I surveyed the courtyard below where everyone was staring. Some covered their mouths in shock, clutching each other with fear.

Fear of my black wings.

A mark of death, as the people believed. As the High Celestials had *made* them believe.

"I'm glad your arrogance in thinking you could win against me brought you here," Auster taunted from the platform. "You make it too easy. All I have are words, and you give them the full display of proof."

I dragged my lethal stare back to him, shaking with a dangerous need to wipe the gleam of triumph from his face. Permanently.

Before I could fly back to the platform again, the sound of fearful murmurs gripped my attention. The people weren't looking at me anymore; they stared past me with wide eyes. Some started pushing each other to get away, then shouting to run.

I twisted my head sideways and gasped at the blazing star hurtling at a deadly speed right toward us. There was no debating if it would miss the city this time. It didn't matter how far away those people below got; I didn't doubt this blast could collapse the city.

I scanned for Auster, but he was gone, now back down on the ground with his brothers in urgent conversation. Their wings were unglamoured, and many celestials were fleeing rapidly with the help of their wings. They and the night-crawlers were the only ones who stood a chance of clearing the blast radius.

The High Celestials wouldn't leave everyone to die here, would they? Together their magick might be able to slow or stop the meteor.

There was no end to my anger that boiled as they just *stood there*.

Fucking cowards.

Landing on the platform, I had no choice. I opened myself to the other-worldly magick that lived within me and hoped it didn't claim or destroy me. Hoped I didn't lose myself to Lightsdeath like Nyte could to his deadly entity of Nightsdeath.

With a long breath, I dove deep into my well of magick, surpassing my limit and letting starlight flood through me. It was all I was. Pure, bright starlight. Enough to drown the world if I wanted to.

I glamoured my wings, shifted my stance, then, as the heat grew, I couldn't tell what source was strongest: the blaze of magick coursing through me or the devastating rock about to obliterate me as I cast out a hand. My magick wrapped around the star, which rebelled against my attempt to stop it from crashing to the land. The world was glowing with silver, and I knew nothing but Lightsdeath.

The rock slowed, but not enough. I pushed more magick out, ignoring the wild pounding that began in my head, my skin that ran too hot, and my stance that trembled. My brow pulled together with the agony tearing through me, but I couldn't give up.

Both my hands pushed out now, and a scream tore from my throat. With the greatest surge of magick ever to unleash in this world, the star finally started breaking. Piece by piece it turned to dust with the starlight ripping through it. Until it was no more than a large boulder that had lost its flame.

I couldn't hold on any more, with no choice but to accept the impact of that piece slamming into me. Then death was a friend that greeted me coldly.

7

Astraea

The ground beneath my body was as firm as I'd expected, gritty and warm as my fingers flexed. The thick air confused my stirring consciousness when I drew a long breath, inhaling thick dust and coughing violently.

I opened my eyes but I wasn't greeted by the red night of my world. My cheek lay against dry, cracked land. Flattening my palms to push myself up, I knew I should be in pain even if only from my position lying on solid ground.

I felt nothing. In fact, my body didn't quite feel . . . wholly here.

I stood and surveyed my surroundings. A sweep of panic choked in my throat when I didn't recognize the neutral toned wasteland with a hazy overcast. The trees in the distance were stripped of all that could bring color and joy, scattered in the field like dark skeletal bodies with crooked fingers reaching to reap the creatures that passed, though only ravens flew, silently, landing on the branches confidently. The wind whistled by me, wailing as though lost souls cried, captured in the drafts.

Hugging myself to fight the prickling sensation that crept over my skin, I turned around and found another person a few paces away with their back to me. Before I could decide whether to let fear or relief dominate after discovering I wasn't alone, both were quelled by a wash of shock. Disbelief.

This couldn't be real.

"Nyte," I whispered.

I would know him from any angle. His tall stature and broad shoulders. The few locks of dark hair long enough to catch in the wind.

I'd been trying to stop the meteor from destroying the central city of Vesitire, but I remembered the final piece that hadn't dissolved in my magick in time and instead pummeled into me.

I hadn't fallen unconscious. What pulled me under after that immediate impact had felt so icily cold and blindingly bright before submersing me in complete darkness. I was sure that impact had killed me.

Nyte turned to my call, but it wasn't him who greeted me. It was Nightsdeath. The black vines crawled his skin and his complexion was paler here. His irises glowed like they trapped the sun. Darkness rolled off him as though he were part flesh, part shadow. Despite his frightening appearance and deathly stare, I inched closer when he didn't move again or speak.

"Astraea."

When I got close enough to reach a hand up to his hauntingly beautiful face, he immediately lashed out. I clawed at his fingers, tight and unforgiving, around my throat.

"You're going to wish you'd never been created, Lightsdeath," he hissed, throwing me to the ground, and I spluttered, my vision peppering.

Could he kill me here? That true fear of possibility, when I didn't think I would awaken in my realm again if he succeeded in ending me in this void between life and death, had me crawling on my elbows while I tried to scramble my thoughts back together. I couldn't leave him here. There had to be a way to reach Nyte through his dark, dominating power, just like I could in my own realm.

Nightsdeath grabbed my ankle, and I grappled for purchase against being dragged back. My fingers only bled, tearing over the dry, serrated slashes of the ground, and I yelped when I was flipped onto my back.

He crouched down, looking over my face and hooking a strand of my silver hair. Even when mirroring Nyte's habits, Nightsdeath held nothing but disgust in his stare. "You made the greatest mistake in thinking you could become something to contend with me, Maiden," he said, his voice a haunting lullaby.

"Where's Nyte?" I breathed, trying to swallow the terror threatening to keep me down.

A wicked smile curved his mouth and his eyes, blazing like twin suns, locked on mine.

"I'm right here. Only now I'm free from the weak, cowardly parts that I've been plagued with for eternity."

I shuffled back a fraction as it started to make sense. This was Nightsdeath. *Only* Nightsdeath. A creation that started as a death-given power that fed on pain and suffering. My eyes stung realizing everything Nyte had endured over his life was what made this side of him so strong.

What stood before me was a raw representation of Nyte's tortured soul given form.

All his pain and suffering had become a creature that wanted to shroud everything in his path. His misery fed his cruelty. To inflict pain on others was the only way to claw out some of the agony festering in himself.

"How are you here if Nyte's body . . . his right mind . . . is not."

"Who are you to say I am not his *right* mind? I think far clearer without the *wrong* side that tries to conform to your ways in a world that is long overdue to be purged of its sins."

It was puzzling, confusing to my heart and mind, to understand that this was Nyte in a way. What stood before me was Nyte with his humanity detached. The part of him I would reach for to pull his humanity back to the surface was gone, but I hoped it lingered somewhere safe. Waiting for me to wake him from his curse.

"What is this place?" I asked.

"The rift between life and death. I was hoping you would make it here sooner or later before you woke me in your realm."

I shuddered, realizing Nightsdeath had been here all along. Waiting for me.

"Why?" I dared to ask.

"Because when you do find a way to break the curse, I want full control of our mortal body. I want the part of me you call Rainyte to be buried so deeply it can never see the light."

"No," I breathed. I would never let that happen.

I had to get out of here.

As I threw out a gale of my violet power, Nightsdeath hissed, conjuring a cloud of pure darkness to engulf it. Unlike when Nyte used shadow magick, this was devoid of stars, another distinguishing feature that separated Nightsdeath from Rainyte.

I scrambled to my feet, racing though I didn't know where I could make it out, only that there was a beast on my heels and I couldn't let him keep me here.

Was this where Nyte went every time he died? The thought of him wandering alone through the lost, barren land ached in my soul.

Had there been a time, perhaps several, he hadn't wished to come back to life? *I've died many times. I'm pretty good at it.*

Of course he was. He was masterful at harboring more pain than any person should have to endure. He had every reason to let Nightsdeath take it all out on the world that hurt him so reprehensibly, yet he fought that part of himself every day.

For him, for his humanity, I would never stop fighting to remind him there was *good* in him, and he deserved far better than the cruel hand life had dealt him so far.

My magick built steps, which I climbed frantically. Shadows crept around my ankles in a soft caress. I couldn't find a direction on land, and so I chased the sky, the only course toward a break of light in the thick, sad clouds.

A whimper fell from my lips when I didn't think I would make it to the bright window of escape that could be a figment of my desperate imagination. I raced the shadows that began to wrap around me, the slow embrace of Nightsdeath like a cold lover's touch.

Then I leaped off my next step right as his hold began to tighten, and I let myself fall to freedom or doom.

8

Astraea

Agony seared through every muscle, each sharp pulse a brutal reminder of the moments before I'd woken here, sprawled in a twisted heap, wedged deep within a narrow crevice. The memory clawed its way back—the catastrophic descent of the falling star, the raw surge of power as I tried to halt it, and then the crushing impact as it slammed into me, driving me down into the earth.

I could still feel the heat radiating from the ground around me, faint traces of the star's energy echoing through the broken rock and debris. My limbs were leaden, pain lancing through every inch of my body as I tried to move, each sensation telling me just how close I'd come to being completely destroyed. My vision blurred and I stopped trying to move.

Wiggling fingers gave me a small sense of control. I had to get up. Yet for a moment, I found serenity in the tinted red sky blinking with stars. I searched the constellations for Cassia and Calix—my two dear lost friends whose souls I'd sent to the stars when they died—to not be alone in my agony.

Shadows crept in the corners of my vision. My lids weighed so heavy that I couldn't be sure if the darkness was my falling consciousness. I hoped it was, eager to welcome sleep to numb the pain. But through the ringing in my ears I heard footsteps crunching through the stone debris toward me.

If it was Auster, I lay here completely at his mercy. I began to fight within myself, grappling for clearer awareness of my senses and scrambling to find any inkling of magick.

My body was too weak to reach for the sparks that tried to ignite within me.

The shadows grew closer, and a familiar sense of dread and utter disbelief slithered through me. My horror was confirmed when the figure knelt, and my head lolled to find such deadly beauty staring down at me.

"Thank you for releasing me, Maiden," Nightsdeath said. "Truthfully, I

didn't think it was possible but you were almost mine in that rift, and you brought me here with you instead of being kept there with me."

How was this possible? Did this mean Nyte had awoken?

That flare of hope was quickly doused under a wave of absolute terror because Nightsdeath was in this realm, separated from Nyte's body.

Oh stars, what have I done?

Unable to fight or protest, I let Nightsdeath lifted me into his arms and I cried out in pain with every movement of my broken body. Next thing I knew we were out of the deep crevice in the courtyard.

"You show yourself too late, Rainyte," Auster called over.

I stiffened as Nightsdeath stopped walking and turned to where Auster, Zephyr, and Notus stood on a flat piece of the courtyard close to the castle.

"Rainyte isn't here," he said, a chilling calm in his tone.

Nightsdeath didn't have a body like a mortal; he was crafted to appear as something between flesh and pure shadow, with amber eyes that glowed permanently, swirling with molten ore.

Auster chuckled menacingly, ignoring that statement. "You will not make it far with her."

"I don't plan to. In fact, I'm about to walk right up those stairs into the castle and take her to rest." His head angled down, caressing me with his ethereal golden eyes. His voice lowered to a whisper of shadow. "We have much to do together before I kill you, my star."

I shivered at the jarring tenderness in his tone coupled with the ominous promise in those words. As I pushed at his chest, he didn't put up any resistance and let me fall clumsily to the ground. I yelped at the sharp pain that shot through every inch of me like the vibrations of a struck gong.

Steps shuffled to me but hesitated; I cast my sight up to find Auster and Zephyr had come forward, but the darkly radiating challenge of Nightsdeath halted them from coming any closer to me. His aura spilled around us like death lingered one touch, one breath, away.

"What are you doing?" Auster spat.

"He has no regard for her in this state," Zephyr deduced.

A muscle in Auster's jaw twitched scanning from me to Nightsdeath. Despite Auster's words and resentment toward me, he was showing his care for me wasn't completely gone. He didn't truly want me dead; he wanted to *fix* me. *Reform* me. He wanted our friendship back, maybe even more, but only on his terms, as the person he wanted me to be.

"He's always been a great danger to you, and this is who you chose to bond with," Auster said with venom. "I suppose you deserve such treatment."

My teeth gritted, and I mustered all the strength I had to lift myself from the ground, swaying to my feet. What stood behind me was *not* a true portrayal of Nyte. Even when Nightsdeath fought viciously to take over his thoughts and actions, there was always the good in him to reach for.

We would all be condemned if we had to let our suffering stand to represent us.

"I will let you live, Auster Nova, as I think we have a common goal for now." Nightsdeath brushed my tangled silver hair over my shoulder. "And we have this one in our possession to help us gain it faster."

"What are you talking about?" It was Zephyr who snapped, his wariness growing as he kept careful track of me.

"We both want to find Rainyte."

That only furrowed the confusion on the High Celestials' brows deeper.

"It's not him," I said, barely a croak.

"You want me to believe you're *not* Rainyte?" Auster said in disbelief. "Do you take me for a fool?"

"Yes. But for far more reasons than this, I assure you. Now get out of my way."

Lightning flashed over Auster's hands, and I tensed, in no fit state to defend myself if chaos broke out.

"You're not stepping a foot inside that castle," Auster snarled, standing between Nightsdeath and the way into Vesitire's stronghold.

"I have very little restraint as it is not to kill you all where you stand and take over this pathetic city, but I would rather not have to spend my time forcing your armies to obey me before I get what I need."

His words made me think that Nyte's ability to manipulate minds had to be something he was born with, not a part of Nightsdeath. Otherwise it wouldn't be difficult to bend the allegiance of the army generals to make the shift of authority believable.

"What is it that you want?" Notus spoke at last, his voice the most devoid of any emotion at all.

"To kill Rainyte."

I thought my heart stopped beating. My breath certainly felt trapped in my lungs from that unthinkable outcome.

This time the High Celestials didn't mock him right away. They kept their confusion but Auster's intrigue was caught now. Why would Nyte himself say such a thing?

Nightsdeath trailed a hand over my nape; his fingers threaded through my hair before I cried out at his tightening grip. "I will break you to find out where Rainyte is," he said, so cold and promising. Then he said to Auster, whose eyes twitched with conflict over his roughness with me, "isn't that what you want as well?"

Auster shifted his weight, considering, while Notus gave little away. Zephyr struggled to contain his anger, and I feared he would slip up and expose his deep care for me.

"It is," Auster finally said, bemused over the situation and untrusting.

A roar broke their tense deliberation, and I gasped, casting my eyes up with a burst of hope. It was followed by a loud crashing of shattered glass and then . . .

Eltanin shot high, and on his back, he carried Drystan.

My eyes pricked with pure relief seeing them.

Until they began to head this way.

No. No, they can't come for me.

Nightsdeath let go of my hair with a shove, and I bit my lip against the throbbing sting. He tracked the black dragon that began to swoop lower, and I could hardly see, *think,* through the fear that drummed in my chest and swayed my vision. Watching Nightsdeath walk so calmly, tracking them carefully, arose a sick, terrible dread over what he might do.

Leave! I yelled in my mind with everything I had. If there was some kind of bond between Eltanin and me, and I was sure I'd felt it before, I hoped he could feel my command. *Go to Nyte; it's the only way to help me. Leave, now!*

The dragon roared again; this time I clutched my chest at his cry of anguish. Eltanin didn't want to obey and leave me, but I kept chanting my urgency.

Darkness gathered toward Nightsdeath, and my pulse beat in my throat as I watched shadow form into a giant, long spear, which hovered the air above his raised palm.

A dry sob escaped me as Eltanin finally changed direction. I caught only a trace of Drystan's pained expression before the duo started gaining distance again.

Nightsdeath gave barely a flick of his wrist, and that huge, lethal spear of dark magick projected toward the black dragon with the velocity of a crossbow.

"NO!" I yelled, throwing my own clumsy flare of light after it, but it wasn't enough to stop the spear.

My hands covered my mouth.

It was going to strike them.

At the last possible second, Eltanin dipped sideways, almost clearing the path of it completely, but it tore the side of his wing. His roar of pain sliced within me, but he kept flying, fast and powerfully.

Nightsdeath didn't try again. Instead he turned around, his expression half lost in the shadows he was partially made of, but it wore nothing but boredom.

In my unthinking rage over his attempt to harm or kill Eltanin and Drystan, I threw another weak attack of my magick at him. He deflected it with a lazy wave of his hand while closing the distance between us in slow, unperturbed strides. I tried again. Again. And again until he reached me, gripping my throat in a near choking grip.

"You can hardly contend with a squirrel right now, but you amuse me," he said calmly, tilting his head while I pinned a hateful glare on him. It ached in me so badly, to look at him, seeing *my* Nyte even at his worst. My heart still reached to love him.

"Why . . . Why do you want to kill Nyte?" I wheezed, digging my nails into his hand around my neck, but it was like he couldn't feel it at all.

His grip slackened, slipping around my nape and bringing our faces intimately close. The warmth of his breath blew across my lips when he answered.

"So I can feel," he said quietly, a whisper of longing. "If I take his heart I will have a true form. Not this—cursed in shadow. I cannot feel a single sensation like this. I know what I should feel, having been tied to Rainyte's form for centuries. Like your flesh; oh how he craves your touch more than anything else when it triggers so much within him. What a peculiar thing you are. Something that can inspire almost as much pain in him as you do pleasure."

That twisted a knot in my chest.

With his proximity, I thought he might kiss me. He spoke privately while my heartbeat pounded over what he might do next.

"He deserved better than to be plagued by you," I seethed.

Nightsdeath smiled cruelly. "I am the darkness that lingers in the hearts of all. There is a *me* inside of *you.* All you have to do is look in the mirror long enough to see your darkness smile back. It's not my fault that he was never given enough light to keep me weak." Then the curve of his mouth fell; his amber eyes searched mine with more thought. "Until you. Things were better when you were gone."

"Release her," Zephyr demanded.

I didn't know how to feel being held by the tormented shadow of Nyte. Maybe I was a fool for thinking there could be a warmth, however small and guarded, to be reached even in Nightsdeath.

"Are you ready to accept my proposal?" Nightsdeath said, stepping away from me to address the High Celestials.

"You want an alliance to find and kill Rainyte?" Zephyr reiterated, the only one still regarding the notion with complete abhorrence in his expression.

"Exactly."

"And what happens to you once we succeed?" Auster asked.

I grappled for composure, hearing how confident Auster was that they would achieve the task. "I will have Rainyte's ability to bend minds. I can make the Maiden forget him, *me,* entirely and she will be yours. In exchange you will return to Althenia and leave the rest of this gluttonous, spiteful world to me."

"What will you do?" Auster dared to ask.

"Purge it."

Horror so piercing staggered my steps back. With Auster's silence, and his shifting gaze to me, I saw him truly contemplate the proposal.

"I will never be yours. With or without my memories, Auster Nova, I will never want you."

My declaration infused his gaze of longing with sinister intent. "We would have wed were it not for Rainyte's poison that swayed you away from it."

I blinked, reaching through my mirage of memories. Had I really accepted the fate of marrying Auster despite my uncertain feelings toward him before I met Nyte? I remembered Nyte's own memory that he'd shared with me, where I'd confessed I didn't harbor the lust and affection of a lover for Auster even though I thought I should. I'd come to develop such feelings and so much deeper for Nyte instead.

In all my tunneling into the past . . . I recalled the engagement with a shallow gasp. White gowns, flower arrangements, the Goddess Temple he insisted on for a venue. There was a time I ran out of reasons to deny a life partnership with Auster, when he was my Bonded, a High Celestial, and we were, in the eyes of everyone, a perfect union.

Seeking out Nyte, the first day we'd met when I'd let myself be captured and held in his prison, hadn't just been out of my concern for the quakes, going to my enemy as a last resort. It had been my final rebellion, an act of desperation to delay the wedding as long as possible. I never anticipated how eager for Nyte's company I became. How addicted to every fascinating thing about the realm's nightmare I became.

"I never truly wanted to marry you," I said, barely a whisper.

Auster reacted as if I'd struck him. I didn't want to feel anything for him after all he'd done, but I did. I thought that would be my eternal punishment: to always be plagued with guilt for my choices. I looked at Auster as if he were a monster I'd created in my selfishness.

"We have a deal," Auster said coldly, not taking his eyes from me.

"You may as well kill me. I'll never tell you where Nyte's body is," I hissed.

Nightsdeath hooked my elbow, but I ripped it away, glaring at him with hatred that tore me apart from seeing him wearing Nyte's face through the shadows.

"You make this too fun for me," he mused.

My teeth clenched tightly as he closed the distance between us. I expected him to use the void to take me inside against my will, but to my horror, he leaned down and swiftly threw me over his shoulder.

"Put me down, or so help me I'll burn you from the inside out," I said, losing pieces of my dignity as I wriggled, but his hold was iron.

"I don't think you have that capability in you right now."

He was right. I was far too drained to have enough effect on him. When he took me past the castle threshold, he didn't put me down, and blood started rushing to my head, disorienting me.

"You can't travel through the void, can you?" I realized.

"When I have Rainyte's form, I will."

The reminder of what he wanted surged adrenaline through me, and I conjured enough magick to make him hiss. He set me down on my feet so roughly that I stumbled, catching myself against the wall.

We glared at each other for a few seconds before Nightsdeath canted his head, watching me curiously. He came closer and I stood defiant.

"It doesn't have to be like this," he said, luring me in with his gentler tone. "When we stood among the wreckage of the Nova castle, I saw it . . . how magnificent we would be together if only you aligned yourself with me. This world doesn't deserve to thrive on greed and power. We can starve them of it and make them bow for us."

"I'm going to make sure you can never control him again," I said venomously.

"I *made* him. I *am* him. Choose your poison, Maiden," he said, coming closer this time only to speak between us after a glance down the hall. The High Celestials stood far enough away at the end, trailing us but remaining very cautious of the shadowy monster they'd allowed within their walls. They talked among themselves, casting suspicious, wary glances at us. "Resist me, and he'll get what he wants. You'll have no memory once again, and I will not interfere. Or let them believe that's what will happen; help me, and we can be conquerors together."

He twirled a lock of my silver hair around his fingers, watching the tendril before holding me with a gaze that was hard to resist. The promise of the world lingered in his eyes. I knew Nightsdeath would rule with me, side by side, as equals. He wouldn't want to silence me like Auster would, to keep me in a trophy case. In those blazing amber eyes I envisioned the world burning around Nightsdeath and Lightsdeath. Two entities that would never be challenged in the new world we raised from the ashes.

It was a powerful vision of temptation.

"No amount of power you could promise would ever be worth giving up Nyte's love."

"You don't think I could love you?"

"You'll only ever be in love with my power."

"Wrong," he said, his breath now fanning across my ear. "I'd love your pain. Your sadness. Your loneliness. In fact, I crave it so much, and this world is full of cruelty for me to feed upon; it's the product it produces."

Of course. He was once only a planted piece of dark power watered by Nyte's every negative emotion. He was nothing without misery, and starving him was impossible in this brutal world.

"I will never give up Nyte's goodness," I said with all the promise in the world.

"We'll see."

Nightsdeath stroked my cheek as he pulled back, the touch and look he bore on me so jarringly tender after his vicious words. Then his other hand reached up and I gasped, anticipating the sharp snap of my neck the same second darkness claimed me.

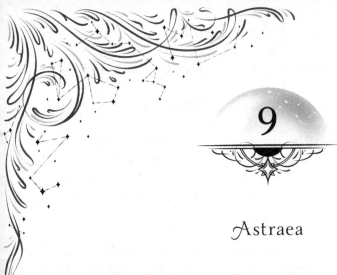

9

Astraea

I was so damn tired of waking up in a state of complete misery. This time I noticed with a choked groan that I was vertical. Lifting my head was like it had been replaced with a boulder too heavy for my shoulders to bear, and my arms . . . they were strung up above my head. Any slight movement shot searing pain through my dormant, awkwardly positioned muscles.

"Why did you come here, Astraea?" a quietly distraught voice asked. My vision came into focus enough to find Zephyr by the door of the wide room.

I didn't answer him right away because my sight started to scan the walls, as I grew more horrified at the stains of crimson around this dark, windowless room. Only two torches were lit on either side of me.

"We had to get Eltanin back," I said, my voice raspy. It ached to speak.

"At this cost? I thought you were smarter than this," he hissed low, coming closer.

My head drooped, but I fought to keep conscious. My wrists were sure to slice more dizzying pain through me if I tried to move, so, to prevent that, I stayed utterly still.

"Has Auster really bought in to an alliance with the realm's most vicious creature?" I asked.

"For now, it seems so."

I couldn't help but chuckle, though it hurt. My laughter was eerie, but I delighted in it.

"Once a desperate fool, always one."

"Speak for yourself," Zephyr countered.

I glared up at him. "I know what I'm doing."

Zephyr's laugh was so far removed from humor. "Sure looks like it."

"What happened to Aquilo? He was absent from the show."

He stared at me, and I could hardly suppress my wicked smile. Zephyr seemed to be deciding whether to be understanding or disapprove of what I'd done to his brother.

"Auster and Notus decided it was only fair to judge him as they would anyone else. He was exiled."

I had to admit I was shocked by that ruling, figuring they would keep him hidden and lie about the exile to keep up the pretense of fairness.

"Good. I hope you exiled him from our sanctuary too if he came crawling."

A muscle in his jaw twitched. "He didn't. I've been away from there too long. Away from Katerina."

"Go back. Please, don't stay for my sake."

"I'm not. Things are tense and uncertain around here, and, after the destruction of the Nova province and the veil gone, Althenia is shaken too. I still have my own people and land that are terrified the same is coming for them."

I sighed sadly. "Everyone is afraid."

Zephyr had a purer heart than I did. I often thought it should be him the world considered their *savior*.

"Aquilo was nothing but a cruel bully," I said coldly.

His hard stare was weighed with judgment, but I wouldn't allow it to inspire guilt for what I'd done—for Aquilo now being without home and title. I was the goddess of justice, and if there was one person I was certain deserved their unfortunate fate, it was Aquilo Sera.

"I know," Zephyr said in a clipped tone.

I groaned, shifting on my knees. Shit, this position was torture in itself and I didn't want to ask how long I'd been *dead* this time. Nightsdeath had snapped my neck so carelessly, and I didn't think it would be the last time he killed me.

"So—" I paused to gather breath when every movement drained incredible energy. "Are you taking first watch of me while your brothers host a tea party with Nightsdeath?"

"Your wits are high, at least."

I hissed at the stinging of my wrists, realizing my shackles had been laced with nebulora. "I'm flattered by all these measures to contain me."

"Nightsdeath wanted to let you roam freely. Said he would enjoy the thrill of you trying to escape or cause chaos. It was Auster and Notus who ordered you here. They've been bleeding you and pushing nebulora into the wounds to weaken your magick in case you managed to free yourself from the bonds." He said the last part with a wince, and only then did I drag my sight up to see the long cuts down my forearms.

This wasn't unexpected, but it was still miserable as hell. There was a spark of delight in me, however, that they believed in my ability to escape.

"My wings," I said. They were glamoured for now, but Auster had promised to remove them when he saw the stark black color of them during the ambush.

"I'd like to believe Auster still cares for you enough to not be so merciless, but if he hands the task of removing them to Notus . . ."

They wouldn't be able to take my wings while I had them glamoured, but a slither of cold fear over what Notus might do to get me to break licked down my spine.

"I don't know what to do," Zephyr said, nearly inaudible. "I can't help you here."

"I don't expect you to," I said softly. "Just . . . don't let them break my spirit, please."

"What do you need me to do?"

"Remind me who I am. Who I love. That's all I need to keep fighting."

Zephyr nodded grimly.

"How long have I been here?" I asked.

"Only an hour or so," Zephyr informed.

I figured the more times I died, the longer I would be wandering between realms before my consciousness found anchor back to this one.

"Dying is really damn taxing," I said, wanting to lie down so badly.

Zephyr grimaced. "I thought *I* nearly died watching him snap your neck so casually. Until he explained that what he'd done put you into, in his words, 'an effective sleep.'"

I scowled, wishing Nightsdeath were here so I could attempt an *effective sleep* on him. Could he be sent back to that veil between life and death? I would damn well try if I got a moment out of these bonds.

I would be at Auster's mercy for a least a week. Until the next full moon when Eltanin would age, and if the stars were aligned for us, he would choose Nyte as his bonded rider, which would wake him from his curse. When he came for me, together we would figure out how to defeat Nightsdeath now that he was a distinct entity from him. Then Auster. Then we'd hunt down his father. Then defeat the gods.

Our list of enemies was long, but together we would claim and right the world no matter the wreckage we might have to salvage it from.

Peace. We'd be reunited to begin our fight for peace down a path of war and terrors, but I wasn't afraid. Not of myself, and not if we were together to face it all.

The door behind Zephyr groaned open, and I shivered like it welcomed death inside. It was Auster, and I couldn't decide if he was the worst of the evils there could have been.

"You're awake," he said, with a confusing note of care and surprise.

"Sorry, not truly dead this time."

That wiped the slipup of emotion from his face as he came closer.

"What is our plan for her?" Zephyr asked him.

I glared at them, needing to keep up a convincing ruse that I despised Zephyr too.

"We need her to tell us where Rainyte is. That's the *thing's* urgent request, and I can't deny it would be a huge thorn out of my side once and for all."

"How can we trust him?" Zephyr asked tightly.

"You can't," I sang, gloating in the irony of them allying with the same person they despised. "Nightsdeath will crush you all when he's done with you. In fact, if you somehow succeed and kill Nyte, I'll gladly side with Nightsdeath to tear apart the world, and you'll be the first to burn within it. Your allegiance with him ends in no favor to you."

"This doesn't concern you," Auster seethed at me, hovering closer. His right fist tightened at his side, and I eyed it carefully.

"On the contrary, all of your plans revolve around me."

"He will take away your memories once again, and you won't remember your vengeance or grief," he snapped, marching to me. I didn't give him the satisfaction of a reaction when he gripped my jaw, forcing me to stare into his brown eyes swirling with humiliation and wrath. "We'll go to Althenia when Rainyte is taken care of. A new veil will be placed around Althenia, and we will govern the celestials as a sovereign nation. All you'll know is me and your people, just how it should have been."

Terror for that possible fate turned me sharp, and before I knew what I was doing I spat in Auster's face.

He growled, letting my face go before a vicious slap followed, snapping my head to the side. I breathed through the explosion of pain, strands of matted, dirty silver hair dancing through my hard pants of rage.

"You are a tyrant, Auster Nova," I said glacially, not looking up. "A root of poison I'm going to weed out from this land."

"You are a spoilt brat I look forward to breaking. Then I'll take pleasure in watching you fall for me."

The mere thought of a life robbed of my memories again and manipulated into loving him made me wish for true death if it ever came to that.

I am Astraea Lightborne. I belong with Nyte. I will not break. I will not forget.

I couldn't let Auster's vile fantasy crumple my composure. I would get out of here. I would be with Nyte again.

I am the star-maiden. I am Lightdeath. I will not break. I will not forget.

I would kill Auster Nova.

"I didn't say you could hurt her without cause." Nightsdeath's voice slithered over me like shadows come to life. He could have stood in the back of the room and been near undetectable were it not for the glow of his eyes.

"What I do with my bonded is none of your business, that was our deal," Auster said, turning to him.

Nightsdeath came closer, not even dignifying Auster with a glance as he kept those amber eyes on me.

"Until I have my full form, she does not belong to you."

"I don't belong to either of you," I snapped.

That earned a slight curl of Nightsdeath's mouth, more like approval than amusement, as he slipped a hand into his pocket.

"Leave us," he said.

I could practically feel Auster's outrage, but he became irrelevant to me in this room with Nightsdeath here. Even though I knew this wasn't my Nyte, not the parts that loved me, it was becoming hard to keep believing this creature was only cruel and merciless and would have killed me by now if I served no purpose.

"We can't waste time," Auster argued.

"What did you plan to do? Strike her until she gave up Rainyte's location? Whip her? I think you forget who you're dealing with, to string her up here for such petty torture. So now that you've had your moment to fantasize about it, she's mine."

Auster audibly spluttered. I didn't think he'd ever been so insultingly over-powered, but he wasn't a fool who'd contend with the pure manifestation of death itself.

I caught Zephyr's look of pained concern and gave a nod of assurance while the other two were occupied in their silent power battle. He and Auster left moments later, but I didn't relax a fraction. Instead my skin pricked with more anticipation in the lone presence of this shadowy mirror of Nyte.

"Make no mistake, my star. You might very well wish for Auster's methods of getting you to talk when you sample mine."

I began to shiver stiffly. Then without warning, he sent a precise slice of darkness toward me. The chain suspending me broke, and I didn't have a second to catch myself. I sobbed when my shoulder took the impact against the hard ground, in so much pain I could hardly stand to be conscious, yet the torture hadn't even begun.

I will not break. I will not break. I will not break.

If it meant keeping Nyte safe, I could withstand whatever they could do to me.

I couldn't get up and surrendered to lying there against the icy stone, hands hugged to my chest with my wrists still in thick manacles and bound with a shorter chain between. The nebulora within my system numbed my ability to reach for my magick. If I really focused, I'd be able to overpower its nullifying effects from my torturous practices to conquer the cosmic plant in my past life. Right now, I had no mental strength to *want* to fight.

Shadows flooded all around me as Nightsdeath crouched. He tenderly brushed the hair over my forehead.

"Such a fragile and breakable thing you appear to be, yet it is your spirit I need to break, and I feel how strong it is."

I'd never been afraid of him. Even when he pushed to the surface of Nyte and threatened my life, I would always reach for his darkness.

"I feel you within me, you know," he said, brushing his knuckles along my bruised cheek. His thumb collected the blood from Auster's slap at the corner of my mouth and his lips parted, tasting it. His eyes closed briefly with a soft sigh, and I shivered at his pleasure. "Our bond. It lingers in me even without the weaker half of me."

"You're nothing more than a parasite he didn't ask to be burdened with. One that delighted and fed on all the pain he never deserved."

"Yet suffer he did, for many centuries, and here I am. He used my power and *enjoyed it*. Don't fool yourself into believing he is better than what you see in me. I gave him the means; he carried out the actions."

"He had no choice."

"Choice, oh there is always a choice. It's what made every transgression he indulged in that much sweeter. It's human nature to blame the lack of *choice* in any wrongdoings to subdue their guilty conscience and avoid full ownership of the unsavory outcome. It's sickening."

I bit my lip with a whimper when he slipped his hands around me, pulling me up, and I couldn't fight it. Not because of the pain shooting through my body with every carful maneuver until he sat there, cradling me to him, but because of the ache in my soul that yearned for Rainyte so terribly that I caved to the illusion of comfort right now. Shadows swirled around us, and that was what kept me knowing this wasn't my Nyte. His touch, his appearance, was whispers of shadows.

"I could save you," he said, so deceptively tender while he stroked tangled hair out of my face. Tears began to blur my vision. "Look how much you're hurting, physically and by the emotions you let plague you. If you give over to Lightsdeath, like when Nyte gave over to me, you'll be free of such weaknesses."

"I thought you would be repelled by an entity of power that is your opposite."

"The dark cannot exist without the light, and light cannot exist without the dark. Acceptance is everything."

"You want to end this world."

"I want to make it stronger. It may take sacrifice, yes. But it is necessary."

"Killing. It would take killing."

"Yes. But death is inevitable, and we are its servants."

I started to fear my understanding of his words. Nightsdeath would eradicate entire species if he saw fit, and not feel a shred of remorse or guilt if the cause justified the means. That's what he was, all he would ever be.

With light fingers under my chin, he guided my head around to peer up at him. Even as death incarnate, I thought him so beautiful it ached in me. So I reached up my joined hands, grazing my fingers over his scar.

"You don't feel me at all? Physically?" I whispered.

"No."

There was a strain in that single word, and maybe I was a desperate fool for any part of Nyte when I clung to it as a piece of the real him. Every flicker of emotion Nightsdeath showed had to be a kernel of the person I loved with all my heart.

Boldly, I leaned up and pressed my lips to his. It was a chaste kiss, and Nightsdeath didn't really react, unmoving as if he didn't know how to. Yet his brow twitched, a note of confusion over what I'd done and perhaps recalling what it *should* feel like.

Then his jaw tightened. "Whatever you think you see or feel, it's only echoes of him. His weak parts I have annoyingly imitated, but I will eradicate them piece by piece."

My heart skipped a beat.

"I won't let you kill every good piece of him."

That removed any flicker of feeling to return the cold, emotionless expression that braced me for his cruelty.

Instead, he stood with me to head out of this underground cell together.

"Where are you taking me?" I said, hating the panic rising in my chest.

"Don't worry, Maiden. I haven't even begun with you yet."

10

Astraea

Nightsdeath had killed me three times now. Each awakening took longer, and the suffering when I returned became more punishing. A tear rolled down the side of my face, falling onto the cold marble I lay against.

My blurry sight could make out only his black boots, spilled with shadows that seemed to writhe and twist around them, alive with an eerie, unnatural motion.

Above me, he lounged upon my purple throne, its once-vivid fabric now dulled in his presence, as though it too had surrendered to his dominion. He leaned back with a casual ease, one hand resting on the arm of the chair, the other draped lazily across his lap. Yet there was nothing casual about the weight of his gaze—though I couldn't lift my head to meet it, I felt its icy pull dragging me down.

And there I was, sprawled at his feet, helpless and humiliated. My chest burned, each breath shallow and painful, but it was nothing compared to the ache in my soul. This was my throne, my kingdom—yet I lay broken, a shattered remnant of the power I once held, as he sat above me like a conqueror surveying his spoils.

It wasn't for my physical pain I cried soundlessly, but for the ache of how every time I awoke from death or sleep, I was being terrorized by every vicious part of Nyte. Worst of all, it hurt because I couldn't even hate Nightsdeath, couldn't fight him; my heart still reached to love him.

"I know you're fighting to contain Lightsdeath. Let it free, Astraea. Let me see how bright you shine," Nightsdeath said, soft as a lullaby.

He was right. That dangerous power rattled within me at the torture he inflicted, and I grappled to keep a tight hold on stopping it from rushing to the surface and taking control of my actions and feelings. The fact that Nightsdeath wanted me to become it gave me enough reason to keep it smothered. If he could speak to Lightsdeath, and they could *ally* together . . . I could lose my right mind as Nyte had lost his battle with Nightsdeath sometimes.

"Why are you so afraid to play with your newfound power? You could turn this castle to stardust with a thought and kill your enemies—the High Celestials—within."

I scrunched my eyes shut and my skin ran hotter to contain the beast inside me. He made it sound so tempting, so easy and without consequence. But there was always a consequence to violence so mindless.

"There are too many innocents. My war is not with them," I rasped.

Nightsdeath groaned. "Your morals are what make you weak and keep you at Auster's mercy. It's a tragedy, to watch one so mighty lie so pitifully."

An ashy taste filled my mouth, and I sucked my lip to keep from crying out at the ache of my dormant muscles trying to peel myself up off the floor. The awful sensations were becoming familiar but no less tolerable no matter how many times I faced this. Coming back from death was akin to, but far worse than, waking from a night of bottomless wine.

His method of torture was what left the burning sensation through my veins, and my cough felt like glass sliced in my throat as I rolled and propped myself up on a shaky elbow. The lingering feeling of his shadows flooding through my body like icy flame left me shivering, yet my skin was slicked with a sheen of sweat.

"I should like to avoid killing you again, I'm growing bored waiting for you to come around. So tell me," he said, leaning his forearms on his thighs to peer down closer. "Where is Rainyte's body?"

I took a few more breaths, trying to draw a clear one free from the sensation of inhaling smoke.

"You can kill me a thousand times, I'll never tell you."

It was a full moon today, and I slipped my sight to the red sphere in the sky out the long stained glass window with a tight yearning in my chest. Part of me was terrified that Nyte would come, in case Nightsdeath managed to kill him and take over his body. He would become more deadly with Nyte's ability to bend minds.

Nyte would win.

I would fight by his side and *we* would win.

Nightsdeath snarled with the snap of his patience. He hauled me up with a tight grip around my throat and I choked. Just as fast as he reacted in violence he switched to quiet tenderness, pulling me flush to his body with an arm around my waist, his shadows caressing my skin, snaking over me curiously. I couldn't decide which side of him was more frightening.

"Why haven't you tried to fight me?" he asked, almost to himself as he studied my face and tucked a lock of hair behind my ear.

"Does it harm Nyte if I do?" I dared to ask.

He sighed, a hint of disappointment. "I almost want to carve out your heart so it can stop being such a pathetic influence to your mind. I expected far more fight from you, but you're perfect prey for me to bend and break here as I wish." His light fingers tipped my chin. "You are so disgustingly, terribly beautiful. I want to have you almost as much as I want to kill you."

Being around Nightsdeath was like walking an endless plank across a deadly ocean. I couldn't predict him—whether the next moment would bring a soft touch, fleeting and disarming, or a poisonous strike sharp enough to cut through me, sending me plummeting into oblivion. His presence was both magnetic and perilous, a constant tension pulling me closer even as survival demanded I keep my distance. My heart raced, not just from fear, but from the maddening thrill of the unknown. Every breath I took in his shadow felt like a gamble, a step deeper into the abyss where I might drown—or worse, never want to leave.

"The feeling is quite mutual," I said, nearly lost in his deadly seduction.

But I had to start figuring out his weaknesses.

Reaching through the void, I retrieved my stormstone dagger and pulled my arm back enough for the momentum to plunge it with both hands through his heart.

My pulse slammed, filling my ears and spiking my anticipation. Nightsdeath made no sound and barely gave a flinch.

"This is more like it," he said in delight. Reaching to wrap his hand around mine, he pulled the blade out slowly.

I didn't know what to expect, but I'd hoped the attack would at least wound him even if it didn't send him back to the veil between life and death.

His amber eyes became more alive, like I'd pleased him with what I'd done. I tore my stare from them to look down at the blade as it slipped out of his body fully. The plunge of it had felt as good as any flesh; it slid out of him with a stomach-churning slickness like a real body . . . yet there was no blood. No wound. He was completely unharmed, confirming the worst of my fears: he couldn't be killed, not even temporarily, nor could he even be wounded by any mortal weapon.

In my horror and fear of his retaliation for my attempt, I summoned my magick on instinct. He anticipated it, instantly smothering my light with his darkness, but I didn't give up.

Lightsdeath hummed through my veins like liquid silver, peeking to the surface.

My next attack pushed distance between us, but he deflected easily, stalking me with a slow smile that dared me to keep trying. *Wanted* me to give in to my world-ending power completely. Only so he could manipulate it for himself.

I stopped, gathering my breath and backing myself against the wall as he closed in.

"Is that all you've got, my star?" he purred.

"I'm not going to give up Nyte, so get on with it," I said coldly.

A muscle in his shadowy jaw flexed. "You desire me too," he said, drawing me closer again with a slithering arm around my back. "With Rainyte, you wanted to see me take over, you wanted me to crave you instead of seeing you as nothing more than an insufferable light to be extinguished. Your heart has always called to darkness."

But you don't get to become it.

That missing line from what Nyte had said to me before was what separated his dark mind from his good. The side of him that wanted to watch the world burn hand in hand with me and the other that wanted to help me salvage this world even if it came to that.

"You're a kernel of dark power that only grew from his pain . . . and that makes you a piece of him I will always love."

"Poetic," he said, inching his lips closer to mine. "Then why do you resist me?"

"Because he could have become you long ago. He could have let his pain take over completely and damn the world. Yet he fought through everything to not be the merciless villain he was portrayed to be, and I won't let that be in vain."

"So weak and vulnerable, your mortal hearts."

"But . . ." My heartbeat picked up as I slipped a hand up his chest. His shadows weaved around my fingers, and there was a certain pleasure to their caress. "You're right. I craved you because I wanted that part of him to love me as much as the rest of him. I wanted to show *him* that Nightsdeath didn't frighten me. If you let me wake him, you'll still be there in him. You'll get to rule with me."

"Why would I want to go back to being suppressed and ignored inside a vessel that refuses to let his pain be avenged like we deserve?"

"Because we all have that inside of us. A suffering we want to unleash upon the world, but, if we all gave up, this world would belong to no one. It would be in ruins."

"That's what you think I am? The embodiment of giving up?"

"Yes."

Nightsdeath smiled, amused. "Oh my star, I haven't even begun. I am not surrender, I am liberation."

His lips brushed softly against mine, and it took all my willpower to not give in. The ways he touched me were always curious, as if he was searching for something though he didn't quite know what.

We had been alone in the throne room all this time but now voices sounded outside. As they grew closer, I distinguished one of them to be Notus's. My heart slammed and I clutched Nightsdeath with a surge of urgency. I was trapped between the bodies of two enemies, but I had to find a way to escape.

"I need your help," I whispered.

His knuckle brushed along my cheek. "Those are beautiful words from you."

My eyes closed, welcoming the peace, as my words escaped my lips in a few final breaths. "We'll find the key together. But I need your help here first."

His eyes flared a fraction at my offer right before the doors were thrown open and several footfalls marched inside.

"She was to be kept chained in the dungeons," Notus bellowed.

Nightsdeath kept an intimate hold of me, tightening as Auster arrived close behind. As Auster noticed our proximity, his jaw tightened.

"So you're a desperate whore even for the most despicable part of him," Auster sneered.

Humiliation from being called that degrading term in front of so many guards standing by flushed me, but it quickly hardened to anger I hoped he felt from my piercing stare.

"Unlike you, I don't need chains to be sure she'll stay by my side."

Nightsdeath goaded them both. Flaunting his power both in magick and the hold he had on my heart.

"You have no authority here," Auster snapped.

"Go ahead, try to take her."

No one moved.

"I thought we had an agreement," Auster ground out.

"I've come to see you offer little to me, Nova," Nightsdeath drawled. He held the power, and everyone knew it.

My mind spun, trying to calculate my own plan between their hostility. Auster had power over the people; Nightsdeath had the power to destroy everything. There was a scale to balance, and I had to have the cunning to hold them both in my palms.

"Men like to bicker over their power when the one with the most is a woman standing behind you both."

Nightsdeath's attention swung to me with mild surprise; Auster pinned me with challenge and caution; Notus could hardly contain his hatred.

As a demonstration, I threw up a sheet of light, separating me from them. Out of their sight, I stepped through the void onto the other side before the wall of light fell like water.

"Always behind you," I said, making all of them whirl around to the main doors where I'd transported myself. The guards all drew their swords, but I smiled calmly. "So you might never know when I'm coming for you."

"Restrain her," Notus demanded to his guards in gold.

I didn't resist, letting them approach with manacles carefully held in rags. I knew then they had to be laced with nebulora and braced for the sting. Gritting my teeth, I didn't let them see my pain, instead widening my smile that might have looked manic considering the way Auster recoiled.

Nightsdeath studied everything with amused intrigue, and, through our stares, I believed we formed a temporary agreement of trust, a plan to be decided, as he let the High Celestials take me away.

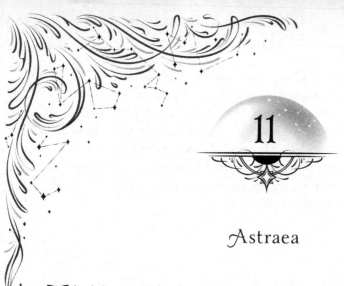

11

Astraea

I hadn't expected to be in the comforts of my rooms in the castle again. The thick red abrasions that already formed around my wrists itched like hell.

Auster lingered near, a predator in the shadows. My manacles had no chains, so I didn't need aid or to be released from them to undress for the bath that awaited me. I eyed the milky steaming waters with suspicion.

"Honey milk soap is your favorite, I recall," he said, stalking closer.

Every measure of swallowed distance between us turned my stomach.

"Times change," I lied, to starve him of any piece of me.

His body warmth radiated into me from behind while his hand slithered across my nape. A hand that had once been a reach of safety to me, a touch I once considered dear, now roiled repulsion in me. His proximity crawled my skin, making me want to abandon my own flesh to escape him.

"You will bathe, and you will dress in the clothing brought for you," he said, a rumbling warning close to my ear.

My gaze slipped to the bed, finding layers of stark white material against the deep purple sheets.

"What for?" I dreaded to ask.

Auster always loved me in white. He would say it was the symbol of my grace and devotion as the star-maiden and insisted I always wore it in front of my people.

"We're going to show the world you can be saved. That your heart isn't beyond returning to righteousness."

He wanted to parade me as a lie. Compliant by his side to atone for all he had condemned of me.

"I won't."

I hissed with the tight grip he took of my hair.

"It wasn't a request. You either kneel or bleed."

"Then bleed me dry, Auster Nova; I will never kneel for you."

He twisted me around by my hair until our loathing clashed in our battling stare. A cool breath of metal touched my collar, but it was my tunic, not my flesh, that tore, his blade cutting down the material to my navel, and my hands lashed up to keep my breasts covered.

"It's not like I haven't seen every inch of you," he said in a shadowy tone.

I hadn't considered the possibility of Auster wanting to violate me, but standing here vulnerable wavered my composure.

"You lay a hand on me and I will kill you," I promised.

"You have already threatened me that way. So laying a hand on you makes no difference."

The handle of the blade twisted in his palm so as not to cut us when both his hands split the rest of my tunic. I stumbled back from him, knocking into the vanity unit in the washroom, keeping myself covered with my arms and the ruined fabric. My heart thundered, but Auster didn't advance for me again.

I stared at him wide-eyed; my blood coursed hot and furious. Auster's unfeeling gaze slipped down my body, and the only relief I had was that he bore no lust or desire. No—if he decided to do something reprehensible and evil against my will it would only be to prove his sick dominance over me.

I swore to every god I would not let him get that far, no matter what I had to do.

In those thick, tense seconds, neither of us moving, I was preparing for the worst.

"Servants will be with you shortly," he said, so cold and calm. "Resist or refuse the attire and this summons, and you will severely regret it, Maiden."

I had words of acid and disdain for that parting statement but I kept them burning in my mouth as I watched his navy cloak billow slightly with the force of his march out of my rooms.

Alone, I felt the tension dissolve from me and dropped my arms and my tunic, leaving me bare-chested. I took a moment to collect myself before floating toward the water, dipping my fingers in. It didn't burn; instead it relaxed me with its soft caress and that irritated me irrationally, simply because Auster had provided the blissful bath.

No, this was *my* castle, and *he* was the invader with no claim on anything.

Reminding myself of that, I bathed in peace.

Servants did come, and I couldn't let any of my outrage out on the gentle hands of the fae who helped me dress in the white garb. The final addition to the long gown of beaded silk and lace was the veil that was draped over my head to cover my face. Was this Auster's idea of punishment? A symbol of my shame? Or did he merely hope to hide my cold loathing for him from the people he was to put me in front of?

I was escorted by two guards in front, two behind, toward the front entrance of the castle. Auster was already outside, along with Zephyr and Notus, standing exactly as they had been when I saw them days ago.

The citizens had gathered again, flooding the courtyard save for the huge crevice from the impact of the meteor. Their quiet chatter increased when I strolled out, and I'd never felt more ashamed than I did as I was presented like an obedient pet to Auster, veiled and hidden.

Still, I kept my shoulders squared and my head held high.

With Auster's hand held out to me when I was close enough, I hoped he could feel the heat of my eyes on him through the lace when I slipped my white-gloved hand into his, glad for the barrier between our skins at least.

Auster's voice amplified to address the people. "I can only take our disruption when last we gathered here as fate. Though lives were lost in the tragic imbalance that is shaking our world, with our Maiden back and willing to reform, we have more hope than ever to stop the stars falling and to restore nature's peace."

I was itching to tear off my veil, not out of rebellion, but to speak to my people rather than through a proxy who had his own selfish goals woven in the name of restoring *peace*.

My hand lifted toward the hem of the veil that reached my navel, but Auster's fingers tightened against mine in warning.

Auster went on. "It is why Astraea Lightborne has agreed to marry me."

I didn't need to utter a sound when the crowd erupted with shock and cheering at that declaration. Now the veil made sense, since I couldn't keep my utter abhorrence of the idea from my expression. It would be clear to all who gushed and gasped that I was not in favor of this movement in the slightest.

Daring to twist my head a fraction, I saw Auster's endearing smile for the crowd, which seemed laced with cunning to me.

How could the people believe this so easily after our confrontation mere days ago? I was beginning to spiral with hopelessness—Auster had won their hearts, their loyalty, so they would always follow him, not me.

I had abandoned them for centuries.

My slip into despair halted when someone stood on something that lifted them a head above everyone else. Their arms thrust into the air, and *my* symbol— the key staff with my constellation over it—was embroidered on the deep purple banner they held in their defiant grip, and what had previously been silver wings were now sewn in *black*.

Pride burst in my chest like a new heartbeat as I looked at the symbol of silent rebellion. It slammed again and again when more purple banners were thrust into the air, littered throughout the crowd as proud beacons of support. Not for Auster. For me. These were people who believed in me alone.

A smile began to lift on my face and unburden a piece of my soul. That was until soldiers started pushing through the crowd, and when the first person who'd stood was pulled down from their small vantage point, I broke.

Throwing the veil over my head, I didn't get one step forward before Auster took a tight grip of my elbow, trying to yank me back into the castle.

"Leave them alone!" I yelled, but my cry and struggle were swallowed by the crowd's unrest.

The gathering quickly became a rowdy scene of distress with celestial soldiers pushing through forcefully and rebels being pulled out. My magick hummed despite the shackles laced with nebulora. I wanted to burn the wings off any celestial who acted to Auster's cruel demands.

I was pulled into the castle, and the doors were swiftly closed, cutting off the sounds of the people. Ripping my arm out of Auster's grip, I blazed at him.

"If you harm a single one of them, I'll make sure their pain is inflicted on you twice as punishingly."

Auster's expression was quietly simmering with resentment. He hadn't expected that display, and that made it all the more satisfying.

"They will be reminded that you are nothing without us. You will be my wife, a counterpart to the House of Nova, nothing above that. The age of the star-maiden is dead."

I dared to shorten the distance between us, never taking my determined stare from him.

"My age is just beginning, Auster Nova. You see that—you *feel* it. All of this is a desperate grapple for what has already slipped from your fingers. Control."

His hand wrapped around my throat, pushing me against the wall. The sudden aggression shifted the guards around us. Auster didn't hurt me despite the tremble in his hold, like he was refraining from choking me. Despite our eyes piercing each other, I didn't think the thread of our past, our friendship, would ever fully burn out in our hatred.

That was a torment that plagued us both.

Auster lowered his voice as not to be overheard. "This marriage won't just be in law. You're quite educated about bargains, aren't you? You'll be familiar with the Greciea Bargain, known as the marriage bond in the common tongue."

My blood ran cold. I did know of it—it was used by those who weren't fated to one another to forge a similar mating bond. It gave them a strong emotional connection and the ability to mind speak to one another.

"That bargain can't be forged without full intimacy."

"That's correct."

"*Willingly,*" I added through my teeth. "And that will never happen."

"You've lost your memories once before," he said.

Auster's throat bobbed as he released me. I wondered if that small reaction was an indicator of disgust over what he implied.

"That's no different than taking me against my will and you know it," I seethed.

"Is it? I wouldn't force you; I'd show you everything we could be together and a land we could build together, free of the burden Rainyte brought into your life."

"He's never been my burden, he's always been my freedom from a cage you tried to keep me in."

I pushed at Auster's chest to gain more steps of distance.

"Escort Astraea back to her rooms," he said to no guard in particular. "She doesn't come out, and no one goes in, without my say."

As he left me, my anger began to simmer when I thought of those purple banners in the courtyard. I was determined to flood the world with them.

I didn't have anything to indicate time, but from the grumbling of my stomach, I assumed it was past supper, and Auster had denied me that meal since his guards locked me in my rooms. I paced in front of the blazing hearth and let my thoughts reel to distract from the hunger pains.

A strange sound made me jump and whirl toward the source. It came again, like a scratch against glass, which drew my cautious attention toward the balcony.

If the moon hadn't cast a permanent hue of dark red I wouldn't have spotted the black cat outside. I blinked at it in confusion, then I gasped, rushing to let it in.

I winced at the quick flare of light as Davina shape-shifted and I stood staring at her, wide-eyed and dumbfounded.

"I'm very mad at you," she said, bracing her hands on her hips. "You leave in the middle of the night and—*oh*—"

I threw my arms around her, cutting her off, but I couldn't help it. She was so warm and sure, and my brow pulled together tightly with my threatening tears. After a few seconds, she sighed away the anger she'd arrived with to hug me back.

"Oh Astraea, you really had to embrace your saviorhood at the worst moment."

"I had to," I choked. "I didn't want to risk any of you, and I thought it would be quicker going alone." I pulled away, holding her arms. "Drystan made it back with Eltanin?"

"Yes."

"Eltanin was injured."

"He's healing well with Lilith's help. The tear in his wing might scar, and he shouldn't fly for a while. She's hoping it won't permanently damage his flight ability when he grows on his next cycle."

I nodded. All I could do was hope for that too.

"Why are you here?" I asked, paranoid that she could be seen. I scanned outside before drawing the curtains on the balcony and leading her into the dining room.

"To check in on you, of course! Stars, we're all so worried about you and—" she gasped as she started taking in the marks on me in my short silk gown. I hugged myself.

"I'll heal just fine. Most of it is from the meteor blast."

Her sad eyes found mine and she cupped my cheek. "I heard. The whole city is talking about it, how you saved them. That was so brave of you."

"It was necessary of me."

"The High Celestials' combined magick might have stopped it too," she argued, with dismay now creasing her expression.

"Maybe they would have tried, but I wasn't going to wager on it."

Davina didn't speak, still silently assessing the state of me. I took her hands.

"I need to tell you something," I said quietly.

I told her what I could about dying and how Nightsdeath had followed me through that thin veil between life and death. I tried my best to explain what he was and all he'd said and done so far, but I was still figuring him out myself.

"Stars above," she muttered, staring at nothing in particular as we sat on my bed and she took it all in.

"Nyte is still . . . as well as he was?"

Davina didn't answer right away, still seeming lost in her own thoughts with all I told her. My anxiety spiked and I shook her arm.

That snapped her back to our conversation. "Nyte? As in Rainyte? I guess using his full name is a good way to distinguish him from his dark counterpart set on conquering the world. Oh, yes! He's as fine as he was before you left."

Relief whooshed out of my next breath.

"Did Drystan tell you about his theory that Nyte could be awoken with a dragon bond? Is he still confident it will work?"

"Yes, but he hasn't spoken much about it. He hasn't said much at all since he got back. He just paces and ponders over his books more distressed than ever; he practically barks at anyone who disrupts him. I think he's most worried about you, yet he won't admit it."

My heart sank. Drystan might continue to pretend he doesn't care and won't invite friendship into his life, but his actions always countered his stubborn resolve.

"He's anxious to wake Nyte. This week of waiting is going to be terrible," I sighed.

In more ways than one, but whatever Nightsdeath or Auster would do to me, I could bear it.

"I can't leave you here," Davina said, squeezing my hand.

"You have to. If Auster or Notus catch you they won't hesitate to kill you, likely after they use you to get me to give up Nyte's location. I can't risk that, and I will not lose you."

Her eyes scrunched shut for a second. "I despise Auster Nova."

"I can handle him."

She squeezed my hands. "I know you can." Then, to my surprise, tears welled in her eyes. "Oh, even as that clueless, frightened Libertatem participant I knew you'd be the most resilient and cunning."

Her words swelled an ache in me, and I was so grateful to this fae for all she'd done for me.

"All right," she said, wiping away any vulnerability in an instant and standing. "Nyte better wake the hell up by the end of the week; then we're all storming this place to come for you."

I smiled, letting my hope bloom a little more. The thought of having Nyte back, the real and whole him, made anything feel possible.

"Tell Drystan I can handle myself here and he needs to be nicer to you all."

I held back my smile as I pictured Drystan's scowl upon hearing that last part.

Davina chuckled before a sly smile curved her lips.

"You saw our message, didn't you? The people haven't abandoned you."

I drew a short gasp. "The banners? That was you?"

"It was *you*, Astraea. Many are from the fae resistance. Humans have joined us too. There's more support for you than you can see. Belief in the star-maiden is all around you. So let it keep growing that strength within you."

My resolve had never been stronger.

Davina had to leave, and I hugged myself as if it would keep the warmth of her last embrace around me for a while longer. I watched her take the form of a small black bird and soar over the balcony.

I followed out into the lashing, icy wind to survey. There were guards outside my door, but as I leaned over the edge of my balcony, I discovered none below. My floor was too high to jump without wings, but my goal wasn't to escape. My time in Goldfell manor had made me adept at climbing, so I inspected the stability of the wall and ledges.

If Auster wasn't going to feed me, I was going to get to the kitchens myself. I didn't even care about being caught after that. In fact, proving I could elude his efforts to contain me would be quite satisfying.

Changing into the most suitable clothing and boots from my wardrobe, I hoisted onto my balcony railing and threw all caution to the wind. The castle had enough narrow ledges, and a gritty texture for grip, that making my way across and around the building slowly wasn't strenuously difficult.

Two floors down, I finally found a window slightly ajar. After deeming it clear, I slipped inside, needing to take a moment to rub my hands together, shivering violently to bring back the warmth to my fingers.

I enjoyed the winter and loved the snow, but unequipped it was absolutely dreadful.

"I need to know where she's hidden that damned key," Auster hissed.

I stiffened, then launched toward the wall as if it might grant passage away from Auster. I'd chosen the wrong hallway to infiltrate, clearly.

"I may have that answer, but what are you going to give me in return?" Tarran said.

His voice was unexpected, and now I wanted to march around the corner their voices drifted from and wring my hands around the vampire's neck.

"I've already promised you reign over the vampires. Don't test my generosity."

Tarran snickered at that and I tensed. Daring to edge closer to their voices, I peeked around the bend and found them standing in close proximity alone. Tarran had his arms folded, completely unafraid of Auster.

"I don't expect your promise to hold true, not with your new allegiance to an unfeeling creature from the depths of Hell itself," Tarran said.

Auster was out of his league, not knowing how to handle Nightsdeath, and that was clear in his hesitation now. His voice turned to a hushed whisper, but I eyed the darkness as if Nightsdeath lingered in every trace.

"We'll take care of him once Rainyte is gone."

Tarran's chuckle was part amused, part sardonic. "If you thought Rainyte was a merciless villain, you're severely outmatched, facing him without a shred of humanity. Because that's what Nightsdeath is."

"He will have a body of flesh that can be killed. That's all we need." Auster's tone turned low and threatening. "Don't question me, *soulless*; I'll easily find someone else to get me this information."

"No, you won't. You're running out of allies and options, Nova. Is she really worth your relentless pursuit?"

That snapped something in Auster, and he wrapped a hand around Tarran's throat and pushed him against the wall. A few strokes of lightning broke over his knuckles, and Tarran gave a pained sound. Then he smiled. Looking almost . . . delighted by the threat. Auster stared loathingly into Tarran's eyes before pushing off the soulless vampire with a rough shove, lingering only for a pause before he twisted and stormed away.

What the hell was that about?

Tarran stared after him for a moment; then to my horror his head turned toward me. My heart leapt up my throat as I jerked back and plastered myself to the wall, praying it would open up and swallow me whole.

My instinct was to take off, but my elbow was caught by a hand before I could take a step. Then I was the one being slammed against the wall, finding pure amused delight spilled over Tarran's face.

"You're a better spy than this," he said playfully.

"How did you know I was here?"

"You know vampire and fae senses are sharper than celestials'. I could scent you before you even slipped in that window."

"Why are you here?" I snapped, not hiding my accusation.

Tarran shrugged. "I never declared I was only on your side."

"Then what are you truly hoping for at the end of all this, regardless of who sits on the throne?"

He ignored me to ask, "Are you risking punishment by leaving your rooms just to prove a point?"

"I was hungry. He neglected to remember I need to be fed."

"He's terrible at keeping pets."

I scowled deeply. Tarran chuckled.

"I know just the place. You might want a cloak."

"I'm not going anywhere with you," I hissed. "Where is Nightsdeath?"

"Beginning the hunt for his . . . physical form, I assume."

My whole body stiffened. "That would be a futile endeavor."

"He thinks he might be able to sense Rainyte if he gets close enough. Though he's causing a lot of disturbance in his wake already."

A sudden terrible realization hit me.

"He needs pain to survive," I muttered, more to myself. "Maybe he even needs death."

There was a monster on the loose, and I couldn't believe Auster and the other High Celestials had become so focused on me that they were letting him terrorize the continent.

"You know he needs to be stopped," Tarran said carefully, as if I might lash out in defense of Nightsdeath.

I had to admit I was conflicted.

"I need to figure out what his being here means. Nyte still hasn't awoken or he would have come for me. I can't do anything to Nightsdeath without risking that it will kill Rainyte too."

Tarran turned and started walking, hands slipping casually into his pockets. It was either follow him or hope my stealth was enough to get me to the kitchens alone, at least.

Internally cursing, I jogged to catch up, trusting he'd sense guards or the High Celestials and warn me.

"Our sister is in Vesitire," Tarran said so nonchalantly, but it slammed into me. I didn't know what shocked me most: the term *our* and *sister* that linked me and Tarran closer than I thought he would be willing to admit right now or the mention of a *sister* that had my mind rapidly sifting through memories to find a name and a face.

"Laviana," I said; the face that accompanied her name unfolded clearly in my mind. Two-toned black and white hair, harsh green eyes, and firm but elegantly beautiful features.

She was the daughter of two of my guardians: a shadowless and a celestial.

None of us were siblings by blood, but we had been raised so closely, with all of them having been born before I came along, that we always considered each other family.

"Where?" I asked.

"Around the outskirts, last I heard."

"Do you know what she's doing here?"

"Likely still leading the vampire movement for equality."

More threads of memory started weaving together in my mind.

"If you're not part of that cause, what are you part of?"

"Who said I wasn't?"

Tarran would never give me full answers or be straight with exactly what he hoped to achieve.

We reached the kitchens with a few stops and Tarran's complete guidance using his heightened sense to make sure I wasn't found before I could at least eat.

I dug into any leftovers I found in various concealed containers or under rags, ending up with a mouth too full of bread, cheese, and meat.

Scanning for water to wash it down, I found Tarran holding a cup out to me with a look between disgust and concern over my ravaging. I took it sheepishly.

I couldn't decide if Tarran's kindness, however negligible, would eventually call for a price.

"I want you on my side," I blurted.

I thought relieved surprise had twitched his brow for a flash. Until his lips firmed and his eyes turned ice cold.

"You killed my Bonded, Astraea. You executed Gresham for killing innocents when your Bonded is no different. How is that just and fair? Your biases make me sick."

I paled. He was right and I think a part of me always questioned my ruling that day long ago. Until I remembered everything that made the crimes of Gresham unforgivable.

"The death on Nyte's hands has always been collateral damage. Innocents, yes. But Gresham led a slaughter on a town full of females and young. He *targeted* them knowing those deaths would hurt the High Celestials and their people the most, and he had no remorse for it."

A muscle in his jaw flexed, and it pained me as much as him to tear open this wound of the past.

"The act is still the same."

"The intentions are all the difference."

I could see the war in his eyes and his pain broke me. I'd seen it before. Tarran had been devastated to learn what his Bonded had done, but I also understood how love blurred morality. Love tried to find reasoning in the cracks of unforgivable sins.

"I'm sorry," I said. A slipped breath of condolence that couldn't offer even a stitch to the permanent tear in his soul.

"I know," he said with no emotion. "Before my parents passed on to their guardian realm, they made all of us swear to keep looking out for you. That's all I'm doing now: fulfilling an obligation. But you're making that damned difficult, as always."

"You and I were close . . . before what happened with Gresham—"

"Before you executed him."

I winced but nodded.

"You don't deserve a thing from me," he said

"I know."

My agreement only flared his irritation, him nearly rolling his eyes.

Tarran said, "You need to kill Nightsdeath."

He made to leave me here with that parting statement.

"I can't be sure it won't kill Nyte!" I called after him.

"He's already as good as dead. Night has fallen in more ways than one. You know what you have to do, Lightsdeath."

12

Astraea

Revulsion for where I was—right outside the familiar white door of Auster's room—rose to the surface. There might be a few new chips in it than I last remembered, or maybe I'd never stalled long enough outside it to notice all the minor imperfections in the wood.

He'd summoned me here and I had to grit my teeth against the desire to run before discovering why. The guard who'd escorted me had left, and that rattled my unease even further.

Don't run. Don't run.

I heard shuffling beyond. *Was that also voices?* My pulse skipped when the footfall grew louder toward the door and a chill gripped me when it swung open.

Auster's deep frown of annoyance at the intrusion smoothed out when he saw me. My jaw locked tighter as he played ignorant as to why I was here.

It wasn't just his presence that urged everything inside me to retreat, it was the fact he stood there shirtless.

My eyes only trailed lower to take in his missing left arm, now replaced by metal and strapped by leather over his shoulder and torso. I started to wonder about the beautiful craftsmanship—how could it not be too heavy when it appeared made entirely of silver?

Then my awe vanished when I remembered what had happened for him to need it. How the key had eroded his arm in punishment for killing me. If I hadn't been his bonded, it would have killed him instead. I couldn't even gloat over his instant penance.

He'd lost an arm, and I'd lost my life.

"What am I doing here?" I ground out.

"I wanted to talk."

He wasn't alone. When the woman came into view, Auster dropped his right hand from the doorframe so she could slip out. My stomach immediately turned.

In all my years I'd never come across anyone with hair like mine, yet here she was, with silver hair and arms covered with silver tattoos that, despite whatever starlight matter enhancement potion she took to imitate me, weren't right at all.

She gave me a sheepish smile, looking perfectly composed with her clothing and hair impeccable despite what I must have intruded on. She slipped out, and I watched after her with a million thoughts.

"A frequent courtesan of yours?" I asked.

"Yes," he answered unashamedly.

I dragged my sight back to him with more disgust from discovering his particular *desires* rolling in me.

Auster stepped aside so I could enter his rooms, and I had to tear my feet from the roots binding me to the floor.

The familiarity hit me, spinning my mind as I took in the surroundings as flashes of memory stole me away. The worst part was that they weren't all unpleasant.

In the armchairs by the blazing fire, we'd talked for endless hours into the night. About our wants, our dreams, about Vesitire and Althenia, and about nothing at all.

In his dining area we'd shared countless meals, and I could almost hear the echoes of our laughter.

On his bed . . .

I spun away from looking at it, having to close my eyes just to *breathe.* I thought back to the times when it was easy between us. Simply as friends. Very good friends. Then we grew up, and the idea of marriage and romance felt expected because of that childhood closeness. For a while, in our early adulthood, we both suspected the bond. Auster started to lean into the idea of a Bonded life together, and I tried to reciprocate.

If I hadn't found love and passion with Nyte, I might never have discovered what that truly meant in a life with Auster. But I still wanted Auster in my life back then; I still loved him on a different level and always would.

"Why wasn't that enough?" The pained whisper slipped out of me before I could bite my tongue. When I opened my eyes, I turned to him, relieved he'd put on a plain white shirt. My voice picked up with grating resentment. "Why was my friendship never enough for you?"

He considered me for a moment, moving idly toward the bed.

"It wasn't that. It was *who* you rejected me for. You'd turned your back on everything we'd built, for *him.*"

"You didn't give me a chance to explain."

"There was nothing to explain."

"Your perception had always been singular and biased. After all we'd been through you didn't give me any grace to explain to you what I saw in him, why I fell for him."

"You think I wanted to hear it?" he snarled. Then he laughed. A single venomous sound. "You really are so fucking selfish, Astraea. And naive. And damn stubborn."

"I'm selfish?" I seethed, feeling livid now. "You can't keep pretending all you've done is in the name of your duty and protection of the people against Nyte. You couldn't set your pride aside and consider the possibility that maybe we were all wrong about him."

We drowned under the flood of our past.

"You could have found love with someone else," I continued, my bitterness festering. "You couldn't let go of me because of the power and status I would grant you above your brothers. You loathe me now, yet you're still grappling with the idea of us. Why?"

"To break you as much as you broke me."

We exchanged our words like knives, and I didn't know who would bleed out the fastest.

"I didn't break you, Auster Nova, you did that yourself. You can pretend all you want, but it wasn't just me who felt passionless when we were together. There was always something else on your mind." I laughed, a little deliriously. "I thought it was me, that you weren't attracted to me. But I felt your love in every way except when we tried to be intimate. So when I felt what was missing with Nyte, I thought . . ." A new piece of my heart broke off as I stood watching our anguish tighten; there was pain in his eyes too. "I thought for one moment of fantasy you might be *happy* for me."

Auster's hand tightened on the bedpost he leaned on. His expression turned scarily firm.

"Happy?" He bathed that word in acid. "You thought I would be happy to hand over a reign that was rightfully mine? My Bonded, a person who was supposed to be *mine*. You thought I would be fucking *happy* to watch the most heinous creature in our land have it all instead? No, Astraea. The moment I learned of it from Nyte's father, I wanted to kill Nyte more than ever before. I wanted to kill you. I wanted to *stop* the plan the two of you started to contrive together when I didn't know how far ahead you had gotten. I saw only one option, and that was that you had to be stopped."

"Nyte's father?" My focus latched onto that one detail that cut me with new shock.

I'd always assumed Auster had found out through a rogue vampire from the resistance or some other slip of intel.

Auster straightened, realizing he hadn't meant to give that up.

"I never would have thought I'd have to ally with his despicable, powerless father just to stop my own mate from ruining this realm."

A wave of nausea threatened my balance, and I had to step away, mulling over the events of the past to figure out how I could have missed it, Auster's shameful alliance, but there was too much. Too much blood and disorder and arguing during that last year of my past life. Everything felt fragile, and I knew in my soul something terrible was coming.

Auster had allied with Nyte's father before . . . it made far more sense that their recent collusion wasn't new. Just rekindled.

"Where is his father now?" I forced the question through my tight throat.

"He has a plan that will help stop you once and for all, should I fail in re-forming you. Our Gods will walk among us."

Stars above. Nyte's father was already working to bringing the God of Dusk and Goddess of Dawn to our realm, and my parents would be coming for me. The race had begun, and we hadn't even started looking for the key pieces. I needed to kill them before they killed me.

I breathed steadily so as not to give away my sinking confidence and rising trepidation.

"The most terrifying villains are those with friendly faces," I said absent-mindedly, staring at the snowstorm outside the window. Then I locked onto Auster's deep brown eyes. "The worst monster is the one standing in plain sight preaching as a saint."

"Unlike you, I have never lost sight of my faith in Dusk and Dawn. It is our gods' grace that blessed us celestials with the power and privilege to protect the people."

"Religion has formed firm roots of arrogance in the celestials. I won't bow to gods who demand I bend for them."

Auster's huff mocked me. "Then you are the arrogant one, to believe yourself above them and beyond facing judgment."

"I'm not arrogant. I'm free."

To my creators, and to Auster, it seemed, I was nothing more than a failed experiment of Dusk and Dawn.

Auster sat on his bed, which I noticed was completely undisturbed despite his prior company. I couldn't stand still, walking around and taking in new trinkets and old, discovering what had changed and what remained from centuries ago.

I said, "All that time I was gone, how could you rest easy with such delusions while the rest of the continent lived through blood and terror."

"I am a High Celestial. My highest duty is to the celestials, and they were protected and thriving."

"Because of *Nyte*," I snapped. "He created your precious veil of protection around Althenia before the key broke after my death."

"Don't expect my appreciation for it when he's the reason our realm collapsed into ruin," he said icily, cutting me a look over his shoulder when I lingered by the nightstand. "Even before he corrupted you, he was a parasite in our realm, and you know that is fact. He doesn't belong here. I might have killed you, and I will admit it was the hardest thing I had to do, but you two left me *no choice.* You fell in love with a creature that damned us all. You abandoned your one sole purpose of creation to love a monster."

Nothing I could say would pierce through his unyielding hatred. I decided he didn't deserve to know how protective, and kind, and resilient Nyte was for those he cared about.

"Is that all I am—a creation and a duty without a heart of my own to follow?"

"Not all, but first and foremost. You forgot yourself, Astraea, and I pity you. You're not born like the rest of us, you were given to us for one role, raised by six carefully chosen guardians for that role, and you threw it all away for *love.*"

My lip wobbled but I turned enough that he wouldn't get to feed on my vulnerability. I found a small bottle on his nightstand, which distracted my broken heart. Lifting it, I discovered it was a sleeping tonic.

"You loved me once. Are you haunted by what you did to me?"

"Yes," he said easily.

"Every night?" I asked, flicking my gaze from the nearly empty bottle to him.

"Most."

"Do you want to know what I think?" I asked, setting the tonic back down. "I think everyone harbors a monster at their core. Restless nights are a warning; that monster claws in the most silent hours because it has your full attention. It's the people who are most composed in the daylight, too perfectly so, that have caged their beast too long and will break from the madness in one way or another."

Auster huffed, running a hand through his unbound brown hair, which rested above his shoulders. "Is that how you rest easy with all you've done?"

"I rest easy because I don't deny nor am I ashamed of anything I've done."

"Once again you display your hubris."

"Only insecure men see hubris in a confident woman."

Auster stood, swallowing the distance between us. His fingers grazed under my chin when he was close enough.

"Everyone has a place in this world; you've lost yours."

I couldn't help my amused smile. "Who's really the one in shackles?"

At my boldness, his eyes flared with disdain.

"Nightsdeath wants you to reveal the locations of the key pieces as much as I do. I think he'll be far more efficient in his methods."

I gritted my teeth. "Because you're a coward."

His knuckle grazed along my cheek in a deceptive show of tenderness.

"Believe me or not, I do not enjoy hurting you."

"Why did you call me to your rooms, Auster?"

"To tell you our wedding is set for three days' time."

I jolted away from him.

His expression turned cold at my reaction. "The bargain will take time, but our marriage in law will set an example for the people. It will put an end to the Dark Maiden rebellion movement when they see your compliance."

I was running out of time. No matter what, I couldn't let this wedding happen.

Auster added, "You will dine with me and the other High Celestials tomorrow evening as part of the pre-wedding ceremonies. We'll receive their blessing."

My stomach was clenching tighter and tighter the more he talked.

"Where is Aquilo?" I took the opportunity to ask. "He hasn't been with you when you appear before the people."

Auster's look darkened on me.

"It was unlawful and despicable what you did to him. You had no right."

"You don't get to preach rights when you've violated all of mine," I said, nearly shaking with anger.

"You are my prisoner."

I stalked to the door without waiting for a dismissal. "I will be your downfall."

13

Astraea

Once again, I was wrapped head to toe in white for the pre-wedding feast with the High Celestials. This delusion Auster paraded around was as laughable as it was humiliating.

I arrived first to the dining hall, leaving my rooms early and giving my guards no choice but to follow. They could have attempted to hold me, but before I dropped the lace veil over my face, they seemed to read the dare in my eyes and thought it wasn't worth the battle. After all, I was heading to exactly where Auster wanted me.

After wandering around the table placements, leaning in to adjust some askew silverware and the awkward reach of some items, I sat next to the head, where Auster would be, and I cast a pleasant smile at the steely-faced celestial guards, who watched me uneasily. I didn't know if they could see it past the lace.

Auster entered, surprised to see me already here until he fixed a mask of indifference on his face.

"You're early," he commented, not hiding his irritation about it.

He took his place, a statement of his rank above me, but I let my irritation about it fade. Auster could wear as many crowns as he wanted, stand where he thought fit; the more his ego grew, the more satisfying it would be when I made him swallow it.

"I'm quite famished. With the lack of meals, I was beginning to grow concerned that the castle was suffering a food shortage. I almost started without you."

He eyed me warily, as if my cheerful tone unnerved him. I merely reached to spear a slice of chicken before scooping helpings of vegetables onto my plate, not waiting to be served. I really was *very* hungry.

I went to uncover my face to eat.

"I didn't say you could remove that," he said.

Holding his stare in challenge, I lifted the lace, letting it fall behind my head.

"How else am I to eat, *Your Majesty*?"

I didn't think Auster was above hurting me here, with the guards as witnesses; I just didn't care. His eyes narrowed, but he let it go.

"Is the veil really necessary anyway?"

"You're supposed to remain covered from all eyes but mine from the moment our wedding is announced until we are wed."

"That's an archaic and bullshit tradition."

"That is your punishment."

My grip tightened around my fork and I itched to stab him with it.

"Am I to be your wife or your child?" I bit out.

Auster gave me a flat look. "The veil remains until the bond is forged."

Every time he reminded me of that vile agenda, I fought against being sick.

Zephyr entered next, his presence cutting through our building tension, and sat opposite me. Thankfully his choice spared me from staring at the hateful gaze of Notus, who joined him by his side. We didn't smile at each other, keeping up appearances that I despised him as much as his brothers, but I was glad to see him.

"Just like old times," I mused, cutting my meat. "Except for one face. I'm not particularly disappointed Aquilo isn't here to sour the food."

Notus pinned me with a sharp look, Auster's hand tightened around his cup, Zephyr slipped a warning look across to me. I held a pleasant smile.

"You had no right or authority to exact that punishment on a High Celestial," Notus snarled.

"I would disagree. Aquilo got what he deserved and so should you."

Notus targeted his rising fury at Auster. "When will she receive punishment for that act of treason?"

Auster chewed on his meat, contemplating. Zephyr took a drink, observing the three of us nervously over the rim.

"We can't afford to have the people know of it right now," Auster said. "As far as they're aware, Aquilo is currently occupied with private matters in his own court."

"The plan was to make them believe she's as villainous as Rainyte, yet the moment you have her in your grasp, she's dining like fucking royalty." Notus slammed his knife down, rattling everything on the table.

"Our plans changed and new advantages were seen when she came to us; we discussed this," Auster answered calmly.

"I'm not royalty," I said. "That's the title you play with. I am a god. The difference comes not with a bigger crown but a power you don't want to provoke from me."

Notus's tangible loathing of me pricked my skin.

"I want her chained in the dungeons where she belongs," Notus snarled. "I demand it. By ruling of the House of Aura. She has threatened me and I will not stand for it."

"Then allow me to threaten you some more. You put a chain between my wrists and I'll kill you with it."

Notus bellowed a sound of outrage, standing abruptly, and the high pitch of steel echoed throughout the hall. We'd barely lasted ten minutes into our food. His stormstone blade pointed at me from across the table, and all the guards shifted closer. Zephyr stood too, tracking Notus and the blade. Auster stopped eating.

I locked an equally hateful stare on Notus as I reached across the table for a piece of bread. He took it as an insult, a mockery of his threat, which I wasn't afraid of, and he intended for his blade to come down on my wrist, which would have severed my hand.

Instead, he met an invisible resistance as every marking over my exposed flesh shone with my magick awakening in a natural defense. It wasn't without great effort to push through the effects of the nebulora they kept me weakened with. My forehead quickly beaded with sweat and a tremor shook through me.

"How is that possible? There's enough nebulora to incapacitate a dozen celestials laced in those manacles," Auster said incredulously.

"You really don't know me very well," I said, my voice starting to waver with exertion. "Not even in our past, or you would have known I'd been building a tolerance to nebulora against my skin for decades."

Lightsdeath whispered dark chants throughout my mind. It could turn these manacles that were still suffocating a lot of my power into dust. Lightsdeath could make rubble of this castle and the High Celestials within it if I just *gave over to it.*

My vision scattered with silver stardust, a warning of that deadly power pushing to the surface of my subconscious. It was too tempting while my rage stirred hot in the presence of Auster and Notus, but my right mind rang with the alarm warning that I had no experience with Lightsdeath, and this fortress held too many innocents for me to risk unleashing reckless magick.

Just let go. The power caressed my thoughts. Dark with intent, but unlike Nightsdeath, it was pure, bright starlight that wanted to become me.

I pulled my hand back, just enough to touch the tip of Notus's blade, still pointed at me. It pierced my flesh, beading a drop of crimson, which only made my magick more potent. I watched my violet light scatter over the length of his sword like lightning before the stormstone shattered over the table.

I am in control. I soothed my own emotions, taming the unhinged magick pushing to take over after that taste of violence. *I do not fear myself.*

Notus pulled his arm back, now only holding the hilt, with absolute shock and fury lining his face. I let go of my magick, panting shallowly to collect steady breath.

He roared, a sound that declared battle between us.

"Guards!" Notus bellowed.

Those bearing his house color of gold advanced, but Auster's guards in navy intercepted them while Zephyr's small force in turquoise stayed put, uncertain but braced in case their High Celestial gave an order to intervene. Conversations faltered, words falling away into uneasy silence as sharp, cautious glances darted across the room. A quiet hum of anticipation pressed against the walls, coiling tighter with every passing second.

Watching Notus and Auster at odds stroked a dark satisfaction in me. Perhaps I didn't have to do much at all to watch their pillars of union collapse, and I planned to make sure they would be buried in their own wreckage.

I stood carefully, facing Auster. "He's always despised me. I have been nothing but compliant here."

A muscle in Auster's jaw worked as he slipped a look at me that softened only for a second before targeting Notus. "I think it's best if you allow me to handle the Maiden here for now. You should return to Althenia."

Triumph gleamed in me.

"You can't be serious," he spat.

Auster hated nothing more than for his authority to be challenged. Ironic, really, when he sat back unfazed as I challenged Notus's jurisdiction.

As the gentle voice of reason over the palpable tension, Zephyr interjected, "Brother, we need a governing figure over there anyway. Your feelings toward Astraea only complicate things here."

Notus's cheeks reddened and his gaze stretched, keeping his outrage from exploding out of him. With a disgruntled sound, he stormed from the room, still humorously clutching his bladeless hilt.

"I should make sure he doesn't take out his anger at you elsewhere," Zephyr said, casting me one look of reprimand before he followed his brother out.

The silence that followed turned heavy. Auster's stare slowly spread over my skin when I didn't meet it.

"So you've been pretending those manacles and the nebulora have kept you incapacitated? You could have escaped any time?"

I didn't want to expose that advantage, but I hadn't wanted to lose a hand to Notus's blade either. Now I had to scramble for an excuse.

"It weakens me greatly. If Notus challenged me to a fight, he would have won while I still have these on," I said flatly.

Raising my hand, the sleeve of my white gown slipped high enough to expose the red torn flesh of my wrists and the manacles. Auster gave no reaction to seeing them; his suspicion still swirled in that brown stare of judgment.

"I don't believe that for a second. You always have been far too cunning," he said. The cold, distant tone braced me, and with the motion of Auster's hand, guards advanced for me. "There's one way to test your capabilities against the effects of nebulora."

My glare heated and became more spiteful as I kept it held on Auster, hearing the sound of chains before they were attached to each of the bonds around my wrists, held by a guard on each side of me like I was a restrained dog.

I thought physical pain would come next, testing my limits before I broke and showed him how I could have killed him and every one of his followers in this castle all along. Lightsdeath couldn't be silenced so easily. While quick and bloody violence would have fulfilled my ultimate goal to kill him, Auster would have won, even in death. Too much of the world still believed in him and the High Celestial order. Dismantling their ages-long reputation and rule would take more care.

Auster didn't use anything physical, but his words were as striking as a fired arrow.

"Your friend was never supposed to die."

There was only one lost friend he could mean. A beautiful face with the brightest smile, raven hair, and large sapphire blue eyes flooded my mind and thumped an ache in my soul.

"It was you who sent those vampires to kill me at the inn," I said vacantly.

How did I not piece that together before? It felt like another lifetime—that carefree night of laughter, games, and drinks between two dear friends, which had turned into the worst nightmare of my existence.

"Not to kill you. Capture you. Zadkiel came to me and told me you were found; by the time I'd sent more people for you, we learned you were heading for Vesitire. So I offered a prize that couldn't be refused to a group of vampires in exchange for bringing you to me alive."

"You killed Cassia."

My vision started to glow around the edges and my hands trembled. Auster knew physical pain wouldn't be enough for me to lose control and show my hand; he slashed at my emotions, which were always my vulnerable spot.

"She was unfortunate collateral damage. Though I learned she had very little time left as it was."

He brushed off her *time* as if it was nothing. As if I wouldn't have given *anything* to have been granted that time to say goodbye, to be with her until the very end of her days, before she was taken by a cruel but natural fate. Instead, she was ripped away from me when I needed her most and when she was close to fulfilling her biggest dream and purpose. That time was precious, and Auster Nova had orchestrated the robbery of it.

"My hate for you grows more incredible by the day," I said with chilling calm.

Lightsdeath pushed too violently this time. I let my control slip, feeling the electric surges of liquid starlight filling my veins, ready to unleash on Auster . . .

A prick in my arm dragged a sharp gasp from me. Whatever was pushed into my body from it smothered the heat in my veins, turning my blood to ice instead. The pain seized me, and my sight fell to find some kind of syringe being drained of a silver liquid.

An image flashed into mind—the time Nyte had crushed one of the pills Goldfell had been supplying me with, which had been starlight matter enchanted to silence my magick all the time I was his pet.

My eyes snapped back to Auster, wide with horror. Though I considered him my enemy right now, I couldn't help the feeling of betrayal that punched through my gut.

"How could you?" I breathed.

Lightsdeath wailed and drifted away from my reach as the starlight matter took effect. The familiar sensation of the drug crept over me, turning my body heavy and my mind tired. Nyte had sat with me for weeks to overcome the addiction, and even now I'd never stopped resenting Goldfell for the abuse.

"You left me no choice," Auster said. Maybe there was pain in his voice for this despicable measure.

"You're a coward." I meant to spit those words with venom but I couldn't.

It wasn't sleep that coaxed me, it was simply a state of fatigue and vulnerability. I vaguely heard my chains being removed, and then Auster's warmth touched me.

"To pave a future we must let go of the past," he said tenderly. Lifting my wrists gently, he even removed the manacles. "I don't want to keep using the Matter, but for now it is necessary. Nebulora in your system instead would hurt you; this only sedates you enough to make you compliant."

I nodded, agreeable. This did feel nice. When the heavy metal was free from my wrists I leaned forward, pressing my cheek to the warm chest in front of me. Auster's hand smoothed over my hair, and his strong arm encircled my waist. The world felt so light and warm.

"Despite all I've done, I know you, Astraea. You can't let go of everything we were to each other. Everything we've been through together. Five years with Cassia is nothing to the life bond we have."

Cassia. My brow furrowed. The delightful warmth around me turned to suffocating heat, and I pushed against Auster's chest as hard as I could, stumbling back, disorientated from the quick movement.

I blinked hard, willing myself to hold onto my mind as it became cloudy. I threw wrath in my stare.

"I would bargain every memory of you away to have five more *days* with Cassia. You killed the person who once loved you. I feel *nothing* for you anymore."

"You'd be far more tolerable with your memories wiped. Permanently."

"So would you," I spat.

We faced off in a battle of heartache and wills. Auster moved so suddenly I gasped, unable to stop him when his hand cupped my nape, forcing our faces inches apart.

"He wanted to kill you once too," he said, his voice a low murmur.

The beat in my chest skipped.

"Nyte never would have followed through. Not even if I'd chosen you."

"You can't know that. What if you could find it in yourself to forgive me like you did him?"

Maybe there was a kernel of me that pitied Auster for his thick delusion.

"You are responsible for the death of Cassia. You almost killed Zathrian. You tore out Nyte's wings and threatened mine. You drove my own weapon through my heart with the belief I would never return. You just *drugged* me knowing I've suffered from substance abuse at the hand of another before. You are no better than Goldfell and far fucking worse than Nyte could ever be. I will never forgive you, Auster. You're staring at your reckoning, pleading to stop my wrath because it's already tightening around your throat."

His jaw worked, eyes flaring wide as if restraining himself from hurting me or himself. I feared for a second he might kiss me.

"I don't want to keep hurting you," he said, so quietly, like a slipped confession while he tried to maintain a ruthless front.

The drug made my thoughts swim and tangle. It made my hate and compassion blur, and I couldn't keep fighting, not with words or magick. But I had one last lick of venom on my tongue.

"Be your best villain, Auster Nova. Because Nyte has always been his, and I will become mine to finish you."

14

Astraea

I'd never been surrounded by so many people while the world seemed to hold its breath in a mournful silence. Even if it weren't for the starlight matter Auster had injected me with again this morning before our pre-wedding walk through the city, the people seemed so quiet.

This day should have been full of cheers and hope, a prospective marriage for the new rulers of Solanis promising a union that would uplift the nation and strengthen protection for them. Yet, instead, my eyes pricked to the occasional face weighed down in sorrow I could make out through the lace veil covering my face, paired with the starlight matter that occasionally blurred my vision.

I was free and walking, yet a prisoner of substance once more. I kept trying to reach Lightsdeath, touching it with sparks emitting from my fingertips, but I couldn't summon enough magick to harness it fully. I thought if I let that power consume me it might expel the starlight matter, and I only hoped once I was freed from it, I wouldn't suffer the addiction again.

With my hand looped through the arm of the man I despised, I thought of many ways I could steal a weapon from him or a nearby guard just to keep myself calm.

As we made it to the lower level of the city, mostly occupied by humans and fae, hands started to reach toward me. I extended a hand, brushing fingers with many of the people, which started to kindle a flame inside me. I retreated, only to remove my glove, and every touch of skin on skin ignited my flame higher.

Auster's hand closed over mine on his arm and gave a warning squeeze, likely for removing my glove, which was uncustomary. I didn't care.

Only now did the crowd's murmurs pick up. My senses were still dulled under the drug, so I couldn't make out their words, but occasionally I caught sad eyes lifting with hope and wonder as I met them. I captured the smiles of all ages as I kept my hand running along the supple flesh of those who hadn't given up on me.

A warm bundle was pressed into my palm. I carefully let the deep purple cloth stretch out, and when I saw the black wings . . . the key and constellation proudly adorned between . . . I stopped walking.

Glancing back, I didn't know who had given it to me—the new banner of the star-maiden—and I almost lifted my veil to glance deeper through the crowd. Auster pulled me closer to him before I could. The guard detail, which followed, tightened around Auster and me, and I wondered if they detected something I couldn't or if it was because Auster saw what had been given to me.

Auster subtly snatched the banner from me. I tried reaching for it, but my movements were too sluggish.

"Drown the world in starlight!"

The yell came from deep in the crowd, a battle cry from one of the people. It caused the guards to arm themselves as what followed engulfed us all in clouds of deep purple smoke from an explosion that rumbled in my ears. It was followed by a succession of blasts, and my senses were too dull to keep up.

I became separated from Auster somehow, pushing through the crowd and coughing on the plumes I inhaled with my panicked breaths.

Pull yourself together.

I ripped off my veil and found my dress and skin smudged with purple streaks. As I shook my head, my adrenaline brought back some sharpness to my senses and I scanned the people pushing around me. Some were *fighting* the celestials. Those in Auster's uniform. My eyes started to find many bands wrapped around biceps—*my banner.*

I flexed my fingers, *searching* for Lightsdeath this time as the only thing that might help me. *I will be in control. I won't hurt innocents.* Once again, only pinpricks reached my fingertips, but I kept plunging deeper and deeper, fighting through the numbing effects of the starlight matter.

"Protect the maiden!" That was Auster's men shouting. They didn't want to protect me; they wanted to capture me.

Through the crowds I searched frantically for Auster, not in concern, but with a flash of anger that didn't want to let him get away so easily. These people rebelled because they didn't believe his lies, and he wasn't getting to slither away from the confrontation like a coward.

There was too much purple smoke, too many bodies. I searched for the tether to him that would always live within me from our bond, unless he was dead. Spinning, I pinned his direction, catching a small, tight band of guards, who could only be guiding one important person.

Pushing through the bodies, my balance was precarious, but adrenaline kept me stumbling through the crowd toward my target.

"AUSTER!" I yelled.

He heard me. His harsh brown eyes cut into me through the gap in his guard detail.

Auster began to face forward again, intending to resume his retreat.

My vengeance overcame my reason.

I swiped a small blade from the belt of an unsuspecting person close to me, acting on nothing but pure instinct and rage. The dagger was only in my possession for a second before it flew through the air, making its mark in the nape of the guard at Auster's back. When that body fell away, Auster whirled to me in outrage.

Running for him, I swiped up the sword of the guard I had killed just as Auster lifted his.

Our blades slammed against each other; the high pitch of steel against steel cried the sound of our anguish.

"You can talk big words, Auster. But your actions are always small and pathetic," I seethed, sliding my blade against his and attacking again as best I could.

I knew I was outmatched right now. The blade I wielded was too heavy for me, the starlight matter still weakened my muscles, my dress made movement difficult, but I was so fucking angry I didn't stop trying anyway.

"Are you behind this?" he demanded, defending himself easily against me. "Look at the bloodshed you've caused. These people's lives are being carelessly lost for your cause, Astraea."

"These people fight with purpose in their hearts. They fight against tyrants like you."

I wanted to strike him so badly I became obsessed, needed to see him bleed even a few drops.

He said, "Your poison runs deep through these lands, but I am the antidote."

I laughed, delirious and beyond exerted. But still my sword continued to lift and swing and fall. Until Auster backed up two long strides to avoid my next attack and I panted, collecting my breath and sanity in that pause in our battle.

"Let's end this, Auster. Right here."

"I won't fight you like this."

"Why? Only when I'm weak do you ever feel powerful."

Auster's stare darkened; blue lightning reflected across his eyes with a storm brewing beneath their surface. I braced, lifting my sword when he threw a bolt of his magick toward me. Shifting my leg back, I tightened my body for the impact, letting the steel absorb the current while the remnants coursed through me. I was no stranger to his magick, and I would not let it strike me down.

Contrary to what he hoped to achieve with the attack, the last of the lightning humming through me helped expel more of the starlight matter's influence, which was holding me back physically and mentally.

"Seize her," Auster commanded.

I snarled at his cowardly order, having to split my attention between him and his guards, who closed in, herding me as I backed away.

Auster's glare threw chips of ice at me before he began to turn, retreating from the fighting and leaving it to others to *detain* me.

"You cannot escape me, Auster Nova," I yelled, causing him to pause, his shoulders to stiffen, but he didn't look back. "For when the dark descends, I will rise from shadow . . . and you will fall into it. Seeing my face as your reckoning when the light goes out."

His hands tightened into fists at his sides, and for a second I thought he might turn back, but he didn't.

A glint in one of the guards' hands caught my attention. More starlight matter. Were they all equipped with it and it was just a matter of who got close enough first to sedate me again?

Beginning to lose my confidence in this confrontation, I tried to calculate a way to run instead, even though the distance that stretched between me and Auster made me want to damn all odds and charge for him.

I was moments from being captured again . . .

Until I saw a little black bird fly over the heads of the celestials in front of me.

I wasn't alone. Never alone. All these people who fought holding my banner now, humans and fae, they knew when to come, because as that bird swooped into the thick of the crowd it disappeared in a flash of light.

Then through the bodies, Davina *winked* at me.

She joined the fighting seamlessly, propelling a dagger from her fan in her graceful battle dance. It was then I knew . . . Rose and Zath would be somewhere here too. Davina used her influence in the fae resistance to turn it into the Maiden's resistance, open to more walks of life than just fae now.

The day Auster stood me in front of the castle and the resistance had ruined his wedding announcement . . . that had been their warning call.

This . . . this was their first call of action in the rebellion against the High Celestial order.

Before Auster's soldiers could reach me, others did, forming a circle around me and bracing bravely with weapons that could not contend with the might of the celestial soldiers. They shouldn't be protecting me; it was my duty to protect *them*.

Drown the world in starlight.

That phrase had become a battle cry for the people, who struck a determined will in me to stand strong for them.

I am Astraea Lightborne. The star-maiden. The Daughter of Dusk and Dawn. The Goddess of Justice. I am Lightsdeath.

My belief sparked enough of my suppressed magick to seize. A scream tore from my throat to drag it out, and I dropped down, slamming a hand to the ground, striking the land, which cracked from the impact that blasted every soldier back outside the radius of people who surrounded me. The scars of the stone flooded with liquid silver, as if my glowing tattoos flowed off my skin to web around me.

I was hypnotized by the glittering silver pools, and my mouth watered at its resemblance to starlight matter potions.

No. I do not crave that.

I do not crave that.

I scrunched my eyes shut, forcing back the creeping desire for the drug that danced metallic notes on my tongue and pricked under my skin.

My fingers flexed against the stone—still braced in position from my strike of magick—when I felt a shadowy caress over them.

As I opened my eyes, darkness spilled over my silver rivers and twined through my fingers. Glancing up, I saw the source of the shadows stalking toward me, so calm among the chaos. I didn't fear Nightsdeath, but to my relief and surprise, the people around me didn't either. They parted, letting him approach until he was close enough to crouch at my level.

"Hello, Starlight," he purred.

He used Nyte's nickname for me, and I bit my lip against a whimper. Nightsdeath plucked the comb of the veil from my hair and tossed it aside. I took his hand when he offered it, rising on shaky knees with him.

I scanned over the mob still resisting the celestials trying to rally order. They used force and magick and every cry of an innocent life fleeing or falling tore soul-deep.

"Save them," I asked him.

Nightsdeath canted his head as if the request was as humorous as it was curious. But if Nightsdeath helped the people while I couldn't, it would show his allegiance. Right here could begin Nyte's redemption for when I finally had all of him back.

"Please," I said, clutching him tighter.

He cupped my check, scanning my eyes.

"Then we will go retrieve the key together," he said, tipping my hair over my shoulder.

"Yes."

"Very well."

Nightsdeath became a slice of shadow that moved with the grace and precision of a blade with no hand to wield it. I watched in fascination and horror as he was less a body and more a thick stroke of pure darkness, with only his piercing gold eyes to track, as he reaped souls and spilled blood before a single enemy saw him coming.

I only lost track of him when a pink flicker caught my eye. Rose stared at the shadows cutting through masses of celestials like her worst nightmare had come. She met my stare, wide and horror-filled. All I could do was shake my head once.

None of them could come to me. Though they'd helped in rallying allies against Auster, and would continue to while we were separated, they could not be seen by Nightsdeath. If he found any of them, he would have a far easier time than he did with me torturing, even killing, any of them to get the location of Nyte's body.

Zath approached, and seeing him made my heart yearn. He hooked Rose's arm, muttering something to her. With Nightsdeath pulling the focus of battle, it was time for them to retreat. Zath's blue eyes found me, and my pulse lurched at his firm expression of concern, fearing he might break the plan and come to me because he was always so damned stubborn and protective. He shouldn't even be here with his injuries still healing.

Zath looked up over my head and toward the sky. I turned, locking onto the blood-red moon that dominated the sky. A brilliant, full sphere.

Then my breath caught, realizing . . .

I whirled back, but Zath's expression sank my quick surge of hope. Then the single shake of his head dropped the weight of the world onto me.

Eltanin was of age to choose his rider, and either the dragon bond hadn't worked to wake Nyte, or Eltanin hadn't chosen him.

Maybe there's still time. It could still work and Nyte would come for me. My desperate hope clawed against my despair.

My knees almost gave out to prevent me from following after Zath and Rose as they were quickly swept out of my sight in the frantically retreating crowds. It was my time to escape as well, hand in hand with the most unfeeling creature in the realm.

"Are you ready to go, my star? Or would you like me to keep tearing through your enemies?"

I looked up, finding no color of flesh in his form, only darkness imitating the shape of Nyte's face with twin suns wild and blazing against the darkness. He was so hauntingly mesmerizing.

For now, this was the only piece of Nyte I had, as terrifying and unpredictable as he was. But as my fingers slipped against his made of swirling shadows, a piece of my soul felt *home*.

PART
TWO

You Were
My Best Friend

15

Astraea—Past

Astraea walked by Nyte's side, about to announce their alliance to the most unlikely of groups first. His hand grazed hers, and her stomach fluttered when he took an assuring hold of her.

"How are you feeling?" he asked, voice low—everything echoed in this dark cave they ventured through.

"Like I'm about to walk into a lair of vampires that want me dead."

She could feel his smile in the dark, accompanied by the promising stroke of his thumb.

"We're hoping to change that. But one move against you will be the last they ever make."

"Why do I get the feeling you're hoping for that?"

"It's been a while."

"Always restless for violence."

"Speak for yourself. At least you've been party to some action recently."

Her unease started to grow when voices echoed ahead.

"How can you be sure there aren't some here who might go to your father?"

"I can't be. I'm just willing to deal with that should he hear of this news. But these are vampires who don't follow him, nor agree with his methods. This is an army of its own, led by elder vampires who want nothing but peace and equality."

He'd been through this with her already, and she trusted Nyte unconditionally. Yet she still struggled to believe such a force of vampires existed when all she'd been told by the High Celestials so far was that they'd all chosen to ally with Nyte's father to overthrow the celestials, and her, for power over Solanis.

"They agreed to see me?"

Nyte's pause before answering snapped her sight up to him with a new wave of caution.

"I might not have told them," he admitted.

She would have voiced her incredulity, but they'd come to the end of the passage and already she spied many bodies through the opening. Nyte merely interlocked their fingers fully, a declaration of their unity as he pulled her unfaltering through the masses of vampires that parted for him the second they laid eyes on him.

Astraea's whole body tensed when she saw so many faces drop into scowls as their eyes fell on her. Her heartbeat jumped erratically at the hisses and murmurs of disdain, which tightened a white-knuckled grip on Nyte's hand. She had her key shorted to a baton strapped to her hip, but this hall was teeming with so many vampires she was far outnumbered.

"Relax," Nyte said through their bond without looking at her.

"You have to be kidding."

The bastard had the audacity to curve a half smile on his face when taking in the tall expanse of the cave. It had several openings with platforms onto which more vampires spilled out to watch them enter. She imagined this is where many nightcrawlers lived as she took in all the red eyes and leathery wings.

When the last of the tightly compacted groups of vampires parted, Nyte slowed to a stop before a massive table that sat eight vampires down each side. All of them regarded her with shocked outrage as they rose from their seats.

All but one.

Astraea watched the vampire who remained seated. Her shoulder-length, straight hair was half toned in black, the other half in white. She looked from their joined hands to their faces before casting curious gray eyes on Astraea.

"What is the meaning of this?" One of the others who had been seated was the first to bellow the obvious thought on everyone's mind.

Nyte replied calmly, "I was under the impression that this was a standard vampire resistance meeting."

"Explain why you have the maiden by the hand and not in shackles," another snarled.

"She's my bonded, and that's all the warning I give to watch how you speak of her, and to her."

Gasps erupted throughout the room. She didn't think it changed much about their distaste toward her, but she had come prepared for gaining trust on both sides to be a long road.

Finally, the vampire who'd remained seated stood slowly.

Astraea said, "I didn't expect to see you here."

She felt Nyte's eyes on her, questioning the greeting, but her small smile finally broke when the vampire's did.

"Nor I you, Astraea Lightborne."

Astraea tried to let go of Nyte's hand but his tightened in reluctance.

She said through their bond, *"Laviana is the daughter of two of my guardians. She won't hurt me."*

With that assurance he let her go, but his tension echoed through her, anticipating any slight foul play.

When Astraea reached the vampire, her steps slowed, uncertain what reception was appropriate after many estranged decades. The shadowless didn't hesitate, however, pulling Astraea into an embrace she didn't know she'd missed until now.

"It's good to see you again, Laviana." Astraea was suddenly choked with emotion when this reunion brought back fond memories of Laviana's parents, her shadowless and celestial guardians.

"Your time governing on your own hasn't been light on you since the guardians left," she said with a note of sympathy.

"I don't think even they could have predicted this turn of fate."

"Nor would they have done any better in keeping things as together as you have."

That burst the warmth of pride in her, especially from one who was like a distant sister in some ways. The six guardians were, for all intents and purposes, her parents too.

"We need your help," Astraea said quietly.

"Then I'm glad you were brave enough to come."

"Have you seen the others?"

Since the guardians left decades ago, their children had long since moved on to live their own lives around Solanis.

"The twins left for North Star not long after our parents left; said they wanted to make a life there. You haven't seen them in Althenia?"

Astraea shook her head. Last she'd seen the nightcrawler brothers was right before her guardians left.

"Tarran?" Astraea asked with a tightening in her chest.

Laviana's face fell with sorrow. "He still doesn't want to be found."

Even if he were here, Astraea figured she was the last person he would want to see. How could he stand to face the person who'd sentenced his mate to death? It had been the hardest choice she'd had to make in all her rule. Tarran's bonded was a nightcrawler who'd allied with Nyte's father decades ago. He was caught with a band of vampires brought to justice. Tarran's begging for his life haunted Astraea still. Tarran had been oblivious to Gresham's contribution to the dark cause.

Even for Tarran, her friend and in some ways her brother, she could not excuse Gresham's crimes that had killed so many innocents, no matter how much it tore her heart. Nyte's hand slipping around her waist eased her stiff muscles. "You never mentioned you knew Astraea personally," he said to La-viana.

"How could I? In the eyes of everyone here, she's as much an enemy to us as the High Celestials."

"Did you believe that too?" Astraea asked.

"Never. I understand the difficult position you're in with this war that's beginning. I just couldn't make that known here," she mused. "I'm glad you finally came."

"You say that like you've been expecting me."

She smiled fondly, and Astraea had missed her. "You're the star-maiden. You speak for us all, and I knew you wouldn't disappoint the guardians by siding with the celestials merely because of your creators."

Laviana's attention flashed to Nyte's hold around her. "This is very unex-pected, however. I anticipated the notorious Nightsdeath would be your big-gest enemy to defeat."

"He still is," Astraea mused, slipping a teasing look up at him.

Nyte's smile hid a note of disturbance, because it was the truth. Nights-death would always want to kill her, and so far they'd been lucky he hadn't lost control to that pure darkness in her presence. The world didn't know *Nyte* coexisted with the harbinger of death and bloodshed. A person whose love and care was so selective that material riches were worthless to him.

"Now let's subdue the restless minds of those here and get this meeting underway," Laviana said.

"What does your bond mean?" a soulless asked, not sounding pleased by Nyte and Astraea's announcement.

The question stirred the tense crowd's emotions, which ranged from outrage to confusion and curiosity. Perhaps hope. They looked at Nyte and Astraea as if they could be the answer they didn't know they were searching for.

"Are you on our side?" another asked her.

"Yes . . . and no," she answered honestly.

The questions and opinions started to flood over each other so much that Astraea couldn't track them.

"You would stand against the High Celestials?"

"Superior scum!"

"What about your allegiance to your father?"

Questions for both of them were thrown from all directions. She could sense Nyte's rising irritation with the aimless commotion right before choking cut off the loudest voices. Nyte's infiltration of several minds as he severed their speech swiftly silenced the rest. It was chilling to watch how effortlessly he could use his invasive ability. Nyte let their minds go seconds later and silence fell for him.

"I called this meeting for you all to understand what our bond and alliance can mean for our objective of achieving equality for the vampires. Astraea is risking everything to be here, so you'll show her your respect or I'll show you my wrath."

Nyte led Astraea around to the other head of the table. He encouraged her to sit, then he perched on the arm of her chair as if it was the most natural arrangement.

He took her hand, staring deeply into her eyes, which eased her nerves from having the attention of a hundred vampires on them.

Nyte said to her mind, *"Show them how bright you shine, my Starlight."*

"That went far better than I'd expected," Nyte commented when they were thick into the woodland they were going through to reach the vampire meeting.

"All I did was listen," Astraea said, not feeling as spirited as he was.

Nyte's hand tightened in hers. "You heard them, and they know change can't be made in a night. But you gave them your time, and that's a meaningful step toward starting to figure out how to make the world fair for them."

The vampires had long been suppressed and used by the celestials. The nightcrawlers hunted Nephilim for them. The shadowless were used for their allurement. When they drank from a person, it released an aphrodisiac, making it easy to uncover traitors and criminals or gain knowledge from adversaries spilling their confessions under its effects. The soulless were used to consume the entire souls of such criminals and the worst of mankind.

Even though they were controlled by and worked for the celestials, they were treated like lowlifes and criminals themselves.

Astraea listened to many accounts that night, and her mind was buzzing with where to begin righting this power imbalance. She was the star-maiden, but the four High Celestials in Althenia were a strong governing body she could easily be overruled by.

"No blood spilled tonight, I'm afraid," Astraea said absentmindedly.

She gasped as Nyte suddenly gripped her waist, twisted her, and pressed her into the nearest tree.

"The night isn't over," he said, fanning a warm breath down her neck suggestively. "Will you bleed for me, Starlight?"

Every instinct in her screamed yes, but more desirable than having him drink from her was the delicious tension she could incite from denying him.

"You want my blood? Earn it."

His lips pressed to her throat, and Astraea's eyes fluttered at the lustful caress. When his teeth dragged a little lower her hand slipped into his hair, but he didn't bite.

"How might I do so?" he asked thickly.

"Don't be a cheater; figure it out."

"I have you all figured out, make no mistake."

His teeth almost punctured, enough to emit a sharp pain, and she braced for the burst of pleasure that would follow if he sank them into her skin. He didn't. His soft lips replaced the subsiding sting and her hand tightened in his hair with frustration.

"Was my good behavior tonight not enough to *earn* it?" he asked, enticing her to break and ask him to bite.

She wouldn't. This was a frequent parry between them that lit a fire in her. Astraea's lust stirred as she recalled how authoritative and downright attractive he had looked at the meeting when he commanded a room of hundreds of vampires. It was the first time she'd ever seen him use his notorious reputation in front of a crowd, but it was more than that. The vampires of the resistance did fear him, that was clear, but they also regarded him with respect and some with *awe*.

Astraea embraced this night as a flicker of hope for their future, believing the possibility of ruling together would be likelier if they could sway the rest of the continent to look at him the same way she did and not just as a merciless monster. "You were very well behaved tonight," she purred in agreement, pulling his jacket to press their bodies tighter.

Her lips were just shy of pressing to his when he stiffened and she heard the crack of branches. Nyte pulled away, turning and curving an arm back as if to shield her from whoever was approaching. Astraea saw one form, a vampire she recognized from around the table at the meeting. He wasn't alone; her eyes darted to find another, then another, then she stopped taking count when they kept creeping out from behind the trees with a slow, predatory approach.

"I'll warn you this once: I'm really not in the mood for problems tonight, Zender," Nyte said calmly.

Astraea placed her hand on Nyte's arm, and he didn't protest as she stepped up beside him.

"We should be using her against them, not entertaining this farce of an alliance based on nothing more than your lustful cravings, *Nightsdeath*," the blood vampire said bitterly.

"So you've come to capture her?" Nyte clarified.

"Give her up and this will be easy."

Nyte slipped a look down at her. "What do you think?"

She suppressed her amusement, giving an overdramatic sigh instead. "I guess I am quite tired."

Astraea stepped forward, holding out her hands to be bound.

The vampires eyed each other warily, not immediately accepting her surrender.

"Never come to a fight with hesitation," Nyte said; then he was the first to attack.

Astraea didn't see, only heard a *crack* and wail of agony behind her; she was moving the second he was.

Her light threw out, slamming into one vampire while she retrieved her key, twisted it in her other hand, which transformed it from a baton to a blade, and sank it into the gut of another.

She'd thought the meeting had gone well, but she'd let a moment of fool's hope cloud her judgment. Of course not everyone would be swayed toward an alliance with the person they blamed most for their misfortune. Astraea blamed herself too, but she also tried to accept that she was one person with many opposing sides to consider.

By now she'd killed five, but they kept coming, and though they wanted to capture her, and she didn't want to imagine their plans from there, she felt sorrow for every life she took. Sometimes the only option was kill or be killed, but all of the people on this land were *her* people. Whether they followed and believed in her or not.

Her fighting began to falter after the eighth. She didn't want to keep killing when she'd come here to avoid this.

"Stop," she demanded, still fighting but switching to completely defensive.

They kept coming, and she warded them off with shields of light and nonfatal strikes.

"I am not your enemy." She tried again to reason.

The council member, Zender, stalked toward her after she fended off another three. There was no mercy to reach in his eyes of loathing. No compromise, no compassion. Killing him might collapse the fragile pillars of union they had tried to build today with the vampire resistance.

"What can I do or say that would make you believe my dedication to your cause as much as everyone else does?" Astraea kept retreating slowly, gathering her breath back.

Until she met the edge of a cliff and there was nowhere to go but down.

"The best thing you can do for any of us is to die."

Zender lunged for her, but before his hand lifted fully, a horizontal stroke of darkness cut right through his neck. His eyes glassed over, wide on her, before his body fell and revealed the haunting sight of Nyte.

No . . . *Nightsdeath.*

She'd never seen this part of him fully. He'd shown her glimpses, just enough for her to know what changed about his appearance, but he was always fully in his right mind. Her mouth turned dry when he just stood there, staring at her with bright gold eyes, hands clamped and near trembling by his sides. Restraining himself.

Then she understood with a slow lick of horror up her spine. He'd warned her before how he hoped to never have cause for Nightsdeath to surface fully when she was around. Because her brightness repelled the dark.

"You need to *run,*" he said, as if on the verge of losing his battle with the monster that wanted to kill her.

"I'm not leaving you," she said, her voice weak and giving away her fear.

His head jerked to the side, face scrunching in pain. "You're too . . . too bright, Astraea."

"Yes, this is what I am," she said as calmly as she could, closing the distance with slow steps.

"Stop." That word broke from him and still he didn't look at her again.

"You need me as much as I need you. I'm not afraid of this side of you."

His eyes snapped to hers then, and there was nothing kind in those blazing suns.

"I don't need you." His voice didn't sound like his own when a low baritone wrapped each cold word.

Astraea's next inhale choked when he ate up the distance between them in a heartbeat and his hand lashed around her throat. She was forced back until her heels slipped off the edge, and all that kept her from falling was her hands gripping his on her neck. He trembled stiffly, refraining from crushing her windpipe.

"It's okay. You're okay," she said, reeling back her panic.

He was terrifying yet absolutely beautiful with the tip of his ears looking like they were dipped in charcoal. Lines of black climbed his neck, beginning to reach over his jaw as if a quill had pierced his skin and ink now flooded his veins. And those eyes . . . she had never been so entranced than in this moment, watching them swirl like liquid gold metal.

Nyte reached for the key strapped at her waist, and only when it answered him, transforming into a glowing dagger without harming him, did she realize the gravity of Bonding to someone with a side of pure darkness. It gave him the ability to harness the one weapon that could truly kill her.

The hum of magick from the weapon as he pressed it between her ribs sent shockwaves that felt so wrong throughout her body.

Until now there had never been a true piece of her that believed him capable of killing her. Despite all his warnings, how fearful he became when he spoke of Nightsdeath and how hard he had fought against letting him surface fully before. Yet now, with the touch of death one plunge away, she couldn't deny the real danger of him.

"It's okay," she repeated, refusing to let this be something that could break them. "I love you, and I trust you."

"How can you say that," he said, his voice splitting between a snarl and a crack of misery. "Your love for me is deadly."

"We'll work through it. The darkness can learn to love the light." Her lips parted, but she smothered the whimper in her throat when the key dagger broke through her leathers, touching her skin now. "Stay with me, Rainyte."

Astraea let the blade cut her flesh as she pushed up and pressed her lips to his. Even the shallow wound was enough to erupt a line like fire, scattering through her whole chest and abdomen.

Then it was gone. The key was sent into the void by Nyte, who cupped her face in both hands now, kissing her back with abandon. Kissing her as if she would die in his arms any second. Kissing her to claim her last breath if she did.

He pulled back, panting and distraught, resting his forehead to hers. Astraea's hands on his chest reached fractions higher to where the black veins retreated past his collar.

"Don't ever stand in the path of me when I'm like that again, do you hear me?" he said, his voice so raw and thick with emotion. She didn't respond, still in a daze over what had happened. The magick from her key started to diffuse from her body but lingered with a pulsing warning within her.

Nyte pulled back, holding her eyes fiercely. "If I tell you to run from me, you fucking *run*. You don't falter; you don't look back. That part of me isn't merciful, least of all to someone as bright and powerful as you. And if I ever— *gods*, if I ever managed to—"

Her hands tightened on his jacket. Nyte couldn't finish, but she knew the grim reality of what could have happened. She'd been reckless, so completely fooled by her love for him that she'd put herself right in the path of death.

Yet she knew she would do it again.

"My heart is yours anyway," she said, looking up to find his beautiful eyes their usual subdued amber shade. "I'm always running with you, never away. We'll figure this out together. Perhaps the more you expose that side of you in tamer doses, the more control you'll have around me. This continent might break with war soon, and I plan to fight by your side. As Nightsdeath if you must be."

Her words seemed to stir conflict in him, like he yearned to be able to fight with her and not lose control of Nightsdeath to turn on her instead, but he also didn't believe it to be possible when he'd never had reason to build restraint with the dark power inside him.

She reached a palm over his cheek. "One day at a time."

Nyte gave a barely there nod. "My infinite days are yours."

16

Astraea

I never would have anticipated my escape from the castle of Vesitire to be in the literal form of Nightsdeath.

So far, none of Auster's forces had come after us. After the bloodshed in the city, it was hard for me to settle my guilt. I'd asked Nightsdeath to attack; I'd all but unleashed him like he was my weapon to wield.

If you're not with me, you're against me.

I sighed, my breath a thick cloud as we trudged through the snowfall just outside the tiered city. Well, I did. Nightsdeath could be mistaken for gliding with how effortlessly he walked. He wore no cloak or gloves either since he was immune to any physical feeling.

Right now, I might even have envied him for that, as the winter had grown so cold my cheeks nipped painfully, and I had to keep sniffing to prevent my nose from running despite my layers: hood, gloves, and thick boots.

I wanted out of the blood-splattered white clothing as soon as possible.

"I can hear your teeth bashing together. It's rather irritating," said Nightsdeath.

Casual conversation from him always made me glance at him as if by some miracle Nyte's full mind could have awoken. The shadows, which drifted off him like thick smoke in his wake, and the ethereal brightness of his irises immediately extinguished that small spark of hope each time.

"Another mortal weakness," I grumbled.

"So become immortal with me. I'm willing to bet Lightsdeath would defy the effects of the miserable seasons like I do."

With that enlightenment, I stopped internally complaining about the cold.

We trekked in silence for a while longer. I hugged myself and my cloak tightly; the exertion of trudging through the snow started to ache in my legs, but I didn't speak this to him when it would only be met with jarringly quippy remarks or temptations for me to join him in an eternal dark reign.

118 CHLOE C. PEÑARANDA

"This may take far longer than a week to retrieve given your slow pace, and you're no good to me if you get ill or die."

"Thanks for the concern. I'm not as weak as I might look right now." My magick was slowly returning and helped to warm me at times.

"I could go alone if you told me where it is."

I didn't divulge the specific location to Nightsdeath, knowing he would do just that.

"Travel is more fun in company."

He gave the most genuine quirk of a smile I'd seen on him.

"You could use the void to escape me, and I wouldn't be able to stop you," he said.

"I figure you'd call me back with blood and bodies until I answered."

"A likely reaction of mine, yes. You know me too well. As I know that the way your heart bleeds for those you do not know makes controlling you easy."

"Innocent people don't deserve to die for no reason."

"All mortals carry unrepented sins. Why should I need to hear them?"

"Because petty crimes don't deserve the same punishment as those of pure evil," I said, exasperated.

Nightsdeath hummed as if he gave it some thought.

"Your soft mortal values are quite entertaining. They also sound exhausting. No wonder you sleep so long. Can that be improved?"

That answered my question: he would never comprehend judgment and reasoning.

"You must need to sleep," I said, hooking a brow at him. Though as I said it, I realized I hadn't actually considered whether he was a being that needed rest.

"No, I don't," he said, and if I didn't know any better, I'd think he sounded disappointed or confused by that. "You're fascinating when you sleep."

I spluttered. "You've been watching me?"

"Almost every night so far. Speaking of which, this eternal red night is glorious, don't you think?"

He walked so seamlessly with his hands in his pockets, now closing his eyes briefly, soaking in the blood moon as one would summer rays.

It was so . . . *normal*. I couldn't prevent the smile that broke out on my face nor the quick pooling in my eyes. I looked away before he could see it and didn't let a single tear fall. Whatever he did to me, whatever he unleashed on the world, he was still a piece of Nyte, and I chose to take dangerous comfort in that truth.

I said, "Honestly, I'm missing the sunshine. It's been like eternal winter for too long."

His brow pulled together as he internally processed my feelings, like he was trying to comprehend them.

"You miss the warmth of it or the brightness?"

"Both, I suppose. I love the night more than the day, but we all need balance. And the warmth . . . well it sounds very appealing right now."

"Are you sure you're adequately dressed for your weak mortal body?"

"Any more layers and I'd be a lot slower. Though I do wish to change into something less horrifying."

"Amusing. You say the layers make you slower, so that means more time in the cold. Forgo the layers; the punishment of the cold might be sharper but shorter."

I was beginning to enjoy the way Nightsdeath thought; the questions he posed I never would have considered.

"Another mortal weakness is catching ill; it's sometimes fatal, even in a short time when exposed to such temperatures without adequate protection. Are you sure you still want the burden of a mortal body?"

"I'll admit I'm reconsidering it as I observe your struggles. Until . . ." Nightsdeath trailed off, abandoning his next words.

"Until what?" I prompted.

He inhaled a long breath. "Rainyte's ability to bend minds would be most advantageous."

I didn't think that was what he was going to say, but I shivered stiffly at the notion.

"Would you read my thoughts?"

"Of course. I'm very curious."

"About what?"

"All the things that cross your face that you leave unspoken."

That he noticed . . . did Nightsdeath have the capacity to care? No. He wanted to know my thoughts to manipulate and find advantage. Yet my soft heart wanted to believe there could be something tender in his desires.

"Nyte would never read my thoughts."

"How can you be certain he hasn't?"

"I trust him."

"Another—"

"Mortal flaw," I finished for him, casting a teasing smirk he didn't react to. "But you're wrong about that one. I trusted Nyte before I fell in love with him."

"I have freed you from Auster, but you don't trust me?"

"You freed me because you want my power. Nyte freed me because he wants *me*."

"You think I don't want you?"

Nightsdeath slipped in front of me, and I nearly collided into him. Our eyes connected, and I couldn't deny the pull to him I felt.

"You want what we could become together," I answered.

"As does the other half of me—Rainyte."

I pondered that for a moment, staring into the golden eyes that were the center of my universe. Even in all his darkness.

I said, "With you—when Nyte gave over to you at times—I always trusted you didn't *want* to kill me. I understand that in our darkest places we are repelled by the idea of light and hope, but at the same time we don't want it to disappear."

Nightsdeath erased the space between us slowly. My hood blew down with the next gust of icy wind, but he caught it, slipping it back over my head tenderly.

Could there be something to reach within Nightsdeath? Could the pain and suffering he embodied be soothed of its sharp edges?

"You'd be a fool to think yourself safe with me. That I wouldn't kill you— *truly* kill you if I had the means."

"I didn't say you wouldn't kill me, I said you wouldn't want to."

"All parts of him that loved you are gone."

Though that squeezed like a fist in my chest, I didn't believe that.

He captured strands of my loose hair tangling in the wind and tucked them under my hood. "Don't make the mistake of thinking I can be merciful, even for a creature as breathtaking as you."

I'd already experienced how merciless he could be. The memories of his torture in the throne room brought back an ashy taste and a sensation of icy flame in my veins.

When we came to some civilian life, I stared longingly at several inns, but Nightsdeath didn't seem in the mood to stop. Hours must have passed, and the cold seizing my body was becoming too much to bear.

"I need to heat up," I said, so grumpy and pathetic from the weather. "Just for an hour at least."

He dragged a lazy look to me, not pleased at all by the idea.

"So we must stop every few hours for you to bask by firelight? Are there any other shortcomings I should prepare for?"

I glowered at him. "I also need to eat every now and then," I groused.

"Ahh yes, as must I. Very well, we shall stop for one hour."

Heading toward an establishment called Starlight Haven, Nightsdeath was about to wander in without a care when I pulled him to a stop. His amber eyes flared a shade brighter on me as if it was a personal offense to do so.

"We're still the most wanted people on the continent, with *very* generous sums for our capture," I hissed under my breath.

"You see a problem with that?"

"We'll barely get five minutes, never mind an hour, if chaos erupts when we're spotted."

"Or we could have peace and quiet when I kill every person who even looked to be contemplating approaching us."

My frown deepened. Nightsdeath glanced away as if gathering patience.

"Then what do you suggest?"

That was a good question. Even if Nightsdeath had a cloak and face covering like I did, the animated darkness that was ever present around him was enough to draw fear and suspicion. I often found myself mesmerized by the shadows snaking around him, wanting to reach out and touch them, but I had a feeling Nightsdeath would highly disapprove of my curiosity.

"We could find a merchant selling starlight matter." As I suggested it, I wondered if a vial enchanted to change his appearance would work on him.

"No," he said flatly; then he slipped from my fingers. Literally. It was like he could make any part of himself become pure smoke as he drifted away, boldly rounding the corner into the main room.

I didn't even catch up to see before I heard the commotion he was causing just by his presence. As I bustled after him, it was like he didn't even notice the scared people, some vacating their seats as if his shadows were snakes priming to strike them. Nightsdeath wandered over to the bar where a man dropped his tankard, sloshing wine or ale over the edge of the wood and backing away wearily.

"We may as well have left Auster a parting note and directions to find us," I hissed when I came to Nightsdeath's side.

He surveyed his surroundings over his shoulder, taking in the disruption for the first time.

"I haven't even given them a reason to be afraid, and yet their fear is a thick aroma tempting my palate. Their blood tastes far sweeter heated and rushing with terror in their veins," he said, eyes roving over the crowd for selection.

My body tensed and I stepped closer to him with a sharp look he ignored.

"You will not harm anyone in here."

"You must eat to survive. So must I."

I realized what he meant then. Nightsdeath needed blood, and with how he observed the people now like they were on a menu, those with the most fear or pain or suffering were what gave him the most sustenance.

"You don't have to kill anyone," I amended. I wouldn't be able to stop him from taking what he needed, but I could try to reason with him.

"Must you take away my fun?"

Someone interrupted us from my other side. "This place has the best starlight mineras. Your favorite, if I recall."

The feminine voice struck a chord of familiarity. I turned and spied the two-toned hair of black and white;, the impact of who I was looking at stole the air from me.

"Laviana?" I choked, wondering for a second if she could be an illusion.

"I've been looking for you, Maiden. At times it's been easy to get a mark on you but impossible to get you alone."

My brow creased but my body fixed in place, conflicted when it had been so long, another lifetime ago, since I'd last seen the daughter of my shadowless and celestial guardians.

She leaned with her forearms on the bar and gave the barkeep a firm order to snap him out of his scared stillness since Nightsdeath had approached. Then she glanced over my shoulder, studying Nightsdeath with curious wariness.

"Are the shadows a new effect to ward off company? I don't think the extra measure is necessary," she said casually.

They knew each other in the past. Laviana was an elder blood vampire. A leader of the vampire resistance. I wasn't sure if the resistance from long ago still existed.

I didn't know how to explain that who accompanied me was only . . . half of Nyte, in a sense.

"Something like that," he said, playing along, though there was a note of irritation in his tone because we were no longer alone. I relaxed a fraction. "Though I guess they're not as efficient as I'd hoped they would be."

Laviana huffed a laugh as the barkeep came over, placing down one tankard of wine and two drinks in clear glasses. Starlight minera had been my drink of choice wherever I could find it. It wasn't common in most inns and taverns since it came with a high price tag because of the dustings of starlight matter infused in the liquor, which gave it quicker effects, and, no matter how much you consumed, you would never wake up with any sickness or headache. I'd completely forgotten my sweet craving until now.

"You have to try better with me, Nyte," she said, sliding one of the mineras past me in offering to him.

He eyed the swirling glittery silver drink as if it were watery ale.

"Actually, I have other plans of indulgence tonight," he said, slipping it in front of me so I had two now.

My gaze slid up to him in warning, but he merely smiled with deceiving endearment. He was a good actor.

"I'll leave you two to catch up and come for you later." Before he slipped behind me, he leaned close to my ear. "Behave, Maiden. I'll catch you if you run. I'll find you if you hide. By all means, take that as a dare, it thrills me to think of hunting you."

My whole body wracked with a shiver as the last lick of his shadows caressed my skin before he disappeared around the bend of the hall. I strained to go after him, scared of what terror he might wreak out of my sight, but more so, I was eager for Laviana's estranged company and to discover why she'd been looking for me.

"He seems . . . different," Laviana said, watching after him as well.

"He's working through some things," I said. It wasn't a lie really. I diverted the conversation. "Did you know about Tarran allying with Auster?" I asked, taking up one of the tall seats at the bar as she did.

Her frown deepened over the rim of her cup and she set the wine down. "Auster Nova? Why in seven hells would Tarran side with him?"

The guardians had four children between them. Laviana, who took after her shadowless mother. Tarran, who took after his soulless father. And twin nightcrawler brothers, also taking their father's heritage. The twins I'd not seen for the longest time, even in my past life we'd become estranged.

Though they had different parents by blood, the guardians' children regarded each other like siblings. They were nearly full-grown adults by the time I was created and given into their parents' care, but the guardians were my parents too, for all intents and purposes, and their children were as close to siblings as I could ever hope to have. It's what made the broken bond with Tarran cut that much deeper.

"I can only think it's because of his hatred for me now, since he doesn't have the king or Drystan to band with toward my demise."

"Ahh, you and the princeling are at odds?"

"I think there's a lot we need to catch up on."

I took a sip of the starlight minera, which quickly turned to a few long gulps when the smooth, sweet, and tingly sensation exploded against my taste buds. Unlike other alcoholic drinks, this had no bitterness, and it was easy to get carried away with it. One would be enough to push me toward drunk, and now I had two since Nightsdeath abandoned his. I finished off mine.

"Drowning your sorrows?" Laviana commented.

"If nothing else, it might take some of the chill away. I can't stay long."

"Where are you heading?"

I thought for a second, scraping through my past with Laviana, but it wasn't easy to recall so much at once. There could be pieces hidden in the corners of my mind I wouldn't remember unless something triggered it.

"We're looking for a way to reach the gods," I said as a quick alternative answer. "My creators, specifically."

Laviana looked at me with humor, but when I didn't match it her expression fell, switching to skepticism

"You can see them in the temple of Vesitire."

I could trust her. At least I thought I could.

"I've . . . misplaced my key. I need it to kill them."

She spluttered into her tankard.

"Are you insane? That's what the mad king wanted to do, and you knew how dire that would be for the world."

"I have no choice," I defended.

Pity filled her eyes as she looked me over. "Oh Astraea, what happened to you?"

My teeth tightened together to force away the prickling in my eyes.

"So much," I whispered. But there was no time for self-grieving. I squared my shoulders. "The king wanted to kill them and damn the unbalance it would throw us into. There must be a way I can do it that would spare our land."

Laviana said softly, "What do you need us to do?"

That question filled me with gratitude. Remembering I was never as alone as I felt sometimes.

"You said you were looking for me, so what can I do for you?"

She drew in a long breath, and I reached for the second minera.

"Word is you have dragons."

It wasn't what I expected her to bring up.

"Only two. One isn't full grown yet."

"Yes, Eltanin. The legendary black celestial dragon."

A note of pride fluttered in me, but I was highly protective of Eltanin.

"Why does that interest you?"

"Because I've also heard the other—a red dragon, am I right?—bonded with Drystan, a blood vampire."

There was no point in denying it. "Yes. He's the one who discovered where they are and how to release them."

"Do you plan to free the others? How many are there? How *do* you release them?"

I didn't like the pressure for information that felt sacred and dangerous. Laviana was like a sister to me in some ways, but trust, after all this time, had to be rebuilt.

"It's the least of our concerns right now," I said, trying not to shake our fragile trust.

My throat itched faintly and I coughed, taking another sip.

"Are you heading to find one with Nyte now?"

"No."

It wasn't a whole lie. While there should be a dragon painting at the temple we headed for, we wouldn't have Eltanin's tears to release it.

Laviana called me out with a hooked brow. "You've always been a terrible liar."

"It's not a lie," I defended. "We have more pressing matters right now. As should you and the vampire rebellion."

Her face turned pained. "Things aren't like what they used to be. After you left and the king took over, more joined his cause. Vampires were finally given an illusion of free will, but myself and a lot of others could see it was just another system of control. After all this time being used and suppressed by the celestials, there were so many that took the opportunity to be the feared ones for once. They made our species seem exactly like the blood-and-soul-thirsty monsters the celestials painted us to be. What remains of the *rebellion* isn't much; we're more like a group at a loss over how to do damage control if we ever see a day without tyrant rulers."

My gut sank with this knowledge. "So why the interest in the dragons?"

"Don't you see what this could mean for us? I was hoping Drystan would be with you; he'd be an invaluable leader to us. Vampires have never in history been documented to bond with dragons. They're the most legendary and powerful creatures to exist, and if more could bond with them . . . it could be the beginning of shifting our reputation and giving us back some power."

That was the most highly sought-after currency: power. People bled for it, betrayed for it, lied and cheated for it. I'd never known a pursuant of power to be worthy of holding it, and those who might have once had noble intentions . . . power could become a corruptive addiction like any drug.

"If you trust me like you once did, then trust there's an order to gaining the peace and equality we've all fought lifetimes for."

Her jaw set; it wasn't what she wanted to hear and I couldn't blame her. To ask for patience now, after all this time, was like asking her to trust the rain would come after centuries of drought.

"Can we accompany you, wherever you might be heading?" she asked.

The casual mention that Laviana wasn't alone made me subtly survey the establishment. It was moderately busy with chatter flowing, tankards thumping, laughter bouncing. I spied a few pointed ears around the room, but they didn't pay us any attention.

"I don't think that's best this time," I said carefully.

"Nyte can't always get what he wants in keeping you to himself. You must long for other friendly company."

"He's not . . . in the best of spirits for extra company right now."

I feared Nightsdeath would sooner kill them all.

The alcohol had been creeping over me slowly until now. I pushed the rest of the second away when a wave of dizziness swept over me, and my throat tickled worse now.

I raised a hand to my neck when the sensation dawned on me and I slipped clumsily off my stool, pinning Laviana with a horrified look.

"I had a feeling you might resist. It's nothing personal, Astraea. You won't be harmed, I promise."

I stumbled back, knocking into a tall form, but as they grabbed me my magick flared to life and a male hissed at the burning of his hands.

Then in my utter shock and *rage*—rage because I would never be someone's captive again—silver and violet flame erupted through the room, but I held control of it so it would not burn anyone or anything.

"You think nebulora in my cup was enough to stop me?" I snarled, not recognizing the sinister malice in my own voice. This was pain, betrayal, and I'd never felt more aligned with Nightsdeath than right now, which only broke me more.

"It was quite a powerful dosage. Far more easily hidden in your favored drink," Laviana said carefully.

I trembled with the hold on my magick and my skin was quickly slicked with sweat. The nebulora had some effect, I had to admit, but now I had Lightsdeath, which infused the edges of my vision with a shimmering silver.

"Everyone get out!" I yelled. Most scrambled for the exit. Those who stayed were on edge, and I assumed they were with Laviana.

"Why?" I said through my teeth. My eyes pricked. Though we'd become estranged over all these years, and I'd broken many promises with my death, it cut deeply to think she would take me by force for her gain.

"If you didn't react so hastily you would have awoken perfectly well back at our camp."

I chuckled without humor, adding heat to my flames licking around all of us. "Then what?"

Her expression began to shift, not from my question but, as she glanced from the magick to me, as she began to reassess exactly who she'd confronted.

"What happened to you?" she asked again, and the gentleness of it nearly broke me down.

"What did you *want* with me?" I bit out again.

"To convince you to join us and show us where the dragons are so the vampires might have the first chance at securing their rider bonds."

"And you thought kidnapping me was a good start to that alliance?"

"I thought there was no chance of Nyte being agreeable and I needed you alone."

"He's not here!"

In more ways than one. I took a breath through the tightness swelling in my throat to stop my voice from breaking.

I warned, "You'd best leave before he returns because I promise he won't be as hesitant as me to destroy you and this whole place."

"Which is why you need to come with us alone."

I pushed my feelings aside to understand her desperation.

"I want to help you, trust me I do. But there are things I need to do first, and the dragons . . . they belong to no one. There is no telling who they will bond with. There could be a courtyard full of vampires and it may not choose any of them. It's not as simple as that."

"It seemed that way with Drystan and you," she said, slipping a hint of bitterness.

"Nothing has been simple or easy," I said steadily. My emotions threatened to make me volatile.

I couldn't hold the magick much longer, but it was all that kept Laviana's people from advancing on me.

"Leave, please," I said. "I'll find you again when I can. We're on the same side of this war against Auster, and I desire equality for the vampires as much as you do."

Her laugh was dripping in bitterness, and that hurt worse than her anger. It was like she'd given up trusting my word, and the worst part was, I didn't know if she should either.

"You might say you're unbiased and fighting for us all, but time and time again you choose a side whether you realize it or not."

Those were her parting words before she motioned with her head and the other vampires started filing out. I held onto my magick with tears pricking my eyes right until I watched the last flick of her dark hair disappear around the corner.

Then I let go with a choked sob.

I had to brace myself on my thighs as my balance wobbled. The surge of magick had burned a lot of the alcohol from my system but not all of it. Paired with the exertion to hold the flames with the nebulora coursing through me . . . I swore.

I'd come in here to get warm and a quick rest; now the thought of trekking through the snow for hours again weighed my eyelids with more fatigue I had to fight.

"Someone upset my star." I shivered at the controlled calm of Nightsdeath easing into the room. "Though it seems you might have upset them worse, considering how vacant this place has become. I like it."

His shadowy fingers curled under my chin, and I forced myself to straighten. I didn't last a few seconds before my balance swayed, but Nightsdeath caught me, lifting me into his arms, and I didn't fight it.

"Do I need to go hunting?" he asked quietly.

"No . . . it was just a misunderstanding." I was suddenly too tired, and though he wasn't warm, I craved the very faint notes of Nyte's scent so much I let my head rest on his shoulder.

"That sounds like a cause to go hunting."

"Can we just go?"

He was already moving, and I braced for the cold to hit us. Outside, it was so surprisingly mild that I lifted my head in confusion. The wind still whistled by, but I could hardly feel it.

"Your shadows are like a shield," I murmured in realization.

Nightsdeath hummed. "If it prevents you from whining for us to stop and find fire for warmth, I will tolerate this closeness, as much as it repulses me."

I didn't take offense at that. Contrary to his words, his arms held me tightly and he marched on carefully while he carried me.

He was still my Nyte, always.

Nightsdeath

She was such a delicate little thing. The star maiden slept soundly, her head right by my lap so the shadows around me could ward off the chill swirling into the mouth of the shallow cave. Astraea insisted we needed to stop here for her to rest. It had been many hours since the inn, but her depleting stamina was a hindrance to our progress toward the temple. I was starting to reconsider this plan.

Astraea stirred gently, tucking her knees up tighter to her chest, as if the air she claimed was icily bitter still caught at her ankles. Every flicker and sound from her while unconscious was fascinating. Unlike when she was awake, every unthinking thing she did was a breath of pure innocence.

I couldn't fathom how she could rest when a thousand ways to kill her surrounded her vulnerable form and she'd drifted off in naive contentment beside the worst of them.

I reached to hook a strand of her glittering silver hair. It looked so soft, weaving through my fingers like the shadows. The itch to truly know what it felt like irritated my mind. She stirred again, and I stiffened to the brush of her hand against my leg, though I couldn't physically feel it. Then, to my complete abhorrence, she lifted her head and wiggled herself up to lay it over my lap where I sat, legs extended with crossed ankles.

My hands hovered, utterly repelled by this bright creature sleeping on me as she settled soundly again. I battled the impulse to remove her since hideous, treacherous feelings disturbed me. Echoes of the weak and smitten parts from the other half of me that were getting harder to ignore the more she was around.

Which, infuriatingly, was all the fucking time.

Rainyte adored her like there was no greater treasure to be found across any galaxy. Her attachment burrowed deep within him, *within us,* far beyond physical attraction. A kind of love that knew no reason; where Astraea was concerned, there existed no measure too great to declare it.

There was a time when I was utterly repelled by the idea of her. Forced to retreat further and further into the shadows of Rainyte's consciousness while he indulged in her light. Before her, we thrived in darkness, we fed on despair, and from the moment she took root in our mind, I became smaller. My voice diminished under her whispering words of betrayal, like *care* and *hope*.

My fingers slipped across the side of her throat now with the thoughts circling viciously. She made us forget about the wrongs done to us, the things that made me darker and more prominent day by day in this wretched world. I could kill her now, and eventually I would find Rainyte's physical body even if I had to collapse this world building by building to do so.

Yet I couldn't. Somehow the thought of smothering this precious star forever seemed so tragic, even to my depraved spirit.

She was my curse, my eternal torment. And so the only way to have her and the body I needed was to convince her to give over to Lightsdeath. It would be a challenge to reach that powerful entity and strike a bargain, but I believed together—as light and dark incarnate—we could dominate the world and make it ours.

The urge to wrap my fingers around her neck eased with that glorious vision, and instead I lost myself in a trance invoked by her starlight hair while my darkness combed through it.

I could have kept torturing her to get her to spill the locations, to seek out the key pieces and leave her behind, but her suffering . . . it wasn't an indulgence like anyone else's. Her pain rebounded into me, and I came to the realization it had to be the mating bond.

She once tried to stab me with a pitiful weapon to hurt me, unaware that she needed no steel to accomplish that. Astraea believed I could not hurt, but there was one way I felt my own pain: when *she* was in pain. Maybe once I killed the beating heart in Rainyte's body I would be free of that wretched weakness.

Until then I tucked back the locks of her hair to see more of her still, peaceful face.

"I want to end you, Astraea Lightborne. All I am is pain, all I know is suffering, and you drown me with your light bright enough to pierce the thickest darkness."

18

Astraea

I suffered five treacherous days of trudging through snow piled up to my knees, each step an act of defiance against the bitter cold cutting like knives through every layer of my clothes. We had climbed deadly mountains, their icy ledges narrow as threads, and crossed endless fringes where the wind howled, tearing at me as if it could pull me back from our goal. By now, my breath was barely mist against the relentless white. Every muscle in my body burned, yet I forced myself to press on.

Nightsdeath, to my irritation, didn't suffer from the weather and climb, which often soured my mood further.

Finally, through the shimmering veil of snowfall, it finally came into view—a structure that seemed to float against the cliffside, carved out of the rock itself or perhaps out of something rarer, older. It was a temple, unmistakably so, its spires piercing the sky, casting shadows that stretched long and sharply over the snowfield below. The building was both haunting and beautiful, an ancient guardian standing resolute against time and weather, as if waiting for those strong enough to reach it.

The sight stole the breath from my chest but wonder quickly turned to dread twisting in me for what we might face lurking within while we retrieved a piece of the key. As we drew closer, I felt a force pressing down—an invisible hand testing our strength, sensing our motives, judging if we were worthy to even set foot inside.

We had come too far to turn back. And so, with nothing left but my resolve and the promise of what lay within, I tightened my grip on my cloak and took the first step forward, the temple's shadow stretching coldly across my path.

I kept to Nightsdeath's side, his darkness a shield against the worst of the weather. At first, I'd tried to keep a little distance, but the closer I was the more tolerable the cold became and so our arms brushed with every step now.

Neither of us gave the closeness any attention, at least not outwardly. Every

now and then I would glance at him and internally sink with the want to link his arm or have him draw his around me like Nyte would. I missed that caring and tender side of him so much the pain was becoming unbearable. At times I wondered if Nightsdeath could feel my sinking despair when, contrary to his unfeeling character, he'd asked at least once a day if I was all right.

"At long last," he drawled.

I stopped walking halfway across the courtyard, not wanting to let go of the cloak I kept hugged tightly around my body, but I needed my magick. If this temple was like the last, I thought the dragon painting should be under my feet, buried under the thick snow. Though I didn't have the means to free it—needing Eltanin's tears—I couldn't pass without confirming another ancient dragon was wondrously hidden for millennia right here.

"What, pray tell, are you doing?" Nightsdeath asked irritably.

"I just have to see something," I muttered absentmindedly as I focused on my thoughts. "You might want to step back; it's about to get a little too bright for your tolerance."

I shivered violently when his shadows drifted away from me, cursing the wretched cold as I brought my hands up. My magick hummed over my skin with a tingling warmth I welcomed and embraced. A gale of wind and light formed. Pushing my palms down on the ground blasted a wide radius around me that revealed exactly what I hoped to find under the blanket of snow.

Dropping to my haunches, I traced a gloved hand over the blue marks of the magnificent dragon. My first thought was to curse myself for not asking Drystan how many types and colors of dragon there were. Would the blue dragon's breath be different from Athebyne's searing red flame or Eltanin's starry smoke?

I groaned in frustration as I rose since I wouldn't get to know today.

"Of course," Nightsdeath said, examining the painting. "I learned of the dragons and their whereabouts from Drystan just before the curse took hold. Why didn't you mention it?"

"I didn't think it would be important to you. You want the key, not dragons."

"Dragons are creatures as old as the gods themselves. Some believe they are gods. An alliance with one is an incredible advantage in battle, never mind over a dozen that could dominate the skies if you free them all."

"There's no predicting which side each dragon will choose if they bond with a rider."

"So why risk freeing them?"

I grazed my fingers over the blue paint. "No creature deserves to be imprisoned."

Nightsdeath cast his sight toward the temple.

"All we can do is get the key piece right now," he said.

Unlike the temple in Alisus that was dedicated to my guardians, and where I spoke to them, this one was unguarded by the skeletal forms that didn't speak. I couldn't decide if it was a relief or more daunting that Nightsdeath accompanied me inside.

There was no predicting what trial the key would manifest for us to claim a piece of it. We couldn't devise a plan or prepare; this challenge had to be taken in blind faith. The key was smart and very protective of itself, even from me since I was the one to break it.

I didn't tell Nightsdeath that even if we completed the trial, the key piece we gained could be a fake.

There were sixteen potential temples, and only five true key pieces to be found.

I didn't know what I was expecting of the interior. This temple had only a few short steps onto a single level with . . . no ceiling. Except it wasn't our red-infused night I stared up at, it was the dark midnight holding a million stars I'd missed the sight of dearly.

When my eyes fell back down, I gasped, stumbling, and even feeling for my wings, but we weren't falling. The ground mimicked the sky now, as if we stood on a sheet of glass and looked down through an endless night.

"How do you suppose we reach it?" Nightsdeath said.

My brow furrowed at his question, and I glanced up, but he still stared down through the glass under his feet. I crouched carefully, searching through the layers of stars with more precision until . . . there it was. The key piece seamlessly disguised as another blinking star. The only thing that gave it away from such a distance was how it spun, catching a glinting light at perfect intervals.

"Auster took your wings . . ." I trailed off with bile rising in my throat.

"He took my celestial wings."

I watched in awe as the shadows swirling around him moved, coming together and climbing his spine before forming into large, stunning wings of darkness. My brow crumpled at the magnificent sight of him.

"You find me more attractive with them?" Nightsdeath queried, studying my reaction.

I find you the most beautiful thing in the world. With or without wings.

I didn't speak those words; he would only ask more questions about why. Always trying to figure out how emotions worked if only to exploit them somehow.

"Physical attraction is human nature."

"I am not human, and I find you attractive." A blush almost crept over my cheeks until he added, "And repulsive."

My near smile dropped to a glower. "Can we just focus?"

Nightsdeath raised his hand without hesitation, and a blast of dark energy erupted from his palm, hurtling toward the glass in a flash of shadowed light. The force of it crashed against the glass, which shuddered but held firm, rebounding the energy back in all directions. The wave slammed into me before I even had a chance to brace myself, knocking me off my feet and sending me backward with dizzying speed.

My back struck the small stone steps behind me, each unforgiving edge digging sharply into my body. Pain lanced through my shoulder, then my hip, as I tumbled, limbs colliding at awkward angles until I lay sprawled on the cold, rough surface. For a moment, everything was still, save for the lingering hum of his dark power vibrating through the air. He hadn't even flinched.

Groaning, I shifted to be sure nothing was broken.

"A little warning next time." My voice was strained from the throbbing aches.

Nightsdeath wasn't even looking at me as he wandered up the steps toward a podium I hadn't noticed before. My irritation swam as I peeled myself off the ground and shuffled over to him.

He held a blindfold, examining it like it was some foreign artifact. On the podium a short verse was carved into the stone.

The dark is unseeing, the light is unfeeling.

It only took a minute of calculation for a breath of laughter to escape me. I straightened from my hunch, trying to stretch out the dull pains throughout my body.

"What?" he asked while I still mulled over my conclusion.

"It's going to test our trust in each other," I said, studying the starry sky below, then above.

"What a humorous thing," he mumbled.

The giggle that escaped me might have been pure delirium, but it chased away some of my nerves. When I looked to Nightsdeath he was staring at me. His frown pinched deep as though he were angry but his amber eyes were searching.

"What?" I asked, touching my face, as perhaps maybe there was a bleeding cut I hadn't felt from my fall.

His jaw worked. "Let's get this over with."

I skipped after him as he descended onto the glass again. "You sure you have it in you to trust me for this task?"

"What is the task?"

That was a good question. I surveyed the blindfold in his hands.

"I think one of us needs to wear that."

He didn't hesitate to hold it out to me, and I scowled.

"The dark is unseeing, the light is unfeeling," I recited from the podium. "I think that means you have to wear it. It's not like I can kill you."

"You might be able to retrieve the key piece and leave me."

I was about to make a sarcastic remark, but something in the tone of those last two words made me stumble internally. I thought they tapered off with vulnerability. Was it possible that the more time he spent with me, the more Nyte's truer, good feelings grew? I'd noticed how irritable and on edge Nightsdeath had become in recent days. How he often looked at me with the will to kill but something was making him hesitate even from torturing me.

"I'm not going anywhere," I said, barely a whisper as I held his glowing amber eyes. "We're getting that thing together."

I snatched the blindfold from him, only to step closer and reach up while standing on my toes to tie it around his eyes. His hands immediately shot over mine as the material stole his sight. We stood there for a few wild heartbeats before his grip relaxed, and he let me tie it behind his head. When I let go, he hissed as the material tightened by some form of magick, making it impossible to remove now until we'd retrieved the key piece.

For a moment I was stunned by his vulnerability. The shadows around him still primed and swirled with more anger than ever, but he'd given his trust to me for this. If I ran out of the temple now, would he ever be free of that blindfold?

"Now what?" he asked, so quietly it was the first inkling of uncertainty he'd ever shown.

I went to reach for his hand, but suddenly the ground disappeared beneath my feet, and I hadn't unglamoured my wings yet. Falling rapidly only lasted a few seconds before an arm wrapped around me, stopping my plummet. Then we were floating around midnight swirls and broken constellations. His wings of shadow suspended us there.

"Might want to release those wings," he commented, a slight huskiness in his tone over how our bodies were forcibly pressed together. My legs wrapped tightly around his waist. Even if he couldn't feel me physically, was he affected by the proximity?

I tried to reach my wings but they felt . . . missing. Then realization dawned.

"I can't," I breathed, clutching him tighter now that I understood he was the only thing that kept me from plunging into an abyss. "Trust has two sides. Don't drop me."

When he realized what I meant, Nightsdeath stiffened, and one terrible note of dread that he might let go slithered up my spine. Instead, his arm tightened, then his other hand hooked under my thigh, prompting me to wrap my legs around him more securely. My pulse skipped, and I was unable to resist pressing myself against him as tightly as I could.

"Best get comfortable then. Who knows what other surprises there might be. So likewise, don't let go," he said. His breath fanned across my lips, and I could have whimpered as I forced back the desire for him to kiss me.

Nightsdeath flew and I glanced over my shoulder to direct him. "Lower." Then, "Left. No, my left, your right." I bit my lip against the amusement bubbling inside me from how ridiculous this was.

"We should have swapped places," he mumbled, but when I caught a glance, I thought a curl fought onto his mouth too.

"That wasn't the instruction. Lower—not that much!"

The fact that I didn't have my own wings to let go so I could dive straight for the floating key piece was becoming increasingly frustrating. Nightsdeath stopped moving to hover in the air with me, and I turned my face back to him. With his eyes covered I couldn't read his expression to understand why he'd stalled.

"I want to feel you," he said, five words that stunned me, coiling in my stomach. The faint flex of his fingers on my waist and thigh left no mistaking what type of *feel* he meant. "It's the only thing that makes me envy Rainyte."

Without thinking, my fingers threaded through the back of his hair. "Physical touch . . . the yearning for it . . . has to come from a feeling within first."

"Lust doesn't need attachment."

"Is that all you feel for me? Lust?"

He thought for a moment. "No. I feel a deep, unending desire to kill you. Because you making me contemplate such trivial things as lust is a terrible distraction. It's what makes Rainyte fail time and time again."

A swelling grew in my chest, perhaps made of sheer desperation that birthed a new hope in my mind. What if reaching the parts of Nyte that were suppressed in Nightsdeath could wake his physical body? Maybe it was a grasp in the dark, but my light was fading further the longer he lay cursed and out of my reach. No, not out of my reach—he was right here. Wrapped around me.

"Come back to me," I whispered, then pressed my lips to his.

It took a second to bend the dark, but then he was kissing me back. Needy and desperate and searching. It was the dark welcoming the light, colliding as night and stars, accepting the inevitability and chaos of each other.

Then, as if he realized what wanting this would cost, his hold slackened, releasing me.

I would have kept my hold on him regardless but a blast hit my body, striking a pain through me that left no option but to let go.

It wasn't Nightsdeath's power that sent me falling.

I saw strikes of blue lightning in the darkness, and I knew who'd come. But soon, I would be lost in complete endless nothing if I kept falling through the abyss, and Nightsdeath and Auster would vanish from my sight. I didn't have wings, but I could still feel my magick.

My survival came in a rush of adrenaline.

As I twisted, my magick created a sheet of light beneath me and I braced to land on it. The impact shook through my body, but I had no time to think, casting out another step of light, and another, and another. Climbing like I'd done in the void between life and death. The key piece floated above me, and I raced up my light steps one by one as they disappeared behind me.

Then, to my horror, my magick started to dull, as if this trial saw it as a cheat, like my wings. Nightsdeath and I had to retrieve the key piece together—a test of trust. But surely we'd passed that part in our willingness to get this far?

I kept going regardless. I was so. Close. Leaping off my final step I was going to reach it . . . I was going to . . .

My fingers grazed the metal, spinning the shard faster. Then I fell again with no way to catch myself this time. Down and down and down. Through a void of lonely dark.

A gust of air enveloped my entire body before something firmer took hold of me. I gripped it back with everything I had; then we were shooting high.

Nightsdeath had come.

"You caught me," I breathed.

He said nothing, and the stars came back around and the key piece was within reach again. This time I clutched it tightly, pulling it to my chest while Nightsdeath cradled me, flying higher and higher.

Emerging into the temple was a new breath of fresh air.

When he landed, the ground beneath our feet was dull, cracked beige stone again. The illusion dizzied me for a second, but we'd done it—retrieved the first key piece.

I beamed at Nightsdeath, who was able to remove his eye cover now, but when he did those amber eyes were blazing with the heat of the sun, targeting me, then over my shoulder. My whole body stiffened as I recalled the intrusion on our trial.

It hadn't been part of the game. Auster was truly here. Along with his two brothers, Tarran, and a guard of celestials.

"We'll take that," Auster said, holding out his hand for the key piece I held.

Nightsdeath stepped toward me, but at the same time, I stepped toward Auster.

My pulse skipped erratically as I reached him and placed the key piece in his awaiting hand. My gut pulled in knots when I turned back. Nightsdeath watched in pure, still fury.

"I see how it is. Trust is more powerful than love," he recited from me.

What I'd said days ago, and it tore deeply in my heart. "Because trust makes the sharpest blade. Well played, Maiden. You almost had me fooled."

My chest could hardly contain the devastating storm behind my ribs. I couldn't stop my quick look toward Tarran. All he gave was a barely detectable nod, and I heard the unspoken words.

You have to kill Nightsdeath.

I'd heard it first from my guardian at the Temple in Alisus and immediately rejected it. Then Tarran recited it back at the castle when we'd found a moment of privacy in the kitchens.

I understood now.

"You of all wicked beings shouldn't be surprised by this," I said coldly to Nightsdeath.

His amber eyes flared a shade brighter. He took a daring step closer. Auster's guards shifted, but I took a step to meet him too.

"Not surprised. Disappointed. You're just as weak as I thought you to be to allow yourself to rule under one so spineless. We could have conquered the world together."

"I rule under no one. I am the star-maiden."

"A title is just a word. In all I see before me, you two deserve each other, and I deserve to break the world apart for all the betrayal it brews, the greed it feeds, and the fucking pain it inflicts."

Light formed in my palms, and Nightsdeath regarded it with his shadows swirling angrily.

Knowing this place would become rubble the moment we unleashed our magick against each other, I channeled through the void. In a heartbeat, the mild temperature of the temple was replaced with the numbing winter air, so sharp and powerful this high, as I enticed Nightsdeath to strike me out here instead.

He didn't waste a breath.

A familiar stroke of dark awareness slithered across my nape, all the warning I had to spin and throw out a bright flare to clash with his starless blast.

The collision was as stunning as it was devastating. When it cut off, we chased each other through the snow that fell, which hindered me but not him. My only advantage was that I could move through the void and he couldn't, leveling the playing field. That started to annoy him as I used the void to dart around him, play with him. The velocity of his attacks amplified.

This was the Nightsdeath that would kill me over and over and not feel a shred of remorse. He was furious, realizing I'd tipped Auster off about where we were heading, and I had to admit, I was torn about the deception I had to play too, but it was just a distraction.

You have to kill Nightsdeath.

My soul cried at the thought, but if it wasn't too late, I had to *try*.

"You lie as prettily as you look; I have to commend you," Nightsdeath called, but there was nothing admiring in his tone.

A stroke of darkness shot for me, and I twisted. It didn't blast past me but rather snaked around my ankles, quickly ensnaring my body. My hand was free enough to send a coil of light around me to extinguish it.

Nightsdeath raised his arms, and in one elegant motion it conjured the darkness around us, flooding in front of him before forming into a giant serpent that loomed high, swallowing the distance to me as his steps did.

I stumbled back from the rippling animated serpent, but I rallied my own magick, conjuring a huge wolf made of light that stood off against the serpent.

Heart thundering and breath heaving, I didn't know how much longer I could contend with him.

Despite the energy of our clashing power unleashing an angry storm around us, a faint caw caught my attention enough to glance up. Through the whorls of dark and light, a large crow flew overhead, circling. It was so peculiar. Almost . . . familiar. With the sight of the dark bird I remembered my guardians. A seemingly jarring drift of my thoughts considering the circumstances.

You have to kill Nightsdeath.

The distraction cost me.

I choked when Nightsdeath's hand wrapped my throat tightly. I clawed at his fingers, snapping my wide eyes to his glowing amber irises. He hissed when my wolf made of light wrapped its powerful jaw around the neck of the serpent. I used that advantage to strike his chest and gain a second to brace for his immediate advance.

As I stared at the hauntingly beautiful version of Nyte that stormed for me, uncertainty stalled me, and I again doubted that killing Nightsdeath could end the shallow heartbeat in his true body.

Shadows grew around me and I took in their wraith-like forms.

Everyone who faced Nightsdeath saw a monster—a merciless killer. No one stopped to see that pain made vicious things. Pain only knew how to fight back. To deflect. To ease some of the suffering so we could survive.

"I love you," I said. The darkness gave no reaction. "I love every version of the night you are."

A tear slipped down my cheek as I braced my stance.

"Love is not a cure; it's a poison," Nightsdeath snarled.

I didn't declare it to reason with him. I knew he would repel anything warm or true. I'd been there before.

Yet I loved all of him anyway.

Nightsdeath reached me, and I didn't try to attack or defend this time. When he gripped me, I slipped a hand over his face, which bore such rage and repulsion for me. Then his darkness started to devour me.

Shadows crept over my body, and my eyes pricked at the devastation that engulfed me. I didn't let go of his blazing amber eyes. The darkness seeped into me—through my eyes and nose and mouth—seizing my whole body with the agony of ash curdling my blood.

I could hardly remain standing with the shadows tearing me apart from the inside, scorching and shredding and consuming. I fought with everything I had to not let death claim me yet.

Just a little more.

I had to absorb as much of him as I could tolerate.

As I pushed up on my toes, Nightsdeath wrapped an arm around me as my lips met his.

It was time to let go—time to let Lightsdeath charge with full force against him.

A cold, silver light began to radiate from beneath my skin. Subtle at first—a shimmer that glinted in the darkness—but then it grew, spreading in intricate, webbed patterns up my arms, filling my veins with liquid starlight. I shuddered, feeling the icy brilliance threading through me like a second heartbeat.

Lightsdeath filled my lungs, my thoughts, my bones with an energy so vast and cold. Somewhere, in the hollow echo of my mind, I heard my own voice—small, distant, and fading fast. It was a plea swallowed by a sky full of stars, a whisper lost to an endless, starlit night.

Every piece of the dark power I'd taken into my body exploded from the light that I became. Nightsdeath gripped me tighter, as if torn between wanting to keep me and push me away. He kissed me back with so much anguish and heartbreak, like he knew it was over as we became starlight and darkness and everything that exists between. As we exploded into a cosmic catastrophe where everything began and all things ended.

When I pulled back, Nightsdeath had never looked so vulnerable. Tears of gold fell like the liquid metal of his irises they spilled over. He was the most beautiful tragedy.

"It's okay," I whispered, caressing a hand over his cheek, which didn't feel so firm. "You don't have to hurt any longer."

He only stared back with misery cleaving his eyes. The black vines crawled around his skin as frighteningly as ever, the shadows he was made of primed angry still, but those eyes . . . they understood. His form started to catch on the wind, slowly slipping from my touch, leaving my body.

I broke. Watching his acceptance, maybe even his reprieve, as he glanced down at his hands, which dissipated too.

With one last farewell in our shared look of sorrow, he was gone.

And then so was I, into a dark, beckoning oblivion.

19

Astraea

I fell to my knees, but instead of the wet snow of my realm, I was met with the cracked dry land of the veil between life and death. I couldn't move, weighed down by anchors of grief, heartache, and exhaustion.

"What have I done?" I whispered.

"Exactly what destiny foretold." Death's echo was a haunting chill through my bones.

Glancing sideways, I saw him approach in mortal size. Depthless hood, fully cloaked, scythe in hand. It wasn't the first time I'd wondered about the chip in his weapon.

"When falls night," I recited. "Nightsdeath?"

Death nodded once. "The world will drown in starlight. It is your time, my child."

But what wasn't clear . . . was whether my starlight would drown in a wrath of destruction or purge the land of evil darkness.

"Is Nyte . . . is he still alive?"

Death did not answer.

"Come," he said instead.

I had nothing to lose by walking by Death's side through his endless landscape.

"You said I would be the end of Dusk and Dawn . . . how can one mortal kill gods?" I asked.

"You are not just one mortal. You never have been. Nor will you be able to do this alone."

"I can't lose any of them. My friends," I said like a plea.

"You can never truly lose what is always carried in your heart."

My lip wobbled when he didn't assure me they would be safe.

"You made me Lightsdeath and want me to kill my creators. Why? I don't know if you're any better than them."

"I am a primordial. The beginning of time and all creation. I am not good nor evil. I am not kind nor cruel. I simply . . . am. People don't fear me; they fear the unknown. But death is just as uncertain as life. A person is born and there is no telling what will become of it. A person dies and there is no foreseeing where they will go next. Life holds just as much to be fearful of and time is the link between us both. Dusk and Dawn have been meddling with a divine order. They have long been stealing from me, for I need souls for my realm to survive. All things must die."

I surveyed the desolation around us, a bleak, endless stretch of cracked earth and twisted, lifeless trees reaching up like skeletal hands clawing at a gloomy gray sky. The ground was parched and fractured, the deep fissures spiderwebbing across the landscape as if the earth itself had once screamed and split open in agony. Dust drifted across the barren plains, stirred only by faint, unfeeling winds that offered no relief from the heavy stillness.

Then for some reason my eyes held on the blank canvas above us and I wondered . . .

"There's more to our stars, isn't there?" I whispered.

"Long ago the archangels worked for me. They would cycle souls to my realm. Until Dusk and Dawn created their own image of such angels: the celestials. Instead, these new imitations would cycle souls to your stars, which created an unparalleled cosmic power in your realm. You will not have heard of the Divine War in which the archangels, those with black wings, were annihilated by the new celestial breed."

"Some are still born that way," I said, piecing together things I knew. "With black wings. They're not a celestial curse, not a brand of sin."

"No. Those born with black wings have archangel blood in their heritage that awakens. The four High Celestials swear to enforce and hold in secrecy this knowledge when they are chosen by Dusk and Dawn, so the tales of their predecessors are never known."

"But the souls we cycle to the stars get a chance to come back in new forms," I said.

"A poetic notion, I agree. Hope is powerful, and when crafted into deception, it is lethal. It is not true of the souls that reside in your stars. For thousands of years, they have served as a power source to heighten solar magick. When they finally have no energy left, what remains falls. Mortals discover the weak pieces of soul energy, and those with magick found they could use it. Starlight Matter, I believe you call it."

"Cassia and Calix . . ."

If what Death told was true . . .

Oh gods, what had I done?

"You have a chance to right this unbalance, Maiden, though it will take your ultimate sacrifice."

"What does that mean?"

"Those whose energy still charges the stars can be laid to rest in peace. It is my purpose. You have my vow that I will grant passage to the souls who linger in your stars, but time is running out. Your true stars are falling. Soon your land will become just as desolate as mine."

"I just need my key back, then I can kill the gods who made me with it?"

"You will need their true names. They will take mortal form temporarily; after all their failed creations and alliances they will move to rectify the land themselves. In their quest to dominate they will make themselves the most vulnerable a primordial can ever be."

"What are their names?"

"I do not know. It is our most guarded secret. The greatest weapon against us when spoken by a mortal becomes a chain of obedience to them."

"There has to be a way to find out."

"If only there were a creature with a sight into minds. But beware: the mind of a god is no easy passage. It is not ventured into without consequence."

We reached a void of light that began to grow, and I knew my consciousness was awakening in my own realm. I turned to Death, unafraid.

"Can I ask you one thing?" He had no eyes to hold, but in an eerie sense, the primordial still seemed like a person. "What does come after death?"

His hood turned to watch the light grow over us. Over me.

"That, dear Maiden, is the most exciting unknown."

20

Nyte

Waking was like plummeting from the heavens, my soul hurtling downward only to be crushed into a body too frail to withstand the impact. Consciousness returned in pieces, cutting through the darkness. I could see, just barely—a fractured haze of light and shadow hovering above me—but no breath came to fill my lungs. My chest felt as though it were encased in stone, each rib straining against some invisible weight that pinned me down, holding me captive within my own flesh.

Every muscle was locked tight, frozen in shock, as if my very bones remembered the fall, the ground rushing up to meet me. My fingers twitched, a faint echo of life pulsing within them, but no more. My lips parted, aching to form a word, a sound, anything to break the silence, but even that simple effort turned to dust.

Panic stirred beneath the stillness, a faint, fluttering thing buried deep within me, but my body refused to heed it. All I could do was stare up at the hazy shapes above, caught in the terrible stillness, bound to a form that felt foreign—as though I were a stranger trapped within my own skin.

And in that moment, suspended between the waking world and whatever lay beyond, I wondered if I had truly returned . . . or if some part of me had been left behind in that endless fall.

Sound trickled into my senses with part of an answer to the questions of where I was and why. At first, there was a gentle wind and shaken foliage. Then peace turned to violence with the mighty unmistakable roar that rattled through my body. The dragon's cry was a rope to grapple and pull myself out of the void I was drifting in.

"We waited as long as we could. Astraea is right: this is the best hope for now." I knew that voice. The little rogue vampire was here—Nadia.

My pain, my confusion, nothing fucking mattered when I heard the one name that forced every weakness away so I could finally take a deep inhale.

Astraea.

Memory of how I lay so disorientated and immobilized came back to me in horrifying flashes of clarity. Dusk and Dawn had won, inflicting their curse of eternal rest on me, but . . . I was awake. How long had I been gone?

Everything in me barked in protest against moving, but my Starlight was out there, and I didn't care if I had to trek to her with shattered bones and my body in flames.

"I don't know if we'll ever get to make it back here." That was Drystan who spoke next.

With the two of them together, not sounding like they were trying to kill each other, was I truly awake?

"If this is you saying you'll miss me, I know you will," Nadia said, but it lacked a little of her usual arrogance.

"Just—" Drystan didn't finish his sentence, but footsteps compacted the soft snow.

I forced my eyes to open and immediately squinted from the light; the pair seemed close. So close that I tried to focus my vision to be sure the rogue didn't have a blade lodged in my brother's chest. I didn't get to confirm that when the ground beneath me moved as I tried to roll onto my side; then I barely registered that I was falling before I slammed with a groan onto snow thick enough to soften the landing, but not completely.

"Shit!" Nadia exclaimed.

I couldn't see them as I blinked up, realizing now I was previously lying on the saddle of a black dragon, but he was too big to be . . .

The fact Eltanin wasn't as small as I remembered bolted me upright against every agonizing pulse in my head and shooting pain in my bones.

"Where is she?" I demanded. Adrenaline was a drug I consumed greedily to numb the warnings of my body.

"How the fuck are you awake?" Drystan said, marching over and staring at me as if I were a ghost.

"No need to sound so thrilled about it, brother," I said hoarsely, losing shreds of dignity with each passing second I lay here.

I tried to look around, hoping but already knowing Astraea wasn't here right now. The cold started to seep into me, and when Drystan leaned down, I accepted his help up, immediately needing to lean against Eltanin. His feathers against my skin tingled, and with that sensation a thread pulled within me.

"How long?" I asked, barely a daunted whisper because I feared the answer. Eltanin was as big as Athebyne now.

"A month," Nadia said. "Give or take. You've been in dreamland for around a month."

I closed my eyes to accept the lost time. It could have been far more . . . it should have been forever. My mind was storming with questions, but only one thing mattered right now.

"Where is Astraea?" I asked again.

Seeing Drystan's wince, I braced for an answer I wasn't going to like.

"She's . . . with Auster."

My fist tightened and I took a pause to collect my sanity.

"Against her will?"

"It's kind of complicated."

"Then uncomplicate it," I snarled.

"Not even months of sleep can make you less grumpy," Nadia muttered, folding her arms.

I knew exactly where I was when I cast a glance sideward and saw a wooden home so tall that my neck ached when I tried to scan to the top of the structure. We were at Nadir's home.

"Where were you taking me?"

Drystan tried to hide another wince, scratching the back of his neck.

"North Star."

My eyes blazed wide. There was only one reason to go to that island in Althenia.

"You were going to try crossing realms with me," I confirmed, barely able to contain the outrage in my tone. "Taking me away from her?"

Drystan shifted his stance, squaring himself defensively.

But it was Nadia who pointed a finger at me, her brow furrowed with anger. "You don't get to wake up and be pissed," she snapped. "He's been studying tirelessly to figure out a way to bring you back from your damned beauty sleep you let yourself get tricked into."

As much as the idea of what Drystan was going to do enraged me, and how the little rogue dared to speak to me, I had to swallow my feelings after hearing this. Slipping a look at my brother, I felt guilt creep in to cool my body as I took in the tiredness of his face now.

"I didn't know the curse would happen so soon," I confessed.

"But you knew it would eventually and told no one," he said resentfully.

"I hoped I would have a few decades at least and perhaps be able to find a way to break it before the eternal night came."

I cast my sight up, scanning over the declining expanse of stars and the broken moon.

"The sky isn't red anymore," Nadia said, like she was airing a thought.

I didn't know what that meant, but Drystan did. "It should be midday, so the imbalance is still active, and the stars are still plummeting."

As he mentioned it, I saw movement, lights that shot across the sky and grew in luminance. I could hear the roars of the land in the distance, but the vibrations of wherever the star hit didn't reach us.

"This happens often?" I inquired.

"Yes. Astraea managed to stop a meteor from destroying Vesitire right before she was taken. The people still talk about it, which reminds me, we've also seen a rebellion in her name. People wearing armbands of deep purple with her sigil on it—the wings are changed to *black*."

My mind spun to absorb all that stunning information about Astraea. It riddled me with deep pride and immense concern.

"I'm going to get her," I said, slipping into a dark calm at the thought of confronting Auster after where we'd left off. I was looking forward to inflicting so much pain upon him he would forget his own damned name before he begged for death.

Eltanin gave a rattle something between a chirp and a growl; his giant head twisted back, and when I met those starry, purple eyes . . . a thread broke in my soul, physically stopping my breath, only for a few seconds as that thread stretched, reaching to forge something new—a bond so brave and triumphant. It was like a star waking up inside me, a quiet burn that sent heat through every vein, pooling into a golden warmth I could barely contain.

Eltanin bonded with me as his rider.

Our minds brushed each other, tentatively and delicately, yet it was impossible to mistake the weight of the dragon's spirit living within me. Thoughts, not words, resonated between us, each one like an echo of my own heartbeat.

"What is happening?" I asked in a whispered breath.

This wasn't possible. Eltanin was Astraea's dragon.

"We were hoping the dragon bond would wake you from the curse, but it didn't."

Drystan explained to me how Eltanin only matured enough to choose a rider after his second moon cycle. I was drawn closer to the dragon by an invisible tether, which linked us. It seemed too good, too much of a gift, to be true. However, I couldn't deny there had been something that intrigued me about the dragon the moment I saw him, which further cast away my denial. Perhaps it had been his darkness, his shadowy magick. I didn't know, but I was beholden to him the moment I heard Eltanin's first communication through our bond, not in our language, maybe not in words ever known to mankind, but somehow I understood.

I will be your wings.

It took everything in me not to fall to my knees with this utter blessing. The weight of my celestial wings wasn't gone; they were right here, mightier than ever before. Wings that would catch me no matter how many times I fell.

My hand reached to caress his feathered mane. Eltanin's large eyes closed, and a soft purr vibrated over his neck.

"Can you take me to her?" I asked him aloud in the common tongue.

Eltanin's purple eyes snapped open, piercing into me with our shared determination and concern with the mention of Astraea. This celestial dragon wasn't mine alone; he was ours, mine and Astraea's, until the end of time.

I recoiled when Eltanin roared, a declaration of anguish knowing Astraea was in trouble. Eyeing his back, I found the impressive saddle he wore.

"You sure you're strong enough to ride, never mind face Auster Nova?" Drystan said skeptically.

"I have one reason to be glad this curse is broken. One fucking reason to want to be awake in this hell right now, and I'm not leaving her alone with him another damned second."

I sized up the climb to the saddle, but when Drystan didn't respond this time, I glanced at him. His expression turned hard and guarded, then I realized the error in my angry words.

"I didn't mean—"

"Forget it. I know she's the only reason you live and breathe, the apple of your eye, the star to your night." Drystan waved me off, heading toward the great red dragon, Athebyne. "Some things never change."

He threw the comment dryly, and I swore inwardly. I was constantly letting him down. Making him feel he was insignificant to me, when it was so far from the truth.

Nadia hesitated, glancing at us in silent debate before she followed Drystan, who was about to mount his dragon.

"I don't know where she is. Last I knew she was in Vesitire's castle, but that was at least a week ago," Drystan said.

I rubbed my chest, reaching to feel our bond, hoping it would to be enough to guide me to her if Auster had moved her from Vesitire.

"Drystan," I called, but I lost what I was going to say when he glanced my way.

It was strange . . . this tension between us. I wanted it gone but didn't know where to start cutting through it to reach him. Drystan read my failure to communicate, casting his sight forward and bracing himself as Athebyne shifted, ready to take flight. Nadia held onto him from behind.

"If you fall off Eltanin, I won't catch you," Drystan said.

I had to shield my eyes with the powerful blasts of wind throwing snow over me as the dragon launched into the sky.

"Let's go get our Starlight," I muttered to the dragon.

Every piece of me ached and strained to be reunited with Astraea. And every ounce of my villainous darkness itched to rain the hell of a thousand ages down upon Auster Nova for all he'd done to her in the past and present.

21

Astraea

I killed Nightsdeath . . . and I mourned for the loss of him. My body was sunk in a frozen embrace as my consciousness stirred, but the only place I wanted to awaken was by Nyte's bedside. Until I remembered he might not be there anymore. He might not be anywhere in my realm for me to find anymore after what I'd done.

When I opened my eyes . . . the sky was the most beautiful color I'd ever seen. A forgotten depthless midnight cradling the lonely stars. The blood moon curse was lifted.

"Nyte." I whispered his name like it might summon him to me from the stars.

Then my eyes pricked with the most dreadful thought that punched through me: what if the blood moon curse was lifted because Nyte was truly dead this time? What if I'd killed the only piece of Nyte I had left?

Lying here, everything within me steadily became as numb as my flesh.

Through the depths of my despair, I heard distant cries of fighting trickled over to me. Pitches of steel, cries of pain. A battle had broken out nearby, and my memory weaved back together to remember Auster was here, but who would he be fighting if Nightsdeath was gone?

I pushed up, wincing at the sharp stabbing in my muscles. Whipping my head around, through the small patch of forestry, I could make out bodies moving. Many of them. Adrenaline started to warm my body enough for me to find my footing on stable legs.

"I should have known your loyalty always has and always will lie in part with him." I tensed at that voice, turning to find Laviana, flanked by two other vampires, approaching me.

"You followed me?"

"Of course. You can't think us all fools who don't know you're hunting dragons that will grant an unparalleled advantage to the side they're on."

"You've wasted your time and lost lives for nothing. The dragon here can't be released," I said through gritted teeth.

"What does it take?"

I pursed my lips. That knowledge wasn't safe to give out when, on top of Auster's bounty that had people out to capture us, Laviana and all the vampires could leverage any of us to get to Eltanin.

"A specific stone. It's well hidden and not with me."

Laviana smiled, but it wasn't friendly. "Like I said, you're a terrible liar, Astraea. We were once allies."

"We still are. You can't expect me to choose sides when there are far greater things at stake right now."

"Our dearest sister always was the one with the least patience." Tarran's smooth voice interrupted us from behind me.

"Last I heard, you're not to be trusted as Auster's little *pet,*" she gibed.

Tarran didn't appreciate the term, and I winced at the look he cut toward me in accusation.

"Sometimes the best way to spy is in plain sight," he said, slipping his hands into his pockets.

"You expect me to believe that?" Laviana scoffed.

Tarran shrugged. "I do not care, little sister."

"Don't call me that. None of us have been close in centuries."

"Is that what it takes then? Severing your roots to rise to power?"

"It takes cutting out weaknesses. You've been gone. Then next I hear of you surfacing you've gathered your own following on the hunt for the key and the maiden. Did you address Astraea as your *sister* to them then?"

I was growing dizzy glancing between them and the air thickened with their rising tension. Distant cries continued to ring out, and I burned to join the battle so I could stop more careless blood from being spilled.

"Call off your forces," I demanded of Laviana.

Her cold sight targeted me, flaring with offense.

"Two of Auster's pets, I see."

"No, not a pet. Your star-maiden. If you don't call them off, I will."

Her stance shifted in challenge to my assertion of authority, but I would not falter. Not anymore.

"Then do what you have to," she said.

A fist remained wrapped around my heart, and it gave a squeeze at her declaration—her firming stance, ready to fight me. Would this always be a curse of war—friends turning into foes on the battlefield?

"She's telling the truth," Tarran called. "The dragon can't be freed right now."

"At least we know where it is, and Astraea is going to fetch what we need. It's not a wasted trip when we'll eliminate a band of Auster's forces in the meantime."

"I don't want to hurt you," I said with a plea in my quiet voice.

It only made Laviana smirk, as if I were an insect she would flick out of her way to join the battle behind me.

"I don't want to hurt you either. But I won't regret it if you leave me no choice."

"Go," I hissed under my breath to Tarran.

He slid a look to me and whatever he read on my face made him nod and take in Laviana one more time with a note of disturbance; then he left.

"Once a coward, always one," Laviana muttered, watching his retreat.

As she stepped forward, so did the eight soldiering vampires with her. For a while now I'd been building the magick in my palms, letting it heat to a prickling sensation through my veins. With her next step, I unleashed my first attack—a blast of violet light that threw them all back. Some hit the trees hard, a few fell over the side of the cliff, and I had to detach my emotions from the casualties.

Harnessing Lightsdeath was the only way to triumph here.

Alone on the cliff, I looked out at the beautiful, snowy mountainscape, sparkling with the moonlight. The central city was so distant from here, but the more Lightsdeath took over . . . everything glittered.

It was only now that I remembered why I loved to dance so much. My body was an instrument and my magick a song. As one would thrash a bow across the strings of a violin, my arms and legs moved, channeling magick like notes, building a melody of heartache and devastation. The snow that had fallen peacefully was awoken from the ground to storm again. Storm for *me*.

The world was bathed in starlight and moonshine. A glittering mono-chrome vessel of life, death, and souls. I didn't fight the rage of power that whispered through my thoughts and burned through my blood. I *listened* to Lightsdeath and joined with it.

When my dance stopped, I turned around, staring up at a huge wolf made of pure starlight towering over me. Its massive form shimmered with an oth-erworldly glow that spilled over the ground in waves of silver and violet. The wolf's head rose above the treetops, its glowing silver eyes twin to mine, await-ing command. The forest was hushed, every creature silent, as if the world itself dared not break the spell. I stood, small beneath the wolf's starlit shadow, but charge of the colossal creature was mine.

"Astraea . . ."

I found the voice that whispered my name and found a shadowless vampire with black and white hair who peeled herself from the ground, staring at me with horror I delighted in. As I approached her, she staggered back, not looking at me but at the giant, looming beast that followed. Reacting to everything I did. The beast was *me*.

For some reason I faltered. Stopping before reaching the shadowless, I contemplated her for a moment.

A loud roar rattled the night sky. The wolf and I looked up, seeing a stroke of darkness cut across the constellations. An impulse to drown that soaring shadow in starlight itched my skin.

So I left the insignificant vampire and headed toward the heart of the chaos where the darkness was headed.

The wolf passed through the trees without harming the precious nature. Breaking through the tree line, we came to an opening with snow as red as it was white.

Vampires, celestials, even some fae fought and fell. I couldn't see bodies anymore, only souls in varying degrees of brightness, and I wanted to cancel out the darkest ones: those that had become nearly black, so there would be no redeeming them now.

The vicious battle started to cease as, one by one, friend and foe acknowledged the face of their reaping.

So many dark souls.

The wolf . . . attacked.

I followed as the souls scattered, trying to outrun their fate. The first dark soul to be reaped struck my chest like a brand and I cried, folding into myself with the pain until it faded. I barely got the chance to recover before another speared me. Then another. I took long, gasping breaths.

This was my purpose.

So I straightened and kept going.

The wolf continued to tear through the darkest first.

Another ear-piercing roar made me recoil, and I spun to eliminate the creature before it could distract me again.

Until I came face to face with the blackest soul on the entire field.

The longer I stared, the more I saw a true face forming through the shadows.

He was so devastatingly beautiful that it stirred a conflict within me, forcing me to fight the instinct to kill him. He just stood there, staring wideeyed, assessing me and the wolf, which had stopped its slaughter to face this being too.

"Astraea." His voice . . . the magick and aura that hummed from him felt like a dark duet with the song that weaved through me now.

I shook my head to expel the distraction. Something changed on his alluring face that turned awe and concern into fear and calculation.

He amended, "Lightsdeath."

That name flared inside me, and I smiled to it.

The wolf of starlight growled behind me, within me; it was priming to devour this soul it could hardly stand to be near.

He seemed to know death was coming for him, and despite all his darkness,
he didn't have the power to contend with it. Not anymore. I thought maybe he
once had, but something had changed in him. I became fascinated, and it seemed
a waste to end him so soon.

"I'm right here," he said, as if those words could soothe the storm coming
for him.

I advanced slowly, but he didn't retreat. The closer I got, the more I became
entranced by the swirling dark mass within him. Something about him pulled
me closer, made me search his soul deeper, as if to find . . . a light.

It was so small and precious, like a star deep in a depthless sky. It wasn't
smothered; it was protected.

I wanted to reach into him and pull it out. He let me walk right up to him
with the wolf behind me. He didn't run like the others. Instead, he approached
me too.

"The darkest night," I whispered, lifting a hand to his chest.

His body tensed and a hiss escaped from him. I was hurting him. The light
burned through the dark. Yet still he didn't run. His hand lifted to my cheek,
and I wanted to feel it.

"My brightest star."

I was captured by his eyes, so brilliant and blazing despite the whorls of
shadow that made his soul. His lips found mine . . . and the night shattered
the stars.

My immediate repulsion dissolved with the scent that soothed my pain.
The warmth that comforted my anger. The name that severed the control
Lightsdeath had over me.

"Nyte," I whimpered, incredulous, against his lips.

Had I died again? Had I done something terrible in my irrepressible state?

"I've got you, Starlight."

"It's not real. You can't be here."

"I'm real, Astraea; I'm right here."

He kissed my forehead and I cried. I broke. My knees gave out, but he
caught me. His hold was so strong and sure, but my mind struggled to believe
this wasn't a trick I would wake from.

What a beautiful dream, I thought. *After all my nightmares, this is such a
beautiful dream.*

But in a world of monsters, dreams were always illusionary, and nightmares were reality. All it took was catching a glimpse of the crimson-tipped arrow over Nyte's shoulder aimed for his heart, to make Lightsdeath surge to the surface and take over once again to save him.

22

Nyte

I'd just reached Astraea through the overwhelming force of Lightsdeath, but something made me lose her to that power again, so fast I couldn't help her.

Even as the air around her began to crackle with raw energy, I held onto her, feeling the heat of her magick thrumming against my skin. She was radiant, a blazing force, as her magick surged up and out, wrapping her in a halo of blinding light that pulsed like a heartbeat. She looked almost otherworldly, fierce and untouchable, every inch of her glowing as though she'd swallowed the stars.

But her bright silver eyes were sharp; fury was carved into her expression with a cold, determined edge. She wasn't just angry—she was ready to unleash whatever storm was building within her. I felt a chill as I looked behind me to see what had seized her furious attention.

She held an arm outstretched; a tendril of light snaked around an arrow that would have struck through my heart . . . and killed me.

Scenting Astraea's blood on the arrow tip washed me with horror; a kind of real terror I'd never felt before slithered through my core.

Because I could die. *Truly* die.

There was a certain relief with that enlightenment. A sense of mortality I'd never had before that made everything in this world seem so much more precious. It made this woman in my arms that much more desperately fragile to me. No, not her; *I* was fragile.

Astraea, harnessing Lightsdeath, used her magick to splinter the arrow, which dropped into the snow, leaving us facing off with Auster Nova.

"Rainyte."

The moment he called my name, a rush of pure rage-filled loathing washed over me.

In my next breath, I stepped through the void, gripped Auster by his clothing, and reached to unleash my full merciless vengeance through Nightsdeath.

Until I felt nothing but an emptiness where that shadow being once resided in my mind. The voice I'd battled with all my life, against its taunts and dark notions, it was silent.

Auster *smiled*. As if he knew.

That curve of his mouth only made my hatred burn hotter. Pushing aside my confusion, I reached for the dangerous ability in me that was my birthright. Auster choked when I shattered clean through his mental barrier, and I threw his body carelessly into the thick snow.

"I don't need anything but breath to make you suffer for all you've done," I snarled, pacing around him like a wild beast.

Now that I had him, I didn't know where to begin. I wanted to hurt him in so many sinister ways that would make the most deplorable man blanch. I wouldn't kill him, not unless Astraea asked me to, since his death was hers to claim first.

"I have a piece of the key," Auster said, as if it could be a bargaining chip.

Too bad for him that it only surged my fury to be reminded of the weapon he'd killed Astraea with. The haunting flashes of memory of when he'd speared it through her right in front of me, keeping me helpless behind a fucking veil to watch . . . it made me so unhinged in my vehemence that I didn't know when I'd kneeled, nor how many times my fists had slammed into his face before they were split and bloody.

"Stop," Astraea's voice was the only thing to reach me through my place of endless violence. I pushed back to my feet, panting and staring at Auster's bloodied face that was still too intact for my satisfaction.

I forced myself to look at Astraea, who was utterly enchanting, still glowing with the power of Lightsdeath, a goddess that demanded fealty.

"Get up," she said to Auster, who lay catching his breath and spitting out blood.

Auster managed to roll over. "Dusk and Dawn will walk among us soon. You won't stand a chance in this war."

Every time this bastard spoke touched a specific trigger in me that made me want to split the world apart and watch him burn in the cracks.

Before my snapped restraint could register with me, I was upon Auster again, hauling his pitiful form up off the ground, only to plunge into his mind to know what he was talking about.

I didn't expect the first thing I found to be my father. But once it was . . . I knew exactly where he was.

I dropped Auster to fall back into the snow. My eyes were wide, staring at nothing at all, as the plan involving my father that could very well already be in motion swirled in my mind. When I came around from my initial shock,

I was about to dive back into his thoughts for more answers, but Astraea cut in first.

"I said *get up*." Astraea commanded her violet light to snake around Auster this time, forcing his body off the ground. "I want you to face me when I kill you. I want you to fly with me so I can tear out your wings and drop you from the heavens."

As much as that pleased me to hear, I knew this was Lightsdeath taking over her thoughts and feeding her merciless violence. Astraea in her true mind would be heartbroken at this confrontation despite all Auster had done to her. She was too pure-hearted and could never forget their long friendship before the betrayal.

She'd never have peace if she killed him as Lightsdeath.

"Astraea. Starlight." I tried to reach her true mind gently, but with my first step she warned me away with a searing sheet of light across my path.

Steel clanged and grew closer; the battle raged once more between the vampires and the celestials. I saw Drystan fighting, but occasionally his darting gaze revealed that he didn't know who his enemies were until they attacked him. Nadia had less hesitation, targeting only the celestials.

Shit. Astraea could handle herself; I knew this, yet I was torn wondering if she wanted, *needed,* me to help bring her back from Lightsdeath before she did something there would be no taking back. Only I knew how deep the claws of such an entity as Lightsdeath sunk into the very core of her being, especially with her storm of anger and retribution.

"Save my people, Rainyte," Astraea said. She watched my contemplation, and in her bright eyes, I understood.

There were no sides on this small battlefield to her; they were all her people, and she was asking me to end it, while she ended Auster.

I bowed my head, accepting that order. She was my mate, my queen, my goddess.

Blinking through the void, I swiped up a sword from one of the fallen and plunged it into the gut of an unsuspecting soulless. Then I became spellbound by my blade and this dance of reaping souls. It all came pouring out of me and I couldn't stop, losing track of Astraea physically, though she was eternally within me. I was so fucking *livid* I didn't know if I would ever feel lighter after all that had been bottled inside me.

I might have been known for being merciless and ruthless, but there were few times I got to unleash my pain and retribution for all that was done to me by my father. And for a fate that tried time and time again to steal the one thing I *needed* to feel a heartbeat in my cold chest and know I harbored a soul worth *something.*

Worth *her*.

If the world had to break apart for me to keep Astraea, then so be it.

My steel drowned in crimson, and I watched the blood drip off it, staining the pure snow. Bodies stopped advancing, and only then did I survey around to gauge why. I was surrounded by death and gore, but those who remained standing weren't looking at me any longer. Their faces paled and eyes turned wide as they retreated backward, tracking something tall behind me.

I felt it within myself first. Then I heard a cracking, felt it beneath my feet. Turning around, I couldn't believe what I was seeing.

The ground came alive. Blue strokes of paint became animated, taking a form that slowly pulled itself from the land it had long been entombed in. I watched in utter fascination as the dragon painting drew breath and became leathery flesh, awakening from its long slumber.

"I will never tire of seeing this," Drystan said, close by me now.

Athebyne's red form peeked over the treetops in another clearing, but Eltanin was right here. He'd freed another of his kin. The blue dragon gave a distinctive roar, a higher pitch than Athebyne's or Eltanin's.

"She's magnificent," Drystan said.

"How do you know it's a she?"

"The females don't have horns."

I'd never noticed that and how it made Eltanin differ from Athebyne. For this wondrous moment in history, battle on the ground didn't exist. But in the sky . . .

A bright collision stole my attention as I realized Astraea battled Auster with unfaltering might above us. I knew she was far more powerful than him, but sometimes all it took was the right precision strike to win.

The blue dragon threw its head back as if watching Astraea and Auster too. Then its roar mixed with a shriek that pierced my ears, causing everyone to wince. We had to shield our eyes next when its wings cast out and sent powerful gusts of wind that threatened to knock all of us off balance as it took flight.

"Where is she going?" Nadia asked.

Dread twisted in him as the blue dragon looked to be heading toward Astraea.

No, not Astraea. The dragon pivoted when space stretched between Auster and Astraea, heading for . . .

"The dragon chose Auster," Drystan breathed in disbelief.

"Why? He has wings!" Nadia cried bitterly.

"They don't choose by species; they go where they feel needed."

I couldn't believe my eyes when Astraea struck Auster hard with her violet light, tumbling his flight. Then the blue dragon *caught him*.

"That bastard," Nyte seethed under his breath.

The dragon's roar shook the stars, and it began to fly away. It was small with an incredible speed that took the cowardly retreating Auster Nova away from Astraea's vengeance fast.

Nyte thought the battle was over, until Astraea began to chase.

23

Astraea

I didn't want to harm the beautiful blue dragon, but when it kept carrying Auster, darting with him to avoid my attempts to knock him off, frustration turned me ruthless.

Gathering a bigger force of light, I projected it toward the dragon instead. It slammed into its side, and the dragon roared its pain, knocked violently off course, which threw Auster off its back.

I didn't waste a breath, diving after him, and when I touched him, I pulled us both through the void.

When the shadows dispersed and our feet felt ground, I summoned enough magick to clash with Auster's lightning. My attack was quick, pushing distance between us.

We both let go, panting to catch our breath, but the air was thick with our heartache and tension.

Auster surveyed the wreckage around him with loathing plastered on his face. I'd brought us to the destruction of his castle, but the devastation didn't end here. His entire province had suffered because of him.

"Why did you bring us here?"

"To remind you of all you've done. You've made a ruin of your lands and an enemy of me." Auster's rage climbed to frightening heights over the accusation I threw and those brown eyes speared me with it.

"You are the cause!" He spat.

I shook my head, despising the *pity* I felt for him after all he'd done.

"I am your blame. But every path you took toward your own spiral of madness was *your* choice."

"You think yourself so mighty and pure when even the gods who created you see your failure to your duty. You were to be a beacon of hope, an example of perfect order, for the people. Instead, you became a symbol of corruption. A rebellious leader with a poisonous influence that had to be stopped."

"I pity you, Auster Nova. To be so alone and power hungry that you ruined everything you could have had."

"You made me this way!"

"More blame. You don't even realize your deflection is a double-edged blade. Killing yourself as much as you tried to kill me."

"Enough of your judgmental words. I can hardly stand to look at you."

Auster's blue lightning broke across his fingers, and I formed a wall of light to deflect his first attack. Then we unleashed our centuries-worth of anguish. We attacked using the shards of our ages long friendship. The love we once harbored for each other turned into knives to bleed each other dry.

I needed the turmoil of him out of my bones, drained from my blood, once and for all. I didn't want to emerge from this battle unscathed when in some ways he was right, and I did blame myself for what he became. With every collision of our magick, I mourned him. Perhaps if I'd been honest sooner, tried to explain in another way why I chose Nyte, but it didn't mean I abandoned Auster, things could have turned out differently. I never wanted to choose between them. I didn't want to believe Auster would *make* me choose.

Tears swam in my eyes, but my movements never faltered. We staggered over the debris of the Nova castle while the night darkened and thunder boomed across the sky with every strike of our power. As if the world were mourning with us. Two lifelong friends turned enemies and only one could emerge from this fight. I wasn't giving up my second life to the one who took my first.

We were a devastating dance of storm and starlight, and our magick was the song building toward a desolate, tragic ending. As we edged closer to each other, Auster was faltering. From the beginning of our fight he wasn't as strong as he should have been, and I could see the panic in his eyes as he wondered why his magick wasn't conjuring as strong as I'd expected.

But his will to survive drove his reckless madness, and his next strike hit my shoulder, sending me sprawling. The strike itself wouldn't have been enough to wound me except the ground was a deadly plane as well. Something impaled my side and I cried out.

Auster marched toward me, pulling a knife with a blade of dried crimson blood free. It had to be Nyte's, and Auster was more than capable of killing me again.

I scrambled to my feet. Adrenaline drove me to grip the wood lodged in me and pull without thinking. The pain threatened my consciousness, but I blinked the darkness away, stumbling over broken stone and wood to gain distance. Time.

Lightsdeath was a pacing white wolf inside me, but I wouldn't let it out. Not yet. This fight meant too much for me to not be aware of what I was doing. After all we'd been through, I needed every memory from our beginning to our end.

"We could have had everything, *been* everything," Auster said, clinging to his hatred.

"Your jealousy ruined us," I said through a pained breath, clutching my bleeding side.

"I was jealous, yes. How could I not be? *I*, not he, was perfect for you. You stood to gain everything: love, a powerful bond, and a long reign over Solanis while I lost everything."

"You were a High Celestial with power over your own province, which I could never take away. You could have found love with someone else. Power drove you to madness."

"Not power itself. The fact you handed it, on a damn silver platter, to the one who had terrorized our land after you spread your legs for him," he seethed.

Those words seeped into me like poison and I lashed out. The flare of light from my palm slammed into his chest while he was caught unawares and he went flying back. His wings unglamoured to catch him in time, sparing him from injury like that I'd sustained from a tumble to the ground.

Auster retaliated with two fingers pointing toward me, and strokes of blue lightning surged toward me. The attack was so weak that I barely used any of my own magick to smother it. Auster stood there in fury and confusion, glancing down at his hands.

"Something wrong?" I taunted.

His jaw locked and he summoned lightning over both palms. He couldn't hold it for long and it faded out.

"What is happening . . . ?" he muttered to himself.

"The nightmares didn't go away, I see. You've been taking that sleeping tonic every night, haven't you?"

Confusion deepened the furrow of his brow. A breathy laugh broke from my lips.

I said, "I didn't think it would work. Or at least I thought you would surely start to feel it before it could truly affect you."

"What are you talking about?" he snapped.

I relished the triumph that straightened my spine.

"The nebulora I added to your sleeping tonic. I tested it first at the wedding feast you forced me to attend in the castle, putting drops in your wine to see if you would detect the taste. You didn't. So I met with your courtesan and bribed her to add it to your sleeping tonic ever since. It's been slowly numbing your power."

When that revelation sank in, it was like every display of fury he'd shown before was nothing compared to what snapped his resolve completely now.

Auster's roar of outrage and disbelief rattled through me, and lightning exploded from him.

I managed to form a shield of defense before it hit me, but it shot far and wide. Hitting distant buildings to crumble his once prosperous land further and striking the heavens to break a violent rainstorm.

His power snuffed out all at once and I released mine. Auster couldn't summon his lightning again; that explosion of violent anguish was the last of his reserves, but he wasn't giving up. Not even close.

The rain started to drown us, and he pulled his mighty sword free. The way he marched for me, his hair unbound with wet strands clinging around his wild eyes, was truly frightening. In all the times I'd faced him in combat, I had still seen the man I once knew and loved beneath all the resentment and hatred; now he was gone. Simply a hollow vessel of all his transgressions and pain, and I was his one true target to blame.

I didn't have a sword, and I only tracked his purple blade with sharp focus to avoid its path. He was so fast it took everything I had, and I would have been lighter on my feet were it not for the uneven ground.

Auster expended himself with powerful throws of agony through his blade, but when they sliced nothing but air, that pain backfired. His face of pure rage slowly started to fall to defeat and misery. That's when I gripped the handle of my dagger at my thigh, gritting my teeth since it was hardly adequate to meet his blade, but our steel cried against one another anyway.

It distracted him, drawing his eyes to the waved stormstone blade, and his attention was stolen by the memory of gifting it to me so long ago.

I had to take my opening. This had to end here.

My magick engulfed his sword, turning it to stardust, and when I lunged forward our wide stares locked on each other.

Time slowed to a crawl.

Auster's stunned and terrified face tore me apart. But even as tears flooded my vision, I gritted my teeth, twisting the waved dagger in his heart. He choked, blood spilling from his mouth, and we both crashed to our knees.

"You were my best friend," I croaked.

His breaths staggered, and I tuned into each one toward his last. The final threads of attachment to him in my soul split during the countdown.

Auster raised a shaky hand, and my first tear spilled to merge with the rain rolling down my face.

"You were my everything," he said.

My heart didn't get the chance to fracture when a pain so all-consuming pierced my stomach. I looked down as Auster's hold on the small dagger slipped and so did my grip on the handle protruding from his chest.

He fell, glass eyes held on the sky as his chest deflated for the last time. A ringing filled my ears and my shaky hands hovered over the small blade that wouldn't have been fatal . . . it wouldn't have been so damning . . . had it not been for Nyte's blood on it.

It wasn't pierced through my heart but panic overcame me that it could still kill me truly.

I found the will to pull the knife out. It was small, but that didn't matter. The wound hurt far worse than the bigger object that had pierced my side. It slipped from my trembling hand.

A dragon roared with a higher pitch conveying pain. I barely managed to flick my sight up as it came in and out of focus, but at the flash of blue falling from the sky, horror shook me.

The blue dragon landed and wailed again; the intensity of it hit me in a gust of wind from her breath. She came so close, sniffing at Auster's body with smaller cries rattling from her. Her head nudged him, but he was lifeless.

For some reason, she'd chosen Auster as her rider. I couldn't understand why this small, delicate dragon would want to bond with someone so wicked. Though perhaps she saw, *felt,* that he wasn't always so.

Discovering he couldn't be saved, she lifted her head and those beautiful blue eyes targeted me. It was then I heard a wonderful name.

Edasich.

My awe quickly turned to fear when she reared up, rattling and crying, preparing to attack me in her heartbreak.

Just as she wailed louder like a declaration before her strike, I plunged deep within myself, summoning an unexplainable voice to speak to her.

"No." It was a single word with the weight of absolute dominance. I didn't know how I had this ability to command dragons, but shit, I was grateful for it right now.

Edasich backed away a few steps, her instinct for vengeance subsiding under my command.

"I'm sorry," I whispered.

I didn't just drown in sorrow for her loss but mine as well. Auster had been a pivotal part of my life; in reflection we had more tender, joyous memories than cruel. For the man he was, I mourned for him. Curling into myself while my body was wracked with sobs, wishing things could have been different.

In part I blamed the gods, my creators, for what Auster became. Their influence in his mind was nothing but a poison of resentment and superiority. And for that I wasn't finished with Auster. I would carry his name until I ended the gods once and for all.

Rising on shaky legs, I didn't look back at the blue dragon curling around Auster's body as I shuffled away. My next step slipped on a piece of sodden wood and I crumpled.

I have to get up.

There was only one face, one name, that I pictured endlessly in my thoughts. Nyte had come for me. Had he been real?

Believing he was gave me the strength to rise.

He'd come back to me.

My wings splayed, ready to take me to the skies, but my consciousness was slipping.

I had to make it back to him.

My wings carried me, but more strenuous than the ache of moving my body was fighting against my mind shutting down. I was so tired. My hand clamped tightly over the wound Auster inflicted, and all that kept my wings beating hard was my panic that I could be dying. As soon as Nyte's blood reached my heart . . . my death would be permanent this time.

I'd slain my monster and still he won. Determined to drag me to hell right behind him.

The clouds were thick and wet, still shedding their sorrow to the land with hard rainfall.

My body was so heavy. *So terribly heavy.*

Nyte. Nyte. Nyte.

My eternal night.

He was all around me. I was all around him. I drifted through the endless night and brilliant stars. Then I was falling through it.

24

Nyte

I mounted Eltanin, and we took to the skies as quickly as we could, following Astraea from the temple, yet she'd gained an impossible distance away from us so fast and I knew then she had to have used the void for some reason.

Desperation to reach her pounded through my blood. Eltanin flew fast and mighty, a stroke of shadow through the night storm that broke. We cut through the rain that fell mercilessly. Astraea was still fighting; the echoes of her anguish and rage pulsed through me.

Then the world stood still. My next breath held as I straightened at the phantom eruption of pain in my side.

Astraea's pain.

A roar of wrath and vengeance tore through me and Eltanin. I leaned forward as the dragon flew *faster.*

"No," I breathed. Because it wasn't just any mortal wound.

That bastard wasn't getting to take her from me again.

I didn't know how far we'd flown as I followed our bond to her. She was close now.

So close.

I found her with a strike of terror in my soul.

Astraea plummeted through the air. I scanned around as if something had struck her, but Auster wasn't in the skies. I reared up on Eltanin.

"Fly!" I yelled. I didn't think he could go any faster, but Eltanin did, and we dived to catch our falling star

She was too far away. Falling too fast. *She is out of my reach.*

The taunts circled my mind as the rain slashed my skin and blurred my vision.

"Come on," I snarled.

She was so. Fucking. Close.

When Eltanin dipped again, challenging his ability to fly low, Astraea was right above us and I'd never felt relief like I did when my arms wrapped around her. Capturing her tightly to me with my legs clamping tighter around the saddle. Eltanin strained to glide up again but couldn't make it without pummeling into the tops of some trees. Astraea's wings hung limp over the saddle sides, but I shielded her body with mine, curling into her as sharp branches tore at my arms and face and legs. It didn't matter. So long as she was safe now.

Eltanin managed to clear the trees and climb high again, and once we broke through the clouds and I could let go of my strenuous purchase on the saddle, I straightened, scanning Astraea for injuries.

Noticing the rise and fall of her chest released my first sane breath.

"Nyte," she said, barely a whisper, so quiet that I thought I'd conjured it from the whistling wind in my desperation.

"I've got you. *Fuck,* I've got you." I kissed her head, and when her eyes fluttered open, everything in me slumped with utter relief.

"You're alive," she croaked.

"I'm alive. We're both alive."

Astraea's hand reached weakly over my chest.

"You're real," she whispered, her eyes glittered with tears, and the first one to fall was like a knife dragged over my heart. "You came back."

"As long as you're here," I said, resting my hand over hers. "I'll always come back to you."

It was the kind of vow that felt almost too fragile for this world, a quiet assurance that transcended distance, even time. And though I knew there would be moments of silence, stretches when she might feel further away, the simple truth of my words was anchoring for both of us.

Gods, I missed her so agonizingly.

Unbuttoning my jacket, I untucked my shirt as the only measure I could think of to help her right now. Her soft sigh when her palm flattened on my bare abdomen was a sound I'd bleed to hear. Her other joined it and I tensed at her frozen touch, but I would endure every measure of pain she was going through now if I could take it all from her.

"Can you glamour your wings? It'll be more comfortable until we get to land," I said gently.

Her face pinched to attempt the glamour and she cried softly, trying not to by biting her lip as her body locked.

"So brave," I murmured, kissing her head and shifting to hold her closer now that her wings were gone.

"I missed you," she said sleepily. "I missed you so much I was dying from it."

"I know. *Gods,* I know. I have you in my arms and I still fucking miss you."

"It worked . . . ? Nightsdeath . . ."

"Is gone. You brought me back."

Astraea watched the stars, her eyes glistening, and I watched her, entranced by the most perfect creature to exist. Right now, she appeared so precious it hurt. I traced a cut along her cheek, and she leaned into my touch. Every mark I found on her built on a need to inflict them a hundred times more on whoever caused them.

"I'm scared . . ." she whispered, haunted.

My sight raked down her body to where her hand pressed against her stomach. Her pale hand drowned in crimson almost made me lose my damned mind. Not just from the wound but from the all-consuming terror that came back to me.

"What happened, Starlight?"

I dreaded hearing the answer I already knew from the cry within my soul.

"The blade, it . . . it had your blood on it."

My world shifted. Cracked. And it took everything in me not to fall into the depths of the despair that clawed from it.

"You're going to be okay," I said. The dark delusion was both cruel and defiant. "You're still here; that must mean something. You're staying with me."

Astraea nodded weakly, and all I could do was hold her despite the terror coiling between us.

"The key piece Auster had was a fake. There are still fifteen temples left we need to search to find all the real pieces," she informed.

"I don't care about the key," I said, stroking her hair. "Auster, is he . . . ?"

"Dead."

Though I rejoiced to that, I couldn't fully bask in it when, despite all he'd done, the bastard's death caused her pain. It was a certain kind of torment to want to kill what was already dead. To loathe someone who was gone so much I wanted to rip into the Nether just to kill him again.

"You did what you had to do. He was never going to stop. He never would have let you go," I consoled.

"I know. I just wish things hadn't turned out this way."

My wish was that the threats against us died with Auster, but the truth was, we were far from done fighting for our peace. For the happiness we deserved. My father was in pursuit of freeing the gods to walk our lands. Two spiteful entities, who would come for Astraea with more ruthlessness than Auster.

"Nyte," she whispered, touching my face so tenderly.

"Starlight."

Her brow crumpled. In the silence that ticked by, with her tender touches and the thoughtful flickers over her features, she was processing that I was truly here.

After I'd left her for a *month*.

"I'm sorry I wasn't here with you," I said, tucking away the wild strands of her hair that whipped across her tired face.

Astraea gripped my jacket. "Don't ever do that again."

She swallowed hard, a soft whimper left her, then she pulled me down to kiss her.

Every misery became insignificant within the wrap of her affection. She didn't know that she was my shield for survival, when I never felt stronger, more filled with purpose, than in every moment of her yearning for me.

Breaking the kiss, she tucked into me tightly and I held her.

"You bonded with Eltanin," she mumbled into me.

"I'm still in shock about it."

"I'm not. Ever since I first held him it was like I could feel you. I think even then I knew he wasn't mine, not in the way he was destined to be yours."

"He's ours," I promised.

Her silver eyes peered up at me with sorrow furrowed between her brows. "Your wings . . ."

I tipped her chin back, kissing her softly.

"I don't care."

That only seemed to drop her expression more and I ached with it.

"That's not right," she said quietly, as if I wasn't meant to hear it. "Your pain and suffering are not right. You speak of it as if it should be, and I want to make your father and this world pay for it."

"Astraea . . . it's not that I believe it's right, it's that I don't care about any of it anymore because everything I've suffered brought me to you in the end. I'd walk every dark path again and again so long as it always led to you."

She kissed me again. Every time she reached for me with a call, a touch, a kiss, I was reminded of the treasure that could be found in the darkest suffering. Her face burrowed into my neck, and her scent healed the broken threads of my soul that had frayed from being parted from her.

"Fuck, I missed you," I muttered again. Every inch of her wrapped around me was what completeness felt like. Two undeniably perfect pieces fit back together.

"I feared you'd never come back," she whispered.

"There's not a realm or time I won't fight with everything I am to make it back to you."

It was a relief to see the spire of Nadir's home. Our whole flight I was antsy, monitoring her heartbeat and breath. Both were labored but still strong considering her wounds.

Astraea teased me over my fussing, but I knew she was trying to hide her pain, both physical and within.

"Oh my—*Nyte!?*" My name came out in a squeak from Davina when she looked at me. "You're . . . you're walking! You're awake!"

"I sure hope I am," I said.

Her gaze widened, skimming over Astraea.

"What happened?" Davina cried.

"She needs Lilith's help, now."

"We've been coming up with all kinds of reckless plans to come for you since Drystan left with Nyte," Lilith said, rushing across the yard to meet them.

She assessed Astraea as I carried her hurriedly into Nadir's home.

Inside, I didn't take her to the table; she needed warmth. Nadir straightened from their lounging position by the fire as I kneeled to lay Astraea on the rug in front. Davina fetched pillows, and Lilith began cutting away Astraea's clothing to better tend to the wounds.

"My blood was on the blade," I informed them.

Lilith's eyes snapped up and the fear in them rocked through me anew.

When she peeled back the layers around Auster's dagger wound . . . the whole room spun. Her skin had turned gray around the thin stab site, webbing-thin vines like those of a leaf reaching over her ribs.

"What does it mean?" I asked desperately.

The terror only grew in Lilith's soft eyes when she looked at me.

"I think . . . I think it's like poison. These vines will continue to grow, and when they reach her heart . . ."

No. I didn't accept that.

"How do we make it stop?" I asked with deceptive calm. When no one answered I growled under my breath, cutting my wrist with my teeth.

Lilith's small hand lashed out to stop me before I could give Astraea my blood.

"That might only make her worse now . . . considering it's your blood that's harming her. Drinking it now could trigger a counter effect to the healing properties it once had."

I looked Astraea over with absolute desolation. Yet she smiled for me, running her touch up my arm.

"How long do I have?" she asked Lilith.

Her friend's brow pulled together with a wash of devastation. Lilith examined the wound more closely for a few long, tense minutes.

"It's not spreading too fast. Three weeks, maybe less."

Astraea blew out a long breath, contemplating her thoughts with her distant sight on the dark, wooden roof.

"Then we need to get moving to stop the gods sooner rather than later." She played the situation off so nonchalantly while I was silently losing my gods-damned mind.

"Never mind that. We going to find a fucking cure."

"Nyte—"

"No. You don't have three weeks, Astraea. You have eternity with me."

Again, she smiled, but she couldn't hide the weight of her doubt. She might accept her time was draining, but I would never.

I let Lilith tend to Astraea while I had to stand, to pace, to begin to figure out how in the hell to save her this time.

"I'm so glad you made it back to us. Even if you are a moody pain in my ass," Davina said tenderly.

There was hardly a breath of warmth in my attempt to smile.

Then someone descended the narrow stairs, and just for a second my grief switched focus.

Elliot was here. The sole survivor of the Golden Guard.

He tried to smile but didn't approach. "Welcome back."

I was slashed with pain so sudden and immediate. The sorrow on his face matched what I felt within. We reflected on the same grim event of being ambushed in the mountains by an attack sent by my father. The vampires had managed to kill Sorleen, Zeik, and Kerrah: the rest of the Golden Guard.

Before I lost Nightsdeath, it would have been easy to use that power to smother any care or feeling. I would have been able to live with the loss of the only people I'd just begun to consider *friends*. Now, I didn't have such darkness to hide in. I couldn't thrust the agony of loss and fear of losing again into the shadowy depths to numb my mind to keep. Fucking. Going.

This vulnerability that had opened in me was so raw and . . . *frightening*. I didn't think I was afraid of anything unless it concerned Astraea's life, but here I was, starting to fear myself and what my emotions could do to me.

The front door burst open before I could begin to process anything. It was only Drystan.

"That was close!" he announced obnoxiously.

Feeling my tangible ire from the fright he inspired, Drystan gave a grimace as an apology.

"What happened with Laviana and Tarran?" Astraea asked, pushing through her fatigue as Nadir propped more pillows behind her.

"There wasn't much of either force left, celestials or vampires, to keep going. It was all a pointless waste of life." Drystan shrugged out of his cloak, seeming at home here, which enlightened me more to the fact all of them had spent a lot of time here while I lay useless.

Astraea explained what had happened and how Auster Nova was dead. It killed me to feel her sorrow when the bastard deserved a far fucking worse death than what he got.

"He's finally dead," Drystan muttered, mostly to himself.

"The city needs a ruler before word spreads," Davina said.

"We have to retrieve the key; I won't sit pretty on a throne keeping it warm and waiting as idle bait for the gods to come for me," Astraea said. Her silver-blue eyes cast to me and my spine locked. "You need to rule when I'm gone, so maybe—"

I didn't feel the ornament in my possession, but the room turned sharp when it shattered against a wall, thrown with a flash of rage I couldn't contain. I had to take a few calming breaths.

"Do you really think I could stand to rule this continent if you were no longer on it?" I said; a familiar, villainous darkness spread through me. "No, Astraea. I'd sooner rip it apart."

She scolded me with a look I found adorable.

"When you're gone?" Drystan echoed.

I could hardly stand to keep hearing the reiteration of Auster Nova's parting curse.

I tuned out everyone's conversation, sitting by Astraea's side and soothing some of the sharp panic in me with her touch.

"You need to rest," Astraea said gently as if she could feel my racing emotions.

Lilith was almost finished with her bandages.

"These will stay in place well enough for you to bathe," she informed. Astraea would want to wash the blood and dirt from her skin after the ordeal.

"We'll meet here in the morning hours to discuss how to get to all these temples to get the key back," Drystan said, accepting a pipe from Nadir and taking a long inhale. "We all need as good a rest as we can get. Something tells me we're going to miss the month you were asleep and we all hung around in our boredom, considering what we face next."

Just as I helped Astraea stand, as she refused to be carried, I sensed the intrusion before the front door swung open.

Zath and Rose stumbled to a halt as the door locked out the winter chill behind them. They both gawked from Astraea to me.

"Thank fuck," Zath muttered, marching across the room.

I intercepted him, knowing his natural response would be to all but throw himself at her in embrace.

"She's gravely injured," I warned. Then I stepped aside.

Zath approached more tentatively, his expression shifting between pain and relief as he scanned her over.

Astraea hugged him, though it hurt her, and I was on edge with an irrational want to rip Zath's arms off for it.

"I'm so damn relieved you're okay. Leaving you behind in Vesitire was the hardest thing I've had to do," Zath said.

"Thank you," she croaked. "For coming and helping to fight."

"I'd have to be dead to sit it out."

She gave a breathy chuckle. "I know."

"I can feel the heat of your stare," Zath mumbled to me.

Peeling away from Astraea, I didn't bother to smooth out my expression when he glanced back at me. Zath only smirked, which made him grimace. I looked at his wound site, but he slipped a hand over it as if I wouldn't notice he wasn't fully healed yet. That he was alive at all from the fatal sword through his gut was a miracle, even for a Nephilim. He was admirably strong willed.

"I won't take the chance of being suffocated by shadow if I tried to hug you, but shit am I glad you're awake. How did you break the curse?"

"I killed Nightsdeath," Astraea admitted quietly, letting go of Rose who'd hugged her next. I hoped her sorrow wasn't because she thought it somehow hurt me.

"What do you mean? He's right there," Rose said. Her familiar irritation around me was strangely missed.

Astraea explained everything that happened with Nightsdeath, and it tore me apart to hear it. I didn't think she admitted to all of what she suffered by *my* hand. As much as Nightsdeath wandered without me, it was merely a source of power until *I* gave it life. It was powerful enough to live without the rest of me.

The concept was difficult to digest. I wandered away from Astraea, not quite knowing how to process it all. Should I grieve? I wasn't sure. I harbored this ache that plunged soul deep, but I didn't know what it was for. Why this wretched self-pity started to fester inside me; I wanted to claw it out with my own hand.

"Nyte." Astraea's soft tone accompanied her warm hand sliding into mine from behind. Only then did I realize I was staring mindlessly right at a wall. "I'm sorry—"

"Don't," I said, it barely left me as a choked plea. "Please don't apologize to me."

"Come with me?" she offered gently, already tugging me, and I followed like a ghost.

Is that what I was now? A shell of weak parts left behind?

Did I *want* Nightsdeath back?

All my life I'd had that heinous power to blame. To use. *Shit* I used it without remorse and I *enjoyed it.*

I was Nightsdeath. In name and glory and all wicked reign.

Now it was gone . . . a part of me was truly dead.

I didn't know how I would cope without the vicious darkness holding me together. My fingers laced through Astraea's, and I squeezed absentmindedly. As if she were the only way I wouldn't float into a lost oblivion when I didn't know who I was anymore. Or perhaps more frighteningly, who I could become.

25

Nyte

Astraea slept, and while my mind spun in turmoil over leaving her just as I'd embraced her in my arms again, I couldn't shake what I'd learned about my father from Auster's mind.

I had to discover if it was true, and worse, if he'd already succeeded in his plan.

After lulling her mind into a deep sleep, hoping she wouldn't wake until I returned, I headed down to the bottom level of Nadir's home, finding the mage lounging by the fire, pipe in hand.

"I'm beginning to think you don't sleep," I commented.

"I usually catch a few hours before dawn rises. My thoughts are too important to silence for too long."

Something about them pricked the hairs over my body. Not in fear, but certainly with a note of caution.

"You're looking for your brother, I presume. He's outside with his dragon, waiting for you."

I frowned out the window but could hardly make out a thing in the thick dark. The clouds smothered the moon tonight.

"How would he know I was coming?"

"Your father needs to be stopped before the gods truly walk our lands."

I approached Nadir, staring as if they were a puzzle I couldn't figure out. "Does the plant you smoke give you clairvoyance?"

Nadir chuckled, the sound turning to a cough as they set the pipe aside. Their vivid green eyes shifted up to me. "There are many gifts in this world; we couldn't begin to comprehend them all."

I hadn't failed to notice how many hidden weapons Nadir harbored around their home. Subtle utensils made of stormstone, lethal to the vampires, or obsidian, deadly to the celestials. Various herbs disguising the cosmic plant, nebulora, also harmful to the celestials. It made me wonder what else they could be hiding, what other materials they could have discovered or created that only served to harm one species or another.

"You do not trust me," Nadir said, glancing at me like I was a book to read.

"I wouldn't trust anyone with an armory disguised as a gentle home."

Nadir smiled broadly. "Very observant."

I kept my guard firm around them, but I couldn't deny they'd been invaluable for shelter for all of us when we needed it most.

Just then, Drystan burst in through the front door. His eyes found me with relief.

"You know where Father is, don't you?"

"I think so," I said grimly.

"Then what are we waiting for—let's go eradicate one foe while we can."

"He's heading to North Star."

That straightened Drystan's posture.

I added, "If he's not already there, or worse, already been and achieved what he'd planned."

Nadir said, "He means to use the Mirror of Passage to summon the Gods of Dusk and Dawn and give them mortal forms long enough for them to kill the star-maiden."

The gravity of that fate slammed down on us all. Fury boiled in my very bones.

"We need to get there before he does," Drystan said, already marching out.

I cast one last look at Nadir as I followed my brother out, not entirely at ease leaving Astraea under their roof. But I did trust Zath and the others to protect her fiercely while she was healing and vulnerable.

Outside, we found Nadia by Athebyne, casually stroking the giant dragon's leg.

"You don't get to have this fun without me," she said, mounting by the rope hanging over the saddle.

My flat look was met with Drystan's shrug. "Another sword hand can't hurt."

"She's your responsibility," I grumbled.

Drystan smirked, heading toward his dragon. "She's her own responsibility."

The island of North Star rose like a dream from the vast expanse of the ocean, its silhouette both serene and imposing against the horizon. Small yet striking, the island was crowned with jagged, mist-cloaked mountains that stretched skyward, their peaks kissed by an eternal shimmer of starlight.

To the west, near the cliffs, ancient stone markers stood in silent rows, weathered by time but unyielding, their carvings glowing faintly with the rays of the moon. Legends whispered that these were sentinels, guarding the secrets of North Star's ethereal presence, and that the island itself was a beacon—not just for sailors lost at sea, but for those seeking the kind of truths only the stars could reveal. The temple holding the ancient Mirror of Passage stood proudly guarded by these stones.

The dragons flew low, preparing to land, and I wasn't concerned about being spotted in Althenia as this island was free land, not ruled over by any of the four High Celestials and uninhabited by mortal creatures.

North Star was where Drystan had planned to take me to cross realms through the artifact called the Mirror of Passage. It had taken a long time to discover its existence when I was searching for a way back to my birth realm. Leaving was the only solution I had left to give Astraea a chance to rebuild her world when she returned to land, but it seemed fate wasn't done with our story yet.

I had allowed myself to be tricked by my father instead, when he claimed to take me to the passage, only to trap me behind a veil under the castle's library where I remained a long, torturous century before Astraea came back to land. My father's mind was strong and guarded against my ability to infiltrate them, but that wasn't what had kept the knowledge of the passage from me. He'd found a mage capable of wiping small parts of memory, and he'd erased the location of the mirror, knowing if I found it, I could leave him anytime.

It was Drystan who had finally discovered the mage our father went to all that time ago and found the location of the mirror in North Star. Unfortunately for me, it was *after* I had been tricked into imprisonment, and Drystan despised me, dangling that knowledge before me when I was helpless to act. Then Astraea came back, and I couldn't deny a selfish part of me was glad I'd never found out where the passage was . . . the moment I saw her I knew I would watch cities burn and worlds collapse to keep her this time.

As soon as we landed, a sense of magick and dread tightened my skin. We dismounted at the same time, but all of our attention fixed on the temple between the sentinel stones.

"As pretty as this place is, I have a real chilling feeling," Nadia said, rubbing her arms.

It had nothing to do with the temperature that froze the surrounding grass and clouded their breath. The sight was breathtaking, and for a moment I was distracted by the thought of how Astraea would adore this place.

It wasn't me who was arrogant enough to stroll nonchalantly between the ancient stones toward the temple. My body tensed watching Nadia as if she might slam into an invisible shield against outsiders, but she made it right to the doors, which we all now noticed were ajar.

"We're not alone," Drystan said. Still, he headed confidently toward Nadia.

It had been wishful thinking that we'd arrive before our father to intercept this dire plan, but we might not be too late to stop him from completing it.

The metallic scent of blood drifted to us immediately past the threshold. The beauty of the outside was now tainted in sin.

At the end of the dark passage, the oppressive shadows fell away, and the space opened into a spectacular hall that seemed to breathe with life. The ceiling soared high above, an intricate mosaic of stone and light filtering down through narrow skylights, creating dapples of gold across the floor. Towering pillars stretched upward like ancient trees, their surfaces alive with climbing greenery that wound around them in an elegant embrace.

In the center of the round space, the shard of mirror loomed impossibly large, a jagged monolith of gleaming silver that caught and fractured the light into shards of brilliance. It stood embedded in the earth, its thinnest edge driven deep into the stone as if it had pierced the ground like a celestial blade. Despite its violent arrival, the surface remained eerily smooth, unmarred by cracks or imperfections, as though it defied the laws of nature itself.

The sight it reflected charged so much emotion through the air, brewing a storm of potent rage and dread.

My father turned to us from staring into the ethereal mirror; his smile spread cruelly, expectant.

"Ah, both my sons reunited with me at last," he drawled. Every note of his voice raked over my skin like knives, itching a near blinding need to slash his throat so he couldn't utter another word.

"This plan is madness," I said, tracking him carefully as I got closer.

He wasn't alone. A man and woman were on their knees at his feet. They were the source of the metallic sting in the air as they bled onto the stone, each sending a thin river of crimson running through the uneven ground as if it raced to be drunk by the colossal mirror.

A small band of vampires lingered in the corners of the room, but I was confident I could shatter their minds if they moved an inch.

That was until I felt a barrier to my ability and realized this place had to be guarded against magick abilities being used within.

My fists tightened as I recalculated. It would take more physical effort to eliminate them, a little more time, but getting to unleash the growing fury in my body physically might be somewhat relieving.

"I see you broke the gods' curse, Rainyte. It's no matter; Dusk and Dawn will achieve a more permanent solution with you when they walk among us."

"Does being your sons mean nothing to you?" Drystan yelled, a fraction of his broken child's heart slipping through.

Drystan and I aren't his only sons.

In my deep dream state . . . I didn't know whether to believe that the vivid memories I had when I awoke were just dreams, or if I had, by some miracle, travelled back to my birth realm in that time I was cursed by Dusk and Dawn.

I realized with a skip in my chest that I didn't need to walk through that mirror to have my answer when I discovered . . .

"You have another son," I stated, watching my father's every flicker of reaction. "One you left behind when you brought me here."

There it was. Confirmation in the narrowing of his eyes that was neither confusion nor denial . . . it was surprised accusation.

I'd never felt this kind of beat in my chest. Nerves, I thought, clashing with disappointment. "Not with my mother but another woman before her. That son wasn't powerful enough for you, was he? Do you want to know what became of him?"

"I don't know what you're talking about," Father spat.

"Malin Ashfyre."

Father recoiled as if it were a blade I'd thrown.

"What the fuck is going on?" Drystan hissed at me, glancing between us.

"Where did you hear that name?" Father asked, so cold and lethal.

"All that matters is that you're a shit awful father, and we're not the first to disappoint you."

"That child died."

"No. Your ruse was almost perfect. Your own brother was to be the next king, but you were nothing, a prince that wouldn't amount to anything. It drove you mad. Enough to fake your death in battle, to abandon your life and son and seek out the one with the greatest power in the land. My mother. You saved her from a tragic fate only to turn on her the moment she gave you a son prophesied to have even greater power than she. So you stole me away in the night, crossing realms with the idea that you and I would conquer another realm together. Because mother would have always reminded you how powerless you truly were. Always lesser, just like with your brother."

I didn't expect the emotions that crashed into me as if I were a rock braced upon a shore of vicious waves. I'd always had Nightsdeath to rise me above before I could drown, turning pain to anger, and it's how I knew to survive.

Now . . . I didn't know what to do with these feelings that were so hideous I wanted to claw them from my chest. I didn't want to feel betrayed or sad—*so fucking sad*. I wanted to reach for the rage that had once been so easy to let take over, inflicting all I felt inside on the world outside before it risked killing me instead.

"How do you know all this?" Father asked; the vacancy in his voice told me everything I'd experienced had been real. Everything I had impossibly discovered during my curse was the truth.

"Doesn't matter," I said, my own voice reduced to a pitiful whisper.

In some ways I related to how Astraea felt as her lost memories were returning. I harbored memories that lingered like threads of a dream—vivid but uncertain—from that month I was cursed into a deep slumber and my conscious mind projected across realms to protect itself. Or because of another meddling entity.

But it didn't matter because I had no desire to ever walk through that mirror. Everything in me, every fiber of my being, belonged right here with my Starlight.

"What I learned is that blood does not mean loyalty," my father said darkly.

"You're right," Drystan said, equally as resentful. "It's not our blood but our actions that make us stand by each other."

In those words, I thought the fraying bond between Drystan and me mended a few threads.

Our father looked at us like we were the biggest disappointment he'd faced.

He said, "It's just about time. The twelfth hour of a full moon. I didn't need you here, but I guess it is fitting you should bear witness to this world-changing event in our history."

"Now would have been a good time for you to unleash that frightening side of you," Drystan said to me.

Nightsdeath wasn't a magickal ability and would have served well here.

"Too bad we're stuck with just this frightening side of me," I said.

Drystan skimmed his eyes over me. "Fine. Do the other thing then."

"Not possible. It seems magick is warded off in here."

"You're too late to stop this." That call came in the voice of my father but his lips didn't move.

A flicker behind him drew my attention to his reflection in the mirror. To my horror, it *moved,* turning around slowly while he stayed exactly where he was, creating an eerie illusion that there were now two of him.

"As if one wasn't insufferable enough to look at," Drystan said, unsheathing his blade with an added curse.

"Nothing can stop me now. My prize for my work here is that I will become the King of the Gods."

His arrogance had truly decended to new levels of utter stupidity.

"No crown you wear will ever transform the coward trembling beneath it," I snarled.

For the first time, I regarded the two on their knees, sensing now that they weren't humans, they were celestials. When the man lifted his head . . . I couldn't sort my shock from my confusion over seeing Aquilo, the High Celestial of House Sera.

"He was captured after the battle," Drystan informed me. "Astraea removed his wings. I assume the other High Celestials had no choice but to outcast him as they do their own citizens. Honestly, I thought they might have been keeping him hidden and just kept up a pretense, but at least Nova wasn't biased in favor of his own in his merciless ruling."

"He is the perfect vessel for Dusk," Father said, glancing down at the High Celestial. Once so proud and mighty, now . . . he was nothing. As frightened and horrified as anyone would be in his situation.

I held no sympathy for him. In fact, I was twitching to claim his life right now, remembering his cruelty to Astraea. He'd *whipped* her and laughed. The echoes of it trembled through me, and if I had my full power I might not have been able to stop myself from doing whatever it took to kill him before my father could use him.

I didn't immediately recognize the woman. A beautiful blonde who hugged herself, casting pleading eyes at me as if I could save her. Her face was muddy and her hair tangled; she'd put up a good fight against being captured.

I wondered why she seemed familiar.

"Zephyr's bonded. Katerina Luna." Drystan filled in the patch of my memory.

Shit. Now I understood why a spark of tragic hope lay in her ocean blue eyes. Zephyr was an ally to Astraea, and Katerina was her friend too. She would beg me to try to save her.

This confrontation had just become so much fucking worse.

"How about you forget this foolish plan and I'll let you live another day," I said to my father as evenly as I could while I was studying everything. Trying to calculate every possible way to get out of here with Katerina alive at least.

More imminently, my father could *not* summon the gods to walk our realm.

To face Astraea's creators . . . I wasn't ready for the wrath that would take me over for all they'd done to her.

"I realize now I've trusted the wrong god all along. Death made you powerful and promised you would conquer lands. But Dusk and Dawn are far more cunning and have a vision for this world of power and prosperity in which I sit the throne of Vesitire. Once I fulfill my bargain to them, Astraea's power will be mine when they kill her."

"Even you can't be this naïve," I spat. "They're using you like the desperate puppet you've always been."

"You're a delusional fool," Drystan muttered.

If he could kill us with his look alone, we'd be dust where we stood, but I delighted in his visceral reactions that gave full weight to his misguided beliefs.

I couldn't reach my ability, but I felt the void, able to step through it and snap the neck of one vampire just as Drystan darted for another, clashing blades before plunging his through their gut.

There were only a half dozen vampires, and they were all dead in a minute.

While we were distracted, taking them out, my father was given a brief moment to act.

Aquilo's wail rang through the temple hall, and my attention swung to him as I released the heart of the final vampire I killed.

The High Celestial's hand had been forcibly plunged *through* the mirror, which rippled around where his arm sank in to his elbow. I could only watch in horror as silver crawled up his skin, like the mirror had liquefied to engulf him.

I blinked through the void. Stepping out of shadow, I gripped my father by his clothing, charging forward with a yell of wrath until his back slammed into the nearest pillar.

"You can't stop this now, Rainyte," he choked in my vise grip.

"You're a spineless, power-hungry bastard," I seethed in his face.

I hadn't been this close to him, staring so ferociously into his brown eyes, in so long that I trembled with fear as much as I did rage. I held the monster who plagued my entire existence, ready to snap his neck once and for all.

"You cannot kill me," Father rasped, struggling for breath and clutching onto the fraying tethers of his consciousness. "Dusk and Dawn not only granted me the ability to use the maiden's key, but they gave me immortality to make sure I lived to kill her with it."

Fury *consumed* me.

I snapped his neck before another thought could cross my mind, letting his body slump in a heap while I gathered myself and sanity in deep, measured breaths.

"Nyte." Drystan said my name so calmly it jarred me out of my rage-induced state.

I twisted my head to him but didn't expect to find him in the compromised position he was in.

Nor could I have predicted who balanced his life between twin blades crossed over his neck from behind.

Nadia strained on her toes while Drystan bent back awkwardly. I could hardly see straight with my violence climbing to unhinged levels.

"What the fuck are you doing?" I said, so cold and dark it was like the remnants of Nightsdeath surfaced within me. Or perhaps that part of me had never truly died. It could resurrect, grow stronger and deadlier as it was fed betrayal, violence, and despair.

"You two are such an idiotic pair," she said, as if angry with us about that opinion.

"Let him go before I make you, little rogue," I warned.

"You welcomed me so easily," she went on.

I understood what was happening, and she was right: I was a damned fool not to have seen this coming.

"That's debatable," I said calmly, though inside I was simmering with wrath.

"You accepted my story about how I found out about the bond. Me, the only fucking person to know," she hissed, more to Drystan now. My brother's face lined with anger but he didn't try to free himself, and I knew he had to feel just as betrayed as I did. Perhaps more so.

Her tone turned so hushed. "I was livid when your father told me about it. He offered me my full freedom from that cave, a place by his side when he would rule. I've never had a place or purpose, so I was lured in by that prospect. I had nothing to lose after having what little shred of myself I had in this world ripped apart and forged into this bloodthirsty monster. He found out all the transitioned vampires were compelled to obey Drystan, and he predicted you would run back to your brother's side eventually. He couldn't allow you to have those kinds of numbers as an army against him that would have no choice but to side with you. It was my mission to sever your power over the transitioned vampires, and you all made it too. Fucking. Easy."

It all made sense. Our father once again being cunning enough to rally the alliances he needed. He was smart, elusive, and so fucking *dead*.

"Bravo," Drystan said at last, but there was something broken in that word. Defeated. "You almost had me."

I realized then . . . despite their bickering and violence, Drystan had begun to fall for her.

"Why do you think he chose me?" she said resentfully. "For how easy males fall to pretty things."

Drystan's laugh was more like a bitter breath. "Trust I would have killed you despite your pretty face long ago if I'd had my way. You have my brother to thank that you made it this far."

Since Nadia had breached my trust, I had no guilt shattering hers. I wanted to see her betrayal for myself; I just needed to get her out of this damned temple to break into her mind.

"It's not too late to choose again," I reasoned with her. I was unfamiliar with this method of negotiation, which would usually be a lot bloodier by now.

"As if you would ever let me live after this," she accused.

"You're right; I'll kill you the moment I get a chance, but I'll make it painless."

"Kind of you."

We were pulled from our standoff by choking sounds from Aquilo. The metallic essence had consumed him, and he knelt there like a statue of solid armor. It reached his mouth, spilling down his throat now, and it was horrifying, even for me, to watch.

Katerina still knelt beside him, trembling and wide-eyed. She'd gone into shock, unable to move.

I took one step toward her . . .

A silver hand lashed out of the mirror, gripping Katerina's throat.

"No—!"

"You can't save her," Drystan yelled to stop me from getting any closer. "The gods' ascension is too far along to stop now."

To both our surprise, Nadia's blades dropped and she pushed Drystan away. He spun around as she held the point of the blade to his heart.

"Idiots. Fucking *run*, will you?" she hissed.

We both stalled in our conflict. I still wanted to rip out her throat, but Drystan backed away from her, closer to me.

"Best we can do is report back and prepare for what this could mean," Drystan said, not taking his eyes off Nadia.

"We're just letting her go?" I said, not in the least pleased with that mercy, given her long betrayal.

"For now. She's nothing more than a desperate rogue."

I felt the hurt behind his words as much as he meant them. Drystan had come to care for Nadia, and the fact that she'd lured him in just made me want to extract vengeance on her all the more.

Aquilo and Katerina became still statues while the liquid silver rippled over their bodies. I hoped they would retain their faces so I knew who to hunt for, and who to hide from.

I hated the thought of hiding at all, but there was no predicting what powers the gods might harness in their mortal forms.

Astraea would be devastated to learn of her friend's fate, and I left that temple with my anger subdued under the weight of my failure to stop my father, for if what he said was true, he would awaken from a broken neck, and my failure to save Katerina Luna.

I wouldn't know liberation until I killed my father, somehow, once and for all.

Auster Nova was dead. Our war was with the gods now.

PART
THREE

A
Wrath of Gods

26

Astraea–Past

Today she would tell Auster about her bond to Nyte. Astraea flew to the Nova province with nerves eating away at her insides the whole way. She didn't expect him to take it well at first, and she was ready to do what it took to heal the pain the news would cause. It was inevitable. But Astraea remained dedicated to him as a dear friend. She couldn't lose him over this, and that was what had kept it a terrible secret to harbor for weeks.

Auster wasn't in his castle, and Astraea followed the direction of a few guards informing her he was in the heart of the city at a small orphanage. It was unexpected to hear he was there.

Inside, she was guided to a room laid out for the children's school hours. The sight of Auster sitting in the middle of a reading area with the attention of over a dozen young celestials on him stole her heart. He read to them with the voice of a compelling storyteller. She didn't know how she'd never seen this side to him before. He was a natural with children, making them laugh and marvel. The room went delicately silent to hear his tale as he flipped pages, but it was bright with the imagination he pulled from the texts.

When his eyes flicked up to her, he faltered his next page turn.

"Don't stop on my account," she mused. "You're getting to the best part."

But story time was over when the children caught sight of her.

"It's the star-maiden!" one gushed, scrambling to their feet, which set off the rest. They bounded over, some more timid while others approached confidently.

She cast a wince at Auster as she stole the attention, but he grinned brightly, setting his book aside and joining them.

"Can you make it rain stars?" A young boy asked her.

"Hmm, let me see," she said, reaching for the key staff that was transformed to a compact baton strapped at her hip. "You'll need to make a little space."

They pushed their small circle around her back a few giddy steps, giving her room to twist the key between her hands as it became its legendary staff form. The children *ooo*'d and *ahhh*'d, but when she tapped the staff to the ground, their joy erupted as a silver flare shot high toward the roof before exploding into a shower of stardust. The children ran toward the center, giggling and trying to catch the dissolving glitter.

"Sorry to steal the show," she said as Auster came up beside her.

He chuckled. "I'm used to it. Your performances always outshine the rest of us."

Astraea sent up another flare of stardust for the children, which kept them happily occupied.

"I didn't expect to find you here," she said.

"I visit from time to time, making sure they have what they need," he answered.

"That's generous of you."

"It's the least I can do. These children have no parents, some by tragic circumstances. They don't deserve to suffer any more hardship."

As she watched the precious children, her heart ached for them. While she appreciated Auster's efforts, she couldn't help but wonder how many were orphaned because their parents had been outcasted by Auster for losing their wings.

Just then a woman came bounding in, carrying a toddler. She looked flustered, searching for another adult, and her eyes bulged when they landed on Astraea. She came over, attempting to bow, but Astraea insisted against it, instinctively reaching her arms out, like the toddler might slip from the cradle against the woman's hip. Somehow, the tiny celestial ended up in Astraea's arms, and she was stunned still, realizing she'd never held a baby before.

"Oh, thank you. I just need a moment; Zadkiel and Jack are going to be the death of me!" the woman screeched. Then she was gone as quickly as she'd arrived.

Bemused, Astraea didn't know what to do with the baby that began grabbing at her. Clothing, hair, jewelry. Auster's chuckle as she held the babe at arm's length made her snap her eyes to him in a plea for help.

"Just relax," he said, his voice coated in mirth as he watched her struggle.

Astraea held the child like the woman had, using her other hand to play with the tiny pincers that constantly wanted to grab. After a moment, the feeling was quite special. The small bundle had big blue eyes and soft blond hair, and her silver wings were so small Astraea's heart squeezed. She wouldn't be able to fly until she was into her teens.

She bounced the child in her arms, feeling an infectious joy spread within her, the likes of which she'd never experienced. When she glanced toward Auster, he was staring at her fondly, and Astraea stopped moving.

"You would make the most amazing mother," he said.

Her sparks of warmth cooled as her eyes searched the room, eager for the woman to return to take the child back.

"What's wrong?" Auster asked, reading her shift of mood.

"I need to talk to you about something."

"I'm all yours."

She swallowed hard.

"Can we go somewhere private?"

To her immense relief the woman came rushing back, taking the child from her. The way Auster had looked at her moments ago churned the guilt she harbored over her bond with Nyte.

His expression slowly firmed, and she could hardly bear her racing anxiety.

The woman rambled to Auster while Astraea was antsy to leave. "Will you speak with him again? Zadkiel has been having a hard time here lately."

Auster promised to visit again soon, and they left.

He pulled her to a stop by her elbow when they'd only gotten a street away.

"You're going to wring your hands dry; tell me what's wrong."

"You're my best friend and I can't bear to lose that," she blurted.

His expression turned guarded. *Shit, how was she supposed to tell him?*

There was no sequence of words that formed right in her mind. Every delivery was a bomb she would have to throw between them and hope they could survive the explosion.

"What have you done?" he asked, but it was like he already knew.

His features darkened in the way she'd seen his loathing at the mere mention of Nyte. He stared at her now as though the imprint of Nyte unveiled before his very eyes.

"I didn't have a choice," she scrambled, but that was a lie. Nyte might have forged their bond to save her but she'd known . . . long before then she'd chosen him.

Astraea shook her head, trying again. "I need you to listen to all I have to say. To try to understand."

She gasped when he crossed the few steps between them and grabbed her arms. Auster pulled them through the void, taking them to an edge of a cliff overlooking his province as the sun was beginning to set.

"You're not about to humiliate me where my people can hear," he said sourly.

Astraea blinked. Her heart pounded wildly.

"You already know?" she asked in disbelief.

His eyes cut into her. "You haven't done a very good job of concealing that vile mark on your neck."

Astraea recoiled, backing a step toward the ledge. She didn't know why. Auster would never hurt her . . . would he? She didn't believe in her heart he was capable of it, but the hatred in his stare that lingered on her neck displayed a frightening side of him she'd never seen aimed at herself.

"Just let me explain—"

"I don't want to hear it," he cut her off. Then his expression completely softened as he took a step toward her. "We can fix this. Let's go to the temple of Dusk and Dawn in Vesitire; they'll know of a way to sever your bond."

"Why didn't you tell me you knew of it before?"

He avoided answering. "He's a master manipulator with an ability of the mind. He's brainwashed you and taken you against your will to spite me. I knew if I mentioned it you would defend it, but I've been trying to find a way to help you. The marriage bargain might—"

"Stop," she said harshly. She couldn't stand to hear another word, in complete disbelief over Auster's conclusions.

Still, he approached her tentatively. His face held nothing but sympathy now.

"I'm going to make this right," he said gently.

"Everything is exactly the way I chose."

Auster winced as though she'd slapped him.

"We'll go to the temple now."

He reached for her and she jerked back before he could pull her through the void. Astraea's parents were the last entities she wanted to confront with this. She had no doubt they had been seething since the bond with Nyte happened.

"If you still regarded me as dearly as you say, you would trust me. Once the bond is broken you'll see it was all a villainous lie to corrupt you onto his side."

Her bond to Nyte physically tugged at the mere thought of being broken.

She couldn't retreat any farther as her heels slipped off the edge of the cliff.

"You're wrong about him. If you were still my friend, you would let me explain it all to you. He hasn't harmed or manipulated me. If that were his intention you know he could have caused far more destruction by now."

"I am more than your damned friend, Astraea, *I'm* your bonded!"

Everything in her rattled at his tone spiked in anger. Did she truly fear Auster right now?

"Please," she croaked.

This had gone so horribly wrong. She knew it wouldn't be easy, but the fact that Auster had known about her bond to Nyte for some time changed everything.

"This is for your own good."

When he reached for her again, she fell back, letting gravity have her instead.

Astraea didn't fall for long, and it wasn't her own wings that came out to catch her. The embrace she was cradled in was both an immense comfort and a terrible dread.

Nyte shot high with her, swooping around before landing across the cliff. Auster whirled to them with rage twisted over his face.

"I believe your problem is with me, not her," Nyte said, darkly but calmly.

"Get away from her," Auster snarled.

Astraea was torn. Auster truly believed he was protecting her, and that only tightened her guilt toward suffocation.

"It's long overdue that we met, Auster Nova."

"I'm going to fucking kill you."

"Good luck with that."

"You need to go," she said to Nyte.

He glanced at her, his cold stare softening just for a moment. "I'm not leaving you here when he's like this. I could feel your terror."

"You're the terror of these lands," Auster spat. She'd never seen him so angry that he was shaking with hatred.

"I am. But never to her."

"Lies."

"I can see your denial spinning into madness. Just accept it, Nova: she chose me."

Nyte reached to slip an arm around her, but a flash of blue accompanied Auster's sound of rage and warning. The key quickly became a staff in her hand to repel Auster's lightning, but Nyte's starry darkness engulfed it first.

Then before she could intervene, Nyte and Auster became engaged in a vicious power struggle of lightning against darkness.

This had gone from bad to much fucking worse.

She had to stop them, but stepping into the middle of their storm would be deadly. Astraea growled under her breath, angry at the both of them for this display of dominance. Using her as the catalyst to unleash the feud between them.

Unglamouring her wings and conjuring a sphere of light around herself, Astraea flew between them before she dropped down, bracing to take full force of their magick battering into both sides of her shield. The darkness swiftly eased, but the lightning grew stronger. Astraea had to shift her legs, twisting her full focus to ward off the violent blue currents that snapped over her gale of light.

She didn't want to hurt him, but he wasn't stopping. Was he so lost in his determined hatred that he didn't see her? Didn't notice he battled light, not dark, now?

Astraea saw only one way to snap him out of it. She let go of her shield, taking the impact of Auster's lightning, which slammed into her chest, projecting her through the air.

Nyte caught her, but Astraea could hardly feel him while her body seized tightly with the remnants of electricity sparking through her. It felt as though she'd held her breath for minutes, so when the shocks finally eased she swallowed air greedily, choking on it.

Nyte was muttering assurances to her, smoothing back her hair as she came around.

"Astraea, I didn't mean to . . ." Auster sounded sincere, and she didn't blame him.

She pushed up to sit and accepted Nyte's help to stand. The wrath from him was palpable, and she feared they'd break into a fight again.

"You need to leave," Astraea said.

Auster's eyes turned desolate, but Astraea shifted her gaze, meaning those words for Nyte.

A muscle in his jaw worked. He said, through their bond, *"I don't think I'm physically capable of it if he's still breathing."*

"I must speak with him. To try to make this right. He won't hurt me."

"He already has."

"I let him."

Astraea's chest hurt with Nyte's resistance.

Nyte let her go. Though he didn't leave without pinning Auster with a lethal warning look.

"If you harm a single hair on her, I'll burn this province to the ground before I throw you into it."

He wasn't helping Astraea's case to acquit him of villainy.

Nyte lifted a tender hand to her face, barely grazing her skin as the void opened up for him to step back into.

"If I don't see you in the bell tower in an hour, or if I feel even a note of fear from you again, I'm coming back for you."

With that, the darkness took him away. Her heart strained to go after him, but it was also yearning to mend her shaken relationship with Auster.

Alone with him, she turned to Auster and it was like gravity demanded their embrace. Relief relaxed her. They could get through this. She believed their bond of friendship forged over many decades could survive.

"I didn't mean to hurt you," he muttered into her hair.

"I know," she whispered.

But as the words left her . . . she didn't know if she believed them. She'd felt his power amplify when it switched from colliding with Nyte's darkness to contending with her light. Astraea wanted to push the most horrible thoughts away, but it was like they fought for her to truly consider . . . could Auster, the man she loved and respected, who'd been her close friend for most of her adult life . . . intend to cause her great harm?

27

Astraea

I hadn't been able to get out of bed when Nyte brought me back to Nadir's home. I was told a few days had passed since. It wasn't the wounds on my body that weighed me down, it was those that were still raw on my soul after my battle with Auster.

You were my everything.

Auster's final words tormented me. Because my heart squeezed at them, but my mind knew that every one of his actions heinously contradicted what those words should have meant.

He hurt me more than anyone. Yet he loved me more than anything.

No, that wasn't true. He loved what I could have given him, or he wouldn't have betrayed me.

At least that was the war raging on in my mind.

Lilith helped with my wounds, and my side was almost healed from being impaled by wood. As for the smaller puncture I'd sustained from the blade that had Nyte's blood on it . . . the skin around it had become gray with dark veins, and we all knew my life was on a countdown if it continued to climb toward my heart.

Someone entered my room. I didn't turn from my position on my side, staring out the window. I knew I couldn't lie here for much longer in my grief.

"Hey, Stray," Zath said gently.

My brow crumpled when I heard his voice, and when the bed dipped I rolled over to face him, wincing from my tender wounds. He cast a warm smile at me and sat against the headboard. Zath reached to brush a lock of my hair from my cheek.

"I've missed you," I croaked with my voice hoarse from days of silence.

"Of course you have; I'm far more delightful company than Nyte," he teased. Then asked, "How you holding up?"

There was something about that kind of question that broke the straining dam holding back my emotions. When I sniffed, his face fell knowingly, and I shuffled closer until my head was partially on him.

"I'm angry that I'm sad," I confessed.

"I understand."

"Auster doesn't deserve my grief after all he did."

"Then why do you cry?"

"Because I miss the person he was." I broke. Ugly sobs wracked through my body, but Zath's gentle strokes along my spine helped soothe the pain. "I wish he didn't have to *become that.*"

"You can't long for the past, or you'll always be stuck there."

"What if it was my fault? It's because of me he ruined himself."

"We cannot shoulder blame for someone else's actions, even someone we love. You're thinking you could have fixed him, but people are not mechanical. You would have always chosen Nyte; nothing would have changed Auster's reception to it in the end. Unless you regret that choice, you have to find peace and let go of anyone else's feelings or actions."

"I would never regret choosing him. Never."

While I'd lain here for days I'd been reliving memories of the past, as if I might find the moment I should have known Auster loathed me enough to want me dead. The vision of the day I told him about Nyte kept replaying, like new details would unveil something then . . .

I pushed up suddenly, wincing at the sharp pain around my ribs.

"Where's Nyte?" I asked.

"I'm not sure. He only said to tell you he'll be back soon if you asked."

I swung my legs off the bed.

"You need to rest," Zath reprimanded.

I was already dressing, too flustered to care that Zath was in the room, but to his credit, he turned his back as I did. Stuffing my feet into boots, I headed out.

My instincts took me through the surrounding woodland until I emerged on a cliff ledge. The same one where I'd found Nyte right before he fell under his curse.

I looked up and I remembered . . .

Burdens are heavy on the ground.

I didn't unglamour my wings before I ran through the snow, pushing with all I had for the best momentum, and then I leapt off the side.

I made sure not to dive in my free fall, instead letting my body fall in a weightless cradle.

Arms caught me, and my anticipation of it had me clamping my arms around his neck.

Nyte was so beautiful my words stalled for a second to take in his subdued pale gold eyes and the wind whipping his midnight hair across them.

"There you are," I whispered.

"That was very bold of you," he said.

"If you hadn't caught me, I do have wings."

He helped me maneuver on Eltanin's saddle to sit facing him, half straddling his legs. Before I could tell him what I suspected from the past, his desolate expression distracted me.

He wasn't looking at me. Instead his fingers lifted the hem of my shirt to examine Auster's stab wound.

"I don't know what to do, and I'm fucking terrified to lose you."

"It might heal. We don't know that it will continue to spread."

It was a grasp of hope in the dark we both knew was weak, but it was all I had.

I said, "Do you remember when I was dying from being ambushed and struck by the key, and I came to you?"

"This is a kind of terror I'll never forget," he answered grimly.

My heart skipped, then squeezed.

"I think the attack was ordered by Auster, that he knew I would have to go to one of you to save me with the bond, and it had been a test."

Nyte frowned. "I thought Auster didn't know about us at that time?"

"So did I . . . but, looking back, it makes sense. Your father must have told him to goad him about us and perhaps to have a new potential ally in his pocket should he need it. To confirm if it was true, Auster staged my ambush by a group of vampires, hoping I would go to him to save me, and he would get what he always want . . . to forge our bond and have access to the key and my power."

Nyte's eyes closed for a moment. Collecting his wrath when the culprit was no longer alive for him to unleash it upon.

"You came to me," he murmured. "Your intuition has never led you astray, even when people you trusted tried to make you doubt yourself."

I held his face in my hands. *"You* have never led me astray, Rainyte."

28

Astraea

We rode Eltanin until our burdens were distant enough to bear the weight of the ground. Now, Nyte's warmth pressed against my back while we lay in the bath in our room in Nadir's home. His bare flesh wrapped around me like a shield against the emptiness that always threatened to creep in.

His touch was slow, deliberate, tracing patterns along my skin that sent shivers through me—not from cold, but from the raw, aching fear that this was fleeting, that he could slip away at any moment.

Every brush of his fingertips felt like a promise he couldn't make. An invisible tether wound us tighter together every day but I was too afraid to trust in its strength not to break us apart again. My breath hitched as his hand skimmed the curve of my arm, his presence so solid, so real, and yet a fragile part of me screamed that it wouldn't last. He'd been taken from me too many times.

Nyte had gone after his father days ago, and though everything he relayed terrified me, and I had been angry because he'd risked himself so soon after coming back to me . . . right now I couldn't be anything but grateful he was here.

"How am I going to tell Zephyr?" I whispered, heartbroken about Katerina, who had been such a light, a brave and encouraging spirit, when we'd been captive together in the Keep of Alisus.

"I'll be right there with you," he said; it was all he could offer.

The more he touched me, the more I ached to hold him tighter. Zephyr had lost his mate, and he hadn't even been there for a chance to save her. That fact ached so deep in my soul.

"Don't leave me." Those words slipped out in my fear. "We do everything together from now on, promise me?"

Nyte's lips pressed to my wet shoulder.

"You and me," he murmured over my skin. "I promise."

After the hellish month without the real and tender parts of him, lying against his authentic self in these hot bath waters made the misery worth bearing to reach this.

The wound from the wood piercing my side was almost healed with Lilith's help. Auster's stab wound had scabbed over too, but the thin black vines of Nyte's blood continued to spread, so slowly it wasn't detectable to most. Nyte noticed every fraction they crawled closer to my heart.

I couldn't let it distract me. While I still had breath in my lungs and fight in my body, I would charge forward in this war to banish the gods for good.

Nyte's lips pressing to my neck pulled a soft sigh of contentment from me. He'd been so tender and careful with me these last few days, but I needed him closer than he'd allowed.

Now that I was healed enough, I rocked my hips back, encouraging him to drink from me. He groaned against my throat.

"You're going to feel me deep inside you," he muttered huskily. "But not like this."

"Please," I begged pathetically.

"I don't need your blood, and I won't risk it harming you in your condition."

I hadn't considered that possibility, and a surge of new rage for the curse Auster set in motion ran through me. Nyte felt my anger and quickly made it melt with the dip of his fingers past my navel while his lips trailed over my shoulder with soft kisses.

"I'll make up for it in many other ways, I assure you."

His fingers slipped between my legs. My back arched into him with the sparks of pleasure as he circled my apex, my legs pushed apart as far as the bath would allow.

Nyte's other hand smothered my cry, anticipating my climax.

"Do you want to announce to the others what I'm doing to you?" he said sinfully. "I won't mind. I'll release you and have you calling out my name for this whole house to hear."

In my cloud of lust, I hardly had consideration for anyone or my own decency, but I was glad Nyte retained enough of his mind to know I'd be hiding in embarrassment when we faced them in the morning. I bit his fingers instead.

"Come for me, Starlight," he whispered by my ear; then his tongue licked over his mating mark.

I became shattering stars in his arms. Nyte held me against him tightly as my body trembled. He kept up the glide of his fingers, which slowed with the comedown of my climax.

"Good girl," he said thickly, planting tender kisses along my collar.

Though I was still panting and shuddering, I wasn't done with him.

I floated around in the water to face him. The tub was big enough, so I straddled him. Sparks of oversensitivity had me gripping the bath's edge from the friction of his hard cock between my legs. His expression pinched in pure lust as he gripped my hips, aiding the slide of me against him.

"Not enough for you, was it?" he taunted.

"Not even close."

"I want to take it slow tonight," he said tenderly. His tongue flicked over my nipple, and he groaned when my chest pushed into him for more. "I'm going to stretch out every hour with you. It seems there's no rest for the wicked since you're adamant that we can't stay here for a few more days."

"It's a race out there. For dragons and for key pieces."

"You're right. Though a part of me still wants to convince you to watch the world burn with me, because I'd still have everything. I'd have you."

It was then, in his beautiful words and unwavering devotion, that I knew no matter what wounded my heart it would always be healed. As long as I could find him, I would never be lost. I was made of many fractured parts, but Nyte was all the light and darkness between the cracks which held me together. That made something broken feel stronger than ever before.

I kissed him deeply. The kind of kiss that warmed and tangled in our souls.

When we broke apart, our faces stayed close, and I traced my finger idly over his scar across his cheek. The one I'd carved on him during a time I thought he'd betrayed me. It was always in the most perfect moments that vulnerability clawed within. Recalling the chaos we'd escaped from at the temple, a new fear had been unsettling me.

"When you found me—when I was *Lightsdeath*—I didn't know who you were. I remember it all now, but at the time . . . your soul was so dark all I wanted to do was *reap it*. I don't ever want to look at you and not remember who you are, and I'm scared I don't know how to control this new power inside me."

Despite my confession, Nyte didn't appear the least bit concerned.

"I know," he said thoughtfully, playing with the wet lengths of my hair. "We've been through this before with Nightsdeath, and you never left me. I'm never leaving you, even when you want to kill me."

His lips twitched in humor, and it released the tension from my body.

"I need to learn to control it. With all we'll face, Lightsdeath is going to surface, and I don't want to be afraid; I don't want it to be a curse. I want to use this power."

"Good. We'll practice every moment we can on our journey."

He kissed my arm, my chest; Nyte was so relaxed and unafraid that it was contagious.

Then something disturbed him. "I can't apologize enough for what you suffered because of me."

I was confused for a moment before I realized what he meant.

"Nightsdeath isn't you."

"You're wrong."

"No. We are not our worst selves. There is so much good in you, Rainyte."

"For you. But if you left me again . . . I wouldn't just watch the world self-destruct, I would collapse it myself. If I'm poison, you're the antidote. If I'm fire, you're water. I am completely destructive without you. That has not changed."

I contemplated his words. "If I'm the star, you're the night. If I'm the rose, you're the vine. I'm completely lost without you. So I think it's in everyone's best interest that we win this war together."

Nyte's smile was so endearing it hurt before he kissed me softly. My fingers threaded through his hair and tightened, my mouth opened for the sweep of his tongue. I moaned lightly in the breaths that shorted between us.

When my hips next rocked forward, his cock lined up perfectly to sink into me unexpectedly when I eased back. I couldn't stop the noise that left me then, breaking our kiss suddenly.

Nyte reprimanded me with his teeth pinching my nipple, which had the opposite effect.

"I wish we were alone so you could scream for me," Nyte said, voice gravely with lust.

Neither of us moved with him seated and fully inside me. Nyte's fingers reached for the tangled wet hair over my shoulder, pushing it behind me so I could marvel at his bite.

"So beautiful," he said. "I missed you so fucking much."

I started lifting my hips, which sloshed the water around us, close to spilling over the edge.

"I want to fuck you, but we'll flood the place if we stay in here," Nyte said.

I gasped, clamping around him tightly when he stood with me from the tub.

"We'll soak the sheets," I protested in a near squeal when he was about to drop me, my skin dripping wet, onto the bed.

"If you want me to fuck you against the wall you need only ask."

He headed over to the side of the room, but instead set me upon a dresser.

"Touch yourself for me," he said, holding one of my ankles to keep me spread wide while he watched.

My cheeks flushed, but I reached between my legs and began circling my apex. Nyte swore, pumping his cock slowly with his other hand, eyes wild with my every movement. I curved two fingers into myself with slow strokes, alternating between fucking myself and rubbing myself.

"You can go deeper," he groaned.

I sank into myself to my knuckles, and Nyte's expression pained pleasure.

The next time I pulled out, Nyte stepped forward, plunging into me fully and without warning. His hand planted on the wall by my head as his rugged breaths broke a shiver down my chest. He stared down to where we joined.

"Fucking incredible." He fucked me slow and deep, savoring how perfectly we fit together, and I was so euphorically full.

Nyte ran his fingers lightly over the black spiderwebbing around my abdomen. I wished I could erase his pain every time he tracked the growth of it with panic in his eyes. He pulled out of me and knelt, pressing his lips over the darkening skin.

"I'm going with you," he muttered. The vibrations scattered over my skin. He kissed the tip of the vines just over my ribs. "Wherever you go, I'm going with you."

Even to death is what he didn't say. The thought inspired a soul-deep ache.

"You can't just give up on life like that," I said quietly.

Nyte sucked my nipple and I bit my lip. He kissed between my collarbones; then his hand cupped my nape and he devoured me with a kiss that left me lightheaded by the time he let me breathe.

"Have I not made myself clear? You are my life."

Nyte sank his cock into me again; this time he picked up pace, which had me clawing at his back. He kissed me to swallow as much of the noise escaping me as he could. With this pace and demand, the noise from the dresser was too much. Nyte seemed to realize that too as he lifted me off, only to drop me next to it and spin me around. I was so delirious in my lust that I barely had time to reorient myself when he kicked my feet to widen my stance.

"Hands on the wall and arch your back for me," he instructed. I did and he wasted no time in sinking back into me. Far less noise in this position, save for his skin against mine and the mixed sounds of breathless pleasure we tried to contain.

It was torturous to be . . . *mindful* of the household.

After a while of building ecstasy, Nyte's hand curled around my throat, testing my flexibility by pulling me up to him with my back still curved so he could fuck me.

"I've dreamed of the home we could have. Not just in the castle. I'd build you whatever you want, wherever you desire. A place that is just ours."

"Yes," I breathed, wanting that more than anything. "Just ours."

The bell tower was high and precious, but if we were triumphant in finding our peace, if I could live through this deadly ailment, there would be nothing to hide from anymore. I wanted a house with water and forest nearby. Somewhere private but not hidden. I wanted that gift for us more than anything, and we deserved it.

Nyte pulled out suddenly, and I stifled a whimper when he released me.

"I need to taste you," he said thickly.

He led me over to the fireplace and knelt on the rug. I copied his movement and he claimed my mouth in a long, deep kiss, coaxing me to lie back. He stopped only to reach for the cushions on the armchair and slip one under my head, then he took another, tucking it under my lower back. I melted over his tender care with me as his mouth descended on my body.

"Quiet, remember. Or I'll have to punish you," he muttered, reaching past my navel, and my hips lifted, greedy for him to reach the growing heat between my legs.

His fingers dipped through my slickness, and a guttural sound resonated in his throat.

"You're soaked for me," he said, kissing the inside of my thigh. "Just as I hoped."

Nyte licked me, and my hand lashed down to grab a fistful of his hair. He took his time at first, teasing me until I was so breathless and needy that I couldn't stop myself from rolling my hips against his face.

"So greedy," he said sinfully. Then he devoured me.

His hands hooked around my thighs, trying to keep me still, but I was quickly chasing an orgasm, undulating my hips in tandem with his assault. His tongue dipped inside me and flicked at my opening. I was conflicted over whether I wanted his fingers or cock inside me to make me finish or if I wanted to come with his mouth alone.

I wasn't getting a choice when his hold tightened and he focused all his attention on the sensitive bud, racing me toward another shattering end. My thighs clamped around his head, and my hands splayed out on either side of me, my back bowing off the ground with a silent scream. I came down in a shaking, helpless mess as Nyte slowed his movements.

The climax was still tingling my skin when his cock pushed inside my tight channel. Then it was like that orgasm wouldn't end, only roll into another with his thrusts hitting a perfect spot inside me.

"Fuck," he rasped, voice strained with his impending release. "Say you're mine."

"I'm yours," I rasped, meeting him stroke for stroke with the lift of my hips. *I'm yours. I'm yours. I'm yours.*

"Ready to come with me again?"

"Yes," I mewled.

"Good fucking girl." He said each word between thrusts before he came, spending himself inside me in long, jutting strokes.

He pulled out abruptly, replacing his cock with his fingers, pushing his release back inside me, and I came again to the primal claim it felt like. He didn't stop until I was a shuddering, sweat-slicked mess. He knelt between my legs with his other hand pumping his cock.

When I deflated from that earth-shattering climax, I lay there near bursting from happiness and love. So much love for Rainyte, who kissed his way slowly back up my body.

Nyte went to retrieve all the cushions from the bed to bring before the fireplace while I was reluctant to move from the warm bliss. When I saw the two angry purple scars from his torn-out wings, a piece of me withered inside.

I pushed up, the black bedsheet half covering me now as he settled back down, arranging the cushions. He stopped moving at my touch on his shoulder.

Neither of us spoke, but as Nyte turned a little more, I took that as permission to trace my fingers over his back.

"I don't miss them," Nyte said, as if that was my concern. "I have a far bigger set of wings now. I can't decide if it should be humorous or not."

He was hiding what losing his wings meant to him. Though he had Eltanin to fly with, I couldn't imagine the void that had been left inside him when his wings were taken. I felt compelled to touch those thick scars, like they called for me to discover something about him.

When I touched his wing scars, I gasped at the tug within me. As if it pulled me through a void. I didn't know where I was, stolen away from our room. It was a similar sensation to when my own memories filtered their way into the present after they'd been lost, trying to get me to understand something I couldn't remember. Except this was Nyte's memory.

I saw a woman with flaming red hair whose beauty was too perfect to be of mortal nature. She seemed so angry, but an anger that was crafted of pain. She reminded me a lot of . . . Nyte.

I was sucked back to the brown surroundings of Nadir's home by Nyte, who held my wrist while fire danced across his concerned expression.

"When you were asleep . . . where did you go?" I asked, a little breathless because the vision had felt so raw and real. Nyte harbored such strong pain and yearning toward that woman that my eyes pricked with the echo of his emotions.

Nyte's face relaxed in surprise. "I think I went . . . home. Or at least my mind did."

"Who was that woman? With the red hair?"

His brow twitched as he stared at nothing in particular. "My mother."

I was slammed with shock. He didn't elaborate, and I tried to read his face, wondering if it had caused him more pain or given him closure to have met her.

"What was she like?" I asked, tracing the golden marks absentmindedly up his forearm.

"She was . . . everything I could have become," he said honestly. His tone was haunted. "I would have . . . if you died and weren't going to come back, I would have fallen down a similar dark path. She started a continent-wide war because of me. Five hundred years ago when I was taken from her. She'd suffered a lot before that, and I guess losing me snapped her for good."

A fist tightened in my chest; my lips pressed to his shoulder where we sat in a comfortable entanglement of limbs.

"Being in that realm, did you find what you were looking for?"

A part of Nyte had always been lost and, while I couldn't comprehend how his experience was possible, I hoped he gained the closure about his mother and the birth realm he didn't know he'd been looking for.

"I think so," he said quietly. "Or at least . . . I know without a doubt I don't want to go back. I learned where I came from, and I also discovered the only place I truly belong is with you. Wherever that might be."

I kissed the corner of his mouth, and he cupped my cheek.

"I belong with you too. I always have," I whispered.

I climbed onto his lap, breaking into a slow grin when I felt him.

"We might have a lot of irritable friends to face in the morning," he murmured huskily, getting the same idea as me. His arm snaked around me, pulling me down fully on his hardening cock.

"Friends," I repeated, then kissed him softly.

The term was so endearing, so hopeful, coming from him. He'd lost most of the golden guard, who he'd only started to regard as such before they were murdered right in front of him. It flared hope in me that his heart hadn't sealed completely because of it.

"They are more like pesky little rodents we can't seem to get rid of," he muttered.

I giggled, and Nyte smiled when I did. He was such a precious sight when he smiled.

"I want to hear more about your realm," I said.

Nyte blew out a long breath, seeming to tunnel back. "It's a very long story."

I lifted my hips and reached between us, taking him into my body again. His fingers dug into my side with his arm still hooked around me, and he groaned, planting his lips on my chest.

"Tell me when we win," I whispered.

29

Astraea

I sat on the floor while Nyte, on the bed, braided my hair. More times than necessary, and slower than I knew he could. I thought he did so in an attempt to slow my thoughts and my heart, which were both racing to get going on the quest ahead. Though I wanted to sit here for hours in this pleasurable relaxation.

"Your infatuation with my hair hasn't changed," I mused. My eyes fluttered at the bliss of his fingers against my scalp.

"Do you remember everything from the past?" he asked, lost in his task.

"Sort of," I said, trying to find the right explanation for how I was both found but still lost in my own mind. "I can't often grasp some of the memories as truth. Sometimes I remember things but as if they were a dream. The life I had before feels like a long, vivid dreamscape that suddenly comes back to me at times. Like when I do something in this life that reminds me I either enjoyed it or hated it in the past."

It surprised me when Nyte insisted on styling my hair this morning. Until flashes of a memory from long ago in the bell tower came back. Me teasing him over his obsession and challenging him to style my hair so he could be useful. Something he'd taken *very* seriously.

"That must be confusing."

"I remember a lot of our times together. Certain activities or things you say, the ways you touch me. They feel even more familiar now. I think I'll always feel like I've lived two lives, but I'm okay with that. I'm ready to focus on this one. Fight for this one. The past has an end I plan not to repeat, so I have to be better than her, smarter."

"You are absolutely perfect," he muttered, not stopping his braiding to lean in and kiss my temple. "Then, now, and always."

"You're biased to think that."

"Some might say you have flaws, I suppose. I just happen to enjoy them."

Nyte tied off the bottom of the braid after finishing several over the crown of my head, which I watched through the full-length mirror in front of me. I had to admit, his love for my hair came in useful considering the skill he'd mastered.

I turned, bracing on his thighs and pushing up on my knees.

"What are my flaws, exactly?"

"You're stubborn as hell."

"So are you."

"And quite reckless."

"Says the one who murders first and considers later."

His wicked side-smile inspired a tingling thrill in me.

"You're attracted to all things bad for you."

"Meaning you?"

Our lips came shy of meeting before someone burst through our door unannounced.

It was Drystan with a rather irate look on his face. "I would apologize but you two have the rest of us waiting around downstairs, promptly by sunrise, despite the disturbances to our rest you caused."

I almost choked at his bold proclamation. We'd been as careful and quiet as we could have been last night . . . hadn't we?

I met Nyte's stare with a blush fanning my face when Drystan left after that announcement, but Nyte wasn't fazed. In fact, I thought he was delighting in it.

"I warned you to be quiet," he said, standing and reaching for my cloak. He used any excuse to touch me, fitting it around me and clasping it at my shoulder. I was too focused on what the mischief in his eyes suggested he was going to say next. "I can't wait to inflict your punishment."

I scowled, pushing him lightly. "You weren't silent either."

"Impossible with you."

Everyone was downstairs; they all sat around a dining table with empty bowls of porridge. Their irritation wasn't subtle, and I kept my head down sheepishly, sitting opposite Zathrian.

Drystan marched over with a large map, pausing expectantly to look over the table. Nadir waved a hand, and the bowls vanished for him to lay the map down.

"We should probably split up. There are fifteen temples left since we've freed Athebyne and Edasich. Athebyne was at the temple in Alisus, and there are no others in the kingdom. The blue dragon, Edasich, was in Vesitire, which leaves two more temples here. One in Astrinus in the north. One each in Fesaris, Arania, and Pyxtia, so that makes three to the west. Leaving most of them, nine, to the east, seven of which are scattered past Althenia borders beyond the Sterling Mountains," Drystan finished explaining, folding his arms and pondering the map.

Glancing over to the side of the room, he found something of interest, stalked toward it, and returned with chess pieces gathered in his arms. He started setting them on the map to give us visuals on the temple locations.

"Lilith and I can cover the three in the west," Davina said, sipping her tea. Lilith smiled at her in agreement.

Zath said, "Rose and I should take the two here in Vesitire."

The scent of warm cinnamon and honey filled my nostrils before Nyte slipped a bowl in front of me. My smile broke out at such a simple pleasure as porridge. A greater pleasure was Nyte's grin in response, and my heart fluttered at the sight of it, not taking a single treasured moment for granted.

"Enough of your flirtations. Silent or otherwise," Drystan muttered sourly. "We have work to do."

"Said work needs sustenance," Nyte countered, slipping onto the bench beside me with his own bowl.

"If you had been prompt, we'd have already covered that."

"I wouldn't mind second breakfast," Zath cut in.

Drystan ignored us all to say, "I'll go north to Astrinus myself; then I can cover the two outside Althenia borders to the east."

"You're not going alone," Nyte said firmly.

"I wasn't asking, brother."

Their standoff hummed with tension. Then I scanned the room.

"Where's Nadia?" I asked.

My inquiry twitched a muscle in Drystan's jaw. "Her allegiance was always elsewhere," he said flatly, not elaborating.

Nyte met my eyes, explaining to me through our bond, *She's been my father's eyes and ears this whole time.*

Denial was my first instinct, but from Drystan's reaction . . . *Oh gods.*

"I can go with Drystan," Elliot offered. He leaned at the side of the room like he didn't know how to integrate himself into this group of new and unlikely friends after losing those he'd bonded with over centuries in the Golden Guard.

"No offense, but I'd rather go myself," Drystan said.

"Not an option," Nyte repeated. "You travel with Elliot, or you'll come with Astraea and me. Elliot can accompany Zath and Rose. No one goes alone; it's too dangerous."

Nyte was becoming more protective of Drystan, though he wouldn't admit that was why he was vehemently against his younger brother going off on his own. Especially not with their father on the loose.

An argument crossed Drystan's face, but thankfully Zath cut in before he could speak it.

"Did you get a piece of your key at the temple with Nightsdeath?" Zath asked.

"Yes, but it was a fake"

"There are only five key pieces; I was hoping you'd know which temples you sent them to," Drystan sighed.

"It doesn't work like that," I said. "It protects itself by challenging the pursuant. For the Libertatem, it took on the mold of the king's ideals to test him by challenging what he believed in most. That greed, envy, lust, wrath, and pride were the worst of mankind's flaws."

"Your weapon has a twisted sense of humor," Rose muttered.

I said, "There's no telling what form each trial will take this time for each of us. No one has attempted them before. For the one I faced with Nightsdeath, it challenged our trust in each other."

Nyte's hand resting on my thigh gave a gentle squeeze. I slipped my hand over his in comfort.

"At least we'll free more dragons, even if certain temples don't have a true piece. Which I'm guessing we'll only discover when we get them all back to you," Drystan pondered.

"Me or Nyte, yes. The key answers to both of us."

"The dragons will change the tide of this war," Zath said hopefully.

"Unless they bond with any of those allied with Auster or the king," Lilith enlightened.

It was possible. Once a dragon was freed there was no predicting where it could decide to attach its allegiance. We'd gotten lucky with Eltanin and Athebyne, but life had taught me to brace for a storm after a blessing of sunshine.

I said, "We'll cover Althenia after Astrinus. It'll be the most dangerous to venture into. And I need . . . I need to see Zephyr."

"What about our snake of a father and his new primordial allies out for vengeance?" Drystan said warily with a look at Nyte.

"We need the key before we can face them. Right now, all we can hope for is to remain out of their sights no matter what they begin to inflict on the land," Nyte said.

"I don't like the sound of that," I said, torn by the notion that I had to let the gods who created me roam while we went on our quest for the weapon to destroy them.

"Then let's not waste anymore time." Drystan swiped my bowl just as I went to lift my spoon, and I reached after it in protest.

Nyte slipped his bowl in front of me, but Drystan was quick to collect that too.

"Another five minutes to eat isn't going to give the gods much of a head start," Nyte remarked, but stood anyway.

"You used to lead armies, and there was a time you spent more time on the battlefield than off; you should know how crucial five minutes can be."

Nyte and I exchanged a look, which had us mutually regretting the insistence he join us instead of one of the other parties on this quest. I bit back my smile. I couldn't help my amusement, even when nothing was truly humorous; it might be the only way to keep myself from buckling under the foreboding pressure of what we had to achieve.

Our farewells to the others outside Nadir's home started to unsettle my stomach.

I hugged Zath tightly for longer than usual.

"Are you sure you're well enough for this?" I whispered, wishing for an answer I wouldn't get. One that would keep him here and safe.

"I bested Thorns in a combat test—"

"No, you didn't," Rose cut in immediately.

"I *almost* bested her," he amended, pulling back with a boyish grin directed at her. "I'm as good as I can be, and there's no way in hell I'm sitting this out while the rest of you are off risking your lives."

When his sight fell back to me, his smile wiped completely. I couldn't stop staring at him with such worry tightening in my chest. For Rosalind too, as I stepped up to embrace her next.

"Look out for each other," I mumbled.

For once Rose didn't scowl or make any remark.

"We will," she said.

"See you on the other side," Drystan said, heading toward Athebyne without any exchanged sentiments.

Nyte finished talking privately to Elliot, clapping a hand on his shoulder, and I almost thought they would give in to an embrace. It dropped sorrow in me to think of their shared losses; they hadn't had the time to truly grieve.

Nadir had provided horses, which Davina and Lilith mounted. Zath and Rose would go by foot since we were already in Vesitire.

"We'll meet back here in two weeks tops, even if we don't cover all the temples," I reminded everyone.

They nodded, and watching them leave strained the many strings attached to my heart for each of them. Nyte tried to soothe my anxiety with his touch, both on my body, with the hand that rested on my back, and through our bond within.

"We'll all be back together before we know it," he said. It wasn't a promise, just a shared desperate hope.

Before we left, I turned to Nadir, who smoked their pipe by the open door, shirtless with only a thin floral robe and pants despite the cold.

"Thank you for all you've done for us," I said, but it wasn't enough to convey what we owed them.

"I'll see your thanks when you break the chain, Maiden. Free us all."

That struck a powerful purpose in me, and I gave a firm nod. Then Nyte and I headed toward Eltanin, who waited patiently.

Thanks to Drystan, he'd spent a long time studying dragons before he was ever certain they would come back into our existence. He knew about saddles from the past, and though it'd taken a lot of coin, provided by Nadir with utmost discretion, he'd had them made for Athebyne and Eltanin by a leathersmith in Vesitire.

Nyte mounted first, and I followed his maneuvers. Exhilaration thrummed within me at the thought of flying on dragonback again. There was a certain power and beauty in it that couldn't compare with my own wings. As I slipped in front of Nyte, he was quick to shift us both until no space remained between us.

"Eltanin might refuse to fly with us if you're inappropriate," I warned.

"What kind of inappropriate things are you thinking of?"

I wiggled to get a better hold of the saddle grip and to prove my point when he squeezed my thigh in warning for the friction of my ass against him.

"Sure you don't want to ride in front?" I asked innocently.

"Absolutely not."

My grip tightened and my stomach fluttered when Eltanin rose in preparation to take flight. He was so much bigger than he was when I'd taken a short flight with him during the battle on the Nova province. Nyte leaned into me, and I had to admit I was intimidated.

"Do you remember the time you stole Auster's Pegasus and returned it with pink hair?" Nyte said, maybe to distract me from my unease as I pressed into him, gripping his forearm around me tightly, as Eltanin launched powerfully into the sky.

Images flooded my mind. I almost giggled until I remembered . . .

"You put the starlight matter into its food to turn its hair pink!"

"Did I? Maybe my memory needs work."

"He was sour for the weeks it took to turn back to white."

"Then I gladly claim full responsibility for it."

Grinning, with the air breezing through us, I valued the lightness he brought because it felt like treasure in light of the terror we ventured out to.

We soared high above the clouds in an attempt to avoid any wandering celestials in the skies. The air was thin and icy sharp, pricking my cheeks and turning my nose numb.

I slipped off my gloves, shivering as I cupped my hands and conjured a warm sphere of light. I hugged it to myself with a soft sigh, dropping one hand to Nyte's thigh behind mine to share some of the heat. Nyte hugged me against him, and if we could forget all else, this was quite romantic.

"I thought the daylight might come back when you woke," I said thoughtfully, staring at the half-moon. At least it wasn't bleeding anymore. The red overcast had gone.

"I quite like the night."

I smiled, closing my eyes and letting my head rest against his chest. "It's my favorite."

30

Astraea

I raised my hand, and with a whisper of magick, the snow began to melt away from the dragon painting. The ice dissolved into rivulets of water, trickling down the stone in shimmering streams. Light gathered at my fingertips, dancing like tiny stars as it moved over the surface, illuminating the hidden masterpiece beneath.

When the glow finally dimmed, a collective gasp rippled through Nyte, Drystan, and me. The painting was magnificent, its color impossibly vivid despite the passage of time. The dragon stretched across the stone floor in sweeping arcs of crimson, its scales catching the faint light like real fire.

We stood in awe, marveling at the artistry, the sheer presence of the creature captured in the stone. Around it, faint etchings of ancient script curled like smoke, whispering secrets we couldn't yet understand. For a moment, the cold and the snow outside were forgotten. All that mattered was the dragon and the strange, thrilling sense that it was watching, waiting for us.

"It's red like Athebyne," I said wondrously, admiring the fiery depiction, alive against the dull gray stone. "How many colors of dragon are there?"

Drystan crouched, running a hand over the long curling horns of its head. He said, "The world began in chaos. A battle of storm, fire, wind, sea, and darkness. From each birthed a creature that embodied the land's wraths. The dragon with scales of flame and a breath that bears the heat of the sun. The dragon with scales of tanzanite and a breath that strikes the lightning of vicious storms. The dragon with scales of the forest and a breath of lethal gales. The dragon that appeared to be made of water that could flood islands. Then the feathered dragons to rule the rest, those of black or white, with breath of starfire that could rob the senses of humans, decay any life it touched, and what kept the other dragons submissive to them was that the celestial dragons could take away the magickal power of any other living thing with their magick."

My mind played out the different descriptions, imagining a time when there once were countless dragons on our land. Now, if what Drystan predicted was true, there were only eighteen in existence if we freed them all.

"How did the age of the dragon fall if they were so unparalleled in power?" Nyte asked, standing cross-armed, as invested as I was in the history.

"The same thing that collapses all empires in the end," Drystan said as he rose. "Greed and envy. Those who couldn't secure dragon bonds started hunting them. Dragon scales, their blood, their bones—it all could be used for various extremely powerful dark magicks and remedies. A civil war broke out, no one species against the other. It was carnage until someone by the name of Master Decotu, along with seventeen other mages, cast the last seventeen dragons into these paintings to protect their legacy. It killed him and the others, leaving his own white celestial dragon, Fesarrah, as the last who would birth an egg foretold to free the dragons again when the Queen of the Kings reigns."

That last part struck a memory. I'd heard it before. Cassia had spoken of the *Queen of the Kings* in the way she liked to tell her favorite stories.

"We'll free it after we get the key piece," Nyte said, the first to step away from the painting to head toward the temple.

Drystan didn't linger either, following his brother, but I stalled, lost for a moment in my own mind, which was swimming with wonder and terror over the tales about the dragons.

"Astraea," Nyte called.

I tore my sight up from the red paint and started toward him, only getting a few paces before I gasped at the energy I collided into that staggered me back. Nyte immediately approached, but an invisible force rippled at his touch too.

We were separated.

"Looks like this trial is ours alone, brother," Drystan said.

Nyte and I exchanged looks of concern. His jaw locked as he looked like he was calculating a way to shatter the veil before he left me here.

"I'll be okay," I insisted.

"Here," Drystan said. I barely caught the glint of him throwing something before I caught it. The bottle of Eltanin's tears. "Free the dragon while we get your precious key piece."

The bottle came to me as if no shield existed, but when I reached tentative fingers toward the veil, it hummed with a static again. *How annoying I must sit out the excitement.*

"You know how to call for me," Nyte said quietly, pained to be leaving me.

I gave him a convincing smile. "I do. Let's not be separated for longer than necessary. Go. I'll be right here."

He answered with a tight nod before he turned, heading toward the temple that was smaller than the others I'd seen before. Only a uniform block which had an opening inside to go underground.

Nyte looked back at me as Drystan slipped inside first. He spoke through our bond: *"Behave."*

"Speak for yourself. Try not to strangle each other."

I shivered at the internal stroke of my senses, like his fingers brushed down the length of my spine. Then when I was alone, I sighed. My seconds of sulking over being left out were forgotten the moment my eyes fell on the vial I held, and I turned back to the painting.

I braced myself to unleash another fantastic beast into this realm. It was the greatest honor.

"Oh, my dear." A familiar feminine voice said with resignation from behind me.

As I spun around, my eyes caught on the blond hair and blue eyes of Katerina, and delight surged in me. Until my growing smile vanished in an instant.

A slam of terror weakened my knees.

If what Nyte and Drystan had seen was true . . . If their father had succeeded . . .

The confirmation became clearer the longer I stared at the face of my friend and recognized nothing in her eyes.

"Dawn," I said through an incredulous breath.

"Have you estranged yourself so far that you would no longer call me mother?"

That term slithered up my spine with cruel intent.

"You don't deserve that title. You are a merciless, unfeeling god, nothing more."

"Merciless? Everything I have done is to create a perfect world. I created you, the greatest gift for mankind, and yet you chose to love a plague. It is not I who is merciless, child."

"What did you do to Katerina?" I asked. My fists balled and trembled, but I had to admit my fear was greater than my courage in this blindsiding confrontation.

"She is still within this vessel for now. Depending how long I have to stay, she will either die or still have enough of her mind to wake when I return to my realm. I guess we could say her life is in your hands."

"What do you want?"

"In bargaining with Death you severed your ties to us, your parental gods. We cannot allow another creature of darkness to taint the perfect order we have come to set right."

"You've come to kill me?"

"Do you remember—?" she said, avoiding an answer, but a tingling formed over my body and panic rose in my chest. "When you were nothing more than stardust?"

My palms grew warm against my control and I raised them, gasping at the glow of them. Panic seized me when my fingertips started to break away as particles of glittering stardust.

"Stop. Please," I breathed, blinking hard and hoping it was just a cruel trick. She couldn't send me back to the stars.

"You only exist because of me and Dusk. You are nothing more than a cosmic energy."

"You're wrong," I croaked.

"You are not human. You are not even a celestial. You are a god and have no place among these beings. I see that now. We chose wrong in placing you here as the pinnacle example of what mankind should aspire to be."

My hands were gone and my arms kept dissolving; the shimmering dust of me flew toward the night sky and I watched in horror, feeling the pull toward the stars.

I can't go back. I can't go back.

This isn't real.

My eyes scrunched shut, but the shallow burn crawling up my arms didn't subside.

I tried desperately to reach within and call for Nyte, but as I thought it, my chest exploded with fire and I cried, sinking to my knees.

I will not let her win. I will not let her diminish who and what I am.

"I am more than stardust. More than just cosmic power," I whispered to myself. My teeth gritted, and I snapped my eyes open to strike Dawn with the heat of my glare. "I am more than what you tried to make me."

A loud caw rang through the adrenaline beginning to pound in my ears. It was quickly followed by a large raven swooping low, and Dawn shrieked when its claws sliced across her cheek. I tracked the bird with awe. A glistening raven too large to be of nature, and by the way it *helped* me . . .

It was a Guardian spirit.

I'd met the panther, the bonded spirit of my human and nightcrawler guardians, in the Sanctuary of the Soundless. Then I remembered the serpent in the maze; it was the bonded spirit of my soulless and fae guardians. Now my eyes watered to watch the bonded spirit of my soulless and celestial guardians aid me now.

The raven struck again and again, and with Dawn distracted, I plunged into my magick. It surged through my veins, coursed over my arms, and spilled into my palms—now flesh once more.

I was skin and bone and breakable in this realm, but I didn't want to be anywhere else.

Gathering the light within me, I breathed deeply, tempting Lightsdeath but not letting it fully unleash. With a bright gale swirling between my palms, I thrust forward, sending it hurtling toward Dawn, but not with enough force to kill. Katerina still lived, and I had to believe there was a way to save her even when I killed Dawn.

I stood there panting as the snow and wind settled.

Dawn wasn't here.

Rushing forward, I scanned desperately, but Katerina's body wasn't lying injured as I'd expected.

Instead, the raven cawed, landing on a tree branch.

"There is one too great of an enemy to waste focus on others who have been misled by human flaws," the raven said, words that passed through my mind like a song instead of aloud.

"What does that mean?" I asked, taking a step closer, desperate for any guidance to navigate the many adversaries I faced.

"You know exactly what I mean, Maiden. Your heart is as human as every mortal on this land. It makes selfish choices and can be blind to those it hurts. You can forgive and never forget, but if you forget you will never forgive."

"Wait—!"

The raven took off too fast, and I clutched a hand to my chest with an ache that beat with every push of the bird's wings as it soared away.

I had to remember they weren't my guardians anymore; they belonged to the realm now and held no sentiment for me. Though it made me yearn to go back to Alisus and see them in their mortal forms again now that I had my memories.

A tear slipped down my cheek and I swiped it away, turning back to the task I had to fulfill.

The dragon, even in its still, silent form, strengthened my shaken resolve. There was no greater ally to secure, but also no deadlier enemy to face.

Every dragon we released: there was no telling to which side of fate their allegiance would bond.

31

Nyte

What if the only way out is for one of us to kill the other?" Drystan pondered, breaking the eerie silence as we descended in darkness.

"Then it was nice knowing you. I can't be killed," I answered flatly.

"I might have Astraea's blood with me."

"You don't."

"You wouldn't scent it in a tightly sealed bottle."

"I would."

Drystan made a disgruntled sound. "Is that all you'd have to say to me?"

"I'd rather not waste time on theoretical last words."

"I suppose we've already been there."

I didn't need to be reminded of that horror. I'd fallen into the curse not long after I heard about Drystan's plan that he'd sworn Astraea to keep in secrecy. When she'd plunged her stormstone dagger though his heart . . . I'd believed it was true. That she'd killed him. And the reminder surged my anger about the ruse, which I hadn't gotten to unleash on either of them.

"Next time I won't waste my breath," I muttered.

"You have to admit, the plan to get Death to transform Astraea was genius."

"It was idiotic with no guarantee. You deserve to be dead for good."

That thought alone tore a phantom wound inside me, but I wouldn't let it show.

"Probably, but hey, we had to have inherited some tricks from our father, right? I swear he's the one true immortal on this godforsaken land."

I grumbled my agreement, content to let the silence settle again. These stairs down were endless.

"Have you ever imagined how you would do it . . . ?" Drystan asked, voice quieter now with a somber topic. "How you would kill him if he was right there?"

"No, actually. I always imagined the opportunity would come with little time to think about it, and I hope that's true."

A tragic tension grew between us.

"Sometimes I've wished that we would have time," he confessed. "To ask him *why*, but then . . . I don't even know what I mean by it. Why was he cruel? Why couldn't he be satisfied with what he had? Why couldn't he love us?"

I didn't like to carry other people's emotions, but with Drystan and Astraea I always captured an echo of their feelings good or bad.

"The truth is often more painful than the unknown."

"Don't you want closure?"

"We've been orphans for a very long time, Drystan. That's all I need to know. There's no *why* that would heal that truth, or even make it more tolerable to harbor. I'm just glad that you . . . that despite all he tried to do you didn't end up like him."

Drystan didn't speak for a long moment.

"You said he has another son," he broke the silence again. "I have another half-brother?"

"Had," I corrected with a faint pinch in my chest. "When I was cursed, my subconscious projected back to where I came from. Nightwalking, in the most incredulous sense—that realm is where that ability is from. In that other realm, I saw our half-brother, but he didn't know who I was. He was everything I feared you or I could have become from the influence of our father, and the irony is that it was the absence of our father that drove our half-brother, Malin, to become a true villain to himself and his country. I think the abandonment is what made him want to prove himself. For us, we watched our father and knew it was everything we never wanted to be, so why would we want to please him?"

Drystan pondered the story in silence for a while. "I suppose we could have turned out worse then."

Finally, light broke at the end of the tunnel, and when it did, it took everything in me not to retreat right away. We walked right into a perfect replica of the drawing room in our former home. The Keep of Bethezal.

"Stay close to me," I said, but the words became lead on my tongue.

My next step swayed my body from a wave of dizziness that came on sharply and suddenly. I blinked, catching myself on the back of a chair.

Stay close to me.

Stay close to me.

My words echoed through the room, mocking me.

When I straightened, I stared down at the hauntingly familiar pattern of a beige and crimson carpet. Then I heard the suppressed sniffling beside me, daring a sidelong glance to find Drystan, just a boy the height of my shoulder. His eyes brimmed red and his bottom lip quivered.

I remembered why he was so devastated right before I looked a little further up the carpet and found the dog with its neck broken.

"You should be training yourself, not some runt," father spat, furious when he'd discovered his younger brother with the animal.

I gritted my teeth recalling his act of cold cruelty just moments ago. Our father had ordered Drystan himself to kill it, but he never would have gone through with it. Instead, he'd knelt by the beast, hugging it while its tail wagged happily, blissfully unaware of its death crawling closer. I stood by and watched the thinning patience of our father, who would have struck out at Drystan, likely beaten him until he conceded. Even then I knew he never would, not when his heart was so pure and innocent.

So I'd reached into the hound's mind, commanding a sharp and painless break of its neck, when father's yelling and Drystan's cries of protest distracted them both for it to easily appear like Drystan had followed through.

If our father knew what I'd done, he said nothing. After all, *I* was his killer.

The look of absolute horror and betrayal Drystan had cast up to me when he held the beast limp in his child arms would go on to haunt me for years to come.

"Nothing is worth your tears. You shed a single one of them, I'll show you what pain really feels like." Those were father's harsh parting words before he left us in his study, the slamming of the door leaving a rumbling echo of his violence.

To his credit, Drystan didn't let a single tear fall after that despite his palpable misery. Drystan stayed put, and I couldn't leave him. So we stood there and let the sorrow creep in slowly. For his fragile heart, there was a part of me that sympathized with him.

"Anything you love is worth your tears," I said at last. "Father has never loved anything."

"I hate you," Drystan said, three words that formed a blade sharp enough to cut through my own emotionless web. With them he shot his heartbroken gaze, now lined with anger, at me,. Then his first tear fell.

"Hate . . . now that is something that only hurts you unless you find a way to craft it into a weapon."

"You sound just like father," he seethed, with a face far too young to experience such agony.

With that, Drystan stormed out of the room, slamming the door in his wake. I didn't try to deny it. I didn't stop him. I didn't comfort him.

Father gave the order; I carried it out.

We *were* one and the same.

Always one and the same.

I'd so long been numb to that acknowledgement, yet right now it was like

Drystan had punched his small, gentle hand through my chest and ripped out my black heart.

I didn't care how father saw me. I didn't care that I was a nightmare whispered among the people.

I did care about Drystan. How he saw me.

Right now, I was *his* monster.

I wanted to go after him, but I never did. I wanted to lock ourselves in his room and explain why I did it.

I didn't do any of those things . . . Because I knew this wouldn't be the last time father's cruel ways came down on Drystan, and I thought it best to let his heart know a few breaks so he might learn to protect it before it could shatter.

I was wrong. He was just a kid.

My first step to go after him shifted the ground, and my limbs flailed, trying to catch myself before I could slam into the wall, when the whole room tilted on its axis.

"Drystan!" I called.

Gods, I'd let him down. I should have fought with him. Instead, I'd not only just stood by to watch the first piece of his innocence get taken, but I'd been the one to steal it.

"I'm sorry, Drystan," I said in defeat, letting my body tumble whichever way the room went.

It stopped spinning and I slammed to my hands and knees, trembling with the aches lancing through my face and abdomen as if I'd taken a fresh beating.

"When I order an assassination, I expect it fulfilled," father's voice bellowed, and I knew then we were in the great hall. I recalled this memory.

Another powerful kick from a nearby guard nearly knocked my smaller body onto my back, but I gritted my teeth, tensed my muscles, and stayed firm.

I dragged my sight up to see Drystan, who barely looked older than twelve mortal years. He stood by father, looking at me with expressionless eyes, but his features occasionally winced at my pain. He'd told father of my failure to kill the enemy he'd given me as a target.

I'd set it up so perfectly when I arrived at the family's home. It was a vampire who'd deserted his place in father's uprising, and in penance he'd ordered him and any family he'd had killed as an example for others. But he had a wife and two innocent children. He'd pleaded endlessly at my feet, and so I staged their deaths instead.

It was the first time I'd taken Drystan on a task with me because he'd begged to go. And perhaps it was because he was with me I'd found the mercy for the cowardly soldier. I wasn't ready to claim another piece of Drystan's innocence.

The irony that almost made me laugh was that I could kill every person in this room with little effort. The guard who'd carried out my beating would die eventually; I'm sure father was even counting on it. Yet I kneeled here and accepted my punishment like the pitiful child he saw me as right now, because if I didn't, he'd warned me before my rebellions that he would inflict it on Drystan instead.

I didn't know why my little brother had betrayed me. Perhaps in revenge for killing his pet. It didn't matter, and in truth, I didn't want to be spared from this beating.

"You two are dismissed; get out of my sight," father hissed, turning away.

I peeled myself off the ground and staggered after Drystan. Part of me understood why he did it, but my anger grew to be too much with the throbbing of my body. When we were alone in the hall, I pushed him against the wall.

"Father's little rat now, are you?" I snapped.

"Better a rat than a cold-hearted *murderer*," Drystan bit back.

I suffered more from that than anything physical. Not the harsh comment, but watching Drystan's heart become ice right before my eyes was something I'd wanted so desperately to prevent from happening. He couldn't turn out like me. One of us had to be good, be *better.*

Forgiveness clawed in my chest, but I couldn't let it out. It would be so easy to tell him I didn't blame him.

Drystan pushed me away, and his eyes threw spears into my chest. He looked like he might say something else, but it seemed we both had claws against kindness growing stronger within us. I watched him walk away with his hate washing over me in waves with every step he took.

Just forgive him.

He's all you have.

Just forgive. Forgive.

I shook my head, remembering again that this was just a memory. *This had already happened.*

Where was I now . . . ?

As I started trying to figure that out, the room spun again, but I held onto my reality, firming my mind against reliving another cruel memory from the past as if it were the present.

This is a trial.

Between me and Drystan . . .

A trial of forgiveness.

To break the vicious cycle we'd grown up with.

Drystan failed when he didn't forgive me for killing his pet even though I had no choice. I failed for not forgiving him for turning me into father. These were only two events in our long history. If I kept falling into full immersion in these memories there'd be centuries worth for this trial to feed on.

We have to make it out. Astraea was waiting, and the thought of her was a thread of light to keep me aware, which I clung to with everything I had.

The next time the room stopped slamming me against its walls, I landed on my feet, gripping something firm between both hands. Only when an impact ricocheted off it with a high pitch did I register it was a blade, and when my eyes adjusted from the disorientation, I stared through crossed swords at the contorted determination of Drystan, my opponent.

"This will not end until one of you draws first blood," father's voice echoed from across the training hall.

Drystan pushed off first, going on the attack, but he was no swordsman. Not even close to contending with me. This wasn't so long after we first met Astraea. Father had been so furious that he took it out on us, on his soldiers, on anything he could use to grapple with his shame over how easily she'd slipped right out of his grasp.

Astraea. My starlight. My light back.

"Drystan, you need to snap out of it; this isn't real," I said, bracing against each of his amateur attacks.

Though he wasn't a novice swordsman now. In this memory he was missing the centuries he would spend training. The centuries during which he would force himself to become something he never wanted to be. A fighter to be a survivor.

"You've always been his favorite."

"That's not a worthy achievement," I bit back.

I shook my head. *Don't let the trial distract you.*

Keeping myself grounded made sweat trickle down my forehead.

"You're far better than this now. You can actually contend with me," I said, parrying around the hall at his onslaught. He had no form and little skill, but his rage was enough to inspire a commendable attack.

"Don't patronize me, brother," he snarled.

Father called over, "You've always been weak, Drystan. You'll never match Nyte."

Fury boiled in me, but I didn't tear my sight from Drystan. Seeing my father was sure to plunge me deep into the clutches of this illusion once more.

"This is what he wants. Us fighting each other. Betraying each other. He wouldn't care if one of us killed the other," I said.

"Seems inevitable," Drystan said, panting through his exertion, and soon he would falter.

"No, it's not. Father has never been able to forgive anything. But I forgive you, and no matter how long it takes, I'm going to keep trying to become something you can forgive too."

Drystan kept advancing, not breaking out of the trial's illusion. I had Astraea to think of and keep me aware, but Drystan . . . did he really have nothing to reach for in this world? Nothing worth coming back to?

The next time he pushed me back . . . I dropped my sword.

Drystan's blade slashed across my front from the right side of my chest to my left hip. A searing line of fire scorched the deep path of his sword. That was real. Our swords were real, not just part of the memory.

I collapsed to my knees, bleeding onto the floor.

"Nyte," Drystan's voice broke.

"I'm-I'm okay," I said, but I wasn't sure. My mind became foggy, and I hoped it was just the trial and I would begin to heal as soon as we were out of it.

"I just wanted to be like you," Drystan confessed. He fell to his knees with me, sword clattering next to mine.

Father's voice became too loud, piercing our ears and rattling through our bones. "You incompetent brats. Get up! Get up and fight!"

I was too consumed by Drystan's words to be affected by the conjuring of our father in his most vicious days.

I said, "All I wanted . . . was to make sure you never ended up like me." Shit, I was losing too much blood. While it wouldn't truly kill me, I didn't want to risk restarting this trial. "I'm sorry that you felt like I abandoned you. That I was cruel and judged you too harshly, like father did. I thought if you saw a monster in me you'd never want to become it."

"I forgive—"

Before Drystan could finish a flicker of movement caught in the side of my vision. A tall form, an unforgiving twisted face, the glint of a blade coming down toward Drystan. Agony roared through my body, lunging me forward to push Drystan out of the path and brace for it to slice through my shoulder instead.

The impact obliterated the world, and I blacked out.

"Nyte!"

The call of my name echoed, muffled and distorted, as though I were drifting through an endless ocean. It repeated, throwing out a line for me to grasp and pull myself to the surface before I could drown.

"Dammit, you bastard, don't fucking die here," Drystan said. His voice became assured and louder as I detected his frustration. Then pressure on my abdomen shot a new wave of pain through me, and I gasped, eyes flying open.

My vision blurred, but I kept blinking, reaching to hold onto my fading consciousness.

"Shit, this is bad. Can't you heal any faster?"

I gulped for breath that didn't come so easily. My body felt heavy and warm and *wet*. I was bathed in my own blood.

"Stop *bleeding*," Drystan groaned, adding pressure again that made me wheeze my next breath.

"Stop trying to kill me fucking faster," I barked, forcing myself up and pushing him off. I quickly scanned him over, then muttered with mild irritation, "At least one of us remained unscathed."

Drystan ignored me, picking up something discarded beside him. The sight of the key piece made me forget my misery for a second."Is it a real one?" Drystan pondered, examining it before holding it out to me.

I snatched it too desperately, coating it with the blood from my hand as I flipped it, waiting for something. *Anything.*

When I felt nothing at all, my hand tightened around it and my body slumped.

"Another fake piece," I confirmed.

Drystan swore, standing now. I started taking in more of the room, which appeared like a long neglected storage room in the temple. Drystan groaned and his patience snapped, causing him to scatter the few old books and paper from a nearby table.

"That was all for nothing then," he seethed.

I strained to push myself to my feet, catching my unsteady balance on a chair, but it crumpled with my weight and I tumbled, finding purchase on the desk before I went sprawling embarrassingly again.

"We need to get you to a healer—"

"It wasn't for nothing," I said through my clenched teeth, breathing through the dizzying blood loss and throbbing pain.

Why wasn't I healing faster?

Drystan began to rant, "The time we wasted to get a dud piece of metal—"

"I meant everything I said in that . . . *trick.*"

I could practically feel Drystan's guard rising at my confession, and I couldn't blame him.

"Well, I suppose it did feel good to finally land a blow against you."

My chuckle turned into a sharp wince. Fuck, laughing hurt my wound, but it was genuine.

"I let you get that in."

"Don't make me challenge you again; I won't hesitate to do worse."

Even though Drystan was diverting himself from the raw feelings that had been dragged to the surface from long buried depths, at least he was still able to have a sense of humor.

"Let's get out of here. We have plenty more of these damn temples to visit. It's likely you'll get another run at combat with me. I warn you: I'm pretty great now."

We headed up the endless stairs, which felt like a climb of the steepest mountain. I leaned against the wall for support, until Drystan slung my arm around his shoulder and took some of my weight. By the time we spied light at the top I was close to falling unconscious. Or dead.

Sweat drenched me, and with a body of lead, the first breath of fresh icy air was utter bliss.

My foggy sight immediately tried to find Astraea, and I blinked more the longer I couldn't find her waiting for us.

"The dragon is gone," Drystan confirmed, but so was Astraea, and that provided enough adrenaline for me to fully straighten, ready to push through anything to find her.

A loud gust of wind snapped my head up to see a red dragon smaller than Athebyne, a horned male, soaring across the treetops. Then, to my immense relief, I heard the most delightful sound of enjoyment and giggling from Astraea atop its back.

"Huh, that's interesting," Drystan said, retrieving a journal from inside his cloak. He flipped a few pages, lost in thought, then found a blank one with a thin stick of charcoal, which he used to scrawl across it. "The dragons don't typically let anyone other than their bonded rider mount them unless accompanied by the rider. Even then they can be highly selective."

"Did it choose Astraea?"

"I don't believe so."

I watched her soar in circles, and it was enough of a beautiful distraction from my wound for a while. When I next winced, the dragon came down; the vibrations of its landing trembled under my feet.

Astraea slipped off the dragon's back and jogged through the snow toward me, her face pinched with concern.

"What the hell happened in there?" she asked, worry thick in her voice. Her mere presence soothed some of the ache.

Astraea cupped my cheek, scanning me all over until she gasped, pressing small gentle hands over part of the slash across my body that annoyingly wasn't healing as well as it should. The bleeding should have stopped by now at least.

"We fought," Drystan said absentmindedly, looking up from his notes toward the dragon before folding his materials away and heading toward it.

Astraea's mouth hung open as she stared at him; then she snapped back to me for more explanation.

"It's the short version of events, yes," I confirmed.

Her face pulled together into adorable disapproval. "I want the very *long* version once we get you somewhere to heal."

She circled her arm around my waist, coaxing me along.

"While I was making sure my brother didn't kill me, you discovered all dragons have a liking for you?" I mused.

We passed Drystan, who approached the dragon tentatively, not nearly as relaxed as he was with Athebyne but expertly composed. He would catch up with us in the town later, as I assumed he would be staying there a while to document whatever he usually did.

"I'm not sure. I used the tears, and it was wonderful to watch the dragon come alive." Astraea stopped at the tree line, turning back to yell to Drystan, "His name is Alrakis!" Then she was guiding us through the small forest again, resuming her story. "I was just waiting around for you two, and Alrakis wouldn't leave. I was glad for the company; strangely it was very soothing. Then at some point I just made my way onto its back and we went flying for a while. Astrinus is beautiful from above. So many mountains with small villages in their valleys."

"Yes, it keeps the kingdom very peaceful and protected from larger army attacks on foot," I recalled.

The trek into the nearest town was arduous. I hadn't felt this weak and exhausted in a long time. We tried the first inn we came across, and they had no lodgings. The next was the same. By the third, Astraea and I shared a look and began to suspect we were being turned away because I looked like trouble in my current state or because people were recognizing us but too afraid to confront us.

"I offered that last one enough money to buy out all the rooms in the wretched place," she grumbled.

"Money wouldn't mean anything if the place got destroyed or they got killed. They fear we'd bring enough trouble for that possibility." My eyelids kept drooping, as much as I tried to keep straight and present while the worry on Astraea's face grew.

She led me around the side of a building, and I slumped onto a snow-covered barrel. It had to be crawling into night hours with how the temperature was plummeting.

"Just try my blood, here," she said, resting on her haunches and pushing up her sleeve.

I wanted to refuse because I risked taking more than I usually would to heal myself, and that would leave her weak. But if I fell unconscious I'd leave her alone with my dead weight, and that was a greater fear.

"You'll need to stop me the moment you feel even a little tired," I warned.

Astraea nodded with a small, assuring smile.

Taking her wrist, I guided it lazily to my lips and sank my teeth into her flesh. The first drop of her blood on my tongue would usually trigger an acute thirst and feverish demand, but something wasn't right. I pulled back, spluttering sideward at the first taste, which was like ash and smoke, turning into flame in my chest.

"Nyte, what's wrong?" Astraea asked in panic, almost holding all my weight now to keep me from tumbling off the barrel.

"I don't know," I gasped.

Was it because of my blood within her that was used to harm her? No. I didn't think that was it. I should have been healing much faster naturally, which led me to believe that the trials were particularly punishing, making sure any wounds sustained in them couldn't be healed so easily.

"Astraea, I-I can't . . . I can't hold on much longer." My fear was for her. To leave her alone and panicked with my dead weight in this unfamiliar territory. "You need to leave me and find Drystan," I said desperately, fighting the dark spots peppering my vision.

"I've got you. It's okay, Nyte."

The flecks of darkness in my sight merged, slowly stealing the beautiful image of her. Still, I fought to keep conscious enough to follow her direction. Her strained sounds from hauling a lot of my weight were muffled in my ears. She managed to sling my arm around her shoulders and we moved forward. The cold wind stopped lashing us for a few moments. Astraea used the void, pulling us both through it, but I didn't know where to.

"We just need shelter; then I'll get help," she said. Astraea was right beside me yet her voice sounded so distant.

Astraea halted us suddenly, and I grappled for the fading edges of my awareness. At first I thought trees surrounded us, until they began to move, inching closer. Too many bodies, and I could hardly see them, never mind brace to fight them.

"Run, Astraea."

Her hold only tightened on me, and my teeth gritted painfully. Some of the faces came in and out of focus; I didn't recognize any, but all I needed to see was the constellation sigil of Astrinus pinned on their cloaks. These were guards of the reigning lord here.

"Looks like you're going to make this collection easy, Nightsdeath," one called out, strolling ahead of the others.

The name he used confirmed I was only known for the reputation that began right in this kingdom.

"Stay back," Astraea warned them.

"Don't fight for me, please," I said, barely able to bring words to my mouth now. "Use your magick and run."

"That's not happening," she answered firmly.

"Maiden," the same soldier greeted; my only relief was that he sounded genuinely respectful toward her. "We mean you no harm, I assure you."

"You mean *us* no harm," she amended, testing him.

"You don't know who you are harboring. The ruins that monster left this part of Astrinus. Our reigning lord, Viscarus, salvaged it after he and his wicked father and brother left."

I remembered exactly how we'd left. My father had spent decades here building his vampire army and granting them the spoils of the humans and celestials here. When Astraea died, and my father occupied the castle of Vesitire, his followers left too, and these lands were left torn apart from too many years of bloodshed and terror.

"I won't let you harm him," Astraea said, and I felt the growing heat of her skin, her magick awakening.

"It's true what they're saying about you, then?" the soldier said, his tone shifting to an unfriendliness that sparked wrath inside me. "You really have forsaken your people and duty to protect and defend a monster?"

"No. Your tales are twisted and we're trying to stop the real threats to this continent," she said. The confidence in her voice stoked my pride.

"I hope you'll forgive me for our measures, Maiden. But it doesn't seem you'll come with us willingly."

I didn't think I had any fight left in me with the severity of my wound. But the threat in those words snapped something in me, a will that defied all physical limitations to seize the minds of everyone who surrounded us. A dozen, maybe more; I couldn't count and would lose consciousness any second.

"Don't kill them!" Astraea's warning blared through the violent pulse in my head.

I only had seconds to decide. They threatened her and I wanted to kill them all, but her voice of reason would always trump my retribution. She was the only damned moral I had left.

"Then please *run!*" I said in defeat, still holding their minds to give her that last chance.

But I knew she wouldn't leave me. It was both the only thing that kept me wanting to live and, in moments like this, the reason I wished I wasn't this weakness that kept her in harm's way because of her love for me.

Astraea sunk to her knees with me, holding my face in her hands. Her stunning silver-blue eyes were the last glint in the darkness that consumed me.

"Let go, Rainyte. I won't let anyone hurt you."

32

Astraea

I stood in front of the reigning lord of east Astrinus, and I'd have the heat of retribution in my stare if he kept me away from Nyte much longer.

After we'd been escorted here, with several guards having to carry Nyte, they'd listened to my demand that he be made comfortable and a healer be fetched. Then I'd been summoned before this man with long white hair merging with his beard. His wrinkled skin flexed, and his worn hand massaged his cheek occasionally as he studied me like I was an artifact.

"I must say I never thought my years would stretch long enough to see the star-maiden in all your stunning glory."

The compliment flushed through me, dissolving some of my hostility with his touchingly gentle tone, which croaked with the impressive years he'd sustained himself as a human.

"Why did you want us to come here?" I demanded.

"I had to see the world's first and only fallen star, of course."

"Is that all?"

Finally, a cautious shift in his gray eyes firmed my guard again.

"I won't insult you, Astraea; I know you're aware of the realm's nightmare you keep in your company. I will be honest and admit my people would heal an old wound by seeing him publicly slain on the lands he defiled."

My magick rushed over me in an instant, prickling the edges of my vision with stardust. Lightsdeath was one reach away from irrepressible things should this lord think to order Nyte's execution.

"If a single hand lands on him in malice, I will sever it from the body that strikes," I warned.

The old man's chin lifted with the threat. "From your legends, you were not one to act out in violence. You are our goddess of justice and peace."

"Then hear me when I say your vengeance is not for Rainyte, it is for his father, who'll you'll learn is a common enemy if you will listen to us. Hear our tale and be our allies."

This hadn't been what we'd come for, but this could become an unforeseen opportunity to rally more forces against the gods and Nyte's father when the time came.

"You want me to declare Nightsdeath an ally? You insult me and everyone in this kingdom," Viscarus seethed, the first slip of his outrage, which seemed so much more unpleasant on his kind, weathered face.

"His name is Rainyte. And I am asking you to trust me as your Maiden. That my judgment is not corrupt, though the High Celestials have tried to make you believe so. Rainyte is not your enemy."

"Your pretty words hold no weight, Maiden. You were gone a long time, taken back by your gods after you failed your duty once. And as I hear, you have slain Auster Nova."

I stiffened. I'd hoped word of his death by my hand hadn't reached this far yet.

"He killed me first," I said.

Viscarus's head titled. His elbows propped on the arms of his deep green cushioned chair and his hands clasped. In his silence, he pondered his judgment of me.

The tension grew too much for me. "What can we do to prove ourselves to you?"

That made his posture lock straighter and I realized this is what he wanted. The reigning lord hadn't taken us in just for trespassing in his territory or to have his retribution against Nyte. There was something he thought we could do for him.

"Once Nights—"

"Rainyte."

Viscarus's eyes flexed. "Once Rainyte is healed enough, I will summon you both again. Judgment will be carried out."

We both knew that if we desired, there was little that could truly hold me and Nyte to this keep. But we needed allies and my mission was to heal the distrust and divide that had been left to crack too deeply through these lands.

I bowed my head in respect to him. "I look forward to seeing you again and helping in whatever way we can. Thank you for your hospitality in the meantime."

He lifted his brows, surprised by my grace, but he gave me a nod back before asking his guards to escort me to Nyte's room.

Amity settled for only a second before I turned around.

Drystan strolled in, escorting a man who appeared drunk, who was leaning on Drystan for support. I'd never seen his company before, but something about Drystan's dark smile made my nerves stand on edge.

"What have you done to my son?" Viscarus bellowed.

Shit. That declaration came close to shattering the fragile peace I'd just gained with the lord for now.

"He's fine," Drystan drawled. When they stopped walking halfway across the hall, Drystan lifted his thumb to the corner of his mouth, wiping a trickle of blood. Then I saw the raw puncture wounds on the disheveled, pulled down collar of Viscarus's son.

What the hell have you done, Drystan?

I didn't voice my irritation and outrage because so much steel chimed through the air. Every guard made a target not just of Drystan, but once again I became a hostile source.

Drystan said, "I heard Lionel here boasting of the capture of Nightsdeath and the star-maiden. Foolish for your heir to flaunt such things in public."

"Release him," Viscarus demanded.

"As you can see, I'm not holding him." It was true. Drystan even tried to gain distance but Lionel hung sleepily onto his side. "Did you know the bite of a blood vampire has a certain aphrodisiac quality? Believe it or not, your son *begged* for it. However—"

Tension shot high with how fast Drystan moved, holding Lionel from behind with the man's neck inclined to the side. Drystan bared his fangs, a threat that he could rip out Lionel's throat in a heartbeat or drain him dry before anyone could stop him.

"I'll ask once for you to release my brother before I kill him."

I was about to reprimand Drystan and try to salvage this situation, but a stunning red-haired woman glided in through the doors behind him. Her fiery hair touched the billowing blue waves of the material of her gown.

"My brother has always had a curious nature and overindulgent palate," she said, her voice a cool melody that calmed the room.

Her sight slipped over Lionel only for a second before she gave me her attention as she passed. There was a certain serenity in her presence. Though she gave away little emotion, I didn't detect any ill will.

"Leave us," she ordered the room. Immediately the guards exited, and I watched her with more fascination.

"This is my heir, Gweneth," Viscarus introduced.

I dipped my head to her. "My name is—"

"Astraea Lightborne. The star-maiden."

I nodded.

Gweneth studied me for a moment, and I didn't know why her assessment made me shift my weight between my legs.

"You're a little smaller than I imagined."

I couldn't help but huff a laugh, glad for some of the thickening tension

Drystan had brought to be dissolved. In my defense, Gweneth was *very* tall for a woman.

She turned her attention to her father. "Show them. There's no reason to keep our request a secret until Rainyte wakes."

Viscarus's expression softened for his daughter, and that exchange made me believe that Gweneth wasn't waiting for her father's death to assume her duty as reigning lady of east Astrinus; she had been slowly filling that role for many years as her father aged.

But there was something else which burdened them, and I knew it was going to be shared with me, with us, as they believed we might be able to help.

"You have no reason to trust me, and even less to trust Nyte and Drystan. But I give you my word that I'll offer whatever we can to help. There can't be trust without taking a leap of good faith," I said.

Viscarus only looked at me briefly, then nodded his agreement to Gweneth.

"Follow me, Maiden," she said. As we headed out, she addressed Drystan as she passed him. "You can either take my brother to bed, as he seems to need rest after his night of indulgence, or come with us."

Drystan let go of Lionel to hook my arm. "This could be a trap," he hissed low to me.

"Trust works both ways," I said. "You've done enough damage to shake that, so you're coming with me."

Grabbing his forearm, I dragged him along after Gweneth.

"Where's Nyte?" Drystan asked, his tone irritable as he tried not to be overheard.

But Gweneth answered before I could. "Our healers are tending to him. He might not wake until morning."

"I want to see him," Drystan demanded.

"First, you'll see why my father hasn't ordered him chained and tortured instead. Make no mistake, you and your brother are enemies of this kingdom, but sometimes even the deepest hate has to be set aside for those we love."

We were treading dangerous ground.

"What you think we can do for you requires Nyte's mind ability, doesn't it?" I concluded.

They could have held him in the dungeons and refused to get him healer help if it were my magick they sought to use.

"Yes," Gweneth answered.

We were approached by servants, and I accepted the thick winter coat offered to me. Drystan declined, retaining his sour expression, which I rolled my eyes at.

Outside, my first breath of the crisp air was stolen by the snow-capped mountains glistening under the pale moonlight, their towering peaks crowned with frost that shimmered. Astrinus was magnificent, and now I had a moment to bask in its beauty. Between the jagged mountain heights, pockets of life thrived—a tapestry of gentle beauty woven into the harsh landscape. Small villages dotted through the snow-dusted ridges, their warm lights flickering against the cold.

It felt as though the mountains themselves had chosen to cradle these sanctuaries, shielding them from the rest of the world. In this secret realm of stone and snow, life blossomed quietly, resilient yet impossibly tender, as if daring the heavens to notice.

I became more antsy the longer we followed Gweneth away from the keep. Glancing back, I tried to measure time in case I had fallen into a trap and had to make it back to Nyte if he were in trouble.

"I should have stayed at the keep," Drystan said after I looked over my shoulder for the third time.

I was beginning to agree with him.

Around the next street corner, my pace slowed after I saw the large building we were heading toward. I'd seen depictions of a place similar to this in books and conjured my own images through words alone from the vivid minds of authors. But this place . . . it was so *sad*. A long abandoned hall that once would have welcomed all walks of life into its gallery to witness performances upon its grand stage.

"What are we doing here?" I asked, growing uneasy now.

"Don't waver your trust now," Gweneth said with a note of amusement that was lost on me. She walked a few paces ahead.

"This isn't a good idea," Drystan said to me.

"You should stay outside," I said.

His lips pursed together as he weighed whether he should immediately help us to fight if we were ambushed inside or if it would be more of an advantage to get aid if he detected foul play from outside, assuming he could escape. "I can't hear your thoughts and feelings like I can hear Nyte's, so scream particularly loud if you need me," he grumbled, crossing his arms and scanning around for any hint of threat.

The eerie creak of the door we entered crawled over my skin. The ominous stillness that held me upon passing the threshold was a cold ghost of the joy that once brightened this place. A dark passage opened up into a grand hall with two levels. I'd been in a theatre like this before—it's where Davina had once held one of her fae resistance meetings in Vesitire. That one had been long neglected too.

An ache built in my soul for what the loss of these venues represented. A world that had been so upturned by war and greed that the time, or perhaps the passion, to enjoy such performances as would be held in these halls ceased to exist.

We weren't alone here. Gweneth stopped past the first couple of rows of torn, dusty velvet seats, and I found what—*who*—held her attention.

A woman with long gray hair was upon the stage. Noise came from the towers of discarded instruments she searched through as she muttered quietly to herself.

"My mother. I am named after her."

Gweneth didn't approach her mother. We stood there merely observing, and then I started to notice her strange behavior. The elderly woman appeared so lost but energized. She moved around the stage, occasionally stopping to smile and bow as if her own audience existed in her mind.

"She is ill?" I asked carefully.

"A sickness of the mind. No mage or healer can help her. She doesn't remember us most days, and every evening she comes here, reluctant to leave, but father comes for her by bedtime."

My heart cracked for this family. How terrible it would be to have a loved one not remember who they are.

"What happened to this place?" I asked, barely a whisper in this space that felt sacred.

"It was destroyed and abandoned long before my father became the reigning lord. But my mother used to perform with a traveling circus. She wanted to restore this place one day but there was so much else to rebuild that it stayed a dream for too long. Then her illness came on fast. We've tried all we could to help her for ten years."

"I'm so sorry," I said.

Gweneth tore her eyes away from her mother to look at me and I felt her sorrow. "Do you think Rainyte could help her?"

I swallowed because hope felt like too fragile a token to give.

"I really hope he can. And one thing is certain—I know he'll try to the very best of his ability."

She smiled, believing me, believing in Nyte despite the scars he left behind on these lands.

"There's a reason you're our Goddess of Justice, Astraea. Our star-maiden. People say you fell for a monster, but you were simply the first to have an open mind and the patience to hear his story. Too often people judge harshly from what they hear and close their eyes to anything that might shed a light on what they've condemned to the dark."

Pride and relief swelled in me. Every new ally we gained brought us closer to the world Nyte and I dreamed of together. My hand hovered over my wound where Nyte's blood was spreading slowly. The ache was dull, but every now and then it would emit a sting like a warning, a cruel taunt never letting me forget my days were numbered. I didn't know if I would get to see the future I wanted to build with Nyte, but I wouldn't stop fighting and living as though I might.

33

Astraea

I sat on the edge of Nyte's bed, changing the cool cloth on his forehead. His fever had been passing over the day he'd been lying here after the healers did all they could yesterday. His torso was bare and bandaged. The slash would have to heal naturally from now, but they were confident he'd be well enough for travel in a few days.

Drystan lingered by the door to the closet, staring intently at the frame. His fingers lifted, brushing down the wood. Curiosity caused me to stand when I finished checking Nyte over, and I drifted carefully when it was like Drystan wasn't present; he stood in a past time.

I understood when I saw the scores in the wood; next to each one were single initials: D or N.

My smile bloomed with a tender skip in my chest at the markers of Nyte and Drystan's physical height growth over the years they grew up here.

"I didn't know these were his old rooms," I said quietly.

Drystan's touch dropped, and he took a long breath, reeling back.

"They weren't. They were mine." Drystan huffed a laugh as he reflected on the markers. "I was so determined to catch up to his height, as if I had any control over it. I made him come here every year for decades."

I laughed too, picturing the moment they got to be ordinary, free from their father's cold ways, in each other's company.

"You almost did," I mused, skimming my fingers just past my own height.

They were both many inches taller now, at their full, permanent height. Sorrow dropped my hand from the highest scores, the last time Drystan made them document their height.

"Bastard still has around two inches on me in the end."

"That's one race that always had a predetermined outcome," I said, feeling the weight of those words. How many other things did we compete for and chase in life that were never our destiny to triumph against?

"True, but I think there's something to be said for the stubbornness of hoping anyway."

Drystan's eyes slipped to me as mine did to him. In this moment I wanted to embrace him, and I thought he might break our tension at last too . . .

"This is one room I hoped to never be in again," Nyte said, his voice thick and pained.

We both whirled to him, and I was by his side before Nyte finished pushing himself up, helping him to sit back against the headboard.

"Better than a cell, however. You two are hopeless without me, getting yourselves caught," Drystan said.

I ignored him, asking Nyte, "How are you feeling?"

"Miserable. This trial wound is a damn hindrance." He cast a glowering look at his brother.

Drystan rolled his eyes, heading for the door.

"Where are you going?" I called.

"To see if Lionel is willing to indulge again."

"He's off limits," I warned.

Drystan smirked at me from the open door. "That's for him to decide."

I glared at the ghost of him.

"I have clearly missed a few things," Nyte said, accompanied by his touch on my back. "Want to fill me in, beginning with how I'm not, as Drystan points out, in a cell, given who ambushed us?"

I shifted deeper onto the bed to be close to him and told him everything that had happened over the last two days.

Nyte idly played with my hair as I talked, taking everything in and making his own queries.

"We have to get moving again." Nyte tried to shift off the bed, doing a commendable job of hiding his pain.

"You have a task to do here first," I reminded him.

He'd agreed to try all he could to help Gweneth's mother, like I knew he would.

"I'm well enough. Let's go there."

As much as I wanted to protest and stretch out his time to simply rest and heal, too many parts of the war were charging forward, and we couldn't afford to be still for long.

"I'm not leaving you again. Even a courtyard of distance is too much," I said.

"The key piece wasn't real," he told me as he dressed.

"I know. I found it in your jacket."

He sighed in defeat. "If one or more of us gets injured like this again . . . it makes all of us vulnerable."

Since Nyte was gravely wounded my antsy concern for our friends facing the same brutal trials, crafted to test them all individually, had risen.

"Your trial . . . what did you have to do that ended with this?" I asked carefully as Nyte pulled his shirt over the bandages.

"We saw memories. Of us and father in this keep. We were young at first. Memories of times we'd betrayed each other. For the final one, our father made us duel, and it took some convincing to snap Drystan out of the illusion."

My heart ached for the brothers who'd had to relive such cold parts of the past.

"He seems in his usual spirits," I said.

"He's not the one who suffered the slice of a blade."

"You let him."

"I had to. You were my anchor to snap out of the illusion and know it wasn't real. I realized during that trial he had nothing to bring him back. But once it might have been me, so I let him land his centuries-long resentment toward me in that blow."

My brow crumpled when I heard that. Thinking back to the temple, I realized I never had the chance to tell him . . .

"I saw Dawn."

Nyte's gold eyes snapped to me, flaring a shade darker, as if the goddess would be here for him to target.

"How did you escape her?"

"She . . . let me go. I can't be certain she wasn't just an illusion to taunt me. I thought she was taking me back to the stars when my flesh . . . it became stardust before my very eyes, and I thought—"

Nyte took my face in his hands, and I hadn't realized I'd been staring at mine, reliving the sensation of losing the body I wanted to keep, to stay here as a mortal, as long as Nyte would be.

"They don't get to take you back. Not ever again. You're mine, and I'm going to wipe the names of Dusk and Dawn from existence to keep you."

I fell into him, letting his warmth and scent soothe away my burst of panic.

"I'm sorry I couldn't save your friend," Nyte said mournfully.

"Dawn taunted me with Katerina's life. She's still alive, but the longer Dawn inhabits her body the weaker she becomes. If Dawn kills me swiftly and leaves, Katerina will live. If I kill Dawn . . . what if that means I kill Katerina?"

"She's manipulating you. It's not possible for two people's consciousness to exist in the same brain. Trust me, I know it isn't."

Nyte was a master of the mind, and he locked my eyes with such certainty I believed him. Which meant there was no saving Katerina; she really was gone, and I had to take the news to Zephyr soon. Had he been looking for her?

I said, "We need the true name of Dawn to be able to kill her."

"I'll be with you next time she shows herself. I'll find it in her mind."

Recalling my walk with Death in His realm, the warning he gave ran a chill through me.

Beware, the mind of a god is no easy passage. It is not ventured without consequence.

"It could hurt you gravely," I said with a spike of worry.

"Are you doubting me, Starlight?" Nyte said it like a tease, squeezing my waist, but I couldn't muster a smile.

"I mean it. Promise me you won't ever push past your limits."

Nyte kissed me softly. "I promise. Not if it means losing you."

In the abandoned theatre, I'd never seen Nyte this gentle and tentative with another person. We all stood on the stage, but Gweneth and I hung back, letting Nyte approach the elderly woman, who was once again searching through the broken and discarded instruments.

He followed her, watching her; occasionally he spoke to her and she spoke back. We couldn't hear their words, but it was tender to witness. I figured Nyte must be searching her thoughts at times, trying to find what could have been severed for a life full of love and experiences to have drowned within her own mind.

"This is the most she's spoken to anyone in months," Gweneth said to me, quiet so as not to disturb them.

"Nyte has his ways," I said tenderly. Even without his ability, when Nyte wanted to give it, his devoted attention had a compelling property.

After a few minutes, Nyte joined in on her search. The clamor of instruments and occasional ping of breaking strings amplified.

He found a case buried deep. Flicking open the latches revealed a violin, untouched by the wreckage he plucked it from. I thought he'd found the working instrument to give to the elder woman, perhaps discovering it was what she'd been looking for all this time.

To my surprise, Nyte lifted the instrument until his chin rested in position and his other hand angled the bow against the strings. He tested a few notes at first, adjusting the pegs until the notes started to sound like beautiful potential. I wanted him to play so badly my soul ached for it. I hadn't known, even in my past life, that Nyte could play the violin, but it was obvious from how he handled the instrument.

"Oh yes!" Gweneth's mother exclaimed, clapping her hands together while she watched Nyte with the violin. The pure joy on her face lit up my own.

"This is what she has been wanting from this place?" Gweneth asked.

Nyte played a few notes, not a song yet, keeping her mother entranced while his gaze slipped to us across the side of the stage.

"There are those who say music is magick itself. That it invokes feelings that touch the soul deeper than anything else can. Your mother, Gweneth, used to play a long time ago. I think her subconscious is searching for a certain feeling, which may spark her memory."

Nyte spoke on a personal level and my heart could hardly contain itself at the breathtaking sight of him with the violin in his hands.

How he slowly lost himself in the notes that started to weave together.

Then Nyte played, boldly and brilliantly.

I didn't think I could feel any closer to him, but this . . . how Nyte could sing me his soul forged a new tie around mine.

Gweneth had floated closer to her mother until her hand reached around her hunched shoulders. As Nyte's short melody finished, the elderly woman stared, as starstruck as I was.

The final note carried even in the silence. Then Gweneth's mother spoke, her words rhyming into a poem.

"Beneath the sky where starlight glows,

Through silver mists, the cold wind blows.

A dawn awaits where beauty shows,

The tender light of the Goddess Eos."

Nyte's shock slammed into mine; our eyes clashed into each other at the same time.

"*Eos,*" I repeated through our bond.

Had we just learned the true name of the Goddess of Dawn?

"Gweneth?" the elderly woman croaked.

"Mother?"

Watching the recognition light up on her mother's face, and in turn the relief and joy on Gweneth's, touched my heart.

"I don't know how permanent it will be. The mind is a very complicated and intricate system. I can keep trying to fuse together threads that have frayed, but I have to warn there's a risk that it carries that could cause her to lose far more of her mind."

"This is enough," Gweneth said, cupping her mother's cheek.

"You've grown," her mother said, scanning her head to toe. Her aged face pinched in guilt as if she'd missed her daughter growing up. "You're so beautiful, my Gwen."

The resemblance between them still showed in the shape of their noses and color of their eyes. It made me think they once shared the same vibrant red hair too.

Nyte said, "This isn't the only instrument that might help bring her back for a while. Music in many forms lingers strong in her mind."

"Thank you," Gweneth said, embracing her mother, whose head tucked under her daughter's chin.

The look she bore on Nyte filled my chest warmly. Nyte would always harbor the capacity to be the realm's nightmare; that would never change, and I didn't want him to. But it was the light in Gweneth's eyes as she looked at him now that proved Nyte could heal as much as he could hurt.

Gweneth left happily with her mother. Nyte wrapped an arm around me as we watched them leave.

"You didn't tell me you could play," I said, my voice choked and shallow.

"This place was in operation for a while when I lived here. I was only a novice at the violin. It's the instrument I was most drawn to."

"Why did you stop playing?"

A muscle in his jaw worked. Nyte sat, letting his legs dance over the ledge and the violin rest on his lap. I dropped down beside him, looking over the expanses of seats over both levels.

Nyte said, "The first person I ever let in—considered a friend despite me being an immortal child and him an elderly human man—was the lead violinist who played on that stage every second day. I was so taken by the music, by his instrument in particular, that I had forgotten to erase myself from his mind, and he caught me where I shouldn't be. He wasn't mad; he didn't even ask why I was there. All he did was hand me his violin, and from that day I kept coming back. He taught me a couple of songs, and I learned a few of my own, but I was nowhere close to his masterful skill with it. Anyone can learn a sequence of notes, but there's a unique tone to every player."

Tears were already gathering in my eyes, as I knew there was no happy ending to this tale.

Nyte's voice reduced a little more to continue. "One night I came and the theatre was shut off. Vampires warded outside, and I learned the entire orchestra had been slaughtered. From then on, the theatre was declared closed indefinitely. My father never confronted me about my time here, but I knew he had ordered the massacre."

I didn't think there was anything monstrous I could learn about Nyte's father that would shock me, but this was at the top of the worst. Taking away a token of freedom Nyte had found in music. Shattering an innocent dream before it had the chance to become a mastered passion. Robbing him of something precious that saved him within while the world tore him apart.

Sitting here as the focus of an imaginary audience that filled the empty seats in my mind, Cassia's spirit came back to me in one of the last memories we shared together.

I like to dance, I'd said to Cassia. *I don't think I've ever told you.*

I can't wait to see you dance, she'd replied. So confident and sure even though she knew she was dying and I'd been so oblivious to that dark countdown. *On a stage someday.*

"How magnificent you would look," Nyte said quietly, catching the edge of my thoughts I left open to him.

"Never thought I'd see one of those in your hands again." Drystan's voice echoed to us from the top level. Nyte set the violin aside. "We've wasted enough time. I've called Athebyne back and Eltanin came too."

"It wasn't wasted time," I said.

Nyte slipped off the stage and braced his hands on my waist to help me down too. He gave me a squeeze, knowing I meant that our time spent here was worth getting to help Gweneth's mother and secure an alliance with Astrinus, which was willing to fight on our side if it came to that.

I told Drystan, "We have the true name of the Goddess of Dawn."

34

Nyte

It was strange to see right through the borders of Althenia. The Sterling Mountains had always acted as a sentry before one would cross the border at the other side onto the celestial territory. Not so long ago we wouldn't have been able to see Althenia even from high atop these mountains, but the tall veil of starlight that kept the celestials protected from outsiders for centuries had shattered when I walked through it in my rage of vengeance after the Golden Guard were killed.

Standing here, I felt more connected to the heavens than the land, watching the pockets of life stretch vastly and endlessly while the rivers wove like threads of silver silk. Althenia was nothing short of a breathtaking masterpiece, with the water breaking the land like a six-pointed star. Yet even the most ethereal and peaceful part of Solanis was tainted by war now. The bloodshed had been blanketed by snow and the ruins of the Nova province were unseen from here.

"This is going to be difficult," Drystan called over.

We'd been scouring the mountain fringes for hours, trying to pinpoint the exact location of the next temple, when Drystan's map indicated it should be right here.

I found him and Astraea by the edge of a large body of water. They were staring down into it, and then I understood.

"How deep?" I asked.

"Far too deep for any of us to go that long without air," Astraea said, crossing her arms and calculating.

"It might even be a fake piece. We should collect the ones we can, then meet back up with the others to see if we're still missing one," Drystan suggested.

I stared into the faintly rippling water . . .

"I might have a way to get to it," I said. Both turned to me. "It would require a temporary diversion."

Drystan said, "How long? We only have one more week until we have to meet up with the others, and there are still six temples left in Althenia."

"I can't be sure. I know I said no one goes alone, but I could meet up with you two when I have this one—"

"No," Astraea cut in firmly. "You said no more separation."

My heart fucking ached at her note of panic.

"Then we could all go—" I tried, but Drystan spoke over me this time.

"I'll get started on the other temples in Althenia alone while you two go on this *diversion*. I'll be just fine."

Astraea agreed with him. "I'll send word to Zephyr; he should be able to help keep you hidden."

"You two are beginning to feel like the parents I never wanted," he said, reaching Athebyne and climbing up expertly.

"Just don't get yourself killed or trapped in a trial," I said flatly.

"What a poor ending that would be," he replied, bracing himself on Athebyne for flight.

Astraea and I shielded our eyes from the blast of the dragon's wings. Eltanin rattled, watching the red dragon fly away. I believed they were beginning to form something of a friendship bond.

I took Astraea's hand, pulling her through the void to mount Eltanin.

"So where are we going?" Astraea asked, more chipper than she had been in the last few days.

"Volanis."

Her body tensed, seated in front of me, and I got a bad fucking feeling, stalling my command for Eltanin to take flight.

"Is there something wrong with that destination?" I didn't know why, but her reaction alone started prickling my wrath.

"It's . . . I don't know the lord there," she prefaced. "But he . . . he wanted to buy me from Goldfell before I escaped. Goldfell was going to let the lord—Vermont, I think his name is—have me and the manor, and, in exchange, Goldfell would have reign over Volanis. But it was a trap, and Goldfell planned to kill the lord and his men, then have me join him in Volanis after the sale."

My hands tightened on her with the absolute rage that surged through me upon hearing those words.

Sale. Buy. Exchange.

I wished that bastard would stop crawling from the grave I'd put him in.

"So we're greeting Vermont with more violence; good to know," I muttered with an edge.

Before we took off, I angled her head back to me, holding her chin.

"I hope you know there's nothing of equal value to you, not even close, in any realm or galaxy." I kissed her hard, and the soft moan in the back of her throat had me aching for her.

"I never met him; I don't know what he's like," she said.

Her hair was mostly loose and I kissed her neck, breathing in the delicious scent of her wild silver tresses.

"He intended to buy you. That's enough for me to know his time is running very short."

I reached into my bond with Eltanin, and he heard my command to leave.

When we crossed over the sea toward the volcanic island, Astraea leaned over to watch the water expand below us. She let herself fall, and I didn't take my eyes off her to watch her magnificent raven black wings come out and catch her. Astraea twisted gracefully with a bright smile, and Eltanin dropped lower to follow her, as she wanted to fly closer over the water.

Her hand reached down until her fingers splashed across the tame surface and she laughed. The most magnificent sight and sound.

This perfect painting of her was shattered when a dark shadow grew in the waters beneath her. I shouted her name through the bond but not fast enough to alert her before a hand lunged up, wrapping around her forearm and pulling her fully underwater in the blink of an eye.

Eltanin roared in distress, darting sideways to turn around, but that would take too long. I used the void, appearing in the air where she'd gone under, and I dived in after her.

Astraea was fighting with all her might, but the creature was too strong. I swam hard as it kept dragging her deeper, and I reached for her, but she was too far. My golden tattoos glowed and her silver ones did too. I felt a type of magick in me I'd never used before, but I didn't think, only seized it at the same time Astraea sent a blast of light toward her assailant, freeing herself from their clutches, and I attacked in the same manner before the next darting up from the depths could reach her.

I could use Astraea's light magick.

I didn't know how; it wasn't something I'd taken from her in the past, but I knew it was possible to share power between some Bonded pairs.

Astraea threw her head back, and her frantic eyes caught mine. She tried desperately to swim up, but she wasn't getting far. Then to my horror I realized it was because she couldn't swim.

The distance between us felt endless. Impossible. But I would never give up.

More bodies came up from below, and my rage was building, already gripping the loose power Astraea was expelling from her survival instinct; perhaps her magick reached for me when it knew she needed help the most.

Her hand strained for mine, and when I reached her, I pulled her to me, about to explode my wrath into these waters.

The creatures, nymphs from their human-like facial features, balked as light glowed from both of us, but it wasn't our magick that frightened them off. Another nymph hissed and clawed at the face of one. A cloud of black blood made me lose track of them, and the rest stopped reaching for us to regard the interference.

I was already kicking away as the burn in my lungs grew. The darkness pressed in, the surface seemed impossibly far, and my vision blurred as clouds edged in. My limbs grew heavy, each movement sluggish, but still I swam with everything I had.

Then we were shooting for the surface faster than I could carry us.

I held Astraea tight as we gasped for air the second it surrounded us. Her head lost balance as she choked, coming in and out of consciousness. Her forehead rested on my shoulder, and all I could do was hold her, smoothing away her wet hair.

"So silly." I knew that voice all too well, had recognized our savior the moment I saw her stark black tail.

Fedora swam around us, and Astraea tensed in fright. The nymph's head canted with a smile of wicked amusement. She reached for Astraea, tucking a lock of her wet hair behind her ear.

She'd visited me more times than I cared for in the cave under the library, accessing it from the passage of water that filled a shallow pool. I'd asked her to take Astraea's dagger and leave it in a place she would find in Goldfell manor, and my end of the bargain, retrieving a powerful trident she was after that was on land, remained unfilled.

"We can scent celestial blood when it touches our waters, even from the depths," she said in that melodic voice of hers.

"How did you scare them off?" I asked.

Eltanin roared above us, but he wouldn't be able to get close enough to help us, and the void to pass through wouldn't open in water.

"There are advantages to being dark and unknown, as you well know," she said.

Her black tail kept them afraid, as her kind thought her a bad omen just like the celestials harbored disdain for black wings. However, fear was a power in itself.

"You have no magick though," I pointed out.

"Yet." She floated closer, resting her hand on my shoulder while the other idly played with Astraea's hair. "I'm waiting for that to change with what you owe me."

Astraea's teeth bashed together, and her lips were turning faintly blue. We had to get out of the water before the icy cold killed us instead of the nymphs.

"As fate has it, that's exactly what I was going to retrieve for you. But I need something more from you."

Her black eyes flared with excitement but quickly narrowed with ire.

"I did my part in making sure your star found her stormstone dagger in Goldfell manor."

"That's hardly a fair trade for what you stand to gain in return."

"It's not my fault you chose such a pathetic request."

Distant voices caught my attention, and I found a ship heading our way.

"After all we've been through, won't you help me just this once to test the power you'll have with the trident?"

That curved a wild smile on her face.

"What do you have in mind?"

"There's a temple underwater beneath the Sterling Mountains; we'll need your help to get inside it once we have the trident."

"Ahh yes, they speak of the cursed temple under the sea. My kind wouldn't dare try to enter such an ancient place. Fortunately for you, angering gods sounds delightful to me."

"Good. Once I've retrieved the trident, we'll meet you there."

Fedora smiled, baring serrated teeth, which was more frightening than endearing. She cupped both my and Astraea's cheeks.

"It's so precious seeing the star and the night together," she doted. Then her eyes flicked up, and her expression turned dark on the approaching ship. "I could take you to shore instead."

"We wouldn't last in these waters for that long," I told her.

She pouted. "Leaving me so soon?"

"How will I call for you when I have the trident?" I asked.

Fedora held such adoring eyes on Astraea, stroking her cheek like a pet. Then before I could stop her, a long sharp nail cut her cheek, making her bleed, and Astraea's grip tightened on me.

My teeth gritted, suppressing my instinct to kill as I watched Fedora bring Astraea's blood, beaded on her nail, to her tongue.

"A drop into the water you're near and I'll be the first to find you," she said, eyes flaring wildly as she sucked her crimson-tipped finger into her mouth. "Like tasting the stars."

Fedora giggled, an eerie sound. "Don't keep me waiting long!" she sang; then she dove sideways, disappearing under the dark water and splashing us with her tail, which surfaced, then plunged back under.

"She's . . . terrifying," Astraea said through chittering breaths.

I stroked a thumb under her bleeding cheek. "She's a thorn in my side."

"I didn't really feel it. My face is quite numb."

The boat was near, and from the actions of the crew preparing a rope ladder over the side, I knew they'd seen us. Glancing skyward, Eltanin fought my inner command for him to leave, but eventually he began soaring away.

I helped Astraea climb onto the ladder first, following right behind until we both felt the bliss of solid wood beneath our feet. Pulling Astraea to me, I surveyed the crew, who watched us warily, like we were unidentified creatures pulled up in their nets.

"There's no other who can claim they caught a star in their waters." A low, gruff voice broke the stiff silence. The deck creaked, giving me their direction to find a tall, broad, middle-aged man with dark hair curling under his tricorn. The captain, I presumed from his confident demeanor.

I anticipated those on board would recognize Astraea, but I could wipe their memories before we got to shore, so I wasn't too concerned.

"We need passage to Volanis and can pay well," I said to the captain.

"We have no coin," Astraea countered through our bond.

"They won't remember."

The captain said, "It was not my intended destination, but I'm intrigued as to what the Maiden and the notorious Nightsdeath would be after on such a prized island."

"It's merely a political endeavor."

"I see. Gathering allies to stand against the High Celestials after killing Auster Nova, I presume? We're not cut off from affairs out at sea."

If only the threats brewing were as simple as that. A war with only two sides. Us and them. The whole world was oblivious to the scale of what threatened their peace.

"Something like that, yes," I said.

The captain's brown eyes roved over Astraea, and I itched to claw them out.

"I'm curious as to how two with wings and a dragon end up helpless and near frozen in the sea between the mainland and Volanis."

Only one with wings, I thought with a twinge in my chest. Astraea shook stiffly, and I was losing patience with being the crew's entertainment while she was suffering.

"If you have a fire we could warm and dry by, we might be more inclined to share a story."

The captain ignored me to address her. "So quiet, Maiden."

Don't do something reckless, I tamed myself.

Astraea answered through chittering teeth, "I have little desire for conversation when I still feel like I'm in the sea."

The captain chuckled deeply. "Very well. Follow me."

I didn't trust this man, though I couldn't place why. We followed with little choice, but I was at ease knowing I could kill everyone on this ship and not feel bad about it if they tried to harm Astraea.

We went below deck, and the warmth drifting through the cabin was already a reprieve. In the captain's quarters, Astraea left my side to go to the fire, immediately sinking to her knees and holding her hands toward it with soft sighs.

I scanned the room, which was very lavishly decorated with red carpet and velvet-clad seating behind a mahogany desk.

"You must trade well," I observed, heading absentmindedly toward Astraea while keeping my full attention on this man.

"I captain the finest ship on the seas, the *Silver Sparrow*," he replied proudly, wandering around his room with hands clasped behind his back.

Kneeling, I unhooked the fastening on Astraea's heavy sodden cloak, and she smiled her thanks when I peeled it away from her.

"You should take off your boots and socks too," I said through our bond.

"You need to dry your clothes as well," she said back.

I took off my cloak, but then I stood, facing the captain.

"What is your name?" I asked.

"Balthezar Corrick," he supplied.

The name rang a faint familiarity, but I couldn't grasp from where.

The captain took up his grand chair behind the desk, far neater than I'd expect. His calm demeanor told me he didn't fear either of us, and I had to wonder what gave him such confidence.

I didn't like it.

Slipping my hands into my pockets, I crossed the room, trying to figure this man out by the things he chose to keep in his private space.

I picked up a perfect silver sphere that had a good weight and tossed it a couple of times.

"I don't appreciate people touching my things," Balthezar said.

Catching and keeping hold of the sphere, I cast him a playful smile. "No point in being so precious about things that don't really have ownership. If I burn this ship and it goes sinking to the bottom of this ocean, yours it would no longer be."

I tossed it to him, delighting in the irritable flex around his eyes when he caught it.

"Do you make a habit of provoking those who aid you?"

Chuckling lightly, I skimmed my hands over more trinkets.

"I guess not all things reach you at sea if you know my name and thought it would greet you with kindness. Let's not be under any pretense here: we both know the fate of every life aboard, including yours, is in my hands right now."

I could feel Astraea's eyes on me; she didn't speak a note of reprimand for my behavior, but I felt it.

"You dare threaten me and my crew?"

Balthezar rose from his chair. I needed his anger, for him to test me, so he knew what I was capable of if given the right motivation. I wouldn't take any chances on a ship full of pirates that had the most precious prize aboard right now and might be tempted to do something *very* foolish to obtain her.

"If you did know of my reputation, you'd know there isn't a person still alive I've threatened."

"Oh I know all about you, Nightsdeath."

I didn't correct the name. That dark presence might be gone, but the reputation remained power in my hands.

"Good."

"Like how to truly kill you." His eyes flicked to Astraea.

I warned, cold and promising, "If a single drop of her blood spills aboard this ship, accidently or otherwise, I'll make sure the nymphs are fed generously with every single one of you."

"Nyte," Astraea said my name, and it worked to tame the violent beast inside me.

I forced myself to add a smile toward Balthezar, but he knew there was nothing friendly in it.

"I should have left you to drown," he hissed, rubbing his throat.

"If you did, I would have had to waste time hunting you down for leaving her to suffer. You would most certainly have felt my threat while in your final breaths then."

"We are grateful for your help," Astraea said.

Balthezar would lean more toward her kind reception; I had played my part in letting him know any action against us would be a final mistake. This was why we made a brilliant team.

"Might I ask where you were heading?" Astraea continued, starting friendly conversation I had no interest in.

Instead, I continued my vague scour of the room, and what caught my attention next jumped a beat in my chest. Rested proudly upon a velvet cloth was a golden monocular telescope. It couldn't be the one I thought of . . .

"Must you touch everything that catches your eye?" Balthezar grumbled.

Ignoring him, I picked it up, scanning to find any indication it might be the one missing from the Wanderer's Trove. I would wager Drystan would know right away somehow.

"My brother has a fascination for such trinkets. He would appreciate a souvenir from our travels, don't you think?" I asked Astraea, holding it up and keeping my interest tame.

"Nothing in this room is for sale," Balthezar warned.

"Oh, he would," Astraea gushed, coming to take it from me. She put on an adoring act. "I even find myself quite taken with it."

"Name your price," I said to the captain.

His eyes narrowed. "It's an heirloom and has been in my family for centuries. That monocular is priceless."

"Nothing of material value is priceless."

His brown eyes flicked to Astraea as if *she* were his asking price, and every nerve cell rattled within me, ready to lunge for his throat again if that request spilled from his mouth next.

"They say the Maiden's blood can cure any ills, and her hair can grant immortality to humans."

"They also say a pirate's soul becomes chained to the wicked depths of the ocean if they're killed aboard, and I'm more than eager to find out if that rumor is true."

Astraea said, "My blood can't cure all ills." Her tone was quiet, being reminded of her friend, Cassia. Astraea's blood had only delayed the inevitable, but Cassia's fatal illness would have taken her life eventually.

"Now you've upset her," I said, teeth grinding with the echoes of Astraea's sadness rippling through me.

Before I could move, her warm hand took mine.

"I apologize," Balthezar said carefully, looking at me like I'd planted a minefield around this office and one wrong step would trigger me to come for him again. "Regardless, my price is a sample of her blood and a lock of her hair."

Astraea's voice filtered through my head. *"You think it might be the monocular from the Wanderer's Trove, don't you?"*

"It's possible, but also just as likely to be a very old and ordinary monocular. I could just erase it from his mind. I was trying to be civil, but I don't like where it gets me."

"We can't keep taking what we want. You never know when the most unexpected acquaintances could come back into your life one day."

I curled a lock of her stunning silver hair around my finger. "I don't like to share," I said aloud.

"That's what we do for friends," she said, casting a sweet smile at Balthezar.

I sighed, pulling a knife from my side and holding it to the lock I held.

"Are you sure?" I asked though the bond.

"It'll grow back."

It pained me to cut even one tress of her hair, and more so to put it in the hands of a man I didn't trust.

"What will you do with it?" I asked, watching him marvel over the lock that kept its unique glittering property even when cut.

"I'm not sure yet," he said, as though his mind was churning through a million options for what would give him the most gain. My fist tightened.

Balthezar opened a drawer of his desk and lifted out a small box. He tied the hair with a purple ribbon—*how fitting*—before storing it away.

Next he produced a small bottle, looking up expectantly. I turned to find Astraea holding her stormstone dagger, but I caught her wrist.

"Let me," I said, slipping into her mind to take away the sting as I cut the palm of her hand.

She realized what I'd done, staring at the cut with surprise, then smiled at me in gratitude. So damn precious. My teeth sharpened in my mouth at the scent of her blood. A feeling of dominance at the thought of another male receiving it clawed within me. More so than the hair, it physically challenged me not to reach across the desk and spill his blood by pulling the heart from his chest.

"You're radiating violence," Astraea said in my mind.

She soothed my senses from within, and I kissed her temple before wandering over to a tapestry on the wall.

"Is this ancient or important?" I asked, indicating the hung material.

Balthezar looked up when he corked the bottle of Astraea's blood. "It was an honorable gift I received from a wealthy—"

He choked on the ending of his tale when I ripped the bottom of it.

"Part of our exchange," I explained, and tied the strip of material around Astraea's cut palm.

"How long until we reach Volanis?" she asked Balthezar.

He regarded a device above the fire that kept time with sand and metallic spheres rolling through it. "Should the sea stay calm, we'll reach shore by morning. But the evernight has made the sea rather angry. I fear the longer this imbalance lasts without daylight, it will surely start to rebel far more viciously."

I didn't fear the imbalance like everyone did. I wouldn't care if this world collapsed when I could take Astraea to another, to as many as it took to find peace. But it was for her I *had* to care. For she had friends and a duty she loved here.

It was past midnight and Astraea spoke for both of our fatigue after the unexpected hitch in our journey.

"Is there a place we can rest for a few hours?" Astraea inquired.

"You can rest here."

"Thank you," she said, smiling kindly and slipping her hand into mine. "I've never been on a boat before; I'd like to see the waters from the deck before I retire."

My knuckle stroked her cheek. "Anything you want."

We left Balthezar, but I couldn't put my mind at ease about the company of strangers, pirates, we were surrounded by. I didn't think I would be resting tonight.

Astraea tried to let go of my hand, heading toward the ship's edge across the deck. I grasped her tighter, so she pulled me along instead.

She watched the stars. More of them shot across the sky than ever before, falling and causing devastation we couldn't see. Occasionally I could hear the land cracking, splitting. If the stars kept pummeling the land, there would be nothing left but rock and ash.

"It was all a lie," she said, not to me or even to herself.

I held her to me around the waist from behind, watching the sky that was both beautiful and heartbreaking. A sky of trapped souls. Death had exposed the lie of this world to her—that the celestials gain higher power than any other being by tapping into the prison of souls.

Astraea's role now as Death's Maiden was to free them all and let them pass onto Death's realm for rest. Time was running out with more souls dying, more true stars falling, and the world as we knew it set on a countdown toward ruin.

"I believe you'll bring the new dawn," I said.

"I have to kill my parents. Dusk and Dawn. What if our world can never find balance again without them?"

"Then I'll bring the new dusk."

She lowered her gaze from the sky, and she turned in my arms.

"I'm scared," she whispered. "I'm scared that my parents are right and I am nothing more than stardust. People look at me and see me as parts of gods. My magick, my blood, my hair."

I cupped her cheek, utterly enamored with her in this moment when I couldn't explain how she made the night alive within me.

"By the stars, you are absolutely exquisite against the moonlight." I had to kiss her for a small relief to my building ache for her. "Do you want to know what I think?"

"Yes."

"That no opinion, even mine, matters but your own. Your parents think you insolent; I think you brave. Auster thought you incapable of leading a kingdom; I think you capable of leading empires. What matters is what you believe about yourself in your heart. And if there's something you aspire to be, I'm going to be with you every step of the way."

Her silver eyes glistened. "I want to be brave and powerful."

"Then what are you going to do about it?"

She took a deep, confident breath. "I wasn't finished."

My mouth quirked.

"I want to be so many things, and I will be. But I want *you*. The past had me believing there was always a sacrifice. That I couldn't be everything I wanted for the people and have you. I refuse that fate."

Hearing that satisfied my soul.

I promised her, "As the dusk and the dawn, as the night and the stars, as darkness and as light, it's you and me defying fate until the end of time."

35

Nyte

Astraea had fallen asleep on a chaise by the fire in Balthezar's quarters. I sat by her side, hyperaware the captain was still in this room.

The door creaked open without a knock and I stood, defensive instincts on alert to the intruder. My sight fell, finding a far smaller person than I expected poking his head around the wood timidly.

"You should be asleep, my boy," Balthezar said, setting down his quill and motioning for him to enter fully.

I didn't expect any youth to be on board.

"I couldn't s-sleep," he said.

His stutter wasn't from his timidness. He rounded the desk toward his father, and I assessed him as no older than twelve.

The boy resembled Balthezar with tousled curly brown hair, but his father didn't have the same scattering of freckles across his nose and cheeks, nor the deep green eye color I assumed was from his mother. With him being alone, I thought his mother was likely dead or at least not aboard this ship.

"What is your name?" I asked the boy, who didn't stop stealing glances of curiosity at me.

"Brody."

"My name is Nyte."

The boy smiled, easing at my company with that token of amity to share names. While I was stuck with this captain, I thought to probe for any information I could get.

"You used to visit Goldfell manor, am I correct?" I asked Balthezar.

The captain's brow raised as he poured out two drinks of what smelled like rum, offering one to me, but I didn't take it.

"A couple of times, yes. For trade negotiations between Volanis and . . . I can't quite remember his name, in fact, but the man who ran that manor was too arrogant and full of himself for my liking."

He couldn't remember because I'd erased Goldfell's birth name from existence, and he would hardly recall what the piece of shit looked like either.

"How many ships and captains act as traders and communicators between Volanis and the mainland?" I asked.

I tensed when Brody left his father's side, wandering over to where Astraea slept peacefully. I'd lulled her mind into a deep rest; she needed it.

Brody boldly sat at the foot of the chaise. "She's very pretty. And her hair sparkles."

Her beautiful soft laugh echoed through my mind as if she had been awake to hear the compliment.

Balthezar said, "To answer your question: Vermont is a very paranoid and guarded man. Many have tried to take his island, which boasts great riches, as I'm sure you know. As far as I know he had trusted no ship other than the *Silver Sparrow* to dock his shore." Balthezar didn't boast this fact; it was just a job to him, regardless of how rich the person was.

"Many months ago, there was to be a particularly precious trade between Vermont and Goldfell," I mentioned cautiously.

He took a drink, looking off to consider. Then he made a noise of recollection.

"Ahh yes, now you mention it. Goldfell was killed in his manor before the transaction could be completed. Vermont was unusually angry about it. He tires of the seclusion and said what Goldfell offered was a prize as valuable as the whole of Volanis. I couldn't fathom what it could be . . ." Balthezar's gaze trailed over to Astraea, casual at first, until he realized she was the missing piece. "I see. Goldfell had her all that time ago?"

"She was without her memories of the past," I said bitterly, despising how he'd stirred up the memory of a failure of mine: when I left her there believing Goldfell was keeping her safe, when he was just as cruel as the world outside his precious manor.

"What a tragic time, to have the most powerful being on the continent caged without knowing her potential. I am glad she escaped, however it was achieved. It seems fate will always have a way of opening the doors we need to pass through, and it takes a strong will to walk through not knowing what could lie beyond."

Brody reached for her hair, and it took conscious effort not to snap at him. "I-is it ma-ma-magick?" he asked innocently.

"She is pure magick," Balthezar answered in a voice like he was reading a bedtime story. It was a side of him I didn't expect. He exchanged a smile with his son, whose eyes filled with wonder because he wanted to hear more.

"She's also just a person," I said, glancing over her. Astraea was so much more than a god's creation. "A person that loves, and fights, and dreams. Just like anyone else."

"I want her to wake up so I can meet her," Brody said.

"It is long past rest hour, son. You should be sleeping as well."

Brody pouted.

"What can you tell me about Vermont?" I asked Balthezar.

Balthezar ran a hand through his untamed locks, seeming to gather what he could.

"Volanis has long been an independent island. Vermont is a king for all intents and purposes. The people treat him like a god; they say he is a man of great fortune and wealth who can bestow such luck on his subjects. Some believe he is a prophet."

I could have laughed. "Is that what you believe?"

"Not at all. He's a man with power and fortune, which is something that can very easily be taken. Might I ask what your business with him entails?"

"He has something I need."

"Another souvenir, like the monocular?"

"You could call it that."

Balthezar huffed. "Then I will warn you that a lock of hair and a sample of blood will not be enough, no matter what it is." His gaze skimmed Astraea head to toe, and I was close to plucking his eyes out of his head. "He'll want all of her."

My jaw tightened. "We can handle him."

"He's a powerful man. He hasn't lived beyond a human lifespan and kept hold of the richest empire by being so easily thwarted. There are those who believe he is a gold-touched god because his fingers appear bathed in the metal . . . If he sets his sights on the Maiden, he will try to collect her."

"A starlight matter enhancement could achieve the gold skin effect."

"Agreed, but there is power in faith and legends. And there are many about Vermont that make the people believe he is someone sacred. As much as you will be tempted to approach with violence, and you're powerful enough to challenge him, I would caution against it. Vermont is as worshiped as the star-maiden by the people of Volanis."

I said, "Then I'll cut him down and make them see Astraea is the one and only *true* god to walk among them."

"I'm sure you could, but exercise caution, Rainyte, for her sake. She needs all the alliances she can get, and a nation *forced* to bow before her will always remember."

I would have to keep my impulses under control for her. Something told me that being around Vermont was going to be an incredible test of my restraint.

"Will you need passage back to the mainland?" Balthezar asked.

"No."

"I saw your dragon. Is it true there are others?"

I cast him a deliberating look. "Yes."

Balthezar said nothing more about it. He stood, indicating with a hand to Brody, who came to his side with the silent request.

"We should dock in a few hours. You'll be safe from potential pirate attacks here."

"You trust us alone in the place that holds all your treasure?"

Balthezar lay a hand on Brody's shoulder, giving the boy a seconds-long fond look.

"I think you of all people know our greatest treasures are people, not items."

36

Astraea

Stepping off the *Silver Sparrow* was like crossing realms, not seas. The temperature was far more pleasant. Warm, even. The weather aside, I was taken by the breathtaking spectacle of wide white buildings in the distance, with circular roofs, which crowned in the middle.

The buildings and arches we had passed so far had been pristine, mostly white architecture with accents of gold. The mountains, which didn't peak quite as sharp as those on the mainland, must be volcanic, like I'd read about. This kingdom appeared so somber in our eternal night, but I could picture how brilliant it would shine with the daylight.

Nyte and I observed the bright streets from a dark alley, quickly realizing how out of place we would look when we were clad in dark, thick clothing while the people here wore beiges and golds and lighter pastel colors.

Glancing back the way we came, I could just make out the harbor where the *Silver Sparrow* was docked.

"Do you think we'll run into Balthezar and his son again?" I asked hopefully. We hadn't had the chance to say goodbye.

"I hope not," Nyte said.

"I found them charming."

"I'm still debating going back and wiping their memory of us."

"Please don't," I said. "I can't explain it, but I trust the captain. We might need allies on the sea someday."

Nyte reluctantly agreed.

"We need suitable attire," he said, scanning the shops for any that might offer what we need.

"We don't have any coin."

"I don't need coin."

I cut him with a look, not enjoying the idea of thievery, but we didn't really have a choice.

Thinking of Nyte wearing anything but black or dark colors made me grin. He rolled his eyes like he knew what I was thinking.

"How are we going to get inside Vermont's palace?" I asked.

Even from here we could glimpse the expansive, prominent gold building that sat above the rest of the island.

"Balthezar said there's a traveling circus due to arrive by the end of the day for Vermont's son's twenty-fifth birthday. They're performing at a banquet tonight."

"And what? We join the circus?" I asked sarcastically.

His pause of silence twitched a smile on his face.

"You'll be a natural with how you can bend," he said.

I blanched at the thought. "I'm not a performer," I hissed.

"Sure you are; I've seen it. And I'm very much looking forward to seeing you dance again."

Nerves bubbled in my stomach. "That's an outlandish plan! They'll have a set, choreography, routines! I'll look like a clueless fool."

"Not when I make the ringleader believe you're his prized performer, who will have her own solo."

I scowled at him. "And what might you be doing?"

"Looking for the trident, of course."

"It could be anywhere."

"I'm hoping a little rifling through a few minds will reveal it."

I had to admit his ability was highly convenient.

"I don't like this plan," I grumbled.

Nyte smiled again, clearly enjoying himself. "I think you will."

We spent the hours waiting for the circus observing the streets and keeping hidden. By the time the circus arrived in town I was giddy over our brash plan of infiltration.

When they stopped their wagons filled with flame throwers, dancers, magicians, and many more obscure and wonderful talents, Nyte easily lured a pair of dancers our way with the intention of *borrowing* their attire. We had to take them into an inn, and as I couldn't stand to trade away the magnificent custom leathers Nadir had gifted me, we had no choice but to leave them sleeping in a room in their undergarments. They'd likely wake and think they'd indulged in too much wine they didn't remember drinking and ended up in bed together.

I harbored a twinge of guilt about it, but I figured it was a small price for them to pay toward the greater cause Nyte and I were trying to stop.

I was dressed in clothing that reminded me of those I wore at the manor. The fuchsia pink top was cropped below the breasts but had long, sheer sleeves.

The skirt was sheer too but with a lining like underwear. The attire was elegant and lightweight. Slipping my feet into the thin sandals, I turned to Nyte. My hand immediately shot over my mouth to smother my laugh but it didn't stop the air escaping my nose.

"Don't ever mention it beyond this night," he said flatly, fitting on a small hat with a pheasant feather sticking out of the side.

His pants fitted at the waist and ankles with loose material between that matched the color of my top. His vest was black, at least, but he was shirtless underneath. Aside from the ridiculous color of pink on him and the unique style of pants that would take getting used to, he was quite a pleasant sight to behold.

"Let's get this over with," he said.

I reached for the open sides of his waistcoat, pulling him to me before he could turn for the door. My smile was all amusement and allurement.

"I think you look quite attractive," I purred.

"Only quite?"

I bit my lip, and his amber eyes fell to my mouth. His thumb reached up to unhook my teeth before his lips slanted against mine hard. The kiss was deep and wild but very short. He pulled away abruptly.

"You look so utterly exquisite that I don't know how I'll contain myself in there. I want to fuck you so badly; I don't think you're ready for when I do."

Need tightened in my lower stomach, and my fists flexed on his clothing.

"When I next let you fuck me, I'm going to be in charge."

The gold of his irises flared a shade brighter. The way his eyes shifted hues was like a language only I understood from the privilege of being so close to him.

"Is that so?"

"We're going to be late," I said coyly, drifting past him, but I barely got a step before I squealed at the hand he hooked around my middle to pull me back against his front.

His warm breath fanned over my ear. "If you want to play games you should know I'm very competitive." His words vibrated along my collar while his hand skimmed over the bare skin of my midriff. Boldly, his palm cupped between my legs; the thin material was hardly any barrier to his ministrations when his fingers moved in teasing strokes.

"You already know I don't lose," I said, a little breathless, but I pushed my ass against his cock, mimicking his motions, which swiftly made him stop, gripping my hip instead.

"Wicked creature," he murmured, kissing my shoulder. "Go before I bend you over that desk and don't let you leave until the gods hear you screaming my name."

I stifled a shiver. Nyte took my hand. "As you said, we're going to be late."

It was strange, sitting opposite four strangers in a jostling wagon; they accepted us warmly but their confusion-filled glances kept my pulse racing. Nyte assured me he'd manipulated their thoughts to see their expected friends' faces, not ours.

"Relax," he said with a note of humor, taking my hand.

"They're official! I knew it!" A brown haired and dark-skinned man across from us shouted suddenly, "Pay up, Trevor," thrusting a hand out to the other man, brown haired with a fair complexion, opposite him.

Now *I* was confused. Until the only other woman with us giggled, and I noticed her smiling at our joined hands.

Nyte's mouth leaned to my ear. "We've either coaxed along something inevitable or caused two people a whole lot of drama to fix when they wake and make it back to their party."

"Why does it sound like you're enjoying this?" I muttered under my breath.

"You have to admit it's entertaining."

"You're troublesome."

"Of all the things I've ever been called, that's by far the tamest of them."

"Devious."

"Insult me like you mean it, Starlight."

The wagon jostled over some uneven path, which had me bracing a hand on his thigh for balance.

"I can't," I said, sharing his breath in our proximity. "I'd be insulting myself when I love everything about you—everything wicked, every flaw."

"Is this what we have to put up with now?" the pale man with red hair, Trevor, grumbled, turning away from us.

I glanced over my shoulder with a sheepish smile, trying to ignore them amidst my growing nerves.

"You're being too kind to me," Nyte said.

I lay my head on his shoulder, not teasing anymore.

"Maybe you just have to get used to it."

The wagon was pulled to a stop by a command outside, and I stiffened. Nyte kept relaxed; his confidence was assuring.

The doors were pulled open, and we were greeted by gold-armored guards.

"Everyone out," one said rather rudely.

The woman in our company seemed to think so too, but she merely stood with a huff and smiled sweetly at the guard, the kind of smile that hid a threat, but he didn't balk in the slightest. They were all tall and broad and looked like they didn't know the concept of kindness.

Nyte and I followed hand in hand behind our company, which was only one group out of several who would be performing tonight. I had to wonder what the particular *talent* of our group was.

"How are you going to sneak away when they think we're their friends and, I presume, we're to perform together," I asked Nyte.

"I'll leave right after it," he said easily. "Then you'll have your solo."

I had to check for the sarcasm, but his expression remained neutral.

"I'm scared to ask what our act involves."

Nyte *grinned*. Oh gods.

As we approached the gates, Nyte swore under his breath.

"What is it?" I whispered with a spike of panic.

"They're taking a sample of blood before we can enter."

I blanched. "Why?"

"To be sure we're human, perhaps. I'm not entirely sure."

I glanced around, realizing for the first time Nyte's was the only set of pointed ears.

"We're not human though," I hissed. Contrary to his manipulation of everyone's minds to see us as such. I couldn't fathom the toll using so much of his ability was taking, despite how powerful he was.

"We might be the only free-roaming fae and celestial on this island," he muttered, pondering it in his mind.

My body locked at the term *free-roaming*. As if it implied the overlord, Vermont, might have caged celestials or others, just like Reihan Vernhalla, Cassia's father, did at Alisus Keep.

"What do we do?" I asked, wracking my own mind for a solution.

"I was hoping to save as much strength as I can, considering the number of minds I have to alter inside."

"It's too much."

"Haven't I told you not to underestimate me?"

I would have rolled my eyes at his playful arrogance, but I was too concerned for him, and the fact that someone could see the real us and raise the alarm any moment.

When it came to our turn, Nyte's thumb stroked my hand, which had turned into an iron grip in his as we held out our fingers out to be pricked.

It wasn't that I doubted our ability to retreat if we had to; I just didn't want this to turn into an altercation that would likely spill blood. If Vermont knew I was here . . . would he try to capture me as the prize he missed out on all that time ago?

They checked our blood on a strip of paper, the opposite tip of which turned blue after a few seconds. Everyone else, the humans, had turned the tip yellow. I risked a glance at Nyte but his expression was unusually bright.

"Next," the man in front of me grunted, already looking past me, and I frowned again at the rudeness of the guards here.

Nyte pulled my hand, stopping me from blurting something that I would likely regret.

"Does wealth breed arrogance and kill manners?" I groused.

"Most of the time, yes. But I think their lack of conversation is likely the opposite; I'm gathering that Vermont is a very greedy individual who doesn't share his wealth, even with those who keep his empire running."

"Then why would anyone worship him?"

"Fear or superstition, perhaps. That he could curse them or damn their souls. I don't know how he's built such a reputation around himself. I'm most excited to find out, aren't you?"

"You're only excited because you know that while Vermont thinks he's the most powerful man in the room, you could show him otherwise."

Nyte didn't try to hide his smile. "So could you. It's fun to demonstrate the difference between arrogance and real power."

"Just . . . don't do anything irrational."

"We might have different opinions on what is considered irrational."

He was impossible.

"No murder."

"Without cause?"

"Try not to find cause."

"It usually finds me."

We entered the golden palace and within was just as gilded. Beautiful sculptures of naked forms lined several wide halls, where I found other statues wearing full suits of golden armor. White pillars and marble floors broke up the gold, but even breathing the air touched my lungs with a sense of richness. The architecture was flawless, every corner, every carving speaking to a level of craft so meticulous it bordered on the divine. Yet, for all its splendor, the place was daunting. A creation so perfect it felt like it had never been meant for human hands. This wasn't a home—it was a monument, a shrine to something heavenly.

To think that this had almost become my home made nausea upset my stomach.

"Are you all right?" Nyte asked softly.

I would pull myself together, but for a moment I had every right to be afraid to face the man who owned this place and once had every intention of owning me. Once my fear for the woman of the manor I might have been had passed, my anger took over for the woman I was now.

"Yes," I answered him, relaxing my hand in his.

In a fancy drawing room, the rest of the crew seemed to be warming up in one way or another. Stretching, chatting, drinking. The latter I could use to calm my performance nerves. I'd never performed in front of an audience, and Nyte still wouldn't tell me what we were doing, only that I didn't need to prepare.

No one bothered us much, thanks to Nyte keeping an intimate hold of me. It lasted for a good amount of time before the two men and the woman from our wagon approached wearing gleaming smiles.

"Soooo," one man sang. "When did it finally happen?"

Nyte told me their names through our bond. The tall, beautiful man with dark skin was Dale, who'd just spoken, and I recalled the pale, shorter man as Trevor.

"Uh, today, I guess," I answered awkwardly.

"It's about time; I've been tiring of hearing you pine after him all day," the woman, Silvia, said, twirling a lock of black hair around her finger.

"The plot thickens," Nyte said to my thoughts. *"I wonder if Jose felt the same."*

My name for this evening was Calista, a red-haired beauty with a pale freckled complexion and green eyes. Nyte's alias was Jose, who was shorter than his own height, with longer blond hair and brown eyes.

I smiled, which Silvia thought was in response to her comment, but I was picturing Nyte with half-tied-back dirty blond locks instead.

"I think I could pull it off," Nyte said in my mind again.

I considered that image with a stoic look, until a giggle escaped me.

"Ugh, we're going to be suffering their flirtations endlessly now, aren't we?" Trevor said, looking away.

"You're on after us. Half an hour, lovebirds. Don't be late, fucking somewhere you shouldn't be," Dale said, spinning on his heel to leave us.

Nyte tugged me by the waist to where he leaned against the wall.

"Now that's an idea," he said, giving no warning before he dragged his teeth along my neck.

I gasped, pushing his chest. His golden eyes were sparkling, so instead of using words, I pressed myself to him to hide my palm dragging along his cock.

"Behave," he said in a tone of pure gravel.

"No."

His irises flared a brighter shade, and my skin tightened at the challenge in them. Nyte shifted his legs until one of his thighs pressed up between mine. I tried to move back, but his hands pinned on my waist, and he smiled innocently at my warning look.

"Whatever game you think you're playing, I will win it," he said thickly. Our bodies were close and angled enough that no one could see the hand he slipped between my thighs.

My lips parted to tell him to stop, but his slow teasing felt good, far too good.

"Look how you give in to me so easily. I could make you come right here and no one would know unless you announced it to them. You're really not good at being quiet."

"Nyte," I panted, needing much more, but this wasn't the place.

"Give it to me."

Even though his fingers were only rubbing me over the material, he had other tricks I hadn't considered. My pleasure accelerated, and I knew then he was influencing my thoughts to amplify my lust, but it felt so good that I didn't care about the cheat.

My fingers dug into his bicep. *I need to tell him to stop. I need to—*

"Five minutes, you two!" someone called over to us.

I whimpered when Nyte paused his movements just as I was on the cusp of reaching an orgasm.

"Is that enough time for me to make you finish?" Nyte whispered sinfully in my ear. "Sounds like a challenge."

"People can see what you're doing," I rasped, hooking a palm around his nape for purchase, with my knees weakening.

"Do you want me to stop?"

No. Gods no, I needed him to keep going.

"Three minutes left," he warned, his voice so thick it turned me on more.

"Please."

His fingers circled my apex a fraction harder. Warmth pricked over my skin, making me climb toward the edge of bliss I couldn't hold back from now.

Nyte gripped my jaw and kissed me deeply as I came. He pressed me tightly into the wall and I clutched him tightly, trying desperately to keep my body from shaking too much with the pleasure rocking through me.

"I can't wait to taste you. Your scent is driving me wild," he growled against my mouth.

I often forgot about his heightened senses. "You're the one who needs to behave," I said, catching my breath.

"Calista, Jose, time to line up," someone hissed under their breath from the open door across the room.

My heart was thundering, and I wiped the thin perspiration Nyte had caused from my brow. He looked over me, eyes dancing with deviance and satisfaction.

"Now will you tell me what we're about to do out there?" I asked.

He took my hand, heading to the exit. "Just trust you have the best partner for it."

37

Nyte

Astraea had a colorful vocabulary of curses for me and a talent for keeping herself smiling for the crowd of eager onlookers around a banquet table. I tightened the strap on her left wrist, which secured her to the wheel, and could hardly contain my grin when her eyes shot me with daggers, but her face was deceivingly pleasant.

"Why can't I strap you to this thing instead?" she hissed under her breath.

"I will certainly not object to you tying me up next, Starlight."

"You might when I pierce a dagger through your chest and leave you there." My thumb brushed her cheek. "Your violence turns me on."

I chuckled lightly at her quick scowl. The hall was full, and the entertainment took turns in the center of banquet tables closing us in from the front and sides. I'd barely caught a glimpse of Vermont, but what I did uncover was that he had a wife or mistress by his side and a son on the other. It made my blood boil to think of what he might have wanted with Astraea, if not as a bride, and it was enough for me to want his head on a pike.

I gave Astraea a once-over assessment, deeming her firmly secured. How marvelous she looked. A delicate prey in my trap. "This is how Jose and Calista do it. Besides, I have better aim."

Her feet were on two narrow planks jutting out of the wheel, and her ankles were strapped to it. Then she gripped two wooden batons attached to the wheel with her wrists bound. Perfectly secure for when it would start spinning. My task was to awe the crowd, throwing daggers at her in dangerous proximity.

Astraea scoffed. "That is a challenge we're revisiting."

"I look forward to it."

I wanted to claim her pouting mouth, but I refrained, turning to walk back the distance to begin. As I did, I surveyed the tables again, taking in more of the gathering. Everyone was adorned with robe-like clothing of white and gold, some with armor, though it was more stylistic than practical. They were a bright contrast to the bold colors of the circus members, making us even more of a standout spectacle.

Vermont was a skinnier man than I'd expected, sickly so, if I had to guess. Yet his dark eyes were cold and his posture remained dominant. He had cropped dark hair and wore a gold circlet over his deeply tanned skin. The woman had a dark brown complexion with gold painted on her body. Her tightly curled dark hair was complimented with golden rings through various braids, and she appeared like a goddess. Their son, I presumed, appeared entirely uninterested in the feast and entertainment thrown in his honor, his elbow propped on the arm of his chair as he held his lazy head against his knuckles. His hair was cut very short, and he wore a less elaborate circlet over his brow. I'd learned from Balthezar that his name was Kairos Lionel.

As I spun back to Astraea, the attention of the room started to pull toward our show about to begin. Astraea's grip tightened on the wooden beams, and she managed one last glare at me before Trevor and Silvia approached the wheel to make it spin.

"You owe me," she said through our bond after her first full turn.

"I'll be quick. Ten daggers. Then you'll enjoy your solo performance to finish the night's entertainment."

I threw the first dagger as easily as drawing breath, but the crowd gasped at the lethal weapon hurtling for the beautiful woman. It struck near her left foot.

"You can do better," she taunted.

"I'm just warming up."

The next two I threw in quick succession, earning a louder murmur from the onlookers. They struck the wood on opposite sides of her right hand.

"I'd be bored to death if I were a spectator," she said.

My next hit between her legs. *"If you really want outrage from the crowd, I could strike you."*

"You wouldn't."

"Is that a dare?"

I threw another two at either side of her hips quickly, followed by two so close to each of her ears she would feel the kiss of the metal. The crowd was far too easily impressed.

Pulling out a blindfold, I met Astraea's surprised look before I tied the material over my eyes. Juggling my last two daggers in one hand, I folded my other arm behind my back.

"Now you're just showing off."

"You wanted more thrills."

"If you miss . . ." Astraea trailed off; the taste of her fear was delightful.

"Any favorable place I should aim, just in case?"

"You're an ass."

I drowned out the growing chatter of the crowd. Focusing as sounds cancelled out, one by one. Voices, clanging silverware, chewing, rustling. Until only two things were tracked in my senses: the intermittent creak of the spinning wheel and Astraea's breathing.

When she was upside down, I threw one, knowing where her braid hung as she came back around. It cut the tie at the bottom. The last dagger wasn't in my hand much longer when I threw it to land right above her head when she was straight again.

The gathering gasped loudly . . . and I didn't hear the thump of the blade into the wood where I was certain my knife had struck precisely.

Swiftly untying my blindfold, my spike of fear that I could have actually *missed* was quickly smothered by pure, blazing pride.

Astraea had managed to undo one of her wrist bonds and *caught* the last blade by the handle. Trevor and Silvia had stopped spinning the wheel, gaping at her. A slow smile of triumph stretched across her face, and I would have kneeled for her right now were it not for the banquet attendees around us who erupted into applause and jeers.

I stalked toward her, undoing the last binding of her wrist when Silvia and Trevor released her ankles. With an arm around her waist, I lifted her down, taking a moment longer than necessary to squeeze her because of the madness she riled in me.

"An exciting show indeed," I purred.

Astraea was beaming so beautifully as our equipment was swiftly taken away. Her sight caught on something over my shoulder, and I glanced back to find Vermont hardly attentive to us but his son having straightened, staring right at us with a deep frown that held more scrutiny than boredom now.

I pulled Astraea along to exit before he switched his intense gaze from Astraea to me and found a possessive threat in my eyes.

"Now what?" Astraea asked when we passed the doors.

"There's one more group performance, then you're back up. Meanwhile, under the excuse of needing to relieve myself, I'll be taking myself on a tour."

"That doesn't seem fair."

She pouted, folding her arms, but now that we were no longer the center of attention, I tugged her to me. She caught her balance against my chest, and I crashed my lips to hers. Her soft moan ached my cock, and it was becoming clear she was far too much of a distraction for serious missions. Then again, I hadn't felt this alive in a very long time. Having Astraea with me to infiltrate, lie, steal, spy, and possibly commit other crimes made an old pastime thrilling instead of deliriously routine.

"Trust I'd rather be watching you dance, and the thought of everyone else getting that privilege instead is making me antsy with jealousy."

She smiled, so delicately I wanted to capture it.

"No murder, remember."

"Unless it finds me."

"Then best remain very hidden." Her hand reached up my chest with a switch of concern. "How are you feeling? Having to alter so many minds must be taxing."

Her care would never fail to surprise me. When I'd spent centuries being used as a weapon that never seemed to be good enough anyway, but never did anyone inquire as to how the power affected my own wellbeing.

"I'm just fine," I said quietly, twirling a lock of her hair around my finger.

In truth, the small pulse in my head I'd arrived here with was starting to become an intense drum, but I wasn't at my limit yet. Keeping our appearances changed in so many minds in the banquet hall was the biggest challenge.

"Final showtime," I murmured, catching the signal of a performer behind Astraea indicating that she would be called back to the stage soon.

"Be careful," she whispered.

I kissed her forehead and reluctantly slipped away.

The palace guards at the door were less than impressed with anyone needing to take a piss. I must have been the biggest inconvenience of their miserable day, but they let me pass. Before they could turn to follow, they'd already forgotten the encounter entirely with my quick erasure of their thoughts.

The first guard I came across immediately stormed for me, but his marching steps faltered when I slipped into his mind, twisting his outraged intention to detain me, violently so, into a kind eagerness to take me wherever I needed to go.

"There must be a room where Vermont keeps prized possessions. A trident, perhaps?" I inquired.

"Of course, he takes great pride in his collections of the world's most coveted items. I believe I have heard mention of a trident that grants control of the sea. Though none of us are allowed in that room, oh no. He has a few very carefully selected guards for that room."

"Excellent, take me."

He spluttered, but I was already heading in the direction from his thoughts.

"Didn't you hear me? It'll be both our heads if we're caught even near that room——literally; Vermont likes to behead his traitors and hang them out front for days as a message."

I wasn't really in the mood for idle conversation so I erased his memory of our entire encounter, leaving him standing in lonely confusion over why he'd left his post to be there as I turned the next corner.

At the designated room there were two guards posted outside. I strolled up confidently, hands in my pockets, ready to make the guards open it for me and walk right in. My steps faltered when I attempted to slip into their minds and was met by a very rare mental barrier. They wouldn't have the discipline to learn how to protect their minds, and there was no point in them trying to when I was the only person with the talent to infiltrate thoughts. These two had been supplied with a starlight matter enhancement I could break through, but it would likely kill them.

No murder.

I hadn't exactly promised Astraea, but I was trying to be good for her.

The guards immediately became alert at my approach, drawing swords. Had I known of their mind protection sooner I wouldn't have sauntered up to them so brazenly without at least attempting to divert them away from the door to avoid a confrontation.

"You're not supposed to be here," one grunted, approaching me with enough hesitation to reveal their fear.

Unease began to crawl my skin. No, something stronger than unease had me resisting the impulse to head right back to Astraea. But I was right here with the trident beyond those doors, and I supposed if cause for murder didn't find me, at least violence always would.

"On behalf of the star-maiden, thanks to the goddess's merciful nature, I'll grant you one opportunity to open those doors, wait until I retrieve what I need, and then scurry off to your master."

They exchanged a glance. The second guard's throat bobbed as he lost his valor.

"You're Him, aren't you?"

"I have a few names; you'll have to be more specific as to which you're hoping for."

His blanching expression was all the confirmation I needed.

"Nightsdeath," the other said, the word like a tremble from his lips.

I smiled cruelly, embodying the reputation that would always instill fear in the minds of men.

"So, do we have a deal?" I asked.

They shifted on their feet, not lowering their swords, but as much as they were loyal to their position, they knew it was over against me.

The second guard moved first, and my rising ire for the delay in getting back to my Starlight melted away the mercy she'd rubbed off on me. I couldn't risk the clamor of a fight or their shrieks of pain, so, right as his sword rose above my head, I shattered through the barrier of his mind, and it killed him instantly. Magick always had a price, a balance, and in taking the Matter for protection, it killed him when it was broken.

I caught his blade before it could clang against the marble his body slumped to like a sack of wheat.

Then it left me, as I grew more impatient by the second, pinning a cold dare on the other guard who stared at his comrade in complete terror.

Specially chosen guards with no spine, I thought.

"Are you joining him or are you opening that damned door?" I said, running low on patience.

He finally straightened, breaking his fighting stance and scrambling to his side, where keys chimed.

In the room I didn't pay the guard much attention; I'd catch his thoughts if he tried to run. It was a hall the size of a ballroom, with an impressive collection of glass cases to display all of his treasures.

I was distracted by some of the items, wondering what other rare things Vermont could have traded over the decades for this volume of objects.

Many were barbaric. I came to each grim discovery with a note of disgust.

Four sets of fangs: three for each vampire race and one for the fae. They almost looked identical, but I was fascinated to discover the differences. The blood vampire's were the longest and narrowest, for a deeper puncture. The nightcrawler's curved at the tapered end, more effective to rip a vein or tear flesh. The soul vampire had shorter fangs, more similar to the fae's, but the fae's were marginally sharper.

There was also a right-hand set of elongated nightcrawler nails; they didn't often use those to attack humans—perhaps in battle against other species, however.

I started skimming past eyes and other body parts, celestial feathers, and hair. There was plenty of trinkets, clothing, and such that seemed interesting, but I didn't have time to read their origins. Drystan would lose his mind in a place like this, lost in the collectables' endless facts and wonders.

Then, around the next bend of cases, I stopped dead in my tracks. Slammed so hard by a wave of dizziness I couldn't have prepared for over what I saw.

At the far end, in a big glass case on its own podium, the large black-feathered wings could have been someone else's.

But they weren't.

I could *feel* them.

My blood roared and my pulse sped up. I wasn't used to this concoctive reaction of outrage and humiliation. I'd fully come to terms with losing my wings, but seeing them *displayed* there . . . *mocking me . . .* I didn't need Nightsdeath's power to lose control to blinding fury.

I glided toward them when I didn't really feel grounded anymore.

How the fuck did Vermont Lionel, overlord of Volanis, come to possess *my* wings?

I was going to fucking kill him.

My wrath must have been tangible, as the guard gave a quivering sound, taking a step to retreat. The villain in me won, as I turned to become the last cold set of eyes the guard saw before he could take another step of retreat. I shattered his mind.

I stormed to the guard, pulling a dagger from his belt, and in the same breath it went flying toward the glass case, which exploded into hundreds of pieces.

My shoes crunched over them as I approached the wings, reaching a hand to them. The moment I did, my teeth gritted and my back arched with the eruption of acute phantom pain from where they'd been brutally torn out. I didn't retreat, reliving that unimaginable agony through tight, hard breaths. My fingers flexed against the lifeless feathers.

There would be no reattaching them. That had never been achieved in history, nor did I think I wanted it. The wings were a brand from Death, and by some miracle and mercy I had Eltanin now to keep flying with Astraea.

Though I wouldn't let anyone have my wings as a fucking trophy.

Thinking of Eltanin and Astraea, I felt warmth grow under my skin deeper than the heat of my anger. This ran through my veins, and I'd felt it before, briefly in my urgency to reach Astraea as she was being dragged deeper into the ocean. Was it her magick? It felt familiar but in more senses than one. A silver thread wrapped in darkness.

I gripped it, feeling that magick rush to my fingertips and then scatter over the wings. It devoured them feather by feather in an inferno of dark starlight.

A fist in my chest squeezed as I watched them turn to smoke and ash, but in some tragic sense . . . it was also liberating.

Before they finished burning, my sight cast lazily to the side, finding a tall empty glass case. Somehow I knew what I was going to find as I approached it; the pieces were already sliding together, and I'd been a damned unwitting fool.

They had been checking our blood before we came in.

The guards at this door hadn't seemed wholly surprised to discover me.

My wings were here . . . because the trident was gone.

38

Astraea

I finished my dance with exhilaration in my chest and lightness in my bones. I'd stepped into the center of the banquet as a trembling mess of nerves, but then the music had started from a violin, lute, and piano ensemble in the corner, and that was all it took for the notes to erase every set of eyes and place me above the clouds among the stars to dance.

For my circus act, I had a lightweight ball I'd performed several tricks with. I threw it in the air while my body curved backward, and it glided seamlessly around my split legs, projecting back up for me to catch when I straightened; that had earned the most awed gasps, one of the few disruptions loud enough to make me aware of the onlookers.

I was beaming, on a high from the adrenaline and the passion the dance had invoked in me. The admiration for my performance beaming through the crowd made me feel proud and I yearned to entertain again and again. I searched for Nyte to share my feelings with, but I quickly remembered he hadn't been watching. He should have been back by now, but perhaps the trident was farther away than we hoped for. If there were any obstacles, I knew he could handle himself. It was my part to distract and stall when necessary.

There was one set of eyes that tingled a line of tension up my spine: the eyes of Vermont's son, Kairos. While most smiled at me and talked among themselves, his deep brown eyes were always fixed firmly on me, and it had to be my own paranoia that thought them accusatory.

A guard came toward Vermont, and I turned to leave. I didn't make it to the doors before guards blocked it and my heart leapt up my throat. But no one came to detain me right away. Looking around in confusion, I noticed them start to gather the circus crew. Those who were in the designated waiting room were brought into the banquet hall with a mix of frightened and confused expressions and I started to sharpen my senses for what might be about to come.

I was pushed with the others, herded into the center of the tables, like we were cattle for the wealthy to scrutinize and bid upon. I stayed calm while calculating every part of my surroundings that I could see from the middle of nearly two dozen circus performers. More guards had been called into the hall, and the guests were various degrees of upset and restless, clueless to the sudden disruption as well, but at least they weren't the ones on trial.

At last Vermont spoke; his voice grated over me in a croak that sounded like death. "I am informed we are honored by infamous guests," he announced, silencing the hall instantly.

Every hair on my body pricked.

How could he know?

Had Nyte been found?

I mentally shook my head, not doubting him for a second. Even if he had been discovered he would have made it back to me by now. I tried to reach through our bond, but it was like there was static interference. I couldn't feel the void either, making a quick escape impossible.

"The traitorous star-maiden and her villainous Nightsdeath are among you now. So cowardly they need to hide themselves."

The circus members looked at each other, completely confused and terrified.

"W-we are only performers, my lord," one man said for the group.

A hand took mine, and I jerked in fright, snapping my head to find Silvia holding onto me tightly while her frightened gaze fixed on Vermont.

"I will offer this one chance for you to reveal yourself," Vermont said coldly.

In the silence, my battering heart filled my ears as I contemplated if I should abide by his demand or call his bluff. I tried to feel for my magick; it was there, but a humming interference was causing me to slip my grip on the threads within me.

Guards moved at the flick of Vermont's chin, and the man who'd spoken in our group was pulled out roughly and pushed to his knees. I squeezed Silvia's hand, and we exchanged a look.

"I'm so sorry," I whispered. Her brow furrowed deeper, then just as quickly it turned up and her hand slacked on mine.

The guard raised his sword above the man's neck—

"Wait," I called out.

The group turned their heads to me, and I pushed forward. Until I stood staring right at the overlord of Volanis. Vermont Lionel. The man who almost bought me.

He blinked a few times, his expression contorting with his mind slowly letting go of the illusion Nyte had placed in it, to see the true image of me. Silver hair, not red. Blue eyes, not green. Every silver marking adorning my skin on full display in this clothing.

When he seemed to finish painting my real image, he didn't immediately speak. I studied him as he did me in those tense seconds. He leaned on the table like he needed the support, or I was sure he would have approached me. His skin was like paper, revealing more bone and veins than a person of his age should. He was sickly.

Then it all made sense.

Had he heard of the effects of my blood? I didn't know what was wrong with him; if it was a fatal illness inside him, my blood would have only given him borrowed time, like it did for Cassia. But time was the most precious currency to mortals with so little of it. So much so he was willing to trade his entire island—buying me in the hope I would grant it to him.

"Astraea Lightborne," he said, my name like a piece of discovered treasure. "The star-maiden, Daughter of Dusk and Dawn, fallen ruler of Solanis, and as I now hear, *Lightsdeath*."

"As you can see, I am not fallen," I said calmly. "I am and always will be the ruler of Solanis."

"You're a far cry from the obedient, shy maiden that was to be my son's bride."

Every nerve cell in my body recoiled at that piece of information he delivered like a hot brand. My attention slipped to Kairos. A muscle in his jaw twitched; not gloating or proud like his father, he almost seemed as uncomfortable over our near betrothal as I was.

"You were misinformed of a lot of things about me, I'm sure," I muttered bitterly.

"I don't think so."

Vermont's eyes left mine, and I didn't have a second to react before the sickening sound of sliced flesh and blood splattering on the marble came from behind me. I whirled to find the man on his knees, clutching his gaping throat, choking on his blood before he fell.

"Why did you do that!" I roared, spinning back and feeling the vibrations of shallow magick at my fingertips.

"You did that, Maiden. You killed everyone here, selfishly using them to infiltrate my palace. They are all guilty of aiding and abetting known fugitives and smuggling enemies past my defenses. My ruling is death."

"Then so is mine," I said, and with those words the dark intent of death overcame me.

"Don't—!" It was Vermont's son who shot up from his seat, but his warning was too late.

As I thrust out a hand, light shot from my palm toward Vermont. Seeing his wicked, icy smile through the gale before it left me doused me with dread.

The lethal blast rebounded off a protective veil around the banquet tables

I'd failed to see. The next second I was airborne, struck by my own magick. Just as fast, I slammed into the back wall; the world around me started to fade.

I clung to every fiber of consciousness, which kept trying to slip away because of the impact to my head, which turned hot. People were screaming. Crying. I had to get up. I had to help them.

I had enough determination to give my bones strength, and I pushed myself up, leaning with a hand on the wall for balance. With what I saw, I wished I were unconscious. That this was a vicious nightmare. There was so much blood all in one place, spilling out of the bodies that piled on top of each other, their flesh slashed in various places. The final scream was cut off, and the ten guards with their white cloaks splattered in blood were all that stood between the banquet tables now.

He'd killed them all.

Every last performer.

I pushed off the wall, staggering toward them. My eyes met the glassy blue of Silvia's, who'd fallen, still holding Trevor's hand.

"What have you done?" I whispered.

"I don't give second chances to traitors," Vermont said, not a shred of regret or remorse.

Most of the others in attendance at his feast had stood, backing themselves to the wall and hugging each other. As if they had anything to be fearful off . . . as if they were the victims.

All I saw next was light. All I felt was *death.*

My black wings shot out as the power of Lightsdeath blasted from me, shattering the veil that protected all those in robes of white and gold. Their bodies became glowing forms of light to me now, revealing the many shades of dark souls I was starving to reap.

I mourned for the innocent lives taken so senselessly.

It was my fault they were killed.

No, Lightsdeath snarled. My sight targeted the darkest soul in the room. *It's his.*

My power sharpened with wrath and grief.

The dark soul tried to retreat, but it was too slow, and I slammed the door behind him shut before he could slip through it.

"You've lived too long, Vermont," I said icily.

His face clarified the more I balanced Lightsdeath with my rational mind. Feeling his soul . . . it was far too old and tainted for the body he had.

"Thanks to you," he said, fearful of me, but still he retained a seed of superiority.

I understood then. "Goldfell had been selling you my blood to heal you and prolong your life, long before you knew what it was. Then you discovered you could try to buy the source."

"Yes," he confirmed.

Disgust roiled in me. "What has sustained you has come to end you."

I hissed at the sting clamping suddenly around my wrist. My palm slammed to the chest of the guard who'd snuck up behind me to fit the shackle, and his wail burned out in the light that set him on fire.

Glaring at the manacle laced with nebulora, I watched it turn to stardust. The more my rage was provoked, the more I slipped away, close to becoming an unfeeling entity that could melt this golden palace to the ground.

Nyte. I was too bright, and I needed him to balance me in the dark.

My soul called for his.

"You are not a villain, Astraea," Vermont taunted. Lightsdeath clawed my mind, threatening to fully unleash and prove to him I could became a nightmare incarnate to anyone capable of spilling innocent blood.

I sensed his movement before he could lunge forward with the vial of silver liquid he braced with. Starlight Matter.

Though it wasn't me who stopped him.

Nyte arrived as a stroke of darkness through my senses.

He slammed Vermont to the wall, and I blinked consciously, taming Lightsdeath to make out their bodies of flesh though the edges of my vision still swirled with light and liquid silver.

Nyte ripped the vial from Vermont's hand, and his fury, as he realized what it was, stoked the inferno already blazing within me.

"You were going to *drug* her with this?" Nyte said, his words cold as death.

"It's the only way she can be tamed," Vermont choked under Nyte's forearm wedged against his neck.

"Tamed? You should *bow* before your queen, your star-maiden, who is not a thing to tame but a goddess to worship."

Nyte gripped him, forcing the lord to his knees before me.

This reaping was mine.

Before I took his life, I turned to the onlookers pressed against the walls, clutching each other. I raised my voice to be sure all could hear me through the storming winds of my magick.

"You've ruled here, draped in arrogance, clinging to the illusion of power like it was handed to you by the heavens. But look at you—you're no god. Gods don't falter when their masks are ripped away. Gods don't need to shout their greatness to be believed. You're just a man. Flesh and bone. Fragile."

"As are you," he spat.

My smile bordered on villainous.

I gripped his wrist. "They whisper that your touch is golden. Call on it to save you now."

Vermont began to scream when my magick spilled down his arm. Then, by Nyte's interference, his ability to voice his agony was stolen.

"He's just a man, trembling under the weight of his own falsehoods," I said calmly as my light flooded into his open mouth, determined to devour the dark mass of his soul harbored in his frail body. I let him fall. "I am your star-maiden, and you are free from a tyrant ruler who fed you lies for decades."

After a pause of silent judgment, the robed citizens started to drop to their knees one by one. They muttered their praises, their prayers, their wishes. But I could hardly hear any of it when Lightsdeath strained to reap more souls, and among these esteemed guests of Vermont's . . . there was too much temptation.

Dozens of innocent lives were piled before me, and all of these people on their knees for me now had just *watched*.

What were they to do? I tried to reason in my mind.

They would have slept soundly after the terror; they have done so before, Lightsdeath hissed as a more prominent voice in my head now.

They've surrendered to us.

Fear is not respect.

Respect can't be gained by slaughter.

My teeth gritted, and I closed my eyes, battling my inner conflict with Lightsdeath.

Although I'd triumphed by slaying one evil, it only fed a hunger to hunt for more. There were endless dark souls in this world, and right now I wanted to comb the lands for them.

A touch on my arm made my eyes snap open.

"Stay with me," the beautiful darkness said.

The darkest night.

I gripped his waistcoat, trying to fight back the otherworldly power trying to dominate me, but it hurt so badly to refuse it.

Because I didn't *want* to.

Right now, I was grieving for the lives that were taken because of me.

"He killed them all," I cried softly.

"I know," Nyte said. "This doesn't bring them back."

Nyte was so dark I could hardly stand it, yet part of me *wanted* him. I tried to push him away, but he kept a tight hold of me.

"I'm not your enemy," he whispered across my ear.

We stood in the eye of the light storm. My soul wept while my mind tore itself apart.

"Yes, you are," I croaked. "Don't you see? We're always doomed to be right back here. Fighting each other. Everything we are repels each other. The savior and the villain. The death cursed and the god blessed. Nightsdeath and Lights-death. It will never end."

Nyte took my face in his hands, and I whimpered at the pain his shadowy aura invoked while Lightsdeath raged through me.

"In every beginning and until every end, I choose you. Say you want to keep fighting for this."

I was torn by the hurt in his voice. It sliced deep, but Lightsdeath delighted in it, wanting to exploit it.

Scrunching my eyes, I pushed against the power more, sobbing with the pain.

"I'm so tired, Nyte," I confessed. "So tired of being underestimated when I could make an example out of the Volanis empire, collapse it right now, so no one would think to doubt or challenge me again."

"If that is your action call, then I am yours to command. But Astraea, look at me."

I forced my eyes to open and held onto his bright gold irises.

"Focus on my eyes."

Despite the shadows hissing and forming around him, his eyes would always shine so brightly. They were my peace, my anchor; they were the dawn that could never be stolen.

He said, "I don't care for a single person in this room, not even those Vermont killed. They were innocents, yes, but they never meant anything to me. It's not who I am, and you knew that when you fell in love with me. For your pain and suffering I would take your hand and burn this place to the ground with everyone it. But this is not who you are. Lightsdeath will let you go, the pain will subside, and you would never be able to live with yourself."

Tears streamed down my face.

"Then I am weak," I croaked.

"No. I am. Vermont is. Auster is. My father is. It's weakness to respond with violence, inflicting pain on others to survive our own. It takes the strongest will to *fight* your pain. To be in control of it before it controls you, and that is why you are so brave, so feared by those like me. You . . . Astraea Lightborne . . . are the fairest who has ever lived. That is why you are the star-maiden that will bring us all peace. And I'm going to be right here with you."

"I want to keep fighting," I said, gripping him back even though it was like he was made of starfire right now. "For us. I want us."

Nyte smiled, and it brightened the darkness his aura was shrouded in. His thumb brushed the wetness on my cheeks.

"You are pure starlight right now," he marveled. My tears were silver against his tanned skin. His other thumb touched my brow. "There's a crescent moon, on its side pointing to the sky, that glows on your brow when you harness

Lightsdeath." Then his fingers combed through a silver tress. "Your hair shines as though the moon bathes within." His golden irises fell to mine. "And your eyes have captured a thousand stars."

Nyte kissed me suddenly and firmly, knowing the power in me would resist.

Lightsdeath hissed, lashing me within, but I gripped Nyte tighter, pressing my body to his, and he held me tight.

We'd been through this before, except Nyte had been the one in pain. He'd fought Nightsdeath for me and won time and time again. And I was going to do the same for him.

The pain began to lessen and relief started to cool my veins. The hurricane of light and wind tamed slowly around us.

"You two have to leave *now* if you want a chance of escaping with your lives," a voice hissed over the gentle storm.

We broke apart to find Vermont's son, Kairos, his arm lifted above his head to protect his eyes as he stood a safe distance away.

"You expect us to trust and follow you?" Nyte snarled. "You tried to buy her."

"That was my father's plan, and right now it's either trust me or risk capture for his death."

I glanced at Vermont for the first time since Lightsdeath had taken over. He lay in a crumpled heap, and I felt nothing but satisfied that his soul faced judgment in Death's realm now. Kairos spoke of his father's death as if it were nothing.

"I killed your father," I said carefully.

"He deserved it."

Nyte exchanged a suspicious look with me, but as the wind eased and guards started to scramble into the room, our time of distraction was up.

I took Nyte's hand. "We don't have time to debate."

He was very reluctant, but I tugged him toward Kairos, having nothing but the intuitive sense that he wouldn't lead us into a trap. Despite his sour mood all day, he'd called out to me, trying to warn me against hitting that veil with my magick.

Vermont's son handed us two white robes, and we slung them on, drawing our hoods. With the palace in chaos, no one paid us any attention as we ran past many guards scrambling in clear violation of protocol, or perhaps they didn't have one for the death of their overlord.

"We can't use the void," I said to Nyte.

"That would be my fault," Kairos answered.

"You're the mage who placed a protection on this place," Nyte realized.

"Yes. You could say veils are a particular specialty of mine."

I was quite taken aback to discover he had magick.

"Then can't you release it, and we could get out of here a lot faster?" I asked.

"It's not as simple as that, I'm afraid. The veil I created around this place is quite advanced and has various talismans. You'd have to find and destroy them all. The opposite of a faster escape, I assure you." We were heading up stairs and I started to grow hesitant. Until he added, "The grounds will be crawling with guards, and there's a strong force of them around the palace outside. I'm counting on you being able to call your dragon."

I slipped a glance at Nyte, who gave me a nod. He could call to Eltanin through their bond, and the dragon was near.

Before we got the to the top of the next staircase, Kairos stopped abruptly, spinning around to us.

"I only have one condition for my help," he said.

Nyte groaned and his hand flexed in mine. "I'm not in a merciful mood for bargaining."

"Take me with you," he blurted anyway.

That hadn't been what either of us expected.

"Not happening," Nyte said, deadly serious.

I tried to consider. "You're the new overlord now. You can make this place better."

"That's never what I've wanted. My mother will take over; she's kind and gentle and nothing like my father, I assure you."

Nyte said, "We're to believe you'd give up ruling this entire empire for what? Becoming a fugitive? If you run with us they'll believe you had something to do with your father's death. So the deal is this: stay out of our way or I'll kill you where you stand."

Nyte stepped past him, ascending the rest of the stairs, and I followed with our hands joined.

"What if no one ever gave you a chance because they assumed you were nothing more than your father's legacy?" Kairos called at our backs.

Nyte stiffened; I did too with how Kairos dug his claws into Nyte's wound.

"No one ever did give me a chance beyond that," he answered coldly.

Until now, I thought. Things were changing; people were starting to see under the many layers that made up Nyte.

"We can't expect that cycle to break until we do it ourselves for others," I said quietly to him.

Nyte's jaw worked; he knew I was right.

"I have never left this palace," Kairos admitted, seeming to grow desperate. "Or the grounds at least. I may as well be another one of his trophies in a fucking glass case."

"Why would you not leave?" I asked.

"You think killing me would be easy, but even with your mind ability I'm willing to bet my life it won't be so effortless. I'm a mage known as a Keraki."

Nyte's laugh was more of a scoff. "We don't have time for fairytales."

Contrary to his response, my interest was hooked. I couldn't recall exactly where I'd heard it before in the deep pool of my old memories, but I knew it was an old term, something powerful and forgotten.

"Of all the coveted things in this palace, I am his greatest prize. I am not his true son. He stole me and raised me as his own just as he planned to double-cross Goldfell to steal you too. He knew of a prophesy: that two of the most powerful magick wielders in all of Solanis would produce an heir greater in power than even you and they would unite the five great continents of the world."

"Now you're really speaking in fables," Nyte snarled.

I was swimming in my own mind, trying to find the knowledge about the other continents he spoke of.

Kairos stared at me, pleading with me when it would be hopeless with Nyte. "You were just the beginning, Astraea."

"First your father planned to buy my mate and now you tell me the goal was to produce an *heir* with you, based on some nonsense prophesy?" Nyte's tone had turned glacial. "I'm willing to prove just how powerless you are against me."

"Don't," I said, tightening my hand in his.

Kairos glanced at our hands, then back up at me. "If there is a prophesy, it was never about me. Regardless, my adoptive father believed it could be. Ironically I kept his palace safe and made sure his *trades* went smoothly, but it was nature, fate if you will, that was destined to kill him. I couldn't understand how the decades kept passing after his fatal diagnosis, which should have claimed him before his time. Now I do, and I'm sorry your blood was taken against your will."

I gave a nod, grateful for the condolence, but I'd buried that abuse of the past with the corpses of the men who violated me.

I spoke to Nyte through our bond. *"He could make a great ally."*

"Or be the mistake that costs us the war."

We'd spent so much time deliberating that guards had found us. Many of them. They kept flooding through the hall, and Nyte pulled my hand, but we only got two more steps before they descended toward us too.

We were trapped.

"Stand down," Kairos ordered firmly.

The guards didn't advance, but they exchanged looks that told me his word wasn't going to be enough.

"My lord, they have murdered your father. We have a right to vengeance."

Nyte's hand tightened in mine, and I looked up to find him rubbing his forehead absentmindedly but with a locked expression that made me realize he was about to seize all of their minds. It was too much. He'd expended that ability for too long, and it was clearly having a detrimental effect on him if he started to show it outwardly.

Lightsdeath wasn't fully caged within me, and the mere thought of plunging into that power to get us out of this made it a struggle to contain it once more.

But it turned out that neither of us had to do anything.

Just as they started advancing again, Kairos snapped his fingers, and I couldn't believe my eyes when the motion of the guards . . . *slowed*. As if our time continued as normal but theirs had been drastically sedated.

"H-how?" I stumbled. It was impossible. Inconceivable.

"I don't think you want to keep standing here while I explain object time parallels to you," Kairos grumbled.

"No, we don't," Nyte said, but even he looked over the guards, dazed by the concept. He snapped out of it quickly to pin Kairos firmly. "If I get even a hint of a suspicion about you, I won't hesitate, I won't ask questions; I will kill you and not think twice about it."

"I would expect no less from the notorious Nightsdeath."

Nyte sighed, but he was already heading up again, and we had to carefully maneuver around the bodies by moving fractions, still in action.

"The effect will only last another minute, so you might want to hurry up," Kairos hissed, following behind me.

We weaved through the bodies until we got to the top and out a wooden door.

Eltanin's roar shook the stars, and pride fluttered in my chest when I saw him, a dark stroke against the night soaring above us.

"Up there!" someone called.

"Get them!" yelled another.

There were guards on the castle wall on either side of us, but if we crossed the intersection before they did, we'd be okay.

I turned towards Kairos. "Follow Nyte. Don't falter."

Then we took off running. Adrenaline pushed my legs as fast as they would go. The guards were closing in on the intersection just as fast but darted past it first.

They turned to follow our straight path, hot on our heels, and I leapt up onto the wall seamlessly, not faltering my pace.

I hissed when an arrow whizzed by and scored my arm. A superficial wound, but it could just as quickly be followed by another arrow piercing through me. We were almost to the end.

Kairos cried out, and, to my horror, he stumbled, falling with the strike of an arrow through his shoulder. I swore, having no time to deliberate as I sent a flare of light toward the guards who were running toward him.

"Leave him," Nyte said through our bond. I met eyes with him from atop the wall.

"You already know we're not going to do that," I responded.

Nyte's jaw tightened, then he changed course and ran back for Kairos. I searched within myself to gather the strength I needed.

Lightsdeath is me. I am Lightsdeath.

My wings unglamoured as I leapt down, sending the force of my magick into the stone, like a star plummeting from above.

It is not a power to control me but to aid me.

The wall cracked immediately, a violent deep line splitting down the center, and the structure began to fail, crumbling toward the guards, who started running away from me now. Some were too late, swallowed in a mass of rock and dust.

It started to crumble my way too, and I spared a glance over my shoulder to be sure Nyte had managed to help Kairos. They were running again, and the sight of them leaping off the edge together was all I needed before I was falling.

Then flying. My senses turned acute with the gentle presence of Lightsdeath coursing through me to help me navigate the falling rocks.

I soared up past Eltanin, relieved to see Nyte and Kairos on his back. Then when I was high enough I turned, staring down at the palace of chaos, but even with the damage and swarming people, screaming and frightened, it was a stunning piece of architecture that didn't deserve to be in the hands of someone as cold and cruel as Vermont.

Slaying him liberated a final piece of me I hadn't realized was still shackled by the ghost of Goldfell. I'd never felt freer, more powerful.

I saw the world in starlight without letting it overwhelm me. I saw people as auras and nature as glittering dust. I didn't know why I stalled in my retreat. Breathing in the calm eternal night air, Lightsdeath slept within me easier now. I'd only used a kernel of its power to break the wall; I was learning to use it without harming those I loved.

I wouldn't let Lightsdeath be a curse. Hand in hand with it, I would win this war.

39

Astraea

We flew to Zephyr's province, hoping we could track down Drystan's movements from there. After our escape from Volanis, my concern for him, and the others still risking themselves to find key pieces, plagued me.

Arriving in the Luna province, I marched right to Zephyr's stronghold while Nyte had to find clearance, landing farther away with Eltanin.

Zephyr's guards stopped me before I could ascend the stairs into his castle.

"I don't think I have to announce who I am. Zephyr wouldn't be pleased to have my arrival questioned," I said to them.

They considered me for a moment, debating if they should yield.

"She's right; let the Maiden pass," said a voice I didn't recognize.

He appeared through the doors, a striking celestial far younger than Zephyr, but his double in appearance of blond hair and ocean-blue eyes. The conclusion seemed obvious but . . . how had I not known he had a son?

"Judging by your surprise, I'm going to assume my father neglected to tell you about me or my sister. He's particularly overprotective these days."

A daughter too?

A young woman around the same youthful age—the early teens, I would guess—strolled up beside him. It was easy to see her mother, Katerina, in her features, so stunning a resemblance that it squeezed a fist in my chest.

"At least you get to go help at the sanctuary. I'm practically a prisoner in this castle," she whined.

"I'm Raider Luna, and this is my brat sister, Antila Luna." His sister whacked his arm because of the comment.

"I'm so glad we get to meet," I said, walking up to them.

Raider and Antila were perfect depictions of a prince and princess, in their finery of white and turquoise.

"Me too!" Antila said in a chirp as she looped her arm around mine, guiding me inside. "Our father told us many stories about you while we were growing up. You're like a fairytale come to life," she gushed.

My cheeks warmed at that, but to know Zephyr treasured our friendship enough to tell his children about me also bloomed pride.

"I wouldn't believe everything he's told you," I said lightheartedly.

"You mean you didn't accidentally free a pen of chickens in Notus's castle?" Raider inquired.

"Of course not," I said, grinning with the memory. "It was entirely purposeful."

Antila giggled. "Oh, please say you'll come by often. I need to hear more about your adventures, and it's so dull around here."

"I don't remember them all very clearly, I'm afraid."

I enjoyed some fond kernels of the past, but with everything that was threatening my present, I didn't want to keep feeling torn between two lives. One of failure and one with an uncertain end.

Antila pouted. "Can you try to convince my father to let me go out on adventures with you? Or him? Please, I swear I've been training and can handle myself. I want to help, just like mother."

The young celestial was so innocent and precious; she harbored a bright new candle I couldn't be the first to extinguish. So I smiled and her eyes lit up.

"I'll try my best, but you know how stubborn he is."

Antila squealed. "He admires you very much; he'll listen to you!"

"I'm here to see him, in fact; could you take me to him?"

"Father's not here. Mother says he's been so busy with the sanctuary lately."

My feet rooted into the ground on my next step, breaking Antila's arm from mine. When she looked at me with concern, I quickly plastered a smile over my fear.

"Where is your mother?" I asked.

Antila glanced down the hall, and my entire body stiffened, but Katerina—or rather, *Dawn*—wasn't there.

"She braided my hair this morning, then said she had a meeting with some lords," Antila informed. She looped her arm through mine again, tugging me to walk. "Maybe she's still in the throne room."

She wasn't.

Zephyr's throne room was much different from Auster's in the Nova province or mine in Vesitire. His throne itself was made of glass like hundreds of icicles had forged together, jutting out at different angles. The hall was empty, but I lost myself in the beauty of his stained glass windows depicting scenes of power and love. Such as the one of a celestial with wings splayed and their sword drawn, or the one that resembled Zephyr and Katerina, joined hands clasped between their chests.

My heart squeezed at the thought of them. If Dawn had successfully taken on Katerina's life, Zephyr still didn't know about the impostor in his wife's body.

I should have come sooner.

There were so many threads of this war pulling me in so many directions I couldn't tend to them all at once.

The familiar blond hair and passive face of my friend entered the hall not long after I arrived, but in those eyes . . . I saw the Goddess of Dawn in all her wicked gloating.

"How lovely for you to come by, Astraea," she greeted kindly.

I didn't know if it was my grip or Antila's that tightened. Raider hovered close to my other side, and though he was nearly a man, I wanted to grab both of them and run.

"Likewise," I lied. "If Zephyr isn't here, I must be going though."

"Maybe I can help in his stead?"

My heart pounded as I tried to calculate how to get Zephyr's kids to safety in case Dawn thought to use them.

"It's nothing urgent. While he's not here, I was thinking of taking Antila and Raider for a while."

"Where?" Dawn asked.

I couldn't raise any alarm with the fragile hearts beside me, unaware of the goddess who'd killed their mother and stolen her face. Zephyr would be able to explain it to them; I just had to find him.

Antila gasped, gripping me excitedly. "Yes, where?!"

I didn't want Dawn to know where I was heading.

"To Vesitire for a while," I decided quickly. I could leave them in the protection of Nadir's home.

"Have you found all your key pieces yet?" Dawn asked. So deceptively innocent it sickened me.

That was another reason to get back to Nadir's and reunite with the others. Perhaps the fates would be in their favor and the others would have all the key pieces. If I had my key right now, along with knowing Dawn's true name, I could kill the goddess.

"No," I had to admit.

"A shame. Time is running out."

Suspicion started to reel in my thoughts. This was the second time I'd stood before Dawn and she hadn't tried to kill me. That was her objective, wasn't it? Did she need the key to do it?

"Best not waste any of it then," I said carefully.

As I began to back away, the tension in my body only grew. Dawn was unpredictable. Her power in a mortal body unknown.

"Take care of my children," she said in farewell.

My jaw worked at the blatant mockery she was of my friend. A protective flare for Zephyr's children made me want to attack and figure out exactly what Dawn was or wasn't capable of against me. But to spare Antila and Raider grief, I had to let her go for now.

My steps hurried though the halls, like Dawn might follow on our heels any moment.

"I'm not going to Vesitire," Raider said. He stopped walking, and I glanced over his shoulder, antsy to be out of here. Raider crossed his arms, narrowing his eyes on me. "Something's going on."

Antila said, "This is an adventure! Stop ruining the mood."

I crossed the few steps to him, begging with my eyes. "It's not safe here for you two. Trust me as a friend of your father's, please."

"Then how is it safe for mother?"

My lips pursed as I tried to come up with some reasonable excuse to take them away from her.

I lowered my voice. "We won't go to Vesitire. I'll take you to your father at the sanctuary."

Antila whined. "That's not as exciting!"

I turned to her, mustering an enticing smile. "What if I said you can ride by dragon with Nyte?"

Her eyes flew wide. "Nightsdeath?" she whispered conspiratorially, checking the corners of the hall like he might emerge from the shadows.

Raider's gaze swept around nervously too. "Is he as scary as people say?"

My mouth quirked at that. "He's scarier."

"Saying nice things about me, Starlight?" Nyte's silvery voice caressed my skin.

A wave of relief soothed me as I saw him strolling toward us. If Dawn came back, these two youths now had more protection.

Nyte sensed my distress immediately. His smile slowly fell and he scanned the hall.

I said through our bond, *"Dawn is here. These are Zephyr's children, and they don't know she's not their mother."*

Nyte's tension wasn't subtle. *"She's just letting you leave with them?"*

"I don't think she has power in this form."

"Then how does she expect to kill you?"

I was beginning to realize there were more nefarious plans that required the key than we were prepared for.

"The key," I said.

Raider said, "So uh . . . are we going?"

Realizing how odd our silence was to them, I nodded, pulling Antila along this time, but she followed with a chipper step.

We made it out the front castle doors when we saw the most unexpected person walking across the courtyard toward us.

Drystan beamed when he saw us.

"Look who's alive," Drystan sang. "I mean me, by the way. A far more impressive feat when you see what I have."

He wiggled a pouch that rattled with metal inside.

"We need to get away from here," I said under my breath.

Nyte's firm nod agreed. He said to Drystan, "Tell us on the way."

We passed him in quick strides. Drystan gave a disgruntled sound before following.

"*Good to see you, Drystan. How heroic you are, Drystan. Thank you for risking your life multiple times, Drystan,*" he ranted to himself.

"It is good to see you," Nyte said once they were through the woodland and heading toward Eltanin. Athebyne was here too. "How many temples did you manage to cover?"

"All of them," Drystan answered with a gleaming smugness.

"That's near impossible," I accused.

Excluding the one in the Sterling Mountains we couldn't reach after failing to secure the trident, there had been six more temples in Althenia for us to reach.

"Count them," he said, tossing the pouch to Nyte. "And please, for the love of stars, tell me there's at least one true piece for the shit I went through. There's only one temple left in Althenia, which is why I came here. I'm glad I get to hand that last trial over to you two."

Nyte pulled the strings loose, and I felt the pulse of the key as he did. "There's one for sure."

"Thank fuck," Drystan muttered.

"Father told us about your key," Raider said, his curiosity pulling him closer. "How many pieces are left?"

"We're not sure," I said.

I held my hands together to hold the pieces while Nyte pulled them out one by one. Drystan indeed had five pieces. It didn't take long to distinguish the real one. It glimmered faintly and hummed against my palm.

"How the hell did you travel across Althenia and achieve all the trials in the time we were gone?" Nyte said.

It hadn't been that long, had it? My hand hovered over my growingly fatal wound. Dawn was right: *I* was running out of time.

Drystan shrugged. "They weren't that hard, but your key is a menace. I got tested with resilience, loyalty, truth, among other things. I am a saint at the end of this."

"Of course you are, brother," Nyte said.

"How was the underwater trial?" Drystan inquired.

Nyte and I shared a shameful look. "The trident was gone from Volanis. We think Auster got to that one first."

Drystan swore. "Damn bastard. We just have to hope it was a fake piece and if not . . . how are we to know where he hid it now that he's dead?"

I was awash with dread over the possibility that Auster could have acquired a key piece that would now be lost since I killed him. Nyte's hand touched my back in consolation.

"We don't need to stress about that unless it comes to it," he said calmly.

Drystan asked, "Why do you have Zephyr's spawn with you?"

My brow furrowed. "How do you know they're Zephyr's children?"

"He came by the castle a few days ago," Antila said cheerfully.

Nyte and I whipped our gazes to Drystan, who looked at us, confused and defensive.

"You said Zephyr could help me, and he did. I wouldn't have made it through Notus's land to the temple without his help for a disguise and escort."

"Was Katerina there?" I asked.

"I don't think I would have made it out if she was. I thought I'd have to tell Zephyr, but he already knew—"

"We should get going," I cut in.

Antila looked confused by Drystan's words, but Raider's eyes turned hard and accusatory.

"What is it you're not telling us?" he demanded.

My mind was spinning. *Zephyr knows about Katerina.* Then how could he leave his children in that castle with the Goddess of Dawn?

"He wouldn't if he had a choice," I muttered aloud. Horror doused me.

"What's wrong?" Nyte asked.

"We need to get to the sanctuary. Now."

40

Astraea

The dragons swooped down to land as I did, but the horror that crashed into me kept me from any immediate step forward. I stared at the cave opening that led into the underground sanctuary . . . and it was completely sealed off by rocks.

"No . . ." I breathed in complete denial.

My movements were jolted into action. I didn't know how long ago it could have happened, but my adrenaline pushed me forward, believing it wasn't too late to save people. My fingers ripped across rocks and debris, pulling some out of the tighly compacted pile, which tumbled others. I couldn't feel the pain, but I saw the blood smearing the stones more with every desperate attempt to shovel my way through the thick mass of broken rock.

Arms clamped around me to prevent my next reach, and I cried out, struggling against them.

"Astraea, stop," Nyte said calmly in my ear. But it was a distant echo through the wild pounding in my ears.

"There were *thousands* of people in there!" I cried.

How did this happen? It couldn't have been natural. No . . . someone had *murdered them*.

"Father . . ." Antila's voice was too young to carry such heartbreak.

Had Dawn been truthful in telling them Zephyr was here?

A new scream tore from me, and I broke free from Nyte's hold to claw at more rocks as if I could reach my friend inside.

Nyte hooked an arm around my middle this time, hauling me away from the slope.

"There's nothing we can do here," Nyte tried to console.

I cried into his chest with that fact beginning to settle.

"Father!" Antila yelled, though it wasn't in pain. It was joyous.

Pushing away from Nyte, I whirled around, gasping at the celestial who descended gracefully.

Zephyr's eyes were wide, trapped with terrors. He kept them on me even as Antila barged into him. Raider embraced him too, and Zephyr snapped his attention from me, checking them over with the panicked worry of a father.

I sniffed, wiping my disbelieving eyes as I approached him. His children let him go, and he reached for me as I did for him.

"I thought you were in there," I croaked.

"I was," he replied, haunted. We released each other. "I got as many out as I could, but there were still so many left behind . . . hundreds of lives . . . I couldn't save them."

"Thanks to you, we have survivors," I said, my heart ached at his devastated look over my shoulder.

"I don't know what happened. The water system . . . it had to have been tampered with. In all the centuries the pipes have never come close to leaking, never mind bursting to flood the place, which inevitably caved the structure in on itself. Even with my ability to control the element of water, it was too much."

The sanctuary column was colossal.

I exchanged a look with Nyte, then Drystan, but they seemed as clueless as me. Until I realized . . .

"The trident was taken by someone to reach the underwater temple," I said, puzzling over *who* could have possession of it.

Nyte's expression fell as he and I combed over the potential list, which wasn't long.

"It has to be our father," Drystan said first. "I just can't figure out how he managed it when last I heard he sits on the throne of Vesitire."

"From whom and when did you gather that intel?" Nyte demanded.

"I've been asking around," Drystan said vaguely. "All that matters is that we find out if he's responsible for this."

"But why?" I asked, mulling it over in my mind. "What reason would your father have to collapse the sanctuary?"

"Maybe he heard about it from Auster somehow and shares the same prejudice against the Nephilim and wingless celestials," Zephyr supplied.

That conclusion didn't settle right with me. The powerless celestials and the Nephilim were shunned by the gods of Dusk and Dawn.

"He didn't do it by Auster's bidding nor his own," I said, drawing only one conclusion. "He's acted on behalf of Dusk or Dawn, maybe both, and Dawn wanted me to see this as a warning."

Nyte's hand caressed my back in comfort. The devastation of losing the sanctuary and the hundreds of innocent souls inside tore a fresh wound in me.

"Well, we know where the bastard is; I say we rain hell on Vesitire to tear him from the throne for the last time," Drystan said resentfully.

"We need the key," I said. "There's one more temple here; then we'll meet back with the others. Your father is no doubt protected by Dusk and Dawn; I need the key before I face them again."

"They need the key to kill you," Zephyr said.

"I've gathered that," I said.

"They need a High Celestial to do it, or using it will kill them too."

The next beat of silence hung heavily. Nyte shifted, ready to block Zephyr's path to me, as if he might produce the full key right now and lunge for me.

"How do you know that?" Nyte asked, his tone edged with a warning.

Zephyr shifted a pained glance to his children, who watched us talk. Antila clasped her hands to her chest, her wide blue eyes fearful. Raider stood cross-armed, attentive, as though he were part of their battles.

"Take your sister to the dragons," Zephyr instructed Raider.

"But Father, I want to—"

"Now, son."

Raider's jaw worked, but he respected his father's order.

"I knew it wasn't her the moment I saw her." Zephyr's voice lowered torn and shallow. "Dawn came to the sanctuary and tried to bargain with me. If I kill you, Katerina will live."

That triggered Nyte *and* Drystan to firm their stance and shuffle closer, almost shielding me.

I didn't want to believe Zephyr was capable of killing me, but this was his wife, who came above his friendship to me.

"After she left, I planned to retrieve my children and look for you, but then the flood happened," Zephyr explained. "I don't know what to do . . . if Dawn is even telling the truth."

"She's not," Nyte said grimly. His protectiveness of me soured any gentleness for the topic. "Katerina is gone. Her mind could not have survived this long with another's consciousness implanted within."

"How can you be certain?" Zephyr said as a plea.

"You either trust me or you don't. But I warn, the latter doesn't end well for you if I think for a second you'd side with the gods on a fool's hope and make an attempt on Astraea's life."

Zephyr's grief-stricken eyes shifted to me. I pushed past the partial blockade of Nyte and Drystan to approach him.

"I'm so sorry," I said, knowing they were three words that couldn't add a stitch to the wound he carried from losing Katerina.

"There's only one way to avenge her then," Zephyr said, his voice a shell of the joy that once filtered it. "She would want me to help you kill Dawn."

I reached for him in solace.

"Drystan will take you somewhere safe while Nyte and I complete the last temple," I said.

Zephyr nodded his agreement.

Nyte rode Eltanin to the temple, and I flew beside them. Landing, I used my magick to clear the snow off the final dragon painting.

I was shocked to find the black painted lines. Yet, unlike Eltanin, this dragon wasn't feathered. It wasn't a celestial dragon.

Eltanin roared behind me, and I whirled at his sudden cry. He paced, clearly distressed, and it was frightening to see such a powerful creature this way when he could destroy things with any wrong flick of his wing or tail or step of his giant taloned feet.

"What's wrong?" I asked with my heart in my throat.

"I'm not sure," Nyte muttered, closing in protectively beside me.

Eltanin roared again, and his tail flicked instinctively, swiping at my ankles before I could jump or avoid it. I went tumbling into Nyte, who was also thrown off balance, and we went crashing to the ground. The glass vial of Eltanin's tears flew out of Nyte's hand and broke against the stone.

Right over the painting, which absorbed it instantly. The ground beneath us rumbled, and the black lines shimmered. I was too awestruck to move but thankful Nyte had his senses as he leaped to his feet, dragging me up clumsily. He pulled me into a run as the painting started coming to life, and we took cover at the tree line.

The black dragon emerged as though pulling itself out of a deep grave. It grew taller and taller, and Eltanin became so anxious it filled me with fear.

"By the gods," Nyte said in disbelief. It was rare for him to sound so stunned and maybe even fearful himself.

The black dragon with leathery wings finished awakening, and its roar trembled the ground, so loud I had to cover my ears with a pained wince.

Eltanin tried to back away, crashing into trees as the bigger dragon turned its head to him.

"What is happening?" I cried, shaken and not knowing what to do.

"It's . . . it's Eltanin's father."

That slammed me with shock. Then complete confusion.

"It doesn't look like a happy reunion," I said, observing the duo that looked primed to fight, which could turn devastating for everything in their surroundings. There were villages nearby.

"Dragons are very primal and territorial. Do you remember how we found his mother long ago? She was wounded very badly, and while I think the wing clipping was done by humans, I'd bet many of her wounds were from fighting. Despite being his blood kin, this dragon doesn't accept Eltanin. In the draconic hierarchy, his father should rank below Eltanin. Celestial dragons are royalty. I think this is him challenging that rank. If he kills Eltanin, even though he's not a celestial dragon, the others will recognize his father as their king in his place."

"We can't allow that."

"I won't," Nyte said, his tone so set and determined.

Both dragons drew breath at the same time, and I reacted out of instinct. I couldn't stop them attacking each other, but I had to *try* to prevent the catastrophic blast of their colliding power from obliterating half of Zephyr's province.

As they let go of their breath, I let Lightsdeath surge to the surface.

My wings shot me high, and a gale of light expelled from me, creating a dome around the small forest the temple was within. The dragon's dark power slammed against my shield, and, in a second of panic, I thought it would break easily.

Lightsdeath wouldn't let the darkness win. It reinforced the shield with more light, and I trembled with the velocity of the magick and the strength it took to hold it against the battering resistance of dragon breath that rippled ferociously against it.

When the dragons ceased their collision, I let go of my magick for a moment to collect myself. I didn't know what to do, how to stop the powerful beasts from destroying each other.

We couldn't lose Eltanin.

Nyte was on the ground near the battling dragons, and my protective instincts flared for him. I dropped down by his side. He scanned me over for injury.

"Eltanin won't leave. He's staying to protect us against his father," he said.

My chest pained for the smaller black dragon. So selfless and brave. The bigger dragon's jaw opened and it lunged for Eltanin, and I screamed, casting out a flare of light. My light stuck the bigger dragon, but though it spared Eltanin from its jaw, its front claws ripped across Eltanin's chest instead.

Both dragons emitted ear-piercing screeches. I winced, folding into myself. Then I remembered . . .

Edasich . . . I'd been able to stop her from attacking me after I'd killed Auster.

Straightening, I didn't know how that command had come out of me then, but I knew I had to try to find the voice again.

My fingertips clasped in front of me as my eyes slipped closed. I took a long, stilling breath, which cancelled out the chaos around me. I didn't know how I was doing it, but I let my instinct guide me. Eltanin wasn't bonded to me, but I could communicate with him. Even with Athebyne there were times I felt her emotions though I'd never had need to intervene with her.

I had a connection to dragons like no one else had, and it was from that acknowledgement, my acceptance of this power, that I found what I needed.

The black dragon's name.

My eyes opened, and a tone that was new to me echoed over my voice as I spoke.

"Rastaban."

The bigger black dragon drew away from Eltanin upon hearing his name. He turned to me, and Nyte stepped forward a little more, bracing with the frightening attention on us now.

"You will not harm him. You will leave, now."

Rastaban's growl rattled through my bones, and he stepped closer, bearing his teeth.

"Astraea," Nyte said my name like a warning that we should run.

I stayed put, challenging a beast over a hundred times my size, and maybe I was delusional to think I could influence something as mighty as the dragons.

"Leave," I warned a final time.

Faith and instinct were all I had in this deadly standoff. It might be the death of me but . . .

Rastaban's head *bowed.*

It wasn't friendly, and his malice still rippled through me, but he submitted. When he straightened, preparing to take off, my heart slammed to a thunderous beat.

"How the hell did you do that?" Nyte said, incredulous as we watched Rastaban fly away.

"I'm not entirely sure," I said, dazed with the reality sinking in as the adrenaline cooled.

Nyte sighed with relief, cupping my nape and resting his forehead to mine.

"You can be incredibly reckless sometimes."

"I never thought releasing any of the dragons could be a bad thing. They're powerful allies when they're with us, but against us . . . they could be catastrophic."

"There are battles for power and dominance in every species. It was a fairytale to think that awakening the dragons again would be without any consequence or conflict. I'm sure Drystan will have more reports on the other freed dragons, which we'll hear about when we catch up with the others after this trial."

"Do you think we have to worry about Rastaban?"

"You can predict that more than I could. I'm still trying to process how you found his name and managed to command him. I could feel it through your voice as you spoke to him . . . even I felt a certain compulsion of obedience from it. I've never experienced anything like it."

"I didn't know I could do that."

"You continue to amaze me." He kissed my forehead.

Eltanin's rattling wails had us running to him. He was bleeding from his neck and front leg, licking the latter wound.

"Let's be quick. Eltanin needs help from Nadir and Lilith to heal these wounds faster," Nyte said, distressed over Eltanin's injuries.

I nodded. "Let's see what wicked final game the key has in store."

41

Nyte

O ur final trial had me and Astraea opposite each other. I lurked in the shadows, which snaked and primed around me, so familiar, while she bathed in brilliant light casting from behind her.

Nightsdeath was gone, yet I glanced at my hands with the creeping sensation of that dark power within taking me over. My fingers were dipped in charcoal, and I laughed, darkly gleeful, letting Nightsdeath return.

With my repulsion of bright things, it made my deadly glare fall on the being opposite me. Not just Astraea . . . *Lightsdeath* had come out of hiding.

"It's about time we faced each other," I called to her.

We were separated by a wide gap in which I could only see intermittent black tiles, like a two-line checkerboard missing the white squares, which would lead Lightsdeath to the middle platform. Over the side of the rock I stood on it was deep and dark, a the faint glimmer revealed water would catch my fall.

"We have met many times, Nightsdeath."

"Yet you refused to play with me. Do I frighten you?"

Lightsdeath's chuckle was a hubristic as mine. I delighted in her.

"You think I, a light that could drown you in a flare, would be afraid of the dark?"

We both paced the edges of our platform, sharing wicked, taunting smiles, like a dare for one of us to somehow cross the distance. I remembered this was a game. A test. I didn't know the rules yet, but I was already having so much fun I didn't really care.

I wanted to possess this creature. To make her bend each ray to the will of my shadows.

"Come to me, then," I coaxed.

Lightsdeath studied the bridge. "I can only see the tiles of light on your side."

"I can only see the tiles of dark on yours."

It was clear then. We had to trust in each other's direction to make it to the middle. The landing of neither dark nor light. The space between us was a shifting threshold, a place where contrasts collided and refused to harmonize.

"You first," I said. Lightsdeath faced me. "A shift to your right—there. Now forward; that is your first tile."

She didn't immediately take the step off her platform. Her glowing silver eyes studied me intently, so hypnotizing I wanted to crawl the distance to bask in them deeper. Only to tear out the light in them.

"To your left—yes. Then forward is your first tile," she instructed.

"I said, you first."

"Now who's afraid?"

My lips curled cruelly. "Together, then."

"I think that's the point."

Either one or both of us could end up plunging into the black waters below. Was there a prize for deception? One of us successfully tricking the other and making it to the middle alone?

"Ready?" she called with an edge of playfulness in her tone.

Yes I was.

My leg lifted as hers did, tension tingled from my toes to my damn head, and I couldn't be sure if I'd be thrilled or enraged if she'd tricked me and I went plummeting.

In unison we took our first long step forward.

Both of us remained on the same level.

We shared a smile, baring teeth.

"Don't get too comfortable," she sang.

"Likewise."

"Your next step is forward," she supplied.

"Yours is to the right."

Once again our stares locked, heating with passion every time we stood here to test each other.

We took our steps . . . and both remained in the game.

"Make no mistake, I only want to reach you so I can smother you," I said darkly.

"I'll only let you reach me so I can banish you. You think yourself my equal, Nightsdeath? I am the source; you are the absence. Without me—the light— you—the dark—are nothing but emptiness."

"And without me you are unrestrained, a tyrant of radiance. I am not your absence; I am your complement. Your light exists only because I give it shape. Together, we are not rivals but the rhythm of the world itself."

"Poetic of you," she mocked.

We exchanged our next steps, and they held us true, bringing the light closer to the dark with every delicious move.

"It is hard to trust you when I see how easily you can consume those who linger too long in your depths," she said, her voice softening now.

Another tile, another slash of distance between us.

I replied, "Perhaps trust is not required—only the wisdom to know when we must share the sky."

One tile left. We stood right in front of each other, a measure of two tiles was all that remained between us.

"I might have underestimated you," she said, close enough now I could almost reach her.

Taste her. Devour her. Possess her.

This next exchange could see one triumph, watching the other drown beneath their feet. I studied her brilliant eyes, trying to find her deception, but her ability to withhold all emotion was as masterful as mine.

"The strongest light casts the deepest shadows," I whispered. "We are inevitable."

"Your step is forward," she said, voice equally as hushed.

"So is yours."

Our legs lifted in unison, our eyes locked on each other, then . . .

The dark and light collided, exploding through the room in a violent storm of night and starlight.

We gripped each other harshly; my hand clutched tightly in her glittering hair, hers fisted the front of my jacket, our stares clashed with such passion and hatred it was pure nirvana.

"Share the sky with me, Astraea," I said, coming around from the effects of the trial I only now remembered we were in.

Nightsdeath wasn't me anymore. That beast that paced in me was slain by Lightsdeath, unable to take over my emotions ever again.

But Lightsdeath was real in this trial and still had a hold on Astraea, who glared at me, debating if she wanted to kill me or kiss me.

I took that decision from her, claiming her mouth as the ground fell away from both of us. Frozen waters sucked us deep into their depths and tried to tear us apart, but I clung to her like she were my last breath.

We were drowning, but panic didn't find me. I pulled Astraea's mouth to mine again and we floated. Water turned to sky, our bodies to constellations, and here we belonged, never against each other, always necessary to each other.

Astraea held me back, her essence wrapped around every inch of me, and I didn't care about anything else so long as she could never drift far from me.

She broke our kiss, lifting her hands that blended seamlessly into the starry night, as did mine. "We are the stars and night itself," she said, observing her starry form.

"Yes, we are," I said, so overcome with emotion.

Astraea's stretching smile faltered as she choked. Panic surged in me, and I held my breath too as we fell, two shooting stars plunged back underwater.

Then . . . *air.*

Too much yet not enough.

We swallowed water and choked until we reached the shallow end and crawled out. Over rocks and snow and . . . *stone.*

Gasping on all fours, I blinked against the dizzying confusion, whipped from one illusion into another, but I thought this was real now. The polished marble beneath my hands seemed fitting for the temple we'd entered. Though despite there being no body of water around us now, we still suffered the effects: wet and frozen.

Glancing up, I saw an altar, which made this temple more like one of worship.

I pushed myself up to my knees, but Astraea wouldn't move from her locked position on all fours, shivering violently, and I could hear her teeth bashing together.

"Here," I said, pulling her upright.

My instinct was to begin removing her clothing and mine; body heat would help while she came out of her shock and became able to reach her magick to warm herself.

Astraea's eyes were so distant, staring at nothing at all, and she didn't respond or react to what I was doing. Her body was shutting down; her mind became unresponsive. It tore me apart.

I spied an old tapestry that was as treasured as a fur blanket in our condition. Ripping it from the wall, I returned, stripping out of my own clothing before kneeling again. Astraea hugged her hands to her naked chest.

"I've got you," I said, panic slithering in my chest.

I sat, pulling her between my legs, where she curled into herself against my chest, and the tapestry was big enough to wrap us both. I hugged her as tightly as I could but it wasn't enough. I was fucking helpless right now, but I could ease some of her pain at least.

Slipping into her mind, I soothed every sharp and icy edge that was hurting her, and I thought she was starting to calm.

"Talk to me, please," I whispered, pressing my lips to her head.

Her hand moved, flattening on my side and slipping around to hug me back. It relaxed a fraction of my body.

"That was awful," she whispered.

"That's putting it lightly. Drowning is one of the worst ways to die."

"You've d-drowned before?" she chittered.

"Once."

"When?"

I didn't know how to respond to that, what she would think if I confessed the truth. It was something I hoped to never have to admit aloud.

"When you were gone," I said tightly.

"W-what happened?"

At least she was engaging, and I didn't want her to stop if I refused to answer.

"I told you I've died many times. There are very few people who hold an assassination number for me."

I didn't know how else to say it when shame started to shrink me. Astraea took a few seconds to contemplate. I could tell she understood my meaning when her fingers added pressure against me.

"You . . . you tried to . . ." she couldn't bring herself to say it.

Neither could I. Not outright.

"I wanted to follow you the moment you left," I said.

"There's so much more to living than just me," she said, her voice croaking now, and that fucking cut me deep.

"Not to me. You know that."

"You have Drystan. You could have found love again. Oh, Nyte."

She wept, and it fucking destroyed me.

"I was born to be a weapon, or to be yours. If you'd seen all I became in your absence . . . there was no living, only pain. To me and to the world I inflicted it upon."

Astraea lifted her head to look at me. Her lips were still faintly blue and her eyes glistened. Her palm reached to my cheek with such sorrow written on her face.

"I see you. You have so much more to give than you realize. I loathe your father for making you unable to open your heart to see others that will love you too. Not as much as me, because I believe that's impossible to reach, but enough to show you more beauty in a world that has been tainted for you."

How could I love something beyond what my mind or soul could comprehend? I liked to believe there were threads of my devotion to her being woven in the fabrics of every universe. That I would recognize her in any life, in any form, in any age. Should we meet again across time and space and beyond, I would look at her and know the path home. I would know the beat in my chest was only borrowed, and I would give it back to her. I would always see beauty in her that made the world around us pale in comparison.

"You are my life, Astraea," I whispered, slipping a hand around her nape and bringing her mouth to mine. "That will never change."

I groaned with the feel of Astraea's magick from her palms heating over my skin.

"Fuck, that's good," I sighed as both our tremors started to subside with the glorious heat.

"Sorry, it took a moment. Everything felt . . . so numb. As if I were dead but aware."

"I know. I did the only thing I could think of, though I'm not sorry about it."

A small laugh escaped her before her brow furrowed and her forehead fell against mine.

"You are my life too, Rainyte."

My eyes closed and my fingers ran up her spine. The heat from her magick was such absolute bliss that the misery from moments ago was already forgotten. All I could think about now was her naked body against mine.

"There are other ways we could get warmer faster," I muttered thickly.

Desire flickered in her silver-blue eyes before she kissed me, shifting around to straddle me, and my cock jutted against her heat.

"You've definitely kept me waiting too long."

I gripped her hair to kiss her deeper, coaxing her hips down more to feel her growing wetter, hotter, for me.

"This is a temple of worship," she panted as my mouth descended on her chest like a starved animal.

"You're a goddess," I said thickly, squeezing her thighs around me. "I'm going to worship you. I'd say we're in the perfect place."

They say the temples are where the veil between our world and the gods who made it is thinnest. It was deplorable of me to find satisfaction in that, when they'd tried to keep me from Astraea at many given turns, and now they would bear witness to how inevitably she was destined to become mine. How many of the worlds and veils and laws I would shatter to have her.

I flicked her nipple with my tongue before sucking, turning wild with the responses of her body writhing against mine and the small sounds she made. Something between a moan and a breath that were small begs for more, and I would happily oblige. Slowly, torturously for us both, but it would make the climax that much more powerful. Delectable things deserved to be savored, and Astraea . . . she was the most exquisite thing to taste, watch, feel. There would never be enough of her in my hands.

"Get up and bend over that altar for me," I ordered before dragging my teeth along her collar.

She gasped, gripping my hair tighter. When the tapestry fell, she shivered, but I was going to make her sweat for me instead.

Astraea did as I asked, and the sight of her was a religious experience in itself. The moonlight spilled perfectly over her body, breasts pressed against the marble altar with her gloriously angled back glistening with silver tattoos. I took my time marveling over every detail of her until I settled on the awaiting pink spot between her legs.

"Widen your stance. Good girl." I ran a hand up her spine, gently pushing her head down to rest between her splayed palms. "Fucking perfect."

My other hand curved over her ass. I watched her face as I circled my palm before bringing it down in a slap that echoed through the temple. Astraea gave something of a gasp that ended in a moan. So I did it again, delighting in how her brow pinched in pleasure as I soothed the heat blooming on the pink flesh of her ass.

I surprised myself with the raging impulse to drop to my knee and didn't think before sinking my teeth into her flesh I'd already marked. Astraea cried out, and her blood flooding down my throat snapped something in me. Her legs were already beginning to shake, and I slipped my fingers through the slickness that was pooling out of her now. So warm and wet. All I did was slide them back and forth, circling her apex, and it didn't take much with my teeth still buried in her for her tremors to turn more violent with the climax that rushed over her. Before she could have it, I let go with a groan of pained pleasure, completely lost in primal lust when I stood, pulling her upright and turning her around.

Astraea's face was clouded in a daze of desire. Her cheeks flushed rose, and I kissed her once, hard and needy, before lifting her onto the altar.

"You're going to lie on this altar and come on my tongue, and when you do, scream my name for every god to hear," I said in a growl.

Hooking Astraea's legs over my shoulders, I licked through the desire she pooled for me. Her hands gripped over the edges of the altar on either side while her back ached beautifully with my first taste. She was a sight worth painting to decorate the grandest palace.

I feasted on her desire and soared to the song of her moans building and changing with every spear of my tongue into her and every suction around her sensitive bud. My hands clamped around her thighs, and I was determined to make her finish from my mouth alone.

"Give it to me," I growled, devouring her deeply.

Her hips undulated more, struggling against my tight hold. I kind of wanted her standing to let her ride my face, as she clearly wanted to, but I couldn't stop. This orgasm was mine. All mine to give.

After dipping into her tight little entrance a few more times, I focused on sucking. That's what threw her over the edge. I groaned as she came undone, screaming my name. Thighs shaking around me, wriggling like she wanted to escape, yet her fingers threading through my hair to keep me between her legs while she rode out the climax that stretched on.

"Nyte," she mewled when I didn't stop my assault, pushing her toward the brink of overstimulation.

Every flick of my tongue caused her body to buck and jerk; her fingers had tightened painfully in my hair to warn me off, but it only turned me feral for *more.*

"Are you warm yet?" I said, my voice barely a gravelly murmur as I kissed the inside of her thigh, then her navel, her chest, before making her taste her own arousal still coating my lips and chin. She moaned into my mouth, deepening the kiss.

"Not enough," she rasped, and my cock twitched painfully.

"Good."

I lifted her, putting her back on her feet and bending her over the altar again. I passed my fingers through her swollen heat again, and she gave a stiff shudder. As I plunged two fingers into her, she gasped, and I leaned over her back, fucking her slowly with them.

"What happened to you being in charge next time we did this?" My breath fanned her ear.

"Given the circumstances, I didn't think either of us would have the patience for a dominance battle."

I chuckled darkly against her skin, pulling my fingers out to pump my aching cock.

"If you want to fight me for dominance we'd best make sure its somewhere not precious to destruction, because I would win, but I know you would not make it an easy triumph."

She gave a breathy sign of pleasure as I coaxed her feet together and slipped my cock between her thighs, not entering her yet, but it felt almost as good, with her slickness and warmth coating me as I thrusted slowly across her apex.

"You feel so fucking good." I watched my cock sliding between her beautiful thighs, and nearly came on the damned spot without even being inside her yet.

She straightened, turning and gripping my cock tightly. I braced my hands on the altar behind her, watching her fist pump me a couple of times before placing me back between her thighs, leaning back to place her hands by mine.

"Fuck," I rasped, thrusting a couple more times before I couldn't take it anymore.

Lifting one of her thighs around my hip, I plunged into her, and she took all of me effortlessly in her tight grip.

Her hand lashed around my nape for purchase as I fucked her fast and hard. The sounds of our skin meeting and breathless desire filled this sacred hall.

I pulled out with a groan, leading her away from the altar and toward the rowed benches.

"Knees on the bench, hold onto the back," I instructed. "That's it, spread yourself a little more. Good girl."

I stepped forward, sinking into her glorious heat again, slower now, savoring every plunge of my cock in her tight channel.

"My shining starlight," I murmured, kissing her shoulder. "My powerful mate." I kissed her other, and my hand snaked around her front, circling her apex, which made her hips push back against me.

Astraea's moans became sharper and more breathless as she climbed toward a climax. I fucked her harder to the demand her body craved. Then when she was about to tip over the edge, her noises strangled and lessened with her focus as she braced for the blissful crash about to overcome her. It was my favorite fucking symphony.

"That's it, come for me."

I thought I could hold on a little longer, but when her heat squeezed the damn life out of me with her orgasm, I lost my control, slipping over that edge with her in an unexpected eruption that had been denied since the moment I touched her.

The sounds of our mixed pleasure roared through the hall, and I was sure nothing would be left to secrecy if anyone was outside. My orgasm stretched longer than I had the fucking breath for. My cock spent inside her with long jutting strokes, and I didn't realize the hold I'd trapped her in, bent over her back with a hand around her throat, holding her right where I needed.

She was still shaking and panting. I couldn't fucking move.

"I'm more than warm now," she said at last, pulling a breathless chuckle from me.

"Me too," I said, pulling out and stepping back. "Stay there. Just for a damn moment."

I stroked my cock at the perfect sight of her splayed and bent over with my release coating her.

"You are fucking exquisite."

Her head tipped shyly with her vulnerable state. It was so damn adorable. Then she watched my hand with renewed sparks of desire, which hardened my cock again even more.

Astraea twisted to sit on the bench. "Come here."

With those two words, the low sultry command of it, I almost passed out.

I would obey her to walk across knives.

When I was close enough, her hand replaced mine and my jaw tightened with the burst of pleasure and pain.

"You don't have to—*fuck*." Astraea's lips wrapped around me without warning, sucking hard.

I'd thought we were finished, but she was so full of surprises, and I was losing my fucking mind because of her. She moaned around my cock, tasting me and herself, and that thought surged me to the brink again already, which I didn't think was even possible.

My fingers threaded through her damp hair. "So needy for my cock it wasn't enough?" I growled.

She hummed, flicking her silver eyes up, and I lost myself. My fingers tightened to hold her head, and I thrust into her mouth. "Your throat feels fucking incredible."

Astraea was touching herself, ass pushed to the edge of the bench, and circling her sensitive bud faster. Her brow pulled together as she neared another climax, and I couldn't believe she was pleasuring herself while swallowing me. My head was spinning, losing all sense of time and gravity to the erotically torturing sight.

I pulled out when I knew she was close, and I came, painting her chest with my release this time as her back arched and I got to witness it in full sight as she brought herself to orgasm. The experience was transcendent. She was so powerful and beautiful like this I lowered to my knees as if she had willed it through my bones.

When her head straightened, a smile stretched across her flushed cheeks.

"That was unexpected," she said.

"Yes," was all I could say, still in a state of awe as I looked up at her naked, silver tattooed body as she reclined back on her hands.

I used a torn-off piece of my wet cloak to help clean her as best as we could before we dressed back into our miserable, sodden clothes.

Astraea hovered by a podium beyond the altar, and her beaming smile found me, key piece in hand.

It was a true piece. I could feel it after her gleeful expression conveyed it.

"A reward for our suffering at last," I mused.

Astraea strolled over to me with it, pressing her body to mine with the key piece humming between us.

"I will always share the sky with you," she promised quietly.

42

Astraea

Emerging from the temple with a true key piece made my spirits soar, and I could hardly stop grinning. Nyte was smiling too, so bright and rare.

Our happiness was always fleeting in this world of terrors, and seeing Fedora, standing on human legs, had us both staggering to a halt.

"The night and the star." She had a unique song in her voice that was deceptively soothing.

The Nymph's raven hair made it appear as if she'd just stepped out of water, but her skin and dress were completely dry. If what she wore could be called such. The black material barely covered her nipples and crossed around her neck, while the skirt was a thin floating strip covering her front and back. Her legs were fully exposed and she was barefoot against the snow. She gave no reaction to the cold.

"You got your prize, I see," Nyte observed.

Fedora's onyx eyes gleamed with mischief and triumph, because in her hand she held the trident, which was propped against the ground and as tall as a scepter.

"With no thanks to you. It seems you fell short on your bargain to me, and I don't like empty promises."

"You know I tried and would have gotten it for you were it not for my father getting there first."

Her dark brows pulled together and she pouted as if offended. Then something switched in her; a maniacal amusement widened her eyes and she smiled with cruel glee.

Fedora approached Nyte like a serpent in the way she glided. I stiffened when she locked a gaze of playful desire on him. She stopped close to him, tipping the forked end of the trident toward him. I jolted a step, but Nyte's arm extended to stop me. My anger clawed at my mind to unleash violence, but I contained it for now, even as the sharp tip of the middle point of the trident grazed under Nyte's chin.

"Do you even know of the power I have at my fingertips now? Enough to rival both of you. I could drown this kingdom with a thought if I so desired."

"Someone has to rule the land and someone the sea; ally with us, Fedora. We will honor you as the Queen of the Sea," Nyte tried to reason.

"I don't need you for that," she hissed. "I don't need anyone."

The trident cut Nyte's flesh, and I shifted again, ready to summon what I needed to so I could contend with her.

"What is it you've come to me for, then?" Nyte asked.

My skin pricked with Nyte's careful tone and approach. I was used to seeing him confident, sure he could contend with any foe, but he was afraid of the weapon and the unhinged Nymph who now possessed it.

She chuckled. Then laughed. A laugh that mocked us for something we were completely oblivious to. It turned the already frozen air that much icier.

"The night and his star. The star and her night," she sang, toying with us now. "Such tragic poetry you are, and so shall your end be. Why would I want to ally with the two who want to return the sun? My seas are never more powerful than when the moon shines."

"Our world is falling apart with the imbalance. The true stars are falling," I snapped.

"Then the land will crumble and my seas will grow."

There was no reasoning with a creature like Fedora. Her emotions were not a human's, and she would have no care for any land species.

"Do you want to know what the first thing I did when I got my hands on this trident was? I assassinated the clan I was born into, which cast me out. I started with my parents, who had two daughters after me, whom they loved instead of loathed. I killed them too. Then I offered the next clan a chance to swear fealty to me as their one true queen. They refused and I killed them all. I still have ways to go to cover the sea, but anyone who opposes me will die."

She was as cold-blooded as the waters she came from, but I also couldn't fathom the pain she'd suffered being in exile all her life. Sometimes I believed everyone's pain made them capable of villainous things if they were given the tools to seek retribution.

"We don't oppose you," Nyte said.

"I like the darkness. I like the night. There is one who has agreed to keep our world bathing in this tranquil moonlight."

"Dusk and Dawn need the daylight. They *are* the beginning and end of daylight. Your allegiance to them won't grant you anything," I said.

Her depthless eyes shifted to me, and a cold smile curled her pale cheeks.

"I wish them dead as much as you do. As much as my king does."

"Your king?" Nyte repeated.

Her smile spread wider with sinister merriment.

"The person who gave me this trident, of course. The one who holds the missing piece of your key from the temple, which I helped him to long before you came calling. During their trade, he warned the Overlord Vermont you would come, but of course you managed to escape his methods to capture you, I had no doubt in that."

Fedora had betrayed us from the start.

"Why would you ally with the king?" I asked bitterly.

Fedora giggled, stepping closer to Nyte, and I was shaking from restraining my magick. His fingers tightening around mine was a warning not to attack her yet.

"We're going to rule the land and the sea together. It could have been us, you know? I would have preferred it, but your father is quite alluring as well."

"You won't win," I said with deadly promise.

Her smile fell. "You're really starting to get on my nerves, Maiden."

Fedora's hand lashed around my throat so fast that not even Nyte detected her shift of movement. I choked with her sharp claws piercing my neck as Nyte gripped the trident, intending to try disarming her and fighting, but power surged through the weapon, and my scream was choked as I watched it throw him back.

My magick burned her hand and she hissed, throwing me to the ground, but I couldn't rally my next attack before water lassoed around me, coiling up my body until it latched itself to me like a rope with the rapid current.

"Nyte!" I yelled, a futile call of fear as he peeled himself up from the snow, which began to animate around him—another influence of the trident.

"You don't want to do this," Nyte growled; his breathlessness gave away how powerful the trident's strike had been.

"But I'm having so much fun," she sang.

The water holding me shifted, and I tried to reach for Lightsdeath, but I was drowning; the water compressed my body, growing over my neck, and I couldn't reach for my magick.

I held Nyte's look of fury and terror before it blurred, and my last breath held. My limbs thrashed as if I could swim out of the suspended ball of water I was submerged in, but it was all wasted energy. I thought I could hear distant voices yelling through the thrashing current. Then a bright blue flare, and I screamed, though it cost me more of the precious air my body held. I couldn't see what was happening, but Nyte was in trouble. Maybe the trident could kill him. or maybe Fedora had my blood and knew how lethal it was to him.

Darkness peppered my vision. My breath choked, and I instinctively tried to draw another gasp, and my throat was set aflame. My lungs burned. Agony became me, and oblivion stole me.

43

Nyte

I was born in the darkness. Crafted by it. So when it came for me, I didn't submit; I *embraced the dark*.

She took my Starlight, and my rage shattered the ice Fedora trapped me in. On one knee I took breaths to organize my fury, not tame it. The storm that was coming for my father was going to end him if it was the last thing I achieved on this fucking land.

Shadows leaked around me. I lifted one hand from the snow, testing if they were real. The familiar sense of animated darkness wove between my fingers like a greeting from an old friend.

Did I have the ability to use them again?

A loud roar dragged my sight up, and I found Eltanin circling like a spiral of smoke; it clicked in me then. Something I should have realized sooner.

Eltanin's breath had always felt familiar, even *looked* familiar.

"Shit, I didn't know if that would work," Drystan said.

I jolted at his sudden company. He wasn't alone, and I blinked my blurry vision before shooting up with lashing wrath to discover the redhead with him.

"When were you going to tell me you could use your dragon's power?" Nadia folded her arms in accusation at Drystan.

My mind was already spinning to a violent storm with Fedora taking Astraea, now faced with the wrath and confusion of seeing Drystan and Nadia together, I was close to passing out.

"One of you better explain before I lose it on both of you," I said in a deadly, controlled calm.

"A thank you for saving your ass would be appreciated," Drystan grumbled.

His posture stiffened when my expression didn't change slightly. I likely resembled a feral beast right now. Drystan shifted nervously before coming closer.

"Honestly, I'm kind of flattered you and Astraea believed I managed to tackle all those temples myself. In truth, our father has been just as busy as us, and Nadia was with him the entire time, ready to swap out any true key pieces if possible."

Drystan's scheming was going to be the damned death of me.

"You couldn't have told us that?"

He shrugged. "The fewer people who knew, the better."

Nadia explained, "Your father wanted me to kill Drystan from the start. It was him who told me about the blood bond that was created between Drystan and the vampires he transitioned; that was all true. I'll admit I truly wanted to kill him for a while."

"So what changed?" I asked bitterly.

"I simply switched my allegiance. You lot might be marginally better company."

Drystan added, "So when she told me back when we were in Alisus, after freeing Athebyne, we decided to keep up the ruse and Nadia spied for us instead."

"You couldn't have warned us sooner about his plan to send a cunning nymph with a powerful trident after us?" I growled.

That shot his brow up in surprise.

Nadia said, "Are you sure it was your father's order?"

"Fedora gloated about it," I snapped.

Nadia and Drystan exchanged a look, communicating silently, which irked me.

I raised a hand swirling with shadows. "Tell me why I have this."

Drystan answered, "I didn't want to mention it in case it didn't happen for you; not all riders can harness their dragon's power. I figured you would have by now if it were possible, but it seems your sulking after losing Nightsdeath might have suppressed it. All it took to unlock was the acute rage of Nightsdeath."

I looked up at the circling black dragon; occasionally Athebyne dipped through the clouds too. It dawned on me . . .

"You can use fire?"

"You might have broken that ice yourself eventually, but I gave you a good helping hand," he said smugly.

"How long have you been able to do that?" I groused.

"Hey, you should be happy for me!"

I had to close my eyes for a moment of sanity.

My brother could use fire magick when Athebyne was around. It was incredible and my sharp irritation was only because of the secrecy.

"Why wouldn't you tell me?" I amended.

"I was waiting to see if you reached Eltanin's magick."

When his reason sank in, I felt like shit. He hadn't wanted to show off his new power for the sake of my feelings. As if I would resent him for it if I couldn't achieve the same with Eltanin.

My anger cooled at that.

"How did you know I was here?"

"Eltanin found us, and we thought to make sure you weren't dead, given how he was wounded," Drystan explained.

"I appreciate it," I mumbled. I would tell him about Rastaban and his fight with Eltanin later.

The shadowy starlight circled and primed around me just as it used to, yet instead of anger and resentment, which usually caused the darkness to answer me, all I felt was peace and wonder.

"Do you know where father is?" Drystan asked.

My jaw and fists clenched.

"I'm willing to bet he's right back where it all started. On the stolen throne that was always his objective."

And he's not getting the villain he created this time. To protect Astraea, I'm much fucking worse.

44

Astraea

Waking after a battle of water and fire was a torture unlike anything I'd felt before. My entire body was burning from the inside, but I was unable to extinguish it with air when I was drowning. Again.

My panic-clouded mind couldn't recall how many times I had died like this. My vision was blurry and darkness threatened to pull me unconscious once more. At least the suffering in between was quick.

Right before the light winked out completely, the water released me, slapping me like a wet blanket against unforgiving ground. I spluttered and gasped, but the fire in my lungs wouldn't extinguish. I never thought I would wish for death just for a period of relief, but the agony was so intense.

"You're already proving yourself very useful."

I knew that voice. It made my consciousness weave together faster when being vulnerable in his company could spill a more permanent end for me.

My elbows trembled violently as I pushed myself up. I recognized the violet pattern in these marble floors that were flooded from the sphere of water that brought me all the way here.

"As promised, my king. A fallen star." Fedora's voice of song floated above me. Her bare foot touched my shoulder before it pushed me onto my back. It wasn't that rough; I was just far too weak.

"You won't have to worry about her death; it seems it's already inevitable." She leaned down and ripped the bottom of my tunic to display the angry wound growing over my ribs now. "Auster Nova dealt it himself. Fitting, really."

"And my son?" Nyte's father asked.

"I couldn't carry them both. He's in a block of ice in the Luna Province."

For Nyte, I pulled myself together faster, letting adrenaline take over even if it would punish my body when I let it go.

Fedora still stood right by me, and my first reaction was to grab her ankle and pull hard. She went crashing onto her back with a shriek, and I straddled her with my hands around her throat, lost in a haze of violent retribution.

I gripped more magick, and her screams were unnatural, so shrill I winced and lost the ability to focus on my surroundings. I was pulled off of her by two guards, but I thrashed like a wild animal. They dropped me too when I scorched their flesh as it touched mine, but my magick was only a burning ember in my exhaustion, close to dying out completely.

A sharp slap snapped my head to the side. I was let go, too disorientated to catch myself, and I fell to the ground in a crumpled heap.

So much pain. It was all I knew right now, and I wanted it to end.

I was kicked by a boot, more roughly this time, which flipped me onto my back. My vision came and went with blurred focus and threats of darkness, but I knew the face that hovered over me with sinister intent.

Nyte's father crouched, studying me in silence for a moment. I jolted to feel his vile fingers grazing my bare skin where Fedora had ripped my tunic. Then searing agony tore a scream from my throat when he pressed hard on the wound Auster had dealt. I could hardly hear my pain echoing through the hall when inside it was like the small dose of Nyte's blood surged up fractions higher from the pressure.

No, no, no. He was stealing my time and I had to *fight.*

My mind didn't feel connected to my body to stop or fight or move. Tears spilled over the corners of my eyes as I writhed on the cold floor. All I could do was flood my thoughts with thoughts of Nyte.

My night. My mate.

I wanted eternity with him, yet it seemed cruel fate was winning. We were two hopeless souls given an hourglass of time, delusional to believe we could break it and have our sand fill a desert. Each grain a new hour, a new day, a new canvas to paint with our endless future.

Darkness surrounded me. My pain didn't ease, but it wasn't climbing to immeasurable heights anymore.

The darkness was so beautiful. Shadowy and filled with stars. It embraced me, and my hand reached to touch it. Maybe I was in some forgotten corner of Death's realm where a small essence of Nightsdeath still lingered. Where the stars and night collided.

"Don't leave me," I whispered to the familiar, comforting dark.

It answered as a tighter wrap around my body, unable to heal my wounds but filling in the cracks of my soul.

My senses began to return, but I didn't want them back yet. This was peaceful and warm whereas the marble floor took some of that away. My hearing flooded with commotion. Clashes and shouts and so much pain and anguish. I whimpered, curling into myself more.

I only wanted one person, and maybe it was my desperation that made me believe he was here. Finding the will to peel my eyes open and squint through the storm of darkness, I knew this had to be a dream. Nyte didn't have his shadows anymore, so the starry darkness that attacked around the room couldn't be real.

Nyte was absolutely furious. Unhinged in a way that didn't resemble anything human anymore. I watched him move like a nightmare given form. Tearing flesh, snapping necks. His face contorted in such a frightening display of wrath I shivered where I lay, watching the scene of darkness and bloodshed unfold.

He wasn't alone. Drystan was here too.

. . . yes, this was definitely a dream.

Because he was wielding *fire.*

An unnatural blood-red flame conjured from his hands and swallowed bodies whole, burning their flesh and bones to nothing in seconds.

I mistook the next flash of red for a lick of flame at first, until a blade glinted between the hands of a form that moved with such speed and grace.

Nadia.

She fought back to back with Drystan, but she had betrayed us by working for Nyte's father all this time. Hadn't she?

This illusion was becoming too ridiculous, yet my consciousness was coming back more and more in grim awe of the way the trio tore through the enemy effortlessly.

Just as I was beginning to muster the awareness and strength to push myself up, I was forced up with a tight grip of my hair, and I screamed, not sure what part of me was hurting most.

"One more move and I snap her pretty neck," Fedora sang chillingly close to my ear.

The fighting ceased, but Nyte, Drystan, and Nadia had finished off the flood of guards anyway. The throne room was a bath of blood and fire and bodies. It was too real . . . *too real.*

It *was* real.

My gaze of horror found Nyte, who stood across the room like a furious storm. Despite all he'd expended, he wasn't close to being finished expending his wrath.

"I will turn this castle to rubble with everyone in it if she's not returned to my side in the next five minutes," Nyte said, his voice so removed from mercy. He wasn't bluffing.

"I only want one thing from you right now, then you're free to leave," his father said.

Nyte's gaze of liquid-gold targeted him.

"You will get nothing but a painful death."

"Give me the key pieces and no innocents have to die."

"I don't care who dies with you."

I hardly had the voice to reason with Nyte. All he knew was vengeance, and he deserved to feel this way. But I couldn't disregard the number of people that were in this castle, with no way to call for an evacuation.

My pleading eyes met Drystan's. He spoke to Nadia, who looked ready to protest, but after a short exchange, she left in a run.

Was she going to try to get as many innocents out as possible?

Time was too quick in this situation. Less than five minutes wouldn't be enough.

"You have a true key piece from the underwater temple," I said to Nyte's father; my voice was a painful croak.

"Indeed. Now hand over the others."

I chuckled dryly even though it hurt. "You really think I would have them with me? I'm not the fool here."

Nyte's father seethed at me, his anger protruding along the vines at his temples and over his neck.

"It's about time you faced your inevitable demise," Nyte said, words that slithered down my spine along with his next. "Time's up."

Those two words were followed by a deafening blast of stone. Only it wasn't caused by Nyte.

He reached me, throwing up a shield of darkness from the fragments of the back wall that tumbled through the throne room. I couldn't believe the sight of the huge taloned foot that had torn through the castle as if it were paper.

Rastaban roared, and in front of the terrifying black dragon, Nyte's father stood. Unafraid. A slow, dark smile started to grow on one corner of his mouth . . .

"That fucking bastard," Drystan seethed behind us.

Rastaban had bonded with their father. Or at least allied with him for now.

"I believe I have you to thank for handing me such a formidable ally," Nyte's father goaded. He turned, beginning to climb over the slope of rocks to mount the huge beast. "Do you want to reevaluate your challenge against me, son?"

"Not in the slightest," Nyte growled.

He stood, sending his shadowy magick hurtling toward beast and rider, but Rastaban heaved a breath, and Nyte was forced to defend again, creating another dome around us with his magick. With the way his stance shifted, the dragon's breath of pure black had to be a reckoning force.

The attack cut off suddenly with more than one mighty dragon roar. We all watched in stunned horror as Eltanin swooped across like a stroke of death, slicing his claws along the neck of Rastaban, who howled in pain and fury. The celestial dragon was gone again in the blink of an eye.

My heart stopped.

Rastaban didn't hesitate. The dragon adjusted his footing, causing more of the castle wall to crumble. Then we were almost thrown back with the wind force of his wings as he took off after Eltanin.

"Stop!" I yelled, trying to command Rastaban, but it was too late; my dragon voice was weak and Rastaban shot too quickly out of range. My head whipped to Nyte. "You have to go!"

Rastaban was too big; his claws or jaw could kill Eltanin, which became the most imminent threat and fear.

Drystan was already running out, but Nyte hesitated, painfully conflicted.

"I'm fine. Please, don't let him die."

A muscle in his jaw worked. "You're injured," he assessed tightly. "Badly."

His furious gaze surveyed around, and he growled, "Where the fuck did Fedora slither off to?"

"I can handle her if she comes back. Nyte—"

More roars shook the sky, and my desperation was immeasurable. Nyte tensed with a groan, balancing a hand against the ground. Eltanin was hurt. Nyte could feel it.

"He'll kill him!" I said desperately.

Steps came rushing into the room, and we found Nadia racing toward us. "I'll stay with her. Drystan is already in pursuit of your father on Athebyne."

Nyte regarded me one last time, his eyes cleaved with misery as he cupped a hand to my cheek.

"Stay alive," I whispered to him.

He nodded; then he was gone through the void.

45

Nyte

When my body began falling rapidly through air, I thought I'd made a foolish error in attempting to mount Eltanin using the void. He was darting too fast through the night sky. But he saw me, *felt me,* and twisted to catch me in a fearless dive.

I was barely able to get a tight grip on the saddle horn and brace my legs on Eltanin before he roared at the tip of Rastaban's claws tearing his chest. It wasn't too deep, as he'd almost glided completely out of range, but his pain lanced through me. The brave younger dragon didn't falter in his flight, and, now that I was with him, we were going to end this together.

The clouds were thick and rolling with the dark anger we expelled up here. We lost track of my father, but it gave us a moment to think and brace. I extended every sense I could through the sharp wind slicing past.

Eltanin sensed his father before I did mine, diving suddenly with a shrill cry, and I twisted a look up to find the horrifying sight of Rastaban, his jaw wide, revealing every razor tooth, diving after us. Twisting in the saddle, I barely got into position to throw out a shield against his breath. My teeth clenched tight, and a roar tore from me this time, straining with every dreg of strength I had against the mighty, shadowy power ramming into my shield made of similar essence. I was slipping . . .

The pressure eased, and when my magick cleared, I saw that a stroke of red was my saving grace. The sight of my brother on the back of Athebyne, who clawed and snapped at an equally vicious Rastaban, stilled my whole fucking world.

The two dragons fighting viciously in flight was a sight of pure carnage and terror.

Flipping back into riding position, I spoke to Eltanin. "We fight. Until the end we fight." We shifted course, heading back toward the battling duo.

Eltanin heaved a breath of starry darkness, which slammed into Rastaban's head. The giant black dragon emitted an ear-splitting roar, flailing in his attempt to maintain his strong flight.

Even against two dragons Rastaban was an undeniably powerful dragon. My father, much to my displeasure, remained on his back.

No matter. I wanted the last dregs of his life to be spilled by my hands.

Rastaban kept falling, and blood poured out of several wounds caused by teeth and claws. I watched until the dark clouds swallowed him.

I exchanged a wary look with Drystan. The silence vibrated.

My heart started to calm until, slipping past our notice, Rastaban surged up from beneath Drystan, and all I could do was watch with horror and complete helpless terror as his jaw clamped around the base of Athebyne's throat.

The red dragon cried as it was dragged up while Drystan was thrown off her back.

It all happened so fast I didn't have time to debate. I couldn't help Athebyne, who used her back claws to shred deeply and brutally into Rastaban's chest and neck, spilling his blood, but he didn't let her go.

I dove after Drystan.

Clamping my legs and leaning over the saddle, I reached out an arm for my brother when we were close enough. He reached back, gripping onto me when I pulled him to me with everything I had, and he made it onto the saddle behind me.

"No," was the first word he spoke in a breath of pained disbelief.

As I glanced up at the chaos in the sky, to my surprise and awe, Athebyne had managed to get free from Rastaban, and she was still fighting back.

"She's too injured," Drystan said, pure agony and anger in his voice.

He was right: she wasn't going to last much longer, and it was a miracle she still held herself in the sky.

Eltanin was already gliding up, heading toward them, but we wouldn't make it. Rastaban's jaw opened and he lunged for the smaller red dragon again.

"NO!" Drystan yelled.

The scene of horror would haunt him forever. He would never recover from the loss of Athebyne, and my soul tore for him.

Just before Rastaban's mouth could rip Athebyne apart, a lightning flash of blue slammed into his head.

"Is that . . . ?"

"Edasich," Drystan filled in.

It was unbelievable. The dragon appeared like a blue spirit of the night, and I couldn't fathom why she would risk her life for this fight.

Eltanin cried, torn to witness his kin fighting so ferociously.

Edasich sank her claws into Rastaban's eye, blinding him on one side, but the black dragon always had the advantage of size. His huge wing slammed into Athebyne, and that was the end of her fight. Not dead yet, but so severely wounded I didn't know if she would be able to survive or even catch herself as she fell from the sky.

Drystan yelled, and I didn't expect him to leap off Eltanin's saddle and fall after her like a damned fool. I snarled, about to dive to catch him again, but, to my shock, he gripped the horn of Athebyne's saddle, managing to haul himself onto it even in a vertical drop.

Athebyne tried to use her wings again, and my adrenaline pumped so hard witnessing their violent plummet. A tumble of wings and pained cries. Until it was my belief that, because of Drystan, because of his devotion to be with her even if their fate was to die, she found enough will to fly. It wasn't any kind of smooth descent, but they were slowing. Drystan could survive the rough landing; Athebyne would make sure he did.

Even if it meant sacrificing herself . . .

My rage amplified with my deep inhale at the thought, and I set my target back on my father.

"This ends now," I said to Eltanin. He didn't need the push of my dragon's voice but he roared in fierce agreement. Eltanin didn't just obey; he was as determined as I was to emerge triumphant. To cut his own father from the sky and keep his rightful place reigning over the dragons.

Pride to be facing this with such an unexpected companion in my life swelled in me. There were three things worth saving this world for. Three things I would always be glad to have the world brand me the villain to protect.

My mate. My brother. And my dragon.

What stood in the way of our freedom and happiness was not so easy to defeat, but I had bled this much, suffered thus far, and I was going to fucking win this time.

Eltanin charged with unfaltering bravery, and shadowy starlight diffused from his feathers. We were a stroke of black death cutting through the air.

Just as we reached Rastaban, his jaw crushed through the small blue dragon's throat. Edasich's sapphire eyes stared right into me, as if they spoke to my soul, and I didn't know why she delivered her last farewell to me. Tragedy speared me, watching her innocent eyes glass over and slowly slip shut. Moonlight electrified the blue of her scales as she fell alone . . . an image of beautiful tragedy I would never forget.

Her death granted the distraction for Eltanin to sink his teeth into Rastaban's neck, and the giant dragon thrashed to shake him off. At the same time, Eltanin's claws slashed again and again over his already gravely wounded chest. Rastaban was incredibly durable.

I waited for my chance, holding on with everything I had as the dragons fought wildly. Eltanin sustained a few deep claws to his wings, legs, and neck, but my fearless dragon didn't relent in his onslaught of attacks.

When Rastaban's head turned to the angle I needed, I had no choice but to let go of Eltanin, knowing I would be thrown off his saddle. Conjuring a spear of dark power, with a battle cry I sent it right into Rastaban's only good eye.

The dragon wailed and we were both falling. I could barely make out my father yelling, holding onto Rastaban with desperate hands, but the giant dragon couldn't find his flight again.

My body cut through the air at a deadly speed. I couldn't see Eltanin anymore as dark clouds swallowed me. The ground closed in fast.

For a moment, I let go of the fear. The panic. I erased everything from my mind, and my only wish was that I could see the stars.

It wasn't Eltanin who saved me.

Hands gripped mine with a touch that felt descended from the heavens itself.

Astraea's wings splayed, and she cried out, trying to stop this rapid descent. *Fuck*, there was no sound I hated more than her pain. The clutches of gravity were too powerful for her to defy now. Instead of letting her keep attempting to pull me up, I reached to pull her down.

The sight of Astraea's desolate eyes made me ache, and I held her around the waist. She unglamoured her wings, and I didn't scold her for it.

The stars were dying, and we were the brightest of them.

There would never be a limit to how much my love could grow for her. When every time my sights set upon her I had to remind myself she was no dream though every part of her embodied the peace of one. She was no fable though her power was unmatched for this world.

She was Astraea Lightborne, and she was mine.

Eltanin roared above us, but there wasn't enough time for him to catch us. Instead I felt magick growing around us, creating a sphere of starry darkness from the dragon's influence, and Astraea's light reinforcing a second shield despite her pain. I wasn't sure if it would be enough to spare us from the impact of hitting the ground, but I held her tighter and we braced ourselves.

It was like the world exploded and we plummeted deep enough to reach its molten core.

Yet . . . I wasn't too badly harmed.

I caught my breaths of disbelief, staring up at the cloudy sky from within a deep crater as the shields of light and dark broke away like stardust.

"Astraea," I said her name as she lay so still against me, head resting against my chest.

"Nyte," she croaked in reply.

My body slumped in relief, still furious about her suffering, but at least she was alive. With the thought, my father filtered back to the forefront of my objectives and I pushed up to sit, not letting her go.

"I need to finish it," I said, absolutely torn to leave her again.

The fall with Rastaban should have killed him, but if there was one thing that was consistent with my father it was that he seemed to have infinite fucking lives.

Eltanin rattled, peering down at us from the edge of the crater in distress. With an arm around Astraea, I pulled us through the void to get us out of there.

"Be free, Nyte," she said, pressing a leather pouch into my hand. "For you and for Drystan."

I stared down at it, clenching my fist around the solid contents, which raked a hum over my skin. I kissed her fiercely, then took a long step back, letting the void swallow me.

When the shadows let me go I sat upon Eltanin and he didn't miss a beat before taking me to the skies again.

Snow started to fall as I searched the grounds for Rastaban. It didn't take long to find him. The great black dragon had fallen just outside the central city of Vesitire, its tail having collapsed the edge of the lower level wall. Eltanin landed and I dismounted swiftly.

Rastaban was dead, and even though it had wanted to kill him, Eltanin still mourned for the loss of kin. I didn't want to feel the same, but when I spied a form that seemed so small next to the dragon, I couldn't move for a moment.

I wasn't ready to confirm his end.

Tipping the key pieces Astraea had given me into my palm, I joined them one by one. Each serrated shard snapped together with a current of raw power growing denser, amplifying with an electric vibration. It rejoiced to be reforged, but there was one missing piece.

As I joined the pieces, I slowly got closer to my father, rallying the courage to retrieve the last shard he possessed. I wished I could turn off my clashing emotions, fixing my sight on him. He deserved absolutely nothing from me.

Father lay on his back, and when I got close enough . . . I couldn't decide if dread or relief pounded in me when I detected the shallow rise and fall of his chest.

Still. Fucking. Alive.

His breaths wheezed and staggered; his sight fixed wide and unblinking on the sky that wept with snowfall.

I couldn't place this moment. Not in words or feelings.

He was the villain of my origin. The nightmare plaguing my rest. He had created me and tried to end me in more ways than one.

Yet he was just . . . a person.

A mortal being drawing final breaths, who had the same value as anyone else in the end.

"S-son," he croaked.

I sank down slowly to a crouch, continuing to study every piece of him as if it might offer an explanation as to *why*.

Why did I ever fear him?

Why did I let him control me?

Why did I ever try to gain his approval?

I didn't mourn for him. I never would. But my chest constricted and emotions so long buried clawed their way around my entire body because I mourned for myself. All the years I let him have of me.

The glowing violet light of the key highlighted his scared face.

"You don't have anyone," I said. "No one who will cry for you. No one will remember you with anything other than loathing. That is the path you always walked no matter how long it was to be. Why would anyone want that?"

"To mean something to myself."

My brow twitched, not expecting an honest answer.

"Your pursuit of meaning poisoned everything in your path."

"I don't expect you to understand. You were always so weak."

I couldn't deny that comment impacted me. After all I'd done under his command and the black soul I harbored for it . . . I was not *weak*.

Patting over his torso, I tried to feel for the distortion of the key piece. With his protection from the gods, the key was the only true weapon to ensure he truly died.

I'd let my guard down, thinking he was teetering too close to the brink of death to be a threat. I didn't detect his movement fast enough to retract my hand back fully when he moved, slicing a blade across my wrist.

I hissed venomously, dropping the partially forged key when this wound burned through me far more intensely than a shallow slice should. There was only one way for such a cut to roar inside me.

The blade had been laced with Astraea's blood.

A surge of otherworldly power distracted me from my urge to lunge for father with all my loathing. The unmistakable eminence of the Maiden's key blasted around me, and when the light dimmed enough I cast my horrified sight up, finding my father on his feet, holding the key aloft like a god triumphant.

"Don't you see, Rainyte? You were merely a bad sample of what I was to become."

I couldn't believe it. Eltanin roared and I detected his preparation to strike. Father pointed the key in his direction, and I yelled, desperate for the dragon to flee, to save himself. I could only watch in horror as the violet flare of the key grew blinding . . .

As the power released, searing red flame clashed with it.

When it cleared and smoke choked the air, father had changed from attack to defense, fashioning a dome shield around himself. His furious sight cast up to Athebyne.

"Looking for me?" Drystan said.

Those words accompanied the fall of his skyward blade.

Father only caught a glimpse of Drystan, who'd expertly managed to creep right up to him with the distraction of Athebyne. Then father's roar of agony stunned me.

The key fell, still gripped in the hand Drystan had severed from his elbow with a single mighty swipe.

I moved like a magnet to Drystan's intentions. My brother caught the key, throwing it to me as father crashed to his knees.

The full glory of the Maiden's key burst through me. Answering me as her mate. It sought vengeance and blood as much as I did, combining our anguish to fuel a wrath of gods.

As soon as Drystan had severed Father's hand, I had launched up into a sprint toward them. Before Father's scream died out, I reached him.

I braced, I cried out, and I plunged the key through his chest.

It lodged deep into him, and he threw his head back with a silent agony. The key flared brighter inside him until light rays shot out from his eyes and wide mouth. It burned him from the inside out.

"The punishment for your greed doesn't end here," I snarled. "Say hello to mother for me."

I twisted the key, causing the crystal in the staff's end to emit the final killing dose of magick that turned flesh to stardust, blood to ash, bone to smoke.

I yanked the key out of him and watched him dissolve into nothing.

When it was finished, I stood there panting and disbelieving.

Part of me waited to wake up from a nightmare. To discover father was still alive and I would never escape him.

A hand on my shoulder snapped me from my terrorized thoughts.

"It's over, brother," Drystan said.

I turned to him fully, and we shared a look of fear, realization, then . . . liberation.

Drystan hugged me, and I held him back, never having truly believed this day would come.

"He's gone," I muttered. "He's really gone."

We broke apart and Drystan smiled. Then he grinned. When a breathy laugh escaped him, it broke my shock into smile too. The terror of our father that had been embedded deep in us from our cruel upbringing dispersed through our delirious echoes of laughter.

"That was impressive," I said to him.

"Did father hit your head? That was too generous of a compliment from you."

I chuckled. "Don't get used to it."

The monster of our childhood and the villain of our adulthood was slain, but I couldn't rest easy yet. Our world was still under the threat of the God of Dusk and Goddess of Dawn, and our star-maiden needed our help to claim her world back once and for all.

46

Nyte

I found Astraea and Nadia together, kneeling somberly by Edasich.

The dragon was gone, lying there so still and tragically as snow gathered over its ethereal blue body.

Astraea was crying. I scented her tears and that pummeled me.

Athebyne's cry of mourning struck deep in the hearts of all. She approached, wounded greatly from the battle, and dropped close to Edasich, nudging her giant head into the blue dragon's body.

"They were friends," Astraea croaked, having heard me closing in behind. "Not in the sense we know, but it's the best way I can describe their bond. In the past, before their entombment, they had a respect for and understanding of each other."

I couldn't comprehend Astraea's connection to all the dragons. She could feel them and command them as their bonded riders could.

"That's why she helped us," I said, reflecting on the dragons' battle in the sky.

"I just can't understand it," Drystan said in defeat, leaning on Athebyne. "Rastaban and our father made sense as a pair, but a dragon as gentle as Edasich choosing Auster Nova . . ."

Astraea sniffed, and I crouched by her with a hand on her waist for any small comfort.

"Sometimes barbed armor guards gentle hearts," she whispered. "After wearing it too long, one won't realize they were slowly bleeding themselves, and pain turns peaceful things vicious. Auster wasn't always the villain he became."

I didn't respond. As much as Astraea despised Auster for all he'd done, I also understood he was once a dear friend, and that she would always grieve for that part of him.

"You need a healer and rest," I said gently.

Astraea nodded, wincing as I helped her to stand.

Eltanin emitted noise, coming closer to us. He bowed his head, rattling toward Athebyne, who appeared so weak it was difficult to know if she would pull through.

"I can't lose her," Drystan whispered, resting his forehead against her giant head.

It would break him completely. This bond he had with the dragon meant more to him than anything. It was everything our father couldn't give him. Devotion, loyalty, love.

I watched Eltanin as he walked closer, and it was then I saw the glistening in his eyes.

He was offering his tears.

Three of them fell over Athebyne, and Astraea's hand tightened on my arm around her when they shimmered over the dragon's red scales.

"His tears can heal," Drystan muttered in fascination. He smiled, breathing a sigh of relief.

Athebyne still had a long way to go to recover fully, but whatever Drystan felt from her now must be enough confidence to know she'd make it.

Astraea took my hand, smiling preciously at me until something caught her attention. She glanced down, gasping as she pushed my sleeve up as far as it could go. The thin black vines of her blood used as poison had already crawled past my elbow from where my Father scored my wrist with the blade.

I tipped her chin with my fingers, and though her eyes were glistening with shock and panic, I smiled.

"Just another matching tattoo." I tried to lighten the situation.

My days were now as numbered as hers, but I didn't fear. I only wished I could give her more time in this world with her friends, but the fates had bound our final hours together, and though that was tragic, I was glad.

Her brow crumpled more.

"Oh, Nyte," she sighed, leaning into me.

I retrieved the key from the void. Astraea felt its pull instantly, straightening to take it from me. Back in her possession, the staff flared brilliantly, blasting a wave of power around us all.

"Now, let's reclaim your throne," I said.

Astraea wouldn't let me carry her, but I kept a firm arm around her waist as we passed through the first gates into the lower level of Vesitire's tiered city.

The streets were ominous and quiet.

Humans, fae, vampires, celestials . . . we passed them all, and they watched us with variations of fear, hope, and curiosity. As if not knowing which figure of power to trust as friend or foe anymore. Some whispered to each other but I didn't know if Astraea could hear them.

"It's the star-maiden."
"She saved us."
"Praise our Maiden."
"Our queen."

Yes, she was. And we took our time for the city to see her heading off to take back her throne.

We passed someone taking down the posters of us Auster had plastered throughout the streets. In their place they began to hang a purple banner. Astraea's constellation with her key through the middle adorned it, her black wings splayed proudly.

They were accepting her. Putting their faith in her. My pride in Astraea grew immeasurably.

Astraea walked, her chin held high with her sight never leaving the glittering black castle that drew closer. Her steps were tired and her eyes fluttered, but she pushed on in silence, and I didn't disturb this moment for her.

Coming home.

We still had the gods to send back, but for now this was victory.

On the castle courtyard, guards littered the grounds, but we paid them no attention. I stiffened when the first one moved, but . . . he lowered to one knee, head bowing.

"Long live the queen," he declared. The first strong voice in our trek of somber silence, and there were no words more perfect.

One by one the guards started kneeling, uttering the same devotion.

Astraea's tears were flowing now, and I wished I could sense they were happy, but something was polluting that emotion.

Only when we made it past the castle doors did she break.

I hugged her tightly, letting her cry into my chest, hands covering her face, until her sobs ran dry.

"What do you need me to do?" I asked gently.

Her arms circled around me. "They're all talking as if it's over. As if I'm here to stay," she whispered.

"Then let's live like we are. Until the very end."

She squeezed me tighter, and I pulled us through the void then, taking us to her rooms. I lay her down on the bed and I had to see . . .

Peeling the torn piece of her tunic up, I tried not to buckle under my wave of cold panic. Her wound had gotten so much worse, with the skin around the puncture site a dark shade of gray, and I couldn't see the end of the vines carrying my blood toward her heart. In my flustered desperation I removed her top layers, finding the end of the graying vines that stopped between her breasts.

"That bad?" she asked quietly.

My fingers traced over her ribs, lingering under her breast until my thumb touched the top of the mark growing to kill her.

"I'm so sorry," I whispered.

It was my blood that would do it, and that fact scored a deep wound in my soul.

"Please don't say that. I can't bear it."

Astraea tugged at my forearm, and I read her signal, leaning over to bring my mouth to hers.

She said, "Lie with me."

"I'm going to get a healer."

"I'm not in pain anymore. I just want you to lie with me."

I knew that was a lie. Whatever my father and Fedora had done to her had made her fatal wound worse and further weakened her body that needed to recover. Her pleading eyes were too much to deny.

I took off her boots first and brought a blanket to cover her naked torso with.

"Your father is dead," she stated more than asked, but her words were gentle.

"Yes."

"How are you feeling?"

"I'm . . . not sure."

She nestled her head against my chest more, tucking herself in comfortably.

"I'm relieved," she confessed. "The two people who hurt us the most are now gone."

"All that's left is a couple of arrogant gods."

I felt her smile.

"Then peace."

"Then our peace."

My fingers combed through the lengths of her tangled hair.

"It pains me to see your stunning hair so neglected. At least let me run you a bath."

She chucked softly, and I collected that sound every time like tiny candles to place in a hall of my mind, a reminder of what true light in this life felt like.

When Astraea stood naked, I helped her into the milky water filling the room with an aroma of honey and lavender. She sighed sitting back, closing her eyes, and I dragged a stool to the edge, unable to keep my hands off her for a moment.

Gliding a sponge over her clavicle, I reached a hand up to her bruised cheek.

"Father or Fedora?" I asked, controlling my wrath.

"Father," she admitted.

My teeth ground. "Perhaps there's a necromancer somewhere. I don't think I'm quite done with him after all."

Astraea took my hand, and her fingers traced over the thin black vines over my forearm. Her lips pressed to the tip of them halfway over my bicep.

"Where do you think Fedora went?" Astraea asked.

"Back to the sea, probably killing off more clans in her anger."

"Do you think she'll be a problem?"

"A creature like Fedora isn't going to stop now. She lost her ally on land because she chose the wrong one, but she's prideful and determined. I don't doubt she might attack us herself again, and we can't underestimate her with the trident."

Astraea nodded, and I wished I could take more of her burden.

"You could join me in this bath," she said.

"Hmm. As tempting as that sounds, we're about to be—"

"What the fuck happened?!"

I groaned against her skin at the intrusion and Astraea's hands lashed over her chest.

"Zath!" Astraea shrieked, twisting her head over her shoulder.

He'd barged in without a knock, along with Rosalind. At least she had an apology on her face for how they'd interrupted us, but Zath didn't seem to care if Astraea was in a bath or otherwise. The primal instinct in me to have another male so close, with my mate so vulnerable right now, itched violence in me no matter who it was.

"I'll give you this one warning to get out while Astraea is naked," I said, taming my wrath.

Rose gripped his bicep with both hands to drag him out.

"Wait! What happened? Did you know it's snowing in the throne room? I need answers—!"

His rambling faded with Rosalind forcing him out of Astraea's rooms entirely, and I never thought I'd be thankful to the one who despised me most.

Astraea giggled, leaning back again as I quelled my irritation with the interruption.

"These are the friends we need to keep by our side?" I grumbled, reaching for a lavender balm for her hair.

"This may sound a little contradictory right now, given their interruption, but they are part of our peace, I'm afraid."

I hooked a finger under her chin to tilt her head back, kissing her lips.

"The things I tolerate for you."

A dear smile bloomed on her. "Your denial that you care for them all is amusing."

"I care that you care for them."

"Mmm-hmm."

I smiled too, though she didn't see it as she ran a sudsy sponge along her leg lifted gloriously out of the water while I rinsed her hair. Her glistening, tattooed silver skin was mesmerizing. If I hadn't been so considerate of her need to heal after her ordeal, I would have acted on the desirous impulses stirring in me.

For now, however, I treasured our gentle touches and this silence filled with contentment far more after what we'd endured today. The war wasn't over, but we deserved to bask in the triumph of an ages long battle against my father finally won.

PART
FOUR

As
the Dusk
and the Dawn

47

Astraea–Past

A straea was holding a quarterly council with the reigning lords throughout the five surrounding kingdoms of Solanis when the news came in.

An ambush. A slaughter. A battle raging on a mountain fringe just past the Sterling Mountains.

She didn't waste a moment.

The informant couldn't tell her who'd led the attack, but she didn't miss the fearful whispers of Nightsdeath from the lords as she left. She didn't pay them any mind. If Nyte's father was behind this, she would have known about it. Unless it was another attack he'd called for without Nyte's knowledge.

She didn't have time to seek out Nyte for an explanation. Astraea flew right to the battle that expanded in a bloodbath below her. This wasn't a battle that had just broken out, and anger surged through her over how it had taken this long for someone to summon her.

Dropping from the sky, she reached into the void for her key, but . . . she couldn't feel it. Astraea had never misplaced the key, but she didn't have a spare breath to consider where else it might be before a nightcrawler made a target out of her.

Astraea only had her dagger, but it was enough.

Launching into the sky at the last moment, she twisted in a flip around the nightcrawler, plunging her dagger into the membrane below his right talon, and it ripped down the full length of his wing as she landed behind him.

He wailed until she grabbed a fistful of his hair, yanking his head back and slicing across his throat. Then she lost herself in a mindless enemy-killing spree.

When she cut down enough of the enemy to take a pause, she scanned for someone in charge on her side, but this field was chaos. No order, only savagery. At least one of the High Celestials should be here, but she couldn't see any of them.

It was as if this battle was secret. A pen of blood and violence tucked into a lonely pass between mountains. The location was odd. Not an attack on a village or city.

A sense of dread started to knot in her stomach.

Astraea turned around, intending to fly to Auster's province for aid. Maybe he would have answers.

A figure dropped into her path before she could unglamour her wings.

They might have passed for an anonymous masked assassin to anyone else, but Astraea would know Auster from any angle, no matter that he wore all black, his hood was drawn, and his face covering left only his hazel eyes on display.

Relief relaxed her tense shoulders.

"I was just about to come to you. Did you know about this?" she asked.

The battle was dying out now. All that was left was the last of the soldiers with too much fury in their bones to retreat and the dying that were strewn across the land.

Auster didn't answer. He didn't move.

Astraea tried to shake the unease he was inspiring in her. She took a step closer, but he stepped too.

She felt the magick too late. Not until it was a bright violet flare between them did she realize what he had in his possession. Not until she dropped her horrified sight from his cold, unfeeling eyes . . . and saw the stone tip of her key lodged in her gut.

No. This was a nightmare. A cruel, despicable nightmare she would wake from.

Because Auster would never do this. Her best friend would never hurt her. A man she loved and trusted would never want her *dead.*

Astraea's trembling hands wrapped around the staff. Light engulfed Auster's hand, and his hiss of pain rattled through her as he let go. She looked up, finding him clutching his left arm to his chest, backing away from her.

"Auster . . ."

He was leaving her here.

"Wait."

Astraea tried to follow, but she only got one step before her knees buckled. *Was this truly real?*

Despite the agony that ripped her apart, cell by cell . . . Despite the blurring sight of Auster retreating . . . she still struggled to conceive it.

But if she was dying . . .

Nyte.

His name became the only thing that mattered to her. The only person she wanted in the world right now. They hadn't had enough time together. She was desperate, greedy, for so much more time with him while her life was draining rapidly.

They were supposed to change the world together. Had already begun making progress toward their ambition for vampire equality. She was going to show the world who Nyte truly was, and he was going to be free from the chains to his father, as was Drystan.

Oh, Drystan . . . he'd become such a dear friend, and she couldn't abandon him now. She couldn't leave them both to their horrific father.

Astraea gripped the key tighter, and the pain from ripping it out of her body stole the last of her strength. She fell, losing more of her consciousness every second. This was worse than the first time she'd felt the key in her body. Auster had made sure to strike deep, pushing as much of the key's magick as he could tolerate into her body before it punished him. She couldn't even use the void one final time to reach Nyte.

There would be no saving her this time anyway, but still . . . she wanted to see his beautiful face just one last time as the darkness pulled at her. She wanted him to hold her in his warmth as her body turned cold. *So cold.*

Instead, she was all alone, lying here as one of many corpses lost in this senseless battle. Death knew no title.

She wanted Nyte to know that she called for him even if it was too late. She wanted to tell him that she would find him again. No matter what, she would find him always.

In those last fleeting seconds, she felt him so strongly she couldn't be sure if it was her desperation, or if he'd come for her. She couldn't see him. *Oh what she wouldn't give to glimpse his golden eyes one last time.* But she took the last notes of his scent with her as she had to leave him for now.

48

Astraea

After all the trials and terrors, being reunited and surrounded by my friends reminded me why every hardship was worth the suffering. As I'd been prescribed bed rest by Lilith, they'd decided to bring the tales of their own ventures to my rooms. This resulted in Davina lying at the foot of my bed, Lilith sitting by the side on the ground with some cushions, and Rose sitting on the armchair by the fire while Zath sat by her feet, his elbow propped on the side of her seat. Drystan was here too, eager to hear about all the dragons that were freed as he scrawled in his journal from his lean against the wall near Nadia, who perched unconventionally on the dresser.

As they told me about their quests to their designated temples, we sipped tea, and I couldn't stop catching the subtle flirtatious movements between Rose and Zath. He tucked closer into her, an arm draped over her thigh, while she played absentmindedly with the short lengths of his hair.

"Is there something else I need to catch up on?" I prompted.

Rose wore a sheepish smile while fighting the instinct to deny what was obvious.

"We might all die in a war against gods, so why deny any of our pleasures, no matter how many thorns they come with," Zath mused, squeezing her thigh.

"Still insufferable," she muttered.

"But you love me."

"Don't get too ahead of yourself."

Zath shifted, laying his head back on her thighs with a sigh. "I'm just waiting for you to catch up."

My heart swelled with so much love for the both of them. For everyone in this room.

Zath was right: war was on our doorstep and we couldn't waste a second on any negative feelings.

"I doubt they've all bonded," Drystan said, completely lost in his own thoughts about the dragons. "There could still be a chance of other vampires finding bonds with them. I'm hoping for it. It's about time the world started to see we are all one people. There are no chosen ones."

My wound from Auster emitted a sharp pain and I rubbed over it absent-mindedly.

"The blue dragon that chose Auster, Edasich . . ." I trailed off.

"She can bond again," Drystan assured. "It might take a while for her to heal and trust again, but it's been recorded in the past that dragons have had multiple riders, or never have had any at all, but those are typically the most vicious dragons. Rastaban is a prime example. They don't crave companionship, only their own power, and they will slay kin for it. They've even been known to lure humans into a false bond for their own gain before killing them."

"All those dragons and we never got one," Zath said to Rose with a sigh.

Drystan knew exactly how many of each color were roaming now, but the knowledge already left me with so much to keep track of.

"Lilith did," Davina said casually.

"You didn't mention that," Drystan accused. "Which one? What's her name?"

Lilith giggled. "*His* name is Altais. The yellow one we freed in Pyxtia."

Wonder filled my mind as I imagined a sky of colorful and colorless dragons dominating our skies.

"That's incredible," I said to her.

"Where is he now?" Drystan quizzed, scribbling more notes.

"Eating or sleeping, I presume. He likes the forest, though he's seemed a little distressed ever since he woke up. I'm still figuring out this bond between us so I can know what's wrong."

"The yellow dragons will be suffering the most without the sunlight," Drystan informed. Then he asked, "Any other particularly vicious or wary looking dragons I should know about?"

Everyone shook their heads.

I turned my attention to Davina, about to ask about the fae resistance, but I was distracted by her fingers lacing with Lilith's. My brows curved in a questioning look, and a blush fanned across Lilith's freckled cheeks.

"Is there something you two have to share as well?" I teased.

Davina smiled fondly at Lilith, brushing her thumb along her fair cheek, like it was habit. "I guess war has a way of making people say 'fuck the doubt and take the leap,'" she said boldly.

We all chuckled at that and I was bursting inside. After this last month of travel and failure and quests and trials, feeling a slow spiral into helplessness, all I needed was to come home. To see all was never lost so long as I had everyone in this room—my family.

Even after two days of mostly rest—since Nyte all but held me hostage in my rooms to heal—I still had to lean a hand on the council table everyone stood around.

Drystan, Nadia, Zathrian, Rosalind, Davina, and Lilith were here. The others had not returned. Filling up the rest of this meeting were generals of the Maiden's resistance from across the continent. Vampire leaders Laviana had sent while she was still working on convincing others, and a couple of celestial higher ups from Auster's court, who swore fealty to me.

We gathered to share knowledge to figure out how the Gods of Dusk and Dawn might plan to attack.

"Katerina—Dawn—has still been sighted in the Luna province, maintaining her guise," Drystan reported.

Zephyr was still being safeguarded with his children in Nadir's home. I didn't want to risk Dawn coming after them. I just couldn't wrap my head around her objective in being idle in the Luna province.

"And Dusk?" I asked.

"He's fully taken on the guise of Aquilo," Elliot informed. Nyte had tasked him with leading a scouting team for Dusk. "The armies of house Sera are gathering, and what's worse, Notus has joined him. I believe he knows he's allying with the God of Dusk and not Aquilo."

"He'll ally with anyone to overthrow me," I muttered sourly.

"But the gods haven't been sighted together?" Drystan said.

There were a few head shakes around the table.

I couldn't fit the puzzle in my head and it was tormenting me. The gods had created me together; now they'd come to land temporarily to destroy me, yet they didn't seem allied themselves for that mission.

Rubbing my temple, I couldn't concentrate with the ache building in my head.

"We'll resume tomorrow," Nyte announced, a subtle dismissal to everyone.

I was about to object, but they had already started leaving. Zath cast me a small smile. Did I really look that unfit? I believed I was maintaining an admirable façade, but inside, my body felt like a sinking weight, as if my very organs were succumbing to the slow, deliberate pull of collapse.

Turning, I leaned back against the table with a defeated sigh. Nyte was in front of me a heartbeat later. When everyone left and the doors groaned shut, Nyte stepped closer to me, saying nothing but leaning his head down and inhaling deeply as if savoring my scent.

"You're tired," he said after a pause.

"I'm fine."

I wasn't though, and we both knew it. Time was slipping away. It was a cruel illusion—how something that never altered its pace seemed to vanish more quickly when we needed it the most.

Nyte took my hand, and I didn't bother to ask where we were going. We wound through a few halls until we came to the broken throne room.

It was icy in here, with most of the back wall and part of the roof caved in. It wasn't snowing right now, but the previous days had flooded white crystal snowfall into the room.

"We'll need to get that fixed," he said.

I didn't think I would see that day.

"I quite like the view," I said anyway.

"Then we'll knock away the rest and fit glass in its place. Any other refurbishments?"

My smile didn't quite reach my face. Imagining this hall bright and warm while watching the seasons pass through the glass wall was a wonderful vision.

The purple throne still sat proudly and untarnished atop the dais. Nyte led me toward it, up the steps; then he coaxed me to sit. Leaving me there, he descended back down, and I didn't know what he was up to.

He simply stood there, staring, his face unreadable.

"You are absolutely exquisite," he said quietly, like the thought had accidentally leaked from his mind.

"Come here," I said, holding out my hand.

Nyte came back up, bracing both hands on the arms of the throne to lean in and kiss me. He seemed so . . . calm. At peace with whatever fate we were headed to. It inspired the same in me, and I kissed him with more need to make every second count.

He lowered, parting my knees with his hands to settle between them before they trailed up my sides, pulling me toward the edge of the throne.

"I want to take you right here," he muttered huskily. "On your throne. Worshipping you." My breath stuttered with his mouth tracing featherlight along my jaw and down my neck. "My Starlight." His fingers reached for the laces of my front bodice. "My mate." He slipped the material off my shoulders with slow attention. I shivered at the whistle of cold from the outside contrasting with his hot breath across my bare chest. "My queen."

"Anyone could walk in," I said breathlessly, but I lacked any true objection.

"They could."

"It's cold."

"I'm going to fix that."

Nyte's fingers grazed over my chest, and I looked down with him. The dark vein crawling toward my heart reached the top of my breast now. When I spent time studying it in the mirror this morning I realized why I found the grim mark of death beautiful. The line heading for my heart was like a barbed stem, and the site where the blade punctured bloomed like dark petals. As is if a stemmed black rose fell down my body.

Nyte's lips pressed to the top of the stem, and I didn't expect him to be so calm at the sight. He pulled back to hold me with eyes of nothing but adoration and promise before claiming my mouth in a surge of passion.

I moaned and let him undress me, tugging at my dress bodice until it came undone enough for him to close his mouth around one nipple while his hand massaged the other. My legs wrapped around him tighter, as I was desperate for friction between my legs. Nyte groaned at my neediness and began to bunch up my skirts, slipping his palm along my inner thigh.

Nyte pulled his head back suddenly when his fingertips brushed along the crease between my thigh and stomach. His golden irises were ablaze with desire.

"Were you expecting this, since you left your rooms this morning without underwear?" he asked thickly.

I smiled coyly. "Not here in particular, but I quite like your choice."

Nyte made a strangled sound, kissing me. "You are the life and death of me, Astraea Lightborne."

Without warning he pushed my skirts around my hips, slipped an arm around my back to pull me right to the edge of the throne; then his tongue lashed at my core, and I cried out unashamedly, driving my fingers tightly through his hair. My other hand gripped the arm of the chair for purchase.

He slipped a finger into me, teasing me slowly while his mouth devoured. Nyte undid the fastens of his pants, and I watched his arm flex, pumping himself while he pleasured me, and that surged me toward a climax.

"Yes, right there," I panted when two fingers hooked into me now, hitting a spot inside me that built pressure in my lower stomach, and his mouth sucked with the right amount of—

Whatever that twist of his fingers was threw me over the edge I was steadily climbing. My back bowed awkwardly with the pleasure seizing my body tight. He kept licking, stretching out my orgasm to near delirious heights.

I had barely had the chance to come around from it when he lifted me by the waist, guiding me to the side of the throne.

"Bend over for me," he ordered.

I did as he asked, planting my hands on the purple velvet cushion with my abdomen folded over the arm. Nyte lifted my skirts around my hips and parted me when I widened my stance.

"So damn beautiful," he murmured.

A blush fanned across my face as he had to be staring between my legs. His cock pressed against my entrance and he pushed inside slowly, savoring every inch until I was full. Nyte fucked me like that for a while, the hall echoing with a mix of our breathless pleasures. He called me sweet names and said scandalous things. Every word he spoke was like vibrations directed right to the sensitive bud at my apex, and I was so close again.

My hand reached back, stopping him from his next plunge into me.

"I want you to sit there this time," I said in a needy breath.

Straightening, I felt there was something so erotic about witnessing Nyte fully clothed on my throne, fisting his cock and watching me with eyes swimming in pure adoration and lust.

I climbed onto his lap and he lined himself up for me to sink back onto his cock. Our eyes kept locked on each other, twisted with pained pleasure, until I took all of him.

"I love you," he murmured, kissing my chest.

"Now, then, and always?" I breathed.

He smiled, as brightly as the moonlight that flooded through the open stone behind us.

"Yes, my love."

I kissed him deeply as I moved, taking my time to feel him and feel powerful. Where we were, on the throne that was ours, I was overwhelmed with joy.

We came together, hearts bruising against each other, passing breath between our mouths hovering shy of touching. Neither of us moved. Nyte showered my skin with tender kisses as the heat we created started to cool.

Right now I had never been more grateful to be mortal. I was created by gods, but they made me in this image. To love and feel and break. I would rather live this fleeting single existence surrounded by love than spend an eternity alone, within the stars, feeling nothing.

It was then I thought I understood . . . the true reason why I was created at all.

49

Astraea

The tall statues of Dusk and Dawn loomed proudly and dominatingly in their temple in Vesitire. The last time I'd stood here to reach out to them, it hadn't been pleasant. Now they had mortal bodies; I didn't know if they would hear me.

Their mortal depictions were a far cry from the faces of Katerina and Aquilo they'd stolen to walk this land. I wondered how they chose these faces to appear to the first of humanity long ago, giving them this image to carve into stone for mankind to kneel and pray before.

"I know why you made me," I said; my voice rebounded eerily through the hall that thickened with judgment. "It wasn't just to lead mankind and set an example for them. That's what you chose to appoint four High Celestials for, long before I came into creation."

I swallowed because my throat kept drying out.

"I was an experiment, wasn't I? A show for you to watch and discover what being mortal meant. If it could be worth giving up godhood for. You tested me time and time again, hoping I would prove that being a god is above being mortal. That I would want to come back to the stars rather than suffer on land below as part of mankind. Yet despite every trial . . . I proved you wrong."

It had been turning over in my mind. Why the gods were being careful.

"You want to stay," I said. "As gods you sit above us, untouched by time, by pain, by death . . . but what is eternity without ever being touched by love? Without feeling a moment as precious when time is endless? You don't hate mortals . . . you envy them. You envy me."

The final part of my theory pricked my skin. I scanned the cold, haunted hall as though Dusk or Dawn could lunge for me any moment.

"The vessels you chose can't sustain you much longer; they were always a temporary solution, and your time is running out. But I'm a fragment of each of you. Created, not born. A vessel strong enough to contain a god. You haven't come to end me, you've come to take my place . . . and only one of you can."

That's why they weren't working together. Why they had to bide their time and coax a High Celestial onto their side to drive the key blade through me.

Dusk had Notus, and Dawn . . .

My heart skipped and I ran from the temple. Now, knowing their objective, I feared more for Zephyr and his children. I'd thought Dawn wouldn't care about Zephyr; she and Dusk still had Notus to wield the key since they couldn't. But the gods were against each other in this race . . . and Dawn needed Zephyr.

I flew fast and desperately, needing to see Zephyr and his children were still safe.

Landing, I burst through the threshold of Nadir's home without a knock.

The scene I faced slammed my steps into a wall of dread.

The calmness contrasted with the company. Everyone was still here. Zephyr sat at the dining table with Raider opposite him. Nadir was in the small kitchen, chopping vegetables, a jarring activity considering the tension that tightened my skin. Because at the head of the table stood Dawn . . . holding a blade to Antila's neck.

"We've been waiting for you," Dawn said kindly. As though Astraea were merely late to dinner.

Antila's eyes were wide and her body trembled stiffly under the knife resting across her skin.

"Let her go," I said carefully, as though any one of my words could trigger the swipe of the blade.

"Give Zephyr your key," Dawn instructed.

Her calmness was chilling. She knew she had me.

Unstrapping the key from my hip, I set the baton it had been condensed to onto the table in front of Zephyr. His face was firmly set and unreadable. He didn't look at me as he picked it up.

"There, now let Antila go," I warned.

Dawn brushed a tender hand down the young celestial's blond hair, making her whimper. I gritted my teeth, but then Dawn obliged, and Antila rushed for me the moment the blade lifted, crashing into my side with a tight embrace.

"How did you find them?" I asked.

"I told her," Nadir chimed in, tossing a piece of cucumber into their mouth.

Rage boiled in me. Had their help always been a deception? To what end? I caught the glimmer of the dark iridescent blade they used . . . it was familiar . . .

"You supplied Auster with the material that greatly harms fae," I accused.

Nadir held up his blade, admiring it. "I have an interest in the dark properties of magick, you could say. This particular material has many names; it is not grown on these lands. I was able to recreate its effects from the odd shard I traded from a merchant years ago. Yes, I may have told Auster Nova about it when he came to me."

"Why?" I seethed, but through my anger I was hurt over the betrayal because I'd come to consider Nadir a good friend and ally.

"The reason that corrupts most, I suppose. Money and power."

It didn't make sense, but I had a bigger threat to deal with right now.

"Go to your brother," I told Antila gently, peeling her arms from around me.

"This exchange will be quick, though I can't promise that it will be painless," Dawn said, coming around the table toward me. "We will bleed our palms and join them. Then Zephyr will strike the key through you, and the transfer will happen. I will have your power, your body, and your life. I wonder how long it will take for Rainyte to notice. The truth? I hope he never does. As much as he has been a meddling force, I can't deny his love and devotion to you is enviable."

Dawn's delusion, to have Nyte worship her in my body, sickened me.

Nadir approached me, wearing a gloating smile as they held a knife out to me. Not the one they were chopping vegetables with, at least. Their arrogant demeanor was a mockery of the dire situation.

Zephyr stood, coming close to where Dawn and I faced off. He barely yielded any emotion. I wanted to tell him I didn't blame him; he had to protect his children, even if it was too late for Katerina.

"Father, you can't," Antila cried. She was held by her brother.

Zephyr's grip tightened on the key, which changed to its staff form in a pulse of light and energy.

"Let them leave," I pleaded.

Dawn regarded the two children with boredom.

"I'll take care of them," Nadir said with an underlying hint that they could harm Antila or Raider if I tried anything.

They led the children upstairs, though I wished they had been taken out of the home.

"Your compliance is refreshing after all your years of insolence," Dawn remarked.

"Your opinion means nothing to me. It never has."

Dawn's eyes flared.

"When I'm the star-maiden I will shape the world exactly the way you should have shaped it."

"What I don't understand . . . is why you chose guardians of all species to raise me when your perfect societal order always favored the celestials."

"Favored? No. The hierarchy was decided by strength and purpose, nothing more."

"You speak with no soul," I said. "You cannot understand righteousness.

Fairness. Equality. You are a god that feeds on greed and power, and that will never change."

Dawn gripped my hand, yanking me toward her. Our stares pierced each other with loathing. My jaw clenched at the sharp sting as she sliced my palm.

"You are nothing but a rebellious tyrant," Dawn said.

"I am everything but a compliant slave to your ideals."

I took Dawn's hand, and she let me slice her palm, unknowing the blade Nadir gave me was made of obsidian; a material incapacitating to the celestials.

Dawn screeched, yanking her hand back and stumbling a step. She recovered fast, and her eyes turned absolutely feral on me.

I shifted my gaze to Zephyr as he threw the key. We were so fast, but Dawn was faster. She avoided my thrust forward with the key, launching back. My adrenaline pounded through my body as I threw out a sharp blast of light from my palm instead. To my relief, it hit her with full force. Dawn was thrown through the air, her body crashing through the back wall of Nadir's home and out into the snowy darkness.

I launched out after her just as a familiar roar shook the sky. I didn't break my focus on Dawn as Eltanin pierced through the void, nor did I let her leave my sight when footfalls stomped over the snow.

After telling Nyte and the others what I suspected about the god's motives with me, we devised a plan to lure out Dawn. Nadir's summons had been too easy for her to accept, believing his allegiance was to the High Celestials when it was true that he'd been the one to craft and supply Auster with the lethal fae material.

Dawn had risen from the snow she'd tumbled through; her ferocious glare targeted me.

Tonight, I would kill a god.

"Did you really believe I have been powerless all this time?" Dawn called.

The cruelty of her smile braced me to fight, but her attention shifted skyward, intending to strike Eltanin with a light that built from her palm as though she held the sun. Starry darkness formed a shield, but, to my horror, the sun shattered clean through it, slamming into Eltanin, who roared in pain.

That was a distraction . . . for me.

Next thing I knew, a searing pain exploded against my chest and I was flying back. The key flew out of my grip, and before I fell, a dome of light encased me.

Dawn trapped us in a globe of piercing sunlight. My eyes stung and watered, hardly able to open fully because of the lashing surge of brightness after being in the night for so long. The dome roared and swirled as though we stood in a hollow half sun, alive and vivid.

"It's over," I said, pushing myself up.

Her strike had melted my leathers and burnt my flesh.

"You thought yourself cunning, but you forget you are a fragment of *me*," Dawn said.

A loud *boom* slammed against the dome encasing us. The darkness that rippled over the sun could not pierce it despite all of Nyte's efforts.

"You can't kill me without Zephyr and the key," I said.

Dawn gave her attention back to me.

"You're right. You have me surrounded." She approached with the predatory intent of a snake. I backed away until I cried out, stumbling forward when I touched the edge of the dome that singed my arm through the leather.

Dawn caught me by my arms, and I stared fearfully into her cruel eyes.

"You are nothing but stardust," she said. "If I can't have you, no one can."

"No." That denial left me in a breath of horror as a familiar tingling began at my fingertips. My eyes snapped down, unable to fight or save my skin, which began to break off in glittering particles.

I scrunched my eyes shut. *It's not real. It's not real.*

When I opened them again, I sobbed, seeing that my hands were gone. Dawn released me, pacing a few strides backward as she watched me disintegrate and the dust float skyward.

"Make it stop," I cried.

"I'll see you in the sky."

A shattering sound crashed at my left and I winced. When I saw the purple flaring tip of the key piecing through the dome, I gasped. Someone retracted it then swiftly thrust into the same impact point which shattered an opening.

To my shock and horror . . . Zephyr lunged through it.

He charged with a mighty roar, holding the key high like a battle spear.

I screamed. I begged him to stop, but he couldn't hear me, lost in his own wrath and need for vengeance.

Dawn conjured a sphere of molten light, but it was smothered by darkness. My head snapped to where Nyte stood in the dome's opening, aiding Zephyr's advance.

But Nyte knew Zephyr couldn't kill her even with the key. It had to be me.

Then time . . . slowed.

Zephyr's raging advance now seemed like he was floating. Advancing only fractions. Dawn's shock and anger started trying to form a defense against his charging wrath but he would win. He would reach her before she could.

I shifted my sight to the opening in the dome. Nyte was captured in slowed time too. Because Kairos was next to him, his hands poised elegantly with his face contorted in concentration.

"I can't hold this for longer than thirty seconds tops," he rasped.

Kairos was granting me this chance to save my friend, but horror flooded over me. Scrambling to my feet, I examined my missing hands. With Dawn's focus stolen, my flesh stopped turning to stardust, beginning to return. But not fast enough.

"You have to hold it longer!" I begged.

Sweat beaded Kairos's forehead. "I'm sorry," he said, his voice strained as though he were lifting a boulder, about to cave under its weight.

I ran. As fast as I could I ran for Zephyr who was about to reach Dawn. I willed my hand to return to flesh, feeling my palms now and that was enough. I just had to reach him before . . .

"I'm so sorry," Kairos said. "I tried."

A scream tore from me as time resumed its natural pace.

Zephyr reached his target before I could reach him.

"How dare you steal her face!" Zephyr cried out, plunging the key through Dawn's chest.

My run staggered to a stop when a flare of blinding light erupted. Forcing my eyes to bear the sting of the bright, I wept at the sight before me, struck deeply by the intensity of Zephyr's pain as he gripped the key, forced to stare into his wife's eyes with an imposter behind them.

There was no greater tragedy to behold.

In his final seconds, Zephyr's terrified eyes met mine. "Protect my children, Astraea."

The key delivered its consequence before I could promise him I would. Having been used by an outsider, it would demand Zephyr's life . . . he knew this.

The moment I could flex my fingers, my grief had me racing toward Dawn and Zephyr once more.

My friend made no sound as his body was engulfed in light, and when it faded . . . he was gone.

The sound that tore from me was anguish pulled from the heavens.

Lightsdeath surged through me as I gripped the key as Dawn fell to her knees, locking her wide eyes with mine.

"You cannot have my life!" I screamed. "You cannot have my friends. You cannot have my world . . . *Eos.*"

I twisted the key as I spoke her name, and Dawn's head was thrown back. As though sunlight grew a sphere inside her, rays pierced through her mortal flesh until she . . . *erupted.*

Nyte reached me right in time to use Eltanin's magick and cast a shield of darkness around us as we crouched and huddled.

The land roared, splitting deeply and vastly around us. Chasms opened, threatening to swallow all life upon its surface because of the imbalance it now suffered without the Goddess of Dawn.

I couldn't scramble to my feet fast enough before I was pulled down by a fresh scar that shot like lightning across the land.

Nyte's hand wrapped my forearm before I could plummet down into the deep tear, and he pulled me up swiftly. I curled into him, feeling his heart beat as violently as mine under my ear.

I couldn't move.

More thunderous cracks echoed distantly, as if the world was tearing itself apart in retribution for what I'd done.

I cupped my hands over my ears and my eyes slammed shut. But in the darkness of my own mind all I could see on repeat was Zephyr's final charge, his brave sacrifice, his absolute devastation.

He didn't deserve that end. Katerina didn't deserve to be a puppet for Dawn.

"I don't want to fight anymore," I croaked.

I was so tired. So terribly tired of the losses stacking in my chest.

"I know, love," Nyte said, his voice utterly heartbroken.

He held me tight, stroking my hair as the world tore itself apart.

"What have I done?" I whispered.

Had it all been a trick? A lie? Had death given me this power to kill Dusk and Dawn knowing it would destroy this world?

I might not have had much time left because of my wound, but I was fighting until my last breath to leave this world brighter for my friends I loved dearly. Now I wasn't sure if I was only making it worse.

Then I became terror-stricken, too aware that these could be our final days, perhaps even our final hours.

"What if we don't find each other again?" I said, pulling back to scan his face when I didn't know how many chances I had left to just *look* at him. "What if we don't recognize each other?"

"Shh." He soothed the sharpness of my near frantic panic. "Do you trust me?"

"More than anything," I said.

"Then fight with me one last time. I promise you we'll reign eternally if we just win one more time."

He was so sure and confident that it was easy to believe him. So I nodded and let Nyte raise us from the tremoring ground.

A loud crack sounded near, jolting me with alarm. We both whirled to find Nadir's home was the cause. It was like one of the cracks in the land surged under the home then shot skyward, splitting through the tall structure.

"No!" I yelled, lunging forward with my magick priming to flood out and hold the wood together myself as Zephyr's children were still inside.

"Astraea!" Antila's cry of my name cooled the heat flooding through my veins.

Even though the sight of her running toward me was a relief, all of us were within the radius of the building's collapse.

"We have to move," Nyte urged.

I ran toward Antila. "You get Raider!" I yelled to Nyte.

I tried not to look at the massive building threatening to crush us but its groans of warning had me pushing my legs through the snow. Then from behind her, Antila was scooped off her feet by a large arm around her middle, and I was both relieved that Zath's long strides closed the distance faster and terrified that his life hung in the balance now too. As soon as I reached them I would pull us all through the void.

But I wouldn't reach them in time.

The building rattled and cracked and split, tumbling down rapidly. My eyes flew wide and a scream bubbled inside me as a huge piece of the structure plummeted toward Zath and Antila.

Then once again, time was held in the mercy of Kairos.

I reached Zath and Antila, touching them at the same time I touched the void, and pulled us all through it. I didn't risk going far as I hadn't travelled the void with two people before. We all landed in tumbling heaps as though spat out.

Scrambling to my feet, I pulled Antila into me as we both winced, curling into each other as Nadir's home came crashing down in real time.

"Nyte!" I yelled as my first instinct to be sure he cleared the danger with Raider.

I saw him before he replied as he marched through the trees toward us. He scanned me head to toe and his expression relaxed to find me unharmed.

"You heroic fool." Rose's grumble was a little breathless as she caught up to us in a jog. She aimed her concern at Zath.

Zath's grin was roguish. "You're impressed though, right?"

"I'm impressed you're still alive when you're constantly chasing death."

My sight drifted and I found Nadir a few paces away, staring at their collapsed and burning home, one hand in their pocket while the other lifted a pipe to their mouth. I wandered over to them.

"I'm sorry about your home," I said.

Nadir blew out smoke. They were so nonchalant despite all they'd lost.

"I've been building this home taller each year. It was like a game to me, wondering how far I could test its stability before it would collapse on me."

I couldn't understand such a *game*. It seemed like a waste to me.

"Besides," Nadir said, slipping me a sidelong glance. "I'm rather hoping for a place within the royal court once you take back your throne. Did you think I suffered the company of your whining and jeering companions all that time with no selfish goal in mind?" They winked and me and I smirked.

"You also aided and abetted my enemies," I pointed out. "Don't expect too high a reward for your help too soon."

I was only partially jesting. Nadir had been invaluable help to all of us in our most desperate time.

"Auster was a powerful man. He threatened all my establishments if I didn't give him what he wanted. He'd heard about my tinkering with the fae incapacitating material and he was relentless in his pursuit of it, knowing it would harm Rainyte greater than any other weapon."

I understood, yet I still resented Nadir's role in creating the material.

A strangled sound from the debris caught my attention, and when a piece of wood lifted, I gasped, racing through the snow toward it.

Nyte was right behind me, helping to lift the thick piece of wood off Kairos, and Zath helped me pull him out of the wreckage. He was bleeding across his temple, and his face was twisted in pain.

"Can you stand?" I asked, only to assess if he had broken bones.

Kairos shifted, propping his weight onto one elbow. He caught his breath. "I think so."

I let go of a breath of relief. "Thank you. Your gift is invaluable and quite incredible."

His eyes turned pained. "Not that incredible. I'm sorry I couldn't hold time long enough to save your friend."

I shook my head. "You gave him a moment to say goodbye." To ask me to look out for his children which I vowed to with the rest of my life.

I said, "You're probably wishing you stayed in Volanis."

Kairos chuckled but it turned to a wince of pain. Zath helped him stand.

"Are you kidding? This is the most action and intrigue I've experienced in my life. I'm just wondering what's next."

That brought back the challenge and obstacle still in the way of reclaiming the throne of Vesitire and vanquishing the gods. I glanced at Nyte who aligned determination with me, though not without notes of fear and uncertainty.

"Next . . . we have one more god to kill."

50

Nyte

I was tricking Astraea's pain receptors, but still she looked away, fighting her nausea with an occasional gag as I carefully removed pieces of leather from her burnt chest and arm. We were back in the castle of Vesitire, but Dusk had already moved in to attack.

"All done with the worst part," I said, plucking the last charred black piece. Her body relaxed a little; she was so damned brave.

I cleaned her skin gently before applying a healing and numbing salve; then I dressed the wounds with bandages. Despite my protests, Astraea was adamant to change into new leathers and join the fighting that had already broken out outside. The enemy forces weren't within the walls, and we hoped to keep it that way.

"Where are the others?" she asked, pulling on a new shirt.

"Zath and Rose are within the inner wall legion; we're hoping they won't need to fight. The vampire and fae armies are fighting outside the walls, led by Laviana, Davina, and Elliot. Lilith is taking charge of the healing tents on the field. Drystan is leading a charge with those on dragonback; Nadia is with him."

"Dusk only wants me. I'm going to seek him out and end this."

I caught her elbow before she could charge out.

"We should stick to the strategy. Dusk isn't being as arrogant as Dawn; he's surrounded himself with allies and armies that will overwhelm you before you can reach him."

"Not if I'm smart. I can lure him away."

"It's not worth the risk—"

Screams breaking from outside in the city grabbed our attention. We didn't exchange another word before we ran onto the balcony.

People were scrambling through the streets as if they could outrun the terrifying wave that grew higher than the lower city wall.

"Fedora," I growled. "Let me handle her."

I was about to summon Eltanin, but Astraea grabbed my hand.

"This may be our final night. We're not separating."

Our final night. Though I knew our time was draining away, spoken aloud it still slammed me with such ache and denial.

I nodded. We would fight until the very last second together.

Hoisting myself onto the railing, I fell as Eltanin swooped in to catch me. Astraea flew by our side with her wings.

The wave was more frightening up close. Its crest frothed with wild, white foam, stretching around the entire west side, stealing the moonlight in its shadow over the city it loomed over to drown. Panicked crowds scrambled in vain, their silhouettes tiny and fragile against the monstrous swell. The salty tang of seawater filled the air, mixing with the acrid scent of fear and chaos.

When the magick of the trident was released, it would cause immense death and devastation.

Eltanin swooped around the colossal wave, and I searched for the vengeful nymph that had to be close by to be controlling it.

The trident's blue glow gave her away, though she wasn't trying to hide. Fedora stood by the city gates. *Within* the walls. Dread started to creep through me as Fedora met my eyes too . . . and she *smiled.*

Astraea dropped down like a shooting star, the key flaring as bright as her skin. My chest pounded as the glow of the trident faded out at the same time Astraea burst into light. The key in her grasp pulsed with a radiant, starlight energy, its intricate engravings glowing as if alive. In an instant, a shimmering shield erupted from the key, expanding outward in a perfect dome of luminous power.

The shield barely solidified before the enormous wave crashed down with a deafening roar, its immense force hammering against the barrier. The impact was monumental—water cascading like a liquid avalanche, its fury spilling over the edges of Astraea's shield. She couldn't prevent the catastrophe fully, but she'd saved many lives and homes with her heroism.

For a heartbeat, it seemed the barrier might fail too soon; the radiant energy flickered under the relentless onslaught. But she stood firm, her feet planted against the trembling ground, the light surrounding her blazing brighter with each surge of the ocean's wrath. The key in her hand burned hot, resonating with an otherworldly hum, as though it drew strength from some ancient and infinite source.

Beyond the shield, the city was a chaos of water and shadow, streets transformed into rivers and buildings groaning against the weight of the flood. But within the dome of light, there was a haven—a fragile, defiant sanctuary against the overwhelming tide.

Her eyes gleamed with determination, and with a whispered command, the shield expanded farther, pushing back the water in a brilliant wave of its own.

Using the void, I was by Astraea's side in my next breath, circling an arm around her as her body trembled and her stance strained.

"You can let go now. You did it," I said gently.

Astraea was burning with Lightsdeath. Her skin glowed with her eyes to harness the power of a god. She was absolutely magnificent. She had learned control quicker than I ever could with Nightsdeath. I never wanted to. But Astraea did . . . she was so brave and brilliant to master her discipline to better the world rather than cave to the destruction it could grant her.

The shield came down as though the wave was reversed, returning the water that remained trapped against her light back into the grand river around the city.

When she let go of her magick, Astraea slumped into me as her tattoos faded out.

"Did you find Fedora?" she asked breathily.

"She used the wave as a distraction. I think she intends to break the city wall and clear a path for enemies outside."

The dormant city was upended into chaos in the span of minutes.

Eltanin roared, hurtling his breath of shadowy starlight through the enemy lines outside the wall, robbing them of all senses before decaying their bodies from the inside out.

More dragon cries cut the night, and I scanned the skies to find both awe and carnage cutting through the clouds. There were too many dragons for me to track. Red and blue and yellow and all of varying sizes. Though not all the dragons were fighting on our side, creating balls of sun and charges of lightning with their breath.

I spied Drystan on Athebyne with Nadia riding behind him, braced precariously, but it was like they'd done this many times before. She aimed her bow and arrow, shooting nightcrawlers and celestials wearing Aquilo's coat of arms out of the sky. I wondered if they even knew it wasn't really their High Celestial they fought for and would lose many lives for.

I couldn't afford to think of that. I wouldn't think of anything but winning against whoever stood in our way, and that was going to take a lot of blood.

Eltanin's next roar was so powerful it shook me to my very bones. I realized what he was doing when two dragons clawing at each other broke apart before he charged between them. He was using his celestial heritage to assert his command over them. It wasn't enough to stop all of them, and some resumed their vicious battling after a pause, defying the order, but it helped slow the carnage.

Athebyne soared down to land outside the city walls, and I took Astraea's hand, pulling her through the void.

Drystan was already dismounting when the darkness cleared.

"We have unexpected friends, thanks to you two, in case you didn't take notice of the boats on the river," he said.

I glanced sideways and saw them then, a half dozen ships surrounding the river that ran around the perimeter of the three-leveled mighty city of Vesitire. One, the *Silver Sparrow*, confirmed it was Balthezar who had rallied the small armada and come to my call I'd sent weeks ago. I didn't really think he would come.

Water surged up from within the wall as Fedora continued her rampant terror. She had always been a creature with no true alliance, and I'd put off finding the trident as long as possible, knowing it shouldn't reach her hands. Still, I felt responsible for what she was doing, and the vengeance to stop her was mine.

"We're going to aid the fae and lead the transitioned vampires; they're being pushed back too strongly by the celestials," Drystan informed.

I nodded and he began to turn.

"Drystan," I called to stop him.

Every muscle in my body locked against it, but every fiber of my soul pushed past the strange discomfort to cross the few steps and pull my brother into an embrace.

"Be careful," I said, then let him go.

His stun was written all over his expression, but he cleared his throat to save from any awkwardness.

"Likewise," he muttered.

Astraea and I headed back into the city.

On the lower level, we tracked the vicious water attacking through the streets. Fedora commanded water that had slipped over Astraea's shield, and this part of the city was a lethal playground for her. She summoned water to cut down innocents that fled from her for nothing more than her appetite to feel powerful.

I tried her mind first, breaching her thoughts enough to intercept her next current, which stopped cutting through the air and rained down harmlessly instead.

The nymph whirled to me with blazing rage in her onyx eyes and pushed me out of her mind effortlessly. Then she smiled, her head tilted down, making her look hauntingly maniacal.

"Have you come to die, my night?" she said in her melodic voice.

"The only thing I am to you is your death."

Her smile was wiped. "After all that time we spent together? I thought there was something of a bond between you and I."

"Yet you betrayed me the moment you had the chance."

"You forget yourself. Forget that I helped your precious star and then you forgot about me the moment you were free."

That part was true. Fedora had become more attached to me than I had realized, and now I was just another who'd abandoned her.

"It's not too late to join us," I said.

It was a lie, but I didn't care. After what she'd done to Astraea, I had no mercy left. She'd harmed her once before in the cave pool under the library where I was captive, and I was willing to forgive that; now her actions against Astraea had become so extreme that she was beyond redemption.

"It's too late for *you*," she said; then she struck.

Her power with the trident was unparalleled. I was beginning to believe it held just as much potential as Astraea's key.

Water slashed in a horizontal wave toward me, fast enough to cut flesh. Eltanin was close enough for me to feel the darkness of his breath and summon it to my own fingertips. As I narrowly ducked to avoid her first attack, my shadow formed a shield against her second attempt at me, which came in the form of a water spear.

We entered a dance of water and darkness, colliding and blocking each other. I had the patience to wear her out, going on the defensive.

Astraea was nearby; I could still feel her.

Fedora cried in frustration, and I knew her desperation to win against me would turn more vicious. A whirlpool formed around her, taking her high above the buildings within its eye, and she watched me from above like a dark spirit of the sea. She didn't throw out simple attacks anymore, and when a new shadow grew high over the wall behind me, I thought we'd face another colossal wave to stop. Instead, what I saw stopped time for a second.

A water dragon.

Drystan hadn't mentioned this type, which had to have been somehow freed from the temple that lay in the depths of the sea between the mountains. My imagination couldn't have conjured this image that was not made of flesh, scales, or feathers like the others. Instead, it was like its body was made of animated glass, shimmering brilliantly, like the moonlight refracted through a prism.

Its horns were jagged and crystalline, sharp spears of ice that gleamed with cold brilliance. Talons, similarly forged of frost and edged like knives, scraped against the ground, leaving trails of frozen land in every step. It bore no wings yet its body exuded a graceful, otherworldly elegance. Its roar was more of a rattling cry, and were it not so large and threatening, it would have been worthy of kneeling in awe for.

But Fedora had summoned it, and the dragon had crawled from the depths of the ocean at the call of her wrath.

As if it were weightless, the water dragon climbed the wall without breaking it. Carelessly, its huge feet stomped over the city and its long tail and body lashed around the streets, not crushing like something solid, but drowning anything in its path. Buildings were washed away; people were fighting for air, scrambling to flee.

As I watched it head toward Fedora, the trident was glowing. So were the dragon's icy eyes, as though hypnotized to obey the power.

Fedora wasn't bonded to it; she was only controlling it with the trident.

Fedora was too high for me to reach. My attacks with shadow would be negligible from here. I searched for Astraea, and my chest fucking tightened when I couldn't immediately see her. Feeling for her, I raced through the streets to find her.

The enemy had broken within our walls because of Fedora's quick slashes at all our meticulous defenses. My rage grew with every vampire and celestial I had to slay in my path to reach Astraea. My blade tore through them like paper and water as I became an unfeeling reaper of steel and shadow.

The next set of celestials, five of them, approached me with their swords drawn, herding me as though they stood a chance against me in their little group. I was about to enjoy proving them wrong when their stances slackened and their gazes flicked up behind me one by one. Their harsh expressions of determination blanked to stunned fear.

When I saw what made them lose focus on the death I was about to deliver, I understood how I'd become an insignificant threat compared to the stunning display behind me. I heard them running off, but I couldn't look away from the giant wolf made of pure glimmering starlight.

I'd seen it before, though in far smaller form. Astraea's light wolf. I'd been in complete awe the first time, but now I couldn't explain the magnificent sight. Astraea was glowing too, standing upon a rooftop as a beacon of heavenly power. Her skin, her hair, her eyes all shimmered like she was the moon given breath.

With a tilt of the trident, by Fedora's command, the water dragon lunged for the wolf.

Astraea's hands moved as she focused on this powerful conjuring of her magick as she used Lightsdeath to its full, unrestrained power.

I had to help her. While Astraea battled the water dragon, I had to sever the control Fedora had over it before they wrecked the city entirely. Their fight shook the ground, and they quickly tore through the walls of all three city levels.

Racing toward Fedora's whirlpool, I had to act fast. Astraea didn't have her key in hand, and I reached through the void. As I was part of Astraea now with our bond, it answered me.

In my grip, I didn't hesitate to throw myself into the lethal whirlpool that caught me, surging me high toward Fedora. Plunging to the surface I was airborne only for a second, swiping the key, which was infused with light and dark under my influence, erupting like a beautiful diffusion of the night sky.

Fedora's scream barely emitted before the key cut clean through her neck. Her last wide-eyed look of shock froze permanently on her face before her head toppled from her shoulders.

The trident slipped from her hand, and the magick stopped channeling through the water. I was falling in an instant, then was caught just as fast.

Light shone around me, beneath me. I was on the giant wolf's snout as it moved gently toward a building, and I eagerly jumped off onto more solid ground.

Astraea watched me from across the rooftop. No, it was *Lightsdeath* who considered me, her expression emotionless. I stiffened, bracing in case she saw me as the enemy right now. A darkness to eradicate under the influence of Lightsdeath.

She didn't advance. Instead, Astraea's dark wings came out. We had promised not to separate, but Astraea's calm wrath as Lightsdeath only knew her own objective.

To seek out Dusk.

"Wait—!" She wouldn't listen to me. Astraea splayed her magnificent wings and shot to the sky.

I was about to call for Eltanin, but the water dragon captured my attention.

It had stopped attacking, but out of the water it was still causing suffering by flooding the city. I jumped across several buildings, racing down until I reached the ground again. Picking up the trident, I was about to attempt to command it back into the river, but the dragon was so still, its attention fixed on something. Not something, someone.

Balthezar stood in the middle of the street as if he challenged the water dragon. My body tensed.

Until it began to bow its head and a familiar sensation rippled over me.

A dragon bond was being forged.

Yet it was not Balthezar who reached to claim it. It was a hand much smaller . . .

His son, Brody.

There were few times in my life I found myself this taken, but witnessing the bond forging between the young boy and the last water dragon was a memory worth storing safely. The dragon rattled gently now, and it turned, heading back to the ocean where it belonged.

I had to tear myself away from the sight, following a tug that had me racing through the streets toward the castle.

Astraea was calling for me. I felt it through our bond. Heard it in my soul.

I stepped through the void to answer.

51

Astraea

I was a star given breath and the night given flesh. A triumphant embodiment of the lunar sky.

My city was crying, my city was in pain, and I crossed the courtyard toward the black castle like a starlight storm to eradicate the poison before it spread any further.

I was Lightsdeath, but I was also in full control of the deadly power coursing through me.

Defeating the God of Dusk was my final task, and then I would let my fate be sealed. Nyte's blood was so close to my heart now. If I wasn't harnessing so much power, the agony would be ripping me apart from the inside as though my heart was clawing at my flesh to escape it.

The god stood proudly across the courtyard. Expecting me. I didn't let that waver my focus.

It wasn't a surprise to see Notus standing with him.

"You are aware that is not Aquilo you ally with," I said to him.

Dusk wore the High Celestial's face, giving him full control of Aquilo Sera's province and armies. Over a dozen archers held aim with crimson-tipped arrows at me. I didn't balk at them in the slightest.

"You need to be stopped once and for all," Notus seethed.

I smiled wickedly.

"I know what fate is now," I said across the eerie silence before the break of battle. "You created me to govern this world to your order, but the irony of life is that every evil inevitably brings about their own downfall. I am yours. I never abandoned my duty or swayed from my path. It was always supposed to lead me here. You created a means to stop your tyranny."

"You are but a child to my existence, Astraea Lightborne. I have lived since the dawn of time, my dear. I am fate."

"You are a god with too much greed. The Dusk that cannot exist without the Dawn, and she is dead."

"So I have felt."

His tone was so stripped of emotion, resembling Dawn in many ways as a god incapable of human feelings.

"You're jealous of what I am. Mortal."

"All your power, even that from Death himself, will be mine. You don't have long; I can feel the countdown of your fragile time. It would be a waste for all you are to simply die. This is a gift, Astraea; your legacy will live on when I take over your form."

"As I told Dawn before I killed her, you cannot have my life."

I needed the true name of Dusk to kill him, and there was only one person who stood a chance of breaching his mind just enough to hear it.

The smile across Dusk's face chilled me. Braced me.

"These arrows were never for you," he said gleefully. "They are for him."

Every aim shifted a few fractions and the archers fired faster than I could take a breath.

The grunt of pain behind me silenced my world.

Turning around stopped time.

My eyes tracked the arrow tips first. Eight of them pierced him. Three in his abdomen, two in his left shoulder, two in the right. And one . . . narrowly missing his heart.

Nyte's wide eyes lifted from the arrows to me and I ran to him.

"You're okay," I said, desperate words that made no sense. They were cruel cold lies, yet more words of delusional reassurance spilled from me as my hands held his face.

"Don't worry about me," he rasped. His gaze lifted and rage sparked through his agony.

Nyte pushed me, somehow twisting around me before more arrows stuck him. I caught him as he fell back this time. Not as many reached him from the second fired round, but another two pierced the right side of his chest and I screamed.

I erupted.

It wasn't just my terror and agony that tore from my throat. It expelled from me in unending waves of power.

Silver flames drowned the world.

They did not burn, not yet, but through the flickering fire glittering like starlight, fear masked the faces of everyone those flames touched.

Silver flame licked up every wall and torched every path. A sphere of energy grew overhead, trapping the world under my rain of furious starlight.

If Nyte died here, this world would feel my grief.

"Don't burn this realm for me, Starlight," Nyte whispered.

"I'm certain you would do worse, so you don't get to scold me for it," I croaked.

His smile was pained as he reached for an arrow and didn't hesitate to pull it free.

"I'm completely villainous, but that's one part of me you're not allowed to become."

"They have my blood on them," I said in panic, wincing as I gripped one in his shoulder and ripped it free when there was no time to be gentle.

"I know. I can feel it."

"I'm—"

"Don't say you're sorry. Make that bastard scream his apologies at your mercy."

"I don't have his name."

Nyte panted. He blinked a few times, gathering strength.

"I'll find it," he promised. "We're ending this together."

I wanted to sob and find another way, but Dusk was storming through my fires toward us. I saw nothing but blind rage as Nyte steadied himself on his knees and I rose, gripping the key.

I gave myself over to Lightsdeath.

The unparalleled power of it. The rage and smoke and flame of it. I spun with the key as if it were a dance. Dusk turned into the wind around me, able to disappear and reappear, trying to disorient me with the goal of disarming me of the only weapon that could kill him.

And the weapon he needed to *become* me.

I was spellbound to track only him, losing sight and sense of anything else. I whirled again, but he'd managed to grip the key this time as I swiped vertically and I stared face to face with the jarring mask of Aquilo.

"Give up," he snarled.

"Never."

He was strong. We struggled until both our hands wrapped the key staff and he managed to flip me with it. My back slammed to the stone. Agony shot up my spine, seizing my body tightly for dire seconds, which slackened my grip on the key. He yanked it from me and I panted hard.

Dusk handed off the key to Notus, who stepped through the silver flames to us.

My eyes widened when he lunged for me with the key staff. I rolled and it slammed to the ground where my chest had been with a vibrating surge of power.

I scrambled to my feet, facing off with the High Celestial.

"Using the key will kill you," I warned, though he knew that.

"You killed my brothers," Notus seethed. It sounded as if he was justifying his allegiance to Dusk as much to himself as to me.

"I killed one them, but that was only fair; he killed me first. Zephyr died nobly to stop the gods you aid now, and you stand beside the one who killed Aquilo to take his place. You are a traitor to them."

Notus's anger pulsed tangibly, but he was at war with himself more than me. His loathing for me won against his logic. He lunged for me again, and I drifted easily around his attacks.

He wouldn't go back on his chosen side now, and I was running out of time.

I didn't need the key to kill Notus; he was trapped in my magick already. All it took was a lift of my hand, a mere thought, and the silver flames he stood in began to burn. Not hot but a slow icy blaze that devoured him. Notus screamed and I caught the key as it fell, not staying to watch as silver engulfed his body and spilled down his mouth to kill his screams. I ran for Dusk, shifting the key to a blade, raising it for a killing blow.

His hand thrust out, fingers jabbing precisely in the wound on my abdomen Auster had dealt me.

First, agony seized me, then my pain surged beyond my limits and I thought I was falling. Endlessly falling. My vision blurred, seeing flickers of the silver flames and a set of boots heading toward me.

It can't end like this.

A battle cry tore through the silence of my suffering.

Nyte. He was still alive. We were still alive, and it couldn't end *like this.*

My will to live for him dragged me to the surface of my awareness. The key was right by my head, and I rolled onto my stomach, slapping my hand over it and rising despite death's grip squeezing my heart.

Nyte was on his knees, his head bowed at Dusk's feet.

He was so still . . . so deathly still.

Then a poem weaved into my mind, a song above the battle that raged around us.

At dusk, the amber heavens sway . . .

Through the flames, a cry of rage and passion cut through. My dying breaths shuddered as I watched Zathrian lunge out of the arms of silver, his blade aloft to come down on Dusk.

The stars emerge, a bright ballet . . .

I staggered forward as Rose emerged too, attacking Dusk from two angles, but they were no match for him. Surges of twilight power struck my friends, and I screamed with heavenly anguish, charging forward as my friends risked their lives distracting Dusk.

Through twilight's veil, where shadows play . . .

The night is crowned with . . .

"Astraeaus!" I yelled his true name with the full force of my power surging in my grasp.

He whirled to me, eyes blazing and wild.

My friends had granted me the opening to race forward with Dusk distracted.

The key shifted to a dagger . . . and I plunged it into his heart.

His mouth opened wide, but no sound came from him. No movement. Dusk became particles of stardust singing in the silver flames that began to die out too.

The key fell from my hand as I crumpled. My eyes barely lifted to see Nyte had fallen, lying so peacefully on his back as he bled out. I tried to crawl, but my elbow gave out as soon as my hand met the ground.

The land rumbled violently, and all I could do was look up at the sky.

The stars were falling more rapidly than ever. I didn't know if they were souls or true cosmic sources. If they were the former, Death had lied. He'd said if I killed Dusk and Dawn he would take the souls trapped in our stars to rest in his realm where they belonged.

My eyes fluttered, too heavy to keep open anymore.

"Nyte . . ." I whispered. The world was breaking around us. "Did we win?"

52

Nyte

Nyte..." I heard a beautiful angel call my name, but it was a pained distant echo in my mind. *"Did we win?"*

I gasped, or coughed—*both*. I spluttered with blood choking my throat, but I forced myself to find consciousness and search for my Starlight.

She wasn't far. A few steps away, but I could hardly bring myself to stand.

The world around us was furious. The ground was splitting and the stars were plummeting. Without Dusk and Dawn, the imbalance was catastrophic.

We didn't have much time before it would all be destroyed.

I crawled to her. Through blood and sweat and agony, I crawled to her.

Both of us were drawing numbered breaths, having each other's blood struck as a weapon through us. It was so fucking tragic and deplorable.

"Astraea," I croaked. As I scanned her chest, the shallow rise and fall was a small dose of relief. "Hang on for me."

Eltanin's cry of distress rattled through the chaos as he landed on the courtyard.

Cradling Astraea to my body, I pulled us through the void, and the moment we were upon Eltanin's saddle, the dragon knew where I needed him to go.

It took everything I had to hold her tight and keep a conscious purchase on the saddle when Eltanin's flight was more unstable than usual, with the meteors he had to dive and swerve around to avoid. The sky was burning.

He landed in North Star in Althenia, and it took the last dreg of magick I had left in me to use the void to reach outside the temple.

Though I had no arrows left in me, every moment was like ten molten-hot rods were being twisted into my body. Sweat slicked my skin, but one glance at Astraea's too-pale face had me barking in agony to lift her more securely in my weakening hold. Clenching my teeth, I carried her through the doors.

The giant shard of mirror still stood against the quaking lands. I got so close before my knees buckled right before it from the shooting pain in my chest. Breathing felt like the air was clogged with ash and fire. If these were to be our last moments as mortals . . .

I brushed the tangled silver hair from her slick forehead and cheeks. Astraea's eyes fluttered open, so tired. Still the most beautiful set of eyes in all of existence.

Her fingertips barely brushed my jaw, and her sight flicked sideward to the dire reflection of us.

"Where are we?" she whispered.

"Do you remember what I said? As the night and the stars, as the dark and the light, as the dusk and the dawn," I said, running out of breaths, but they were all hers anyway.

"Yes."

"We are inevitable, Astraea. Will you be infinite with me?"

Her glistening eyes filled with puzzlement; then she understood.

"As the dusk and the dawn . . ." she recited.

"After your battle with Auster, when he condemned you with that blade of my blood before you killed him, I was beside myself. I couldn't sleep or eat; I had to know there was a way to save you, but Drystan had nothing. I visited every mage or seer I knew of in a single night and only one gave me a riddle I think I figured out. They mentioned the dusk and the dawn. I think we can take their place, and though it takes us from this realm and our friends, we'll be together, and their land will be restored to its balance."

"Our friends," she repeated, cupping her hand more firmly onto my face. It was a touch of bliss against the misery.

Her tears spilled as she came to terms with everything. It wasn't a favored fate—to become gods that would watch over this realm and others as every dawn and every dusk in existence—but it was still an end, or in some ways a beginning, that kept our promise to stay together.

"But how will we . . . ?" Astraea was split between heartbreak and hope.

"When I figured it out, I only needed one thing. The blood of Dusk and Dawn. It wasn't easy to get, but tracking them down was. They didn't even know I was there as I influenced two others to draw their blood for me." I dipped into my pocket and produced the two vials of blood, pressing Dawn's into her palm for after we stepped through the mirror.

She was stunned speechless, staring down at the sample in her hand. When she looked back at me, she was about to speak before her back arched and her breath caught in her throat.

"Nyte," she said through labored breaths.

I pulled down her collar, seeing we were out of time and the blackness was no longer just a vine crawling toward her heart. It reached its destination and started to spread over the left side of her chest like the veins in a translucent black rose.

"I claim you, Astraea. In every lifetime, I love you. Till kingdom come."

I kissed her one last time, and with my mouth on hers, I took her hand and reached through the mirror.

PART FIVE

The Stars and Night Itself

The realms were breaking without the Dusk and the Dawn, and the bonded souls responsible now faced judgment in the Hall of the Gods. They were also perhaps the only hope to restore balance.

Astraea Lightborne; the star-maiden. Godkiller. Lightsdeath. The Daughter of Dusk and Dawn come to take their place. Is that the destiny you embrace?
    "Yes."

Rainyte Azreal Ashfyre; the lost first son. Nightsdeath. The Realm Walker come to sacrifice himself to stay with his Maiden. Is that the destiny you embrace?
    "I do."

So their punishment shall be their blessing. The tale of two souls that defied time and killed gods would live for eternity in the legends of men. Such triumph wrapped in tragedy.

    Such a tale . . . that was not finished.

53

Nyte

I didn't know where I was. I didn't care.

All I could do was stare at my vacant hands, in complete denial about how Astraea had drifted away from me like stardust. I knelt here alone when seconds ago she was cradled against me.

I had been wrong.

"Give her back to me," I said through a breath, barely able to speak from the grief building in my throat and wracking a chill through my body. "Please."

"Rainyte." A feminine voice spoke my name.

It sounded familiar, echoing around me like an embrace I didn't want. The delicate resonance hung in the air like a half-remembered dream, wavering and unsteady, as though it were a fragile thing that could vanish at any moment.

I didn't care. She was not the one I wanted to turn around and see.

"Give her back!" I yelled, tightening my hands into fists and doubling over with the agony.

"My son."

Those two words softened my hard breaths. I couldn't understand why I was facing my mother. Was it truly her or the call of my reaching subconscious that brought the Goddess here?

Straightening, I didn't even know where *here* was. There was no beginning and no end to the vast bright canvas around me.

My body felt fragmented, as if pieces of me had been scattered beyond reach. I turned, and there she was—the flaming-haired fae, her figure hazy and ethereal, flickering with an otherworldly glow. She looked like she was made of light and shadow, less a solid form than a lingering spirit, the ghost of the being she once was.

Her face held a quiet sadness, a centuries-old weight that spoke of choices and sacrifices I couldn't begin to understand. She'd once been bound to a sacred duty, but she had abandoned it long ago, forsaking the realm she'd sworn to balance and protect to chase a love on land that had turned to dust in her hands. Again and again, the life on land had betrayed her, and yet here she stood, unwhole but unyielding, a relic of her own defiance.

I was one of those betrayals—a harm done to her. Both in the way I was a love taken from her and how I'd almost been the hand to end her once and for all when I'd traveled back to the land I came from during my death-like curse.

"Mother," I said, still finding the term so unusual.

I had her eyes, of course. She was not just the origin of these bright golden irises but the shape of them too.

"My boy," she whispered.

That claim was a punch through my silent chest. It was so . . . gentle. I'd never been claimed so gently, never known what being someone's *child* felt like.

It did nothing for me now.

"Was it worth it?" I asked. "All you did to the realm I was born in?"

"Yes," she answered without hesitation. "My kind have always believed there is a time for and order to everything. I always rebelled against that idea, but now I see. Now I see, Rainyte."

"That your demise was inevitable."

"Our lives connect to so much more than we could ever fathom. I am at peace with my end."

"So even the villains find solace despite all the suffering they caused?"

"Not all. Your father will never be free of his torment."

"Then why are you?"

"Because of you," she said, stepping closer and reaching a hand to my face. "I might not have had the time with you I wanted, but I created you, and you lived for great things. You captured something I never could. A love so true it riles jealousy in gods. How could I not feel fulfilled by that?"

I didn't know what to say. Her explanation was contrary to all I'd learned from my father. He had wanted the prize and glory, and he used me to get it for him.

"She's gone," I said miserably. "Astraea is gone from me."

"She's waiting," Mother amended.

She reached for my hand, taking the vial of Dusk's blood.

"I'll take it from here. Your time isn't finished in your realm. You have so much more to give and to feel."

"Mother," I breathed. This time the word came from the child she lost.

"I was wrong," she said. "You are the dark she needs to find passion. For she has always been the light you have needed for guidance."

She wrapped her arms around me. This embrace was unlike any other I'd felt before, and I didn't really know how to return it. Until she started to fade away; her form became more opaque. I wouldn't ever get this chance again, and so I hugged her back. My mother, from the realm I was born in, who'd come to make sure I could stay in the realm I chose.

Then she was gone.

I was alone holding the true ending of Marvellas, and her new beginning.

The Spirit of Souls and Goddess of the Stars. Mortal mother of the gold-eyed children. . . .

Now she was the Primordial of Dusk across all realms and ages.

54

Astraea

I'd soared through nights so clear they felt like endless oceans of stars, but this was different. Here, I stood motionless, the brilliance of midnight wrapping around me in perfect stillness. It was as if I'd been placed in the heart of a vast, shimmering snow globe, each star a delicate fleck of light suspended in the dark, turning the world into something quiet and magical.

My hand reached out, so weightless, like water carried me. I could feel the vastness stretching out on all sides, yet I was cocooned, held in a moment that felt impossibly pure. The air was crisp, every breath tasting of cold and wonder, while the silence settled like snow around me.

"Oh, Astraea."

I whirled, my breath caught, but my heart . . . I had no beat in my chest in this place.

"Cassia?" I said in denial. She wasn't the only face to shock me. "Calix?"

My dear lost friends smiled. Cassia's was a kind so personal to her delicate face, one I never thought I'd see again, and my eyes welled with tears. I didn't know where I was, and though I was overjoyed to be reunited with Cassia in my death, Nyte was absent and that began to split my soul.

We were supposed to stay together.

"Are you real?" I dared to ask.

She didn't answer in words. Her hand reached to my face, and her palm felt firm. The moment I knew that, I fell into her, holding her tightly as I sobbed.

"It's not your time to pass yet," she said gently.

When I found the will to let her go, Cassia wiped my tears tenderly. The warmth in her deep blue eyes freed some of the ache in me; she always did have that effect, a comforting aura that could lift the world off my shoulders when I was in her company.

"I think it's long past my time," I said. "But I have to find Nyte. Do you know where he is?"

"You'll be with him soon."

Cassia's assurance eased my soul.

"Have you come to take me?"

She held my hands. Calix stood patiently by her side, his face a mask of pure contentment. I was so relieved to see their souls had reunited after their mortal time.

"We've come to take your place," he said.

More confusion deepened my brow.

"I don't understand."

"You harbored our souls," Calix explained. "We have enough of your essence and your power to take your place as the God of Dawn. We just need the one thing you're holding onto."

My next inhale staggered.

Take my place as Dawn?

No. That wasn't the plan. If Nyte had to give himself to become Dusk, I was going with him.

As the Dawn and the Dusk. That was our promise.

"I'm so proud of you, Astraea," Cassia said. "Watching all you've become . . . you're living for both of us."

My vision flooded again; the wound of losing her tore open to bleed me freely.

"I couldn't have done it without you," I croaked. Then my gaze slipped to Calix, who smiled. "Both of you."

"I don't believe that," Cassia mused playfully. Her expression turned into bittersweet gratitude. "Thank you for sending him to me. For keeping us both safe even when you didn't realize it."

Cassia took her hands back from mine, now holding the vial of Dawn's blood that Nyte had given me.

"Keep shining brightly. We'll always be with you in every dawn."

"What are you—?"

Cassia uncorked the bottle and brought it to her lips. An invisible hold kept me back, and I watched with growing dread as she handed the rest to Calix, who finished it.

"I need it!" I cried. "I need it to be with him."

Oh gods. Nyte had found a way for us to stay together, and I'd let it slip from my hands. My friends thought they were helping, but they didn't understand I wanted this. I couldn't return to the mortal realm without him.

Calix took Cassia's hand, and their forms began to fade.

"Please!" I cried.

I lost him. I lost everyone.

I was once again all alone in this void of night and starlight. Alone with my sobs rattling in my hollow chest and shredding at my split soul.

I lost.

I lost him.

"Nyte!" I yelled. I called his name again and again until my throat was hoarse and my cheeks were stained with endless tears.

He couldn't leave me. I couldn't leave him.

"We were supposed to be infinite together," I whispered, an unheard breath of shattered hope lost in this void.

I stood alone and lost. So terribly lost. The silence grew thick with my building grief and complete denial. My knees threatened to buckle because I didn't want to go back. I would rather stay here in torment for my failure to Nyte than face a world where he didn't exist.

"I told you I'd always reach you when you call."

My next breath left me in disbelief, and I was afraid to turn around and have him be a figment of my desperate imagination.

"Starlight."

I couldn't fight the pull of that name, which lassoed around me, and faced the only person to ever call me that.

Nyte stood just a short distance away, watching me with an expression that pulled me forward, my steps shaky at first as I stumbled toward him. His image was perfect. All dark hair, ethereal gold eyes, and that scar . . . the most perfectly imperfect piece of him he'd kept to remember us. That our story was love and war. It was many battles, many heartbreaks, and in every trial and tribulation, it was triumphant.

Before I knew it, my pace quickened—I was running. The space between us closed with every step, and then he was moving too, his strides mirroring my own, closing the distance with an intensity that made the void blur around us.

We were stars colliding and night defying.

My arms wrapped around his neck, and Nyte's powerful arms lifted me. I clamped around him, too afraid that he would disappear, that this embrace was as fragile as a dream.

"Astraea," he sighed into my hair; his warm breath fanned my neck.

"Nyte," I whispered, clutching him tighter. "Oh, Nyte."

"Yes."

His arms slackened, and my toes set back on the ground.

"Yes?" I questioned.

Nyte's golden eyes were the most beautiful things in the world. My North Star. My guide home.

"Yes . . . we won."

My face crumpled with the pure joy that pierced me.

"We won," I echoed. "Is this real? Are you real? Cassia and Calix took Dawn's blood, and I couldn't . . . I thought I'd lost you and I—"

Nyte's lips slanted over mine, dissolving my frantic web of words. I kissed him back desperately, as if our last breath was shared within it.

He was the one to pull back, resting his forehead against mine.

"We win, Astraea. Not to sacrifice ourselves this time; we're going home together. To your lands that you will restore as the people's queen, as their star-maiden. And I'm going to be right there beside you, as the darkness that will always make sure you shine your brightest."

I sobbed in pure joy and elation.

A bright light began to grow over his face, making him shine with the night in his hair and the sun in his eyes.

"Let's go home to our friends," I said, not quite believing my precious words would come true yet. Then the term didn't feel strong enough, and I amended, "Our family."

Nyte cupped my cheek and inched his face closer to mine. "Yes," he said as the light devoured us both. "Our friends. Our family."

55

Astraea

When I opened my eyes, I winced at the piercing amber glow hitting my face and streaking across my fingers over Nyte's chest. The color was so beautiful, the shine of forgotten treasure. My fingers flexed against him, and I felt his heartbeat, strong and sure, under my palm.

I dared to twist my gaze toward the source of the amber light, squinting as I tried to make sense of its brilliance. And there it was—the sun, breaking over the distant horizon, spilling its golden warmth across the land. The world seemed to hold its breath, bathed in hues of fire and honey, every shadow dissolving into the glow. I stood transfixed, utterly captivated, realizing that I'd never felt so humbled by the simple beauty of a rising dawn.

"Is this real?" I whispered.

Nyte's idle caress up my arm was convincing. He seemed too lost in thought to speak, perhaps contemplating the same, as we both stared out over the scene of serenity.

In the distance below, the castle of Vesitire glinted with dark beauty against the stunning rays. The daylight was finally restored to our realm, which no longer quaked with anguish. The land was so still, peaceful. We were high on a mountainside with the most perfect view over the entire central city of Vesitire.

I watched the dawn rise with tears in my eyes and the picture of Cassia and Calix in my thoughts.

We'll be with you in every dawn.

I would always miss having them with me, but every day the sun promised a new beginning, a new day, their spirits within the rays would forever bless me.

Nyte's hand cupped my nape, and I looked up, finding his golden eyes ablaze with the streaks of sunlight against them and . . . glistening. Right as a tear spilled over his cheek, he crushed his lips to mine, and my heart erupted like the break of the first new dawn.

It was a kiss of triumph and devotion. Of defiance that finally *won*.

"We're real," he said, resting his forehead against mine, his smile so bright.

I laughed first and he joined me. We stood there holding each other and *laughing* in pure delirious joy. The ground wasn't rumbling against our happiness anymore; there were no cries of pain or anguish from below.

The war was over.

And we were free.

Nyte lifted me, and there had never been such liberation over his face. He was glowing with so much hope he'd never dared to express before.

"Right here," he said.

My brow furrowed, but my smile couldn't fade in the slightest as I scanned around.

"Here?" I questioned.

"It's a perfect view of the city. Easy to fly down to. We have the forest; there's a nearby stream and enough clearings for Eltanin. I think we should build our home right here."

I didn't think my heart could swell in my chest anymore before it might explode. Casting my sight over the cliff edge, I thought the view held so much more meaning now. My life with Nyte began to build at this very vantage point, starting now.

"It's perfect," I said, barely a choked whisper. "But shouldn't we stay in the castle?"

"We will be there plenty, and we're only one short flight down, with your wings or with Eltanin. I want this home as privacy for us. A safe haven for our friends too. But we can share the castle with them, as a home they can stay in permanently. Drystan can act as your lead counsel, if you choose and he accepts."

I loved that idea, and I hoped the others would too.

Nyte sank to his knees, holding me straddled over them.

"We need to make sure everyone is okay." As I said it, I couldn't bring myself to move.

"We've done enough for the world. Right now, all we have to do is watch the first sunrise."

It was the first dawn of so many hopeful prospects. Most of all, I watched it with him as the first of our new life. The life we'd chosen and might not be done fighting for, but for now . . . we were the stars and night itself; anything was possible and everything was inevitable with us.

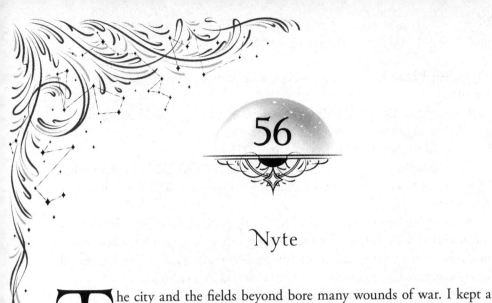

56

Nyte

The city and the fields beyond bore many wounds of war. I kept a tight grip of Astraea's hand as we walked over the bridge, as she insisted we see it all—that we owed that to them.

I would disagree, but I kept my selfish thoughts to myself this time in consideration of all the sorrow we walked through. Astraea had given more to the world than they would ever thank her for. That's not why she did it—stayed resilient in her duty as the star-maiden to a world that had all but given up on her—I knew this. She didn't do it for praise or glory or power. She did it because her heart was too precious for any realm.

So it was my sworn duty until the end of our days to make sure she knew how utterly remarkable she was.

"So many deaths," she said quietly.

I squeezed her hand, watching her survey the survivors tending to their wounded and mourning their fallen. I couldn't share the depth of her sorrow for strangers; it would always be a level I couldn't meet her on, and for a while I'd felt guilty about that incompatibility, believing she might see I was still a monster after all. Until I realized this was another perfect balance between us: as Astraea mourned with them, I was wholly focused on her, soothing her mind without taking any of her emotions, simply wrapping myself around her sorrow and filling myself in every small crack of the heart I swore to protect.

Astraea tugged me toward a grieving mother and her fallen son, a grown human man, but I was beginning to see it didn't matter how many years passed or what they did in life: a parent's child was always just that. A child.

My boy, Marvellas had called me. I couldn't stop picturing her face. Though she didn't wear her broken heart for the world to see like this human did, I'd never felt a heart so broken that nothing would have mended it.

My mother was at peace now. At least that's what I chose to believe. As for my father, I hoped his chains in Hell were melting through his flesh for all eternity.

I thought of Drystan, with an impatient glance up toward the castle. My skin itched to confirm he was still alive after all this.

"Go, I'll be right behind you," Astraea said gently.

That brought my attention back to her and I smiled. Fuck, I couldn't stop this new light in my chest from flaring at the mere sight of her, as if it was the first time.

She kneeled by the fallen man, lifting a beige sheet over his body while the mother cried hard with the finality of this goodbye. I slipped into the woman's mind, not taking her grief but soothing it. Reminding her that he fought valiantly and gave his life bravely for a better world for everyone.

Her crying eased, and Astraea flicked a look up at me, knowing what I'd done.

We continued through the city, stopping occasionally when Astraea couldn't stand to pass by any citizen alone in their deep mourning or anyone who needed help. She directed many of them toward the castle, where we'd immediately get an infirmary set up and call every healer we could there imminently.

I kissed her head, and we kept walking in silence while she gave her thoughts to the people. She gasped and I turned rigid, but upon spying Rosalind's distinct pink hair across the torn street of rubble and dust, I relaxed.

I didn't know how much I'd allowed myself to care about the survival of Rosalind and Zathrian until an immense relief lifted upon seeing them alive. It wasn't just for Astraea I harbored these emotions either, and it would take time to let myself acknowledge—whether they tested the very limits of my patience or inspired bouts of amusement—that I *wanted* these people in my life.

When Rosalind spotted Astraea, I thought I'd never seen such relief and joy over Rosalind's face before. I had to let go of Astraea's hand as they jogged to meet each other, colliding with bright smiles and soft laugher; it was impossible not to find it contagious.

"Look at you," Zath mused, catching up to me. "I think that's the most expression I've ever seen on you."

"Don't get used to it."

He chuckled. "I wouldn't dream of it."

I scanned him subtly; he appeared unharmed for the most part, save for a few superficial wounds. He caught my assessment.

"You do care about me; I knew it!"

To my complete dismay, Zathrian *hugged* me. He was almost the same height as me, with a broad build, and his embrace was far more aggressive than a woman's.

"Hug me back, you bastard. We just survived war against fucking gods."

I couldn't help the single laugh that escaped me; then I allowed the embrace. It was a strange feeling. *Friends.*

Zath pulled back, or rather pushed me back, jostling me a little and patting my shoulder because I was starting to get offended.

"You'll get better at it," he said, not dropping his beaming grin in the slightest, so I relaxed.

When Astraea returned, Zath's playfully aggressive affection amplified, not giving her a second of warning before sweeping her off her feet. My irritable objection flared until she started giggling, such a beautiful sound, as he spun with her because it was precious to witness.

My attention fell to Rosalind, who was already staring at me. I smirked at her familiar scowl, one that felt unique for me personally.

"Are we calling a truce?" I said.

Her face relaxed and she crossed her arms. "For now. Unless you do something to piss her off."

"I'm sure I'll give you plenty of opportunities to despise me."

Rosalind yielded a partial smile, watching Astraea and Zath.

"You're not completely terrible, I suppose," she said.

"That's quite a compliment coming from you."

When Astraea was back by my side I relaxed from the tension I hadn't realized was growing in me, even when my eyes were on her. There'd been so many times I'd had to watch her in enemy clutches that I didn't think I would ever lose the subconscious fear Astraea could be taken from me when she was out of my reach.

My arm slipped around her waist as we continued making our way up to the top level of the city.

Many walls and structures needed to be repaired and rebuilt, but as I studied the wreckage I didn't feel anything but potential. To rebuild better, stronger. War was not without mass desolation and destruction, but the only way to honor the fallen and heal the land was to remember what we fought for and not waste a moment to push forward on the bright path victory had opened.

In the courtyard we found Eltanin and Athebyne, which distracted me from the bodies strewn around and the amount of repair needed.

Eltanin gave something of a loud rattle in greeting; his joy vibrated through me when he saw us. As he shifted his large head down, Astraea giggled, stroking his feathers, when his gentle nudge stumbled her footing. He didn't grow again when the next full moon passed, leaving his mature size just a little bigger than Athebyne's, which in truth was a relief. He would have barely fit in this courtyard himself if he'd grown any bigger.

"Where have you two been?" Drystan called.

My brother's voice had never made me feel such peace before.

Turning my head back, he stormed to us with Nadia close behind.

"I've been worried sick! I knew that goodbye during the battle was suspicious and you'd likely be plotting some bullshit to sacrifice yourself or holding secrets I didn't know about. You're good at that—always keeping me out—"

I pulled Drystan into an embrace when he marched close enough, shocking even myself with the uncharacteristic impulse. Drystan was absolutely stiff against me, and I patted his back with a chuckle before letting him go.

"What is happening?" Drystan muttered, looking me over as if I were a foreign invader in his brother's body.

"We got you something," I said casually.

Reaching into the void, I pulled out the monocular telescope.

Drystan's eyes widened on the item, then on me.

"Is that—?"

I nodded and it had been so long since I'd seen that particular stare of joyous wonder on his face as he snatched it from me.

"What is it?" Nadia inquired, seeming unimpressed as Drystan inspected every inch of the metal.

"An eye for the unseeing," a different voice answered for us.

I turned to find Balthezar strolling onto the courtyard, his hand guiding his son by the shoulder.

"N-Nyte! Astraea!" Brody cried cheerfully, leaving his father's side to skip to us. "Did-did you see? I-I have a Dra-dragon!"

Astraea looked to me for confirmation, and for the first time I smiled at the boy.

"I did. It seems you've been chosen as the King of the Seas," I said to him.

I reached through the void again and felt the collective stun around me at the trident, which radiated with dangerous power even idle in my grasp.

"I think your father should hold onto this for now though," I said, offering it to the captain.

He looked at it in surprise. "You would hand over such a powerful weapon?"

"We have no use for it. Though I only ask you swear on your life to make sure it never reaches nefarious hands. Certainly never those of a nymph."

Balthezar took the trident cautiously. "I will guard it with my life and that of my crew."

Astraea's hand slipped into mine, and she gave me one of her most endearing smiles, which sparkled the stars in her silver-blue eyes.

The next presence I detected washed a new wave of relief over me; it was becoming exhausting to keep up with these fluctuating emotions. As I flicked my gaze toward the direction I sensed, the sight of Elliot filled me with gratitude because he'd made it, but it was tragic to watch him walk alone. Battle-worn and tired. I wouldn't let him walk alone anymore, not when our circle grew on this courtyard with people who would welcome him as easily as the Golden Guard did.

I approached him myself. Neither of us smiled, but we shared our grief.

"Zeik was always the most confident that we all would make it," he said.

That slashed me within, but the wound was welcome when we could remember our . . . *friends.*

"He always was the most optimistic bastard," I said.

Elliot huffed, shy of breaking into laughter.

"I keep trying to convince myself their deaths meant something, that they contributed to the war we've won, but I can't. Sorleen . . . she didn't even get to *live.* How does time mean anything when it isn't filled with any dreams or desires, only suffering?"

I didn't have any condolences or wisdom to soothe his loss and pain. Not when I'd existed before without any care for time myself.

"None of them got to live the lives they deserved. It will forever be one of my greatest failures."

"And mine," Elliot said.

I placed a hand on his shoulder, sharing that burden for a moment.

Behind Elliot, a flicker of red hair caught my attention. Tarran also arrived alone. I still didn't trust him, nor was I particularly pleased to see him, but I returned to Astraea's side because of the expression he wore as he tried not to display his grief, but it was there.

Astraea saw it too, and she walked to meet him.

"She didn't make it," he informed us, his voice reducing on the last words.

With the way he only spoke to Astraea, as if it was something personal to them, I knew who he meant.

Laviana was like a sister to Astraea.

The resilient elder vampire had been a pivotal leader for the vampires, devoted to seeing them achieve the equality they deserved and to not be seen as vicious monsters.

For her, I mourned silently.

Astraea covered her mouth and tears glistened in her eyes. The aftermath of battle was always so desolate and would linger in the air for weeks to come. This was only the beginning of discovering all their losses.

"Take me to her," she whispered.

57

Astraea

I couldn't place my feelings. The war was won, but sorrow filled my chest too heavily to allow any room for victory.

Staring at Laviana's peaceful face upon the pyre, I mourned for her.

"I'm sorry we weren't there," a male voice said from behind me. I turned, finding two nightcrawlers with faces so uncannily alike they had to be twins.

Then the memory flooded back to me with a gasp. They were the children of my nightcrawler and human guardians.

"Kenton," I whispered, in case I was wrong, but the slightly taller dark-haired nightcrawler smiled at the name. "Ethan," I greeted the other brother.

Ethan said, "Phew. We weren't certain you would remember us."

"Where have you been?" I didn't mean to sound disappointed, but they had known the war we faced, and they hadn't come.

Both their expressions fell as they came closer and glanced at Laviana's body.

"It's selfish of us to admit, but the island we live on in Althenia was untouched by the war. The forgotten isles are ungoverned, and it's the one place people like us have found peace. We were able to raise our own families."

I couldn't blame them for choosing to protect their peace, but a kernel of resentment lingered as I looked at Laviana. She'd fought for so long. Fought for all vampires to be able to live a life like Kenton and Ethan had found in a secluded corner of the continent.

"Why did you come now?" I asked, trying to keep my bitterness at bay, but part of me didn't think they deserved to mourn for Laviana when they'd abandoned her.

"Tarran found us. He told us everything," Kenton said.

"You've come too late," I snapped. It was my grief lashing out, but I wasn't sorry for it.

"I know," Ethan said.

"We want to help. Though we're not fighters, we want to help you in any way we can to restore the world for the vampires. We are yours to serve."

The war might be won, but there was a long road to rebuilding all that was broken. I expected to face resistance, and the fight for equality wasn't over. New order took time.

All I could do was nod in agreement for now. My soul was too burdened with loss to push away a hand of help.

My light burned through the wood Laviana was laid to rest upon. There were many more deaths to honor, but I'd made this pyre just for her. For all she'd given for us to win.

Tarran approached after a few minutes, when the flames devoured the structure and the night glowed in Laviana's memory. His presence was silent and careful, as if he didn't want to be noticed and would slip away again after he finished grieving.

He might cast me away, but I couldn't leave him alone in this somber moment.

"I'm glad you're alive," he said, but there was no warmth to it.

"I know you can't ever forgive me for what I did to you in the past, but I miss you. I'm always here for you."

"Touching. If I ever need a favor, I'll keep that in mind."

His words stung. It was a rejection of friendship but a promise he wouldn't disappear out of my life completely.

Tarran turned to leave, and maybe it was a step out of line but I couldn't stop myself. I all but threw myself at him, hugging him around the waist when I didn't know how long he would withdraw from me this time.

I didn't need him to return the embrace, but to my surprise, after a few seconds, he did.

"You're a good leader, Astraea. Maybe even a great one," he said.

My arms tightened before I had to let him go. Tarran despised my leadership for the rift it caused between us when I had to order his mate killed for his crimes, but that parting comment meant the world to me. It wasn't forgiveness, but his understanding was just as valuable.

As I watched Tarran leave, a new figure emerging from the trees stunned me still.

"Zadkiel." I said his name in a partial whimper of relief that he was alive.

Last I'd seen him was when the battle broke out on the Nova province and Auster's betrayals came to light. He approached mournfully, as though he was fighting against being here at all.

He stopped a few paces away down the hill, and I read his need for space though my gut twisted.

"Auster was like a father to me," he said.

That twist tuned into a punch straight through me.

"I'm so sorry," I choked.

"I know what he did. I know you deserved your vengeance. But I still can't bring myself to accept it. After the battle on Auster's province . . . I didn't recognize him. He left his lands in ruin when that wasn't the man I knew. The orphanage where I grew up was destroyed and I spent my time since helping to rebuild what I could over there. Auster would come back from time to time and I saw glimpses of who I knew he was at his core. He mourned for his lands . . . but he was the cause of their destruction."

Zadkiel paused. His head bowed, weighed with conflict and sorrow.

"I miss the man he was too," I said carefully. "He was kind and caring, and I will always be to blame for what he became. Even though it was not my fault, his spiral all links back to me."

Zadkiel's jaw tensed.

"I don't know if I can forgive you," he said honestly.

"I understand."

There was a part of myself I would never be able to forgive either.

Zadkiel nodded. "I don't know why I came. Honestly, I wasn't sure what I would say to you. I've been angry and sad and just . . . disappointed. In Auster for what he became, but then I feel guilt because he's not here to explain and I . . ." Zadkiel hissed, at war with his own emotions.

I closed the distance between us tentatively. Then I reached out a hand to rest on his arm, relieved when he didn't shrug me off.

"Time has a way of softening the edges of pain, healing wounds, and even offering forgiveness to those who once seemed beyond redemption. Auster did terrible things, but his heart . . . I choose to believe it loved with pure intentions despite his actions. I hope in time you'll forgive me too."

Zadkiel finally looked up, staring closely into my eyes. To my relief and surprise, he approached me for an embrace. There was something healing in it, as though the wound Auster left in me had been stitched closed. Zadkiel was a living reminder of Auster's love. A young celestial he raised like a son.

When we pulled away, and gave him a fond smile.

"You should take his place on the Nova province," I said.

Zadkiel's eyes widened. "Me? I'm not a High Celestial. I can't do what he did."

"Yes, you can. You have the makings of a fair and righteous ruler, Zadkiel Nova. Only you can carry on his legacy for the *good* it inspired before the clutches of evil took hold."

His eyes glistened and I fought my own tears.

"Thank you," he whispered.

"No, thank you," I said. "I don't know what's to come. The construct of the High Celestials will be no more, but the provinces still stand, and the people need a guiding light."

"Isn't that you?"

"A beacon of light casts many rays; I hope you'll be one of them to help me restore these lands."

Zadkiel smiled fondly, and even though he had a long path of healing, the lift of his spirit was the first sign of hope in the aftermath of all we suffered.

Nyte had left me alone to say goodbye to Laviana, but as I walked down the hill after Zadkiel left to go back to Althenia, I found him waiting at the bottom for me. My chest ignited in a way I didn't think would ever tame.

The long night of mass funeral pyres lay ahead, but I was ready to bear the stacking grief for the fallen so long as he was with me.

Nyte

By midnight we stood watching the final funeral pyres burning on the hills outside the city. The people gathered all around them, and Astraea lit the one in front of us.

It wasn't the first time I'd witnessed such funerals, but it was the first time I'd felt anything personally. Astraea gave her attention to the mourning citizens while the fires blazed. Taking their hands, exchanging words of condolence and gratitude. I followed right beside her silently. A few cast me wary looks and quickly made themselves scarce. My reputation as Nightsdeath would not be so easily dismissed, but I was prepared to keep *trying*. For Astraea, I had to keep working toward making them see me as their protector, not their villain.

But during Astraea's new reign as the Ruler of Solanis, there would come new enemies, new resistance, and I would always be willing and ready to unleash the monster that would always live within me against anything or anyone who opposed her.

By the time we left the scene of mourning and retired to the castle, Astraea was exhausted. All the emotions of the day and night, so much shared loss and sorrow, made her collapse the moment we stepped into her rooms. I caught her, but she didn't speak. Didn't do anything but let me lift her into my arms and carry her into the bathing room.

She hadn't let me convince her to take a moment to bathe and tend to her wounds before the funerals. Now I wasn't asking. Astraea was so lost in her own unpleasant thoughts she let me begin to undress her, but her distant silence was killing me inside.

"Please talk to me," I said, taking her chin.

Her silver-blue eyes finally met mine, and the trouble in them was tearing me apart.

"I'm happy . . ." she confessed.

"But?"

"With all the devastation, it feels selfish."

I sighed. Her heart was the purest and most delicate thing I would ever possess.

Undoing her torn leathers, I took my time to count every cut, bruise, and minor scratch. While the bath filled, I traced my hands over her marked skin, pressing my lips to every blemish on her naked upper body.

"I know you won't agree, so I'm going to be selfish for you," I said, consuming her soft sighs. "You gave your life to this realm and every person within it. Twice. This time you're mine, and I'm going to make sure your life is full of everything you ever desire. Happiness is a constant pursuit, not a final destination. But I swear to you, Astraea, I'm never letting you stray from the bright path you deserve."

Her fingers threaded through my hair, coaxing my face to hers. She kissed me deeply and I burned for her.

"As long as you're with me, I want to walk that path."

The clouds of war would dissipate, and the hearts that bled would find stitches. It wouldn't be easy nor quick, but we would find our way through the dark times together.

When Astraea stood naked in front of me, I couldn't help my hands exploring the beautiful curves of her tenderly. She reached her delicate fingers to begin undoing the fastenings of my leathers. I wasn't going to object; we were both in need of bathing and I didn't plan to release her for a second tonight.

Once bathed, she wore a short silver silk nightgown and climbed into bed.

I lay beside her, folding a blanket over her bare legs. One hooked over me as I settled under with her.

"Do you want to hear a story?" I mumbled, idly playing with her damp hair.

Astraea hummed. "Is it a nice one?"

"It has a happy ending, I promise."

Astraea smiled and I traced the creases around her mouth.

"Go on then," she said, nestling further into me.

I took a long breath and cast my eyes to the bed canopy. I flooded her mind to make her see stars and all the constellations she loved.

"Once upon a time, there was a war between stars."

End.

EPILOGUE

Astraea

I don't think I've ever seen you so nervous," I remarked, running my fingers along the edges of Nyte's coat.

He looked . . . *gods,* there were no words for how impeccably he stood. His jacket was a deep jet-black, tailored to perfection, with accents of rich purple tracing the lapels and cuffs. Silver filigree adorned the edges, intricate patterns that added an air of regality to his attire.

Draped over his shoulders was a ceremonial cloak, matching my own in its deep, velvety purple, the fabric heavy with tradition. It flowed behind him like liquid dusk, its hem embroidered with threads of silver that formed elegant, swirling designs resembling constellations.

Perched upon his head was a simple yet striking crown—a polished silver band rising to a peak at the center like a blade reaching skyward. It rested seamlessly over his sleek, black hair, its simplicity a testament to understated power and grace.

He stood with quiet authority, his presence commanding without need for flourish, a figure of poise and purpose wrapped in the colors of royalty and shadow.

"I don't think I've ever been this nervous," he said.

Today Rainyte Azreal Ashfyre would officially be crowned king consort of Vesitire, and I its queen.

Nyte held my hand as we stood out of view from the balcony where life roared beyond, waiting for us. He admired the ring he'd adorned my marital finger with nine months ago. A proud eight-pointed silver star with a purple diamond center. We waited to have our ceremony and join it for our coronation. After the war, healing and rebuilding had been our priority.

Now . . . it was time to begin living in our peace.

I cupped his cheek, so taken by the stunning sight of him. As the sun kissed its golden rays over his face, it transformed him. The light danced across his features, warming the sharp angles and casting a soft glow over the deep pools of his eyes. He was a harmony of light and dark, a paradox that made him seem untouchable and profoundly human all at once.

His nerves were because he wasn't forced to hide in shadow anymore. He didn't have a vicious name that masked the real person behind it.

Nyte was ready to show the world who he wanted to be.

"I love you," I said. It wasn't enough for what I felt for him, how proud I was of him, but I would say it every day for the rest of our lives.

Nyte's eyes skimmed over every inch of me. My hair was meticulously braided, each strand woven into intricate patterns to hold the weight of an elaborate crown. The crown itself was a masterpiece—clear and purple diamonds catching the light like fragments of a shattered sunrise. My gown was elegant black adorned with the same regal finesse in silver and purple detailed embroidery. The sleeves were sheer and the neckline dipped low, exposing the powerful silver markings of the star-maiden over my skin.

"I love you, my Starlight. It is my honor to stand by your side in this world."

He kissed me in promise.

Then our hands clasped as we faced the open balcony doors. His fingers tightened around mine with our first step toward those awaiting us, gathered in the city of Vesitire.

A smile broke on my face. "I wouldn't have thought you'd suffer stage fright."

His hand gave mine a purposeful squeeze in jest.

"Fear is a powerful thing to have to hide behind," he said.

Nyte had led and commanded thousands in an army. He was no stranger to being the focus of attention, but he'd always worn a mask. Now . . . he was free. That vulnerability he embraced was what made Nyte as fragile as the rest of us.

We stepped into the midday sun, and the crowds erupted the moment they caught a glimpse of us. I'd sworn to everyone this morning that I wouldn't cry, but I was already fighting back the prickling in my eyes.

Banners rippled through the warm air, proudly flying the new black-winged banner of the star-maiden. I waved, overwhelmed with joy seeing the flood of smiles and happiness pouring through the endless throng of people.

Nyte was rigid beside me, and I let go of his hand to slip it across his back. It worked to relax him some, but as he waved with me, I could hardly contain my laughter.

"Am I really that bad at this?" he asked, smiling so brightly I was taken by him.

"Kiss me," I said.

"Are you trying to start a frenzy down there?"

I bit my lip and his eyes darkened. "Our love isn't destruction anymore. It's hope. I want the world to feel it too."

Nyte's hand slipped along my jaw, and he was right, that movement alone stirred the ground impossibly louder.

"There is no dawn that breaks as brilliantly as you," he murmured, inching his mouth closer to mine.

"There's no dusk that falls as peacefully as you," I whispered before our kiss sealed.

As the dusk and the dawn. As the night and the stars. As the dark and the light. History would remember the two fragments of gods, opposite in every catastrophic and triumphant way, who defied fate to become one.

Nyte pulled back; his grin shone brighter than the brilliant sun.

"Do we really have to do this six more times?" he complained playfully.

After our celebration ball here in Vesitire, we'd be leaving on a coronation and wedding tour for the next few weeks. Visiting all the kingdoms and their reigning lords to gain their blessings for our union and reign.

Then we would go to Althenia, the land with the most to rebuild. Without the High Celestial order, I'd stepped in, dividing my time between Vesitire and Althenia to rebuild after the war. The celestials in Althenia were the most wary of me and Nyte, with many believing we'd killed all the High Celestials to take their thrones. The province least shaken was Zephyr's, as his son, Raider Luna, had taken over ruling with the close advisement of his council. Auster's land had the most infrastructure to rebuild still, but the people were thriving under Zadkiel's leadership.

Notus and Aquilo also had children to take over their fathers' places, but unlike Raider Luna and Zadkiel Nova, they were not as forthcoming with me. Nyte and I were expecting to face resistance from them in some way or another. It was a power struggle we were preparing for and not frightened by. Our mission for peace was stronger than ever, and our pillars of allies grew every day.

After our appearance on the balcony, we barely got inside before I was torn away from Nyte when Rosalind, then Davina, then Lilith pummeled into me. We embraced in a chaotic heap of arms, laughing out of nothing more than the pure happiness spilling uncontrollably out of us.

When we released each other, I spied Nadia nearby as she'd decided against joining in the surge of affection. She didn't wear a dress like the rest of us, opting for a more formal rendition of her usual pants and tunic. I didn't think she planned to join us for the ball this evening.

"Heading out so soon?" I mused to her.

Nadia smirked. "A night of stuffy ball gowns and tasteless food sounds like an absolutely dire time."

The food would be divine, but to a vampire . . . I supposed her palate would be seeking out blood instead.

"We're going to Althenia," Drystan cut in, coming over after speaking with Nyte and Zathrian.

"Why there?" I quizzed.

Drystan pulled the monocular telescope from his side, twisting it in his hand. "There's so much unexplored about the ungoverned lands of Althenia. Who knows what secrets could be hidden in plain sight," he said mischievously.

"Don't get into any trouble," I warned playfully.

Drystan's twinkling eyes took that as a challenge.

The ball was as extravagant as I had braced for. Nyte and I barely got to dance with how often we were pulled aside to talk to lords and ladies and gushing citizens. The hope and joy sparking through the hall was worth the endless talking and slow pull of exhaustion.

Before the end of the dancing and feasting, Nyte stole me away as we managed to elude the guests and slip out of the ballroom. He took me up higher in the castle until we stepped outside and I found Eltanin, barely able to fit on the wall, waiting for us.

"Are we going somewhere?" I asked.

"Yes," was all he provided.

Giddy to discover the surprise, I eagerly mounted Eltanin and he slipped in behind me.

After a few moments enjoying the embrace of falling dusk, I leaned over to discover we were flying over Althenia now.

A gasp left me at the prism of color that expanded below.

"Is this North Star?" I asked.

Nyte had told me about this place. It's where the Mirror of Passage was. This is exactly where Nyte had arrived in my realm centuries ago, and that fact turned these grounds even more precious.

He led me inside the temple, and I followed like a ghost on a leash, with our hands joined. There was a sacred aura surrounding this temple, and I treaded lightly toward the colossal shard of mirror that pierced the land as if it had descended from the heavens.

"This is the last part of me I haven't been able to share with you until now. A glimpse into the realm where I came from."

Nyte reached a hand toward the mirror, and my heart lurched as though it might swallow him.

He paused, letting go of my hand to slip his arm around my waist. A promise that, should it try to take him from this realm, it would never take him from me.

My heart thundered as I watched him reach his fingers toward the mirror again. When he made contact, I gripped his jacket when it rippled as though it were made of liquid silver.

Then color started to flood as though a painting formed across the surface. Stroke by stroke, images came together in a breathtakingly vivid reel.

I saw red-peaked mountains rising sharply against a molten sky, their jagged summits kissed by the glow of sunlight. Between them, phoenixes soared, their blazing forms streaking trails of flame like triumphant comets. Each flap of their immense, fiery wings sent cascades of embers spiraling downward, illuminating the valleys below in a dance of light and shadow.

It was as if the mountains guarded a vast, commanding city, encircled by a massive circular wall, much like Vesitire's though on a single level. The stone of its fortifications glowed faintly as if it had absorbed the fire of the phoenixes themselves over centuries.

At the city's heart stood a castle unlike anything I had ever seen. It wasn't blackened stone nor cold in design like ours. Instead, its structure seemed forged to embrace the sky and the creatures that ruled it. Broad arches and towering spires gave it an open, regal air; its dominating courtyard was designed so the phoenixes could land with ease. A massive phoenix emblem was painted in its center.

The castle seemed like a haven that welcomed the firebirds home from the endless skies they dominated, a place where power and grace intertwined in perfect harmony.

"It's beautiful," I breathed.

Tearing my eyes away from the stunning scenes unfolding, I reached my fingers across his neck, tugging his collar down until I could trace the points of the constellation he wore.

"Constellation phoenix," I muttered to myself. "It makes sense now."

The scene changed again, and I was drawn to see a couple standing there now. Their ears were pointed, but I couldn't tell if they were vampire or fae.

The woman had gold eyes, not as bright as Nyte's, but their likeness was uncanny, as were the golden tattoos peeking out from her crimson attire. She wore a halo crown that rose behind her like the sun. Her dress-like coat was a deep red, and the phoenix emblem I'd seen before adorned the pin at her shoulder. She stood with a man who clearly adored her, holding her close. He too wore fiery colors and a simple gold-band crown. Undeniably, they were royalty.

"My cousin," Nyte said at last. The note of fondness he spoke with warmed me. "Faythe Ashfyre."

"You met them during your sleep-curse?" I concluded.

"Yes."

"Do you want to . . . go back?"

Nyte guided my chin away from the mirror to look at him. His eyes spoke of endless horizons, of battles fought and won, and of dreams yet to be realized. Nyte's tender smile wasn't just a curve of lips; it was a vow.

"Never. My place is right here with you. This is our perfect world, and that is my promise."

PRONUNCIATION GUIDE

NAMES
Astraea: ah-stray-ah
Nyte/Rainyte: night/ray-night
Drystan: dry-stan
Cassia: ca-see-ah
Calix: cal-ix
Zathrian: zath-ree-an
Rosalind: rose-ah-lind
Lilith: lil-ith
Davina: da-veen-ah
Auster: au-ster
Nadia: na-dee-ah
Zephyr: zeh-fer
Aquilo: Ah-quil-oh
Notus: No-tus
Eltanin (Eli): Elle-tan-in (eel-eye)
Athebyne: Athe-bine
Tarran: tar-an

PLACES
Solanis: so-lan-is
Alisus: ae-lis-us
Vesitire: ves-eh-tier
Althenia: al-then-ee-a
Pyxtia: pix-tea-ah
Arania: ah-ran-ee-a
Fesaris: fe-sar-is
Astrinus: as-stry-nus

OTHER
Crocotta: crow-cot-ah
Hasseria: has-er-ee-ah

ACKNOWLEDGMENTS

Of this whole book, I'm finding these acknowledgments the hardest and most emotional part to write. I can't thank you readers enough for championing this trilogy that changed my life. Nyte and Astraea will forever hold a place in my heart.

To my mum, who is the bravest most resilient woman I know. This year has been so tough on your health but your will to fight your illness is so admirably strong. Thank you for being such a light and inspiration in my life.

To my best friend across the pond, Lyssa, you've always been my rock through the hard times. An ear to rant and plot and cry to. I wouldn't be a soldier through it all without you.

To my agent, Jessica, thank you for all you do for me. For believing my stories could be more and finding the Nytefall trilogy its perfect publishing homes. I can't wait for what the future holds.

To Nick, Jennifer, and the team at Sandra Dijkstra Agency, thank you for all your devotion to helping to find homes across the globe for my books.

To my editor Erika, thank you for making these books shine and being such an absolute delight to work with. You crush my doubts and I couldn't have asked for a better editor for these books.

To my entire team at Bramble: Monique, Tessa, Tyrinne, Devi, Lucille, Eileen, Laura, Sarah, Emily, and all the incredible talents who worked on these books, thank you endlessly for all your dedication and cheerleading. I'm incredibly proud to be a Bramble author.

To Areen, Ana, and the whole team at Wildfire, thank you for your amazing efforts in the UK and Commonwealth for this trilogy. I'm so honored to have such a wonderful, dedicated publishing team cheering on these books.

To Lila for another incredible US cover design, and for being an incredible friend, supporter, and bright light.

To Alice for the incredible character artwork on the US hardcover. You've been with me since my very first book, which gets me emotional, and I hope in one way or another, we'll always be working together.

Once again, I come back to thank you, my dear reader. There's no me without you, and I hope you'll follow me into the next magickal adventure, wherever that may be. From the very bottom of my heart, THANK YOU for reading my stories.

ABOUT THE AUTHOR

Eva Peñaranda

CHLOE C. PEÑARANDA is the *New York Times* and *USA Today* bestselling Scottish author of the Nytefall trilogy and An Heir Comes to Rise series. A lifelong avid reader and writer, her stories have been spun from years of building on fictional characters and exploring Tolkien-like quests in made-up worlds from her quiet pocket of Scotland with her dogs. During her time at the University of the West of Scotland, Peñaranda immersed herself in writing for short film, producing animations, and spending class time dreaming of far-off lands.

ccpenaranda.com
Instagram: @chloecpenaranda